SOMEONE SHOULD KNOW THIS STORY

Selected Stories

MERRILL JOAN GERBER

Set in Bembo with LaTeX.

These stories first appeared, sometimes in slightly different form, in the following publications:

Anna in Chains (Syracuse University Press, 1998): "Anna in Chains"

Anna in the Afterlife (Syracuse University Press, 2002): "Anna's Archive"; "The Desert of the Mysteries"

Atlantic Monthly: '"I Don't Believe This"' (October 1984. Also reprinted in *Prize Stories: The O. Henry Awards 1986*)

The Chattahoochee Review: "Anna Gets Wings" (Winter 2002); "Hear No Entreaties, Speak No Consolations" (Spring 1996); '"This Is A Voice From Your Past"' (Summer 1997. Also reprinted in *The Best American Mystery Stories 1998*)

Chattering Man (Longstreet, 1991): "Tabu"

Honeymoon (University of Illinois Press, 1985): "Memorial Service"; "Someone Should Know This Story"

Mademoiselle: "The Cost Depends on What You Reckon It In" (April 1963)

McCall's: "Honest Mistakes" (October 1991)

The New Yorker: "We Know That Your Hearts Are Heavy" (April 1963)

Wascana Review: "Starry Night" (Fall 1985)

Prairie Schooner: "Chicken Skin Sandwiches" (Summer 1988, winner of the Readers' Choice Award)

Redbook: "A Daughter of My Own" (January 1964); "Good-bye, Arny Goldstone" (January 1982)

Shenandoah: "Night Stalker" (Summer 1987)

Sewanee Review: "At the Fence" (Winter 1985. Winner of the Andrew Lytle Fiction Prize); "Comes an Earthquake" (Fall 1987); "Honeymoon" (Winter 1984); "Mozart You Can't Give Them" (Summer 1986)

The Southwest Review: "Anna Passes On" (86, nos. 2 and 3, 2001. Winner of the McGinnis Ritchie Prize); "Tell Me Your Secret" (January 2000)

Stop Here, My Friend (Houghton Mifflin, 1965): "How Love Came to Grandmother"

ISBN: 978-1-963846-53-9 (paperback)
ISBN: 978-1-963846-54-6 (ebook)
Library of Congress Control Number: 2025944282

Sagging Meniscus Press
Montclair, New Jersey
saggingmeniscus.com

For Ilana and Natalie,
bright lights for the future

Contents

A Few Words From the Author

While living in Boston, nine months pregnant and expecting the birth of my first baby in the spring of 1962, I received a letter from Wallace Stegner at Stanford University. "I'm happy to tell you . . ." it read, and I thought, "Oh no, not now!" I had applied for a fellowship to the Stegner writing program at Stanford but never imagined winning one. But NOW? I could not accept . . . I was not available!

I talked with my husband. Could we possibly do this? Of course! He was absolutely in favor of our going to Stanford. This kind of opportunity comes only once in a lifetime, he said. I should not let it go by.

Our baby, a beautiful little girl, was born May 3rd. My mother took a trip to stay with us and help, but I was unhappy to have her there. Her intrusiveness was overwhelming. I turned away from her. She could not help but feel unwelcome and decided to leave early.

When the baby was three months old, we flew to California and in September I entered Wallace Stegner's writing workshop at Stanford. What would I write about? I had earned my BA in English from the University of Florida, where I'd studied with my beloved teacher, Andrew Lytle. His advice was this: "There is only one way to write: you must follow the thread back into the labyrinth; there and only there you will find the meaning." "Follow the thread . . ." Well, I'd just given birth to a baby. Could I write about that? A sentence came to me: "If I never have another baby . . . it will be because I won't know what to do about my mother."

There! I was in the labyrinth now and following the thread. Would it be fair to reveal the details of our unhappy visit? A writer must not allow herself to worry about hurting someone's feelings when art calls for honesty. I wrote fast, sharing parts of my story in the workshop. When I finished it, I titled it "A Daughter of My Own," and—since writers yearn to be published—I submitted the story to *Redbook Magazine*.

Once I put my story in the mail, I was ready to begin another. What else absorbed my attention, struck deeply to my core? Stories often germinate from an experience one thinks about incessantly. A lover lost. A friendship betrayed. A period of fear—perhaps fear of death. At once, I saw another possibility. My father's brother had died the year before, and I had been to his funeral in New York. My dead uncle had looked to me almost like a twin of my father. I could barely glance at his body in his casket. I'd dreamed of that dead face. I would try to write something of what I'd seen and experienced; a complicated, devastating, heart-breaking story.

I typed page after page on my portable typewriter while my husband took care of our new baby. At last, when I read the story in our workshop, my fellow students looked somber. One young woman wiped tears from her eyes. Wallace Stegner nodded approval and added, "But one mustn't get too confident. Anything can happen, and it will, you know. Writers must have a tough hide. They must expect dozens of rejections." I thought perhaps I had a tough enough hide. I took a chance and mailed my story to *The New Yorker.*

Within the next month, the extraordinary thing happened. Redbook bought "A Daughter of My Own," and The New Yorker bought "We Know That Your Hearts are Heavy." My friends in the workshop hugged me! Wallace Stegner was proud! How lucky and fortunate I was! My life as a writer had begun in earnest. But Wallace Stegner was right about one thing—rejection squads were lining up to challenge me on many a day in the future.

Eventually, my husband took a position at a community college, and we had two more daughters. Raising three little girls under the age of five consumed almost all my energy, while at the same time giving me the experiences to write stories about young families and the complications of marriage. In time, I published forty-two stories in *Redbook* alone, and dozens more in literary magazines and journals.

I also began teaching. The poet Pablo Neruda, when receiving the Nobel Prize in 1971, said: "All paths lead to the same goal: to convey to others what we are." What was I doing, or trying to do, if not that? I taught for ten years at a community college and later for thirty-two years at the California Institute of Technology.

Sometimes a story is not a large enough canvas on which to paint a vast and devastating loss. When my father was stricken by leukemia and died at the age of fifty-six, I was unable to regain my balance till I had written the many details of his struggle in my first novel *An Antique Man*.

My mother lived a long life, to ninety, while I accompanied her through her many iterations, from widow, to retirement home, to nursing home, and to death. As witness to her life, I wrote a group of "Anna" stories, several of which are in this volume.

Writers move through many seasons and in the more than sixty years since that letter arrived from Wallace Stegner, I have published novels, story collections, memoirs and most recently, a book of essays: *Revelation at the Food Bank*.

"Someone Should Know This Story" is both the name of this book and the wish of my heart.

—Merrill Joan Gerber

SOMEONE SHOULD KNOW THIS STORY

"This Is a Voice from Your Past"

Every woman gets a call like this sooner or later. The phone rings, a man says: "This is a voice from your past." If you're in the mood and the caller doesn't find you in a room where other people are (particularly your husband), and if you have some time to spare, you might enjoy playing the game.

"Who *is* this?" I said, when my call came.

"Don't you recognize my voice?"

"Not exactly."

"Alvord's class? Florida? Your senior year?"

I paused. There had been a number of young men in my life in college, in Florida, in my senior year—and most of them were in Alvord's class.

This call—the first from Ricky—came just after I had given birth to my second daughter; I was living in California. When the phone rang I was in the kitchen cutting a hot dog into little greasy pieces for my two-year-old's lunch and at the same time I felt my milk coming down, that sharp burning pain in both nipples, like an ooze of fire.

"Janet?" His voice was husky, or he was whispering. "This is a serious voice from your past. You know who I am. I think of you all the time. And I work at the phone company, I get free calls, so don't worry about this long-distance shit, I can talk to you all night if I want to."

"Tell me who you are," I said, just stalling for time, but suddenly I knew and was truly astounded. I had thought of Ricky often in the kind of reveries in which we all engage when we count the lives that never were meant to be for us.

"You must know. I know you know."

"Well, it must be you, Ricky, isn't it? But *I* don't have all night. I have two babies now, and I'm feeding them right this minute."

"Is your old man there?"

"No."

"Good, get the kids settled down and I'll hold on. And don't worry, I'm not going to complicate your life. I can't even get to you. I'm in Pennsylvania—and out of money."

"Hang on." I did some things I had to do for the children and then talked to him with my big girl eating in her high chair a foot away from the frayed green couch where I reclined on a pillow, letting the baby suck from my breast. Ricky told me then that he couldn't write a word anymore, it was killing him, he was drinking all the time, he had six kids, his wife was running around with someone else, and could I believe it, he, *he*, was working for the fucking phone company.

"I'm sorry," I said. "I'm really sorry, Ricky."

It occurred to me that anything else I said would sound trite, like: "We all have to make compromises," or "Maybe at some point we have to give up our dreams." The fact was, I hadn't given up mine but pursued it with a kind of dauntless energy. I didn't count the dream that he might have been my true love because I knew even then, all those years ago, that it was impossible. When he read his brilliant stories in class, he was married and living with his wife in a trailer on the outskirts of the campus. He'd already written his prize-winning story that had brought our writing-class to its knees, the one that was chosen later for an O. Henry Award.

Alvord, our professor, a famous and esteemed novelist himself, had informed us in class, in front of Ricky, that the boy had been touched by the wand of the muse—he spoke of Ricky as if a halo gleamed over his head. He made it clear that none of us would ever reach the heights (and should not hope to) for which this golden boy was destined. "A talent like his," he told us once, "is like a comet. It appears only once every hundred years or so."

I clung to my own modest talent and I was working on it; I couldn't envy Ricky his, based as it was in Catholic guilt to which I had no access (his stories were all about sin and redemption); what I envied during that hungry, virginal senior year of college was his wife, the woman he held in his arms each night, the one whose face was caressed by the gaze of his deep-seeing, supernaturally wise marble-blue eyes.

The day he called me in California as I sat nursing my baby girl, feeling the electric suck of her pulsing lips sizzle in a lightning rod strike from nipple to womb, I remembered an image of Ricky that rose up like an illumination—we were in the university library. Ricky had come in alone and had chosen to sit across from me at one of the long, mahogany tables where I was studying. He had his magic pencil in his long fingers and was bent over his lined notebook paper to create whatever piece of brilliant, remorse-filled prose he was writing. A long lock of his dirty-blond hair fell across his forehead, and his fingers scribbled, bent like crab pincers racing over the lined notebook page, wrote words that according to Alvord would turn out to be second only to James Joyce's.

Ricky had told me that his wife worked in some office, typing business documents. He explained, in his breathy East Coast accent, that she was ordinary and dull and he had too young been seduced by her beauty, her astonishing breasts, and his own fierce desire. He assured me I knew him in a way that she never could. We had long earnest discussions after Alvord's class, and in the cafeteria over coffee, and on benches in front of the library—debates about literature and genius (who knows now if their content held anything more remarkable than youth and idealism cooked up in a predictable collegiate stew?)

Still, that night in the library, he stopped his work to stare intensely at me across the table time after time—but didn't smile. We were like conspirators, we knew we shared a plan, an ingenious plot to outfox time, mortality, death—we were both going to be famous writers, and we would—by our words alone—live forever.

At some point that evening—in his frenzy of writing—Ricky's cramped fingers relaxed, his head dropped sideways onto his arm on the table-top, and he fell asleep in the library. He remained there, vulnerable and naked in my gaze, breathing as I knew he must breathe as he slept beside his wife in that trailer, his mouth slightly open, his blue-veined eyelids closed over his blue eyes, his nostrils flaring slightly with each breath.

I watched him till the library closed, watched his face and memorized every line of his fair cheek, the angle of his chin, watched fascinated as a thin thread of drool spooled from his slightly parted lips to the tabletop. I looked around me to be sure no one was near or watching. Then, before he woke, I very slowly moved my hand across the table and anointed the tip of my pencil with his silver spit.

The second time Ricky called me my husband *was* in the room. It was thirty years later, a day in late August. I—with a slow but certain fortitude—had written and published a number of novels by then. My three daughters were grown. The baby who had been at my breast at the time of his first call was in graduate school, and older than I had been when Ricky slept opposite my gaze in the library.

"Janet? This is a voice from your past."

A warning bell rang in my chest. At that moment I was busy talking to my husband about some family troubles (my mother had had a stroke and we were about to put her in a nursing home) and I felt rudely interrupted. I wasn't ready to engage in the game he wanted to play.

"Which past?" I said. "I have many."

"It's Ricky, your old buddy."

"Ricky! How are you?" I said his name with some enthusiasm because he expected it, but I felt my heart sink because I knew I would have to listen to his troubles and I had no patience just then. The game of "remember what we meant to each other" had lost its appeal since by this time everyone I loved filled up my life completely. I had not even a small chink of space left for a latecomer. "Are you still living in Pennsylvania?"

"No, I'm right here!"

"Right here?" I looked down into my lap as if I might find him there.

"In sunny California. In your very city. And I'm here for good."

"How did you know where to reach me? My number isn't even listed!"

"I found one of your books back east and on the cover it said what city you lived in. So when I got here—and I want you to know I picked this city to settle in because of *you*—I went to the library and asked the librarian. I knew a librarian was bound to know where the city's most famous writer lived. I told her I was your old buddy and she gave me your phone number."

"I'm not famous, Ricky."

"Me neither," he said. "How about that?"

I told him I would call him back in a half hour—and in that time I explained to my husband, more or less, who he was. An old college friend. A used-to-be-writer. A drunk. I don't know why I dismissed Ricky so unfairly. Something in his voice had put me on guard. And I could see that this tag with time was a game there was no sense in playing. I had settled into my ordained life like concrete setting in a mold, and I no longer trifled with the idea that I might want to change it. At least not by trailing after romantic visions. With a sense of duty, though, I phoned him back . . . and braced myself.

"You won't believe the stuff that's happened to me," he said. He laughed—he almost cackled—and I shivered. "Can we get together?"

When I hesitated, he said, "I've been through AA, I'm a new person. I'm going to join up here, too, of course. The pity is that before I turned myself around I lost every friend I ever had."

"How come?"

"How come? Because an alcoholic will steal from his best friend if he has to, he'll lie with an innocent face like a newborn baby. There's nothing I haven't stooped to, Janet. I've been to the bottom, that's where you have to be before you can come back. I've rented a little room in town here, and I'm hoping . . . well, I'm hoping that we can be friends again."

"Well, why not," I said. I had the sense my house had become a tunnel and I was getting lost in the dark.

"But mainly—I'm hoping you'll let me come to your class. I want to get started writing again."

"How did you know I teach a class?"

"It says on your book, Janet. That you teach writing at some university or other."

"Well, you certainly are a detective, aren't you?"

"I'm sly as a fox."

"I guess you could visit my class when it begins again after Labor Day. I'll tell my students that you studied with me in Alvord's class. Since most of my old students will be coming back to take the advanced class, they already know about Alvord. In fact, I quote him all the time. We use all his old terms—'action proper,' 'enveloping action'—his dedication to point of view. Maybe we can even get a copy of your old prize story and discuss it."

"Great. So when can we get this friendship on the road again?"

"Look—I'm having a Labor Day barbecue for my family and some friends on Sunday—why don't you come? Do you have a car?"

"I can borrow one."

"Do you need directions? I'll have my husband give them to you."

I called Danny to the phone and handed him the receiver. "Tell my friend Ricky the best way to get here." I wanted Ricky to hear Danny's voice, to know unequivocally that I was taken, connected, committed . . . that I wasn't under any circumstances available.

A stranger rang the doorbell, a man eighty years old, skin jaundiced, skeletal bones shaping his face. The golden hair was thin and gray. Only his voice, with an accent on his tongue like the young Frank Sinatra, convinced me he was the same Ricky. When I shook his hand, I felt his skin to be leathery, dry. When I looked down, the nails were bitten to the quick.

He came inside. I felt him take in the living room in one practiced glance—the art work, the decorations, the furniture—and then we passed out the screen door to the backyard where the party was in progress.

Danny was on the patio, grilling hamburgers and hot dogs over the coals. My three daughters, one already married, and two home from their respective graduate schools, looked beautiful in their summer blouses and white shorts. I saw the backyard as Ricky must have seen it—alive with summer beauty, the plum tree heavy with purple fruit, the jasmine in bloom, the huge cactus plants in Mexican painted bowls growing new little shoots, fierce with baby spines.

My other guests included my sister and her sons, my eldest daughter's husband, a few of my students, several women I had been in a book club with for the last fifteen years. Ricky looked around; I could feel him adding up my life and registering it in his bloodshot eyes.

I took him over to meet Danny and then said: "Let's go sit on the swings and talk." We tramped across the brilliant green of the grass to the old swingset where my daughters used to play. Ricky was wearing a formal gray wool suit, his bony frame almost lost inside its wide shoulders. He swung slowly back and forth, sitting on the splintery wood seat, his hands clutching the rusty chains. He talked looking forward, into air.

"My son Bobby is the one who invited me out to California. He made it big-time," Ricky said, and laughed.

"Is he in movies?" I asked.

"Not exactly. He dove into a city pool in Philly and broke his spine. Now he's in a wheelchair for life. I got him a sharp lawyer who brought a deep pockets lawsuit against the city. Bobby was awarded a million and a half bucks, enough to take care of him the rest of his life and, if I play it right, take care of me, too! My other kids don't talk to me, so Bobby is my only salvation."

"But why is he in California?"

"He's living in a fantastic halfway house out here—the best in the world for paraplegics; Bobby gets all kinds of services, I even can bring my laundry over there and he'll get it done for me free. And he's got enough extra pocket money to help me pay my rent for a while till I get a job."

"What a terrible thing to happen to him."

"No, just the opposite. He was a beach bum, a loser. Now he's got it all together, the whole future taken care of. I think he's relieved. He can use his arms—he plays wheelchair basketball. He lifts weights. He gets counseling, he gets his meals served. Sometimes I wish I could change places with him. But no, I'm back at square one, looking for a job again."

"No more phone company?"

Ricky made a strangling noise in his throat. "I'm going to write my novel, Janet. Finally. I'm going to get it together before I die. If I can sit in on your class, I figure it will start my motor again. You probably teach something like the way Alvord taught us. That old magic. Maybe I can feel that excitement again. I'm counting on it, it's my last hope."

"Do you ever hear from Alvord? Did you stay in touch?"

"In touch! I *lived* with him for a year in Florida when I was really down and out. He took me in, told me he loved me like a son. The trouble was he didn't feed me, Janet. He offered me a place to stay on this farm of his, and then all I could find to eat in the house was Campbell's soup. I think one day he actually hid the bacon from me so I couldn't get my hands on it. So I had to take his truck into town with some money of his to get some food, but I'd been drinking again and I totaled it. He told me I had to leave. He gave me fifty bucks and bought me a train ticket back to Philly. But he was a pain, anyway, preaching to me all the time about being a man, taking responsibility for my kids. I swear, the man was a genius but he's losing it, Janet. He's in his eighties now. He used to think I walked on water."

"We all did."

"That's why I came to live near you. You're the only one on earth who really knows my genius."

I didn't actually count, but I had the sense Ricky ate at least five hamburgers, and as many hot dogs. He hung around the food table, his mouth going, not talking to anyone, but looking at my women friends, their faces, their forms. He looked my daughters up and down—there was no way to stop him. At one point he came to me and said, "Your daughters are really beautiful. All three of them. They have your soul in their eyes." I wanted to distract him. I asked him how often he saw his son; he said, "As often as I can, he gives me CARE packages. I don't have much food in the new place."

After our guests left, I packed up all the leftovers for Ricky: potato chips, lukewarm baked beans, the remaining coleslaw, a package of raw hot dogs and buns to go with them, a quarter of a watermelon, lettuce and sliced tomatoes, even pickles, even mustard and ketchup.

"Listen, thanks," he said. "You're a lifesaver. You don't know how lucky I feel to have found you again. Could I ask you one more favor, though? Would you mind if I came back tomorrow and used your typewriter? I need to write a letter to apply for a job. Someone gave me a tip about a job being night watchman in a truck yard. All I would have to do is sit in a little shed and watch for thieves. I figure I could write all night if I get it."

My reaction was instinctive; I knew I didn't want him back in my house again. "Why don't you let me lend you my electric typewriter? I use a computer now, so I won't need it for a while. I do love it, though—it's the typewriter I wrote my first novel on."

"Then maybe it will be lucky for me. I'll guard it with my life."

"Okay, give me a minute, I'll go put it in its case." I left him standing in the living room with my husband, but I heard no conversation at all—not even ordinary chatter. I could see why Danny was unable to think of a single thing to say to him.

Ricky finally left, laden like an immigrant—bags of food, paper, carbon paper, envelopes, stamps, my typewriter. He stuffed it all into the trunk of an old red car.

Danny and I watched him drive away. He didn't wave—he tore from the curb like one possessed.

"Funny guy," Danny said.

"I don't think we know the half of it," I told him.

I found Ricky's O. Henry prize story in a book and had thirty photocopies made for my students. At the start of class I distributed the copies and told my students that at 7:30 a guest was arriving, a writer of unique skill and vision, a man we were honored to have visit our class. I warned them about the pitfalls of the writer's life, how one could not count on it to earn a living, how so many talented writers fell by the wayside due to pressures of ordinary life. This visitor, I said, a very close friend of mine from the past who had missed what you might call "his window of opportunity," hoped to join our class and work as hard as anyone in it. "He had a whole life in between of doing something else he had to do. All of you are young, at the start of your first life, and if you really want this, this is the time to do it."

When Ricky arrived at my classroom, it was already almost nine PM. He apologized, saying the bus had been late. He was wearing a red V-necked sweater, and looked less cadaverous than at the barbecue, but still much older than his years. He seemed elated to find that a copy of his story was on every desk, and when one of the students asked him how he got the idea for it, he said, simply, "I had thought many times of murdering my brother."

By then, we were already in the midst of having another student read his story; I told the class that next week we would discuss Ricky's story.

I nodded for Harold to go on reading; his story was about a day in the cotton fields of Arkansas, and how the men, women and children picking cotton on a burning hot day reacted when the truck that delivered them failed to leave off drinking water. When the last line had been read, Ricky spoke out in the exact tones of our teacher, Alvord.

"It comes alive on the last page, finally, you see, because it uses all the senses. Since a crying baby can seduce a reader from the very death of Hamlet himself, the writer must bring everything to life. And you do, young man! You do!"

The class was silent, and then a few students applauded Harold and then everyone did—till his embarrassed smile lit up the room. I announced that we would take our usual ten minute break. When the class had filed out, I thought I would find Ricky waiting to talk to me about my students, to tell me how the class had seemed to him, if it would suit his purposes. But he left the room without a glance in my direction, and when I looked out into the hall, I saw him in deep conversation with one of my students, a young woman. When the class reconvened, neither one of them returned for the second half.

At seven the next morning, my student phoned me. "This is Alice Miller. I'm so sorry to disturb you," she said, "but your friend, the famous writer, borrowed my car last night. We went out for coffee and afterward he said he had an urgent errand to go on, he practically got on his knees to beg to borrow the car. He said that although he knew I didn't know him very well, *you* could vouch for him, and he promised he would have my car back in my carport by midnight. He borrowed ten dollars, too. He never came back. And I can't get to work without it!"

"I'll see if I can reach him at the number I have for him," I told her. "I'm so sorry. I'll call you right back."

But his landlady did not find him in his room. I called Alice back and told her I could only imagine that there was some emergency with his son who was a paraplegic. I reassured her that he would surely have the car back to her very shortly but in the meantime to take a taxi to work, that I would pay for it.

I learned later that when finally Ricky did return the car to Alice, he never even rang her bell. He left the car at the curb. She found the inside of it littered with cigarette butts, racing forms, empty paper cups, and the greasy wrappers from McDonald's hamburgers. The gas tank was totally empty. There was not even enough gas left in the tank for Alice to get to a gas station to fill it up.

Toward the end of September, I was about to apply for a fellowship and realized that I needed my typewriter to fill out the application form. My anger overcame my revulsion, and I dialed the number Ricky had originally given me. His landlady answered and informed me that he'd moved out bag and baggage—that "he shipped out to sea."

"To sea!" I imagined him on a whaling ship, thinking he was Melville, or more likely that he was one of the sailors in Stephen Crane's story about men doomed at sea, "The Open Boat," a piece of work whose first line Alvord had often quoted: "None of them knew the color of the sky."

But my typewriter! I wanted it, it was mine. I felt as if Ricky had kidnapped one of my children.

"Let it go," my husband said. "It's an old typewriter, I'll get you a new one, it doesn't matter. Write it off as a business loss. Write him off—your old friend—if you can as one of those mistakes we all make in life."

In the days following, I had trouble sleeping. I held imaginary conversations with Ricky, by turns furious, accusatory, damning, murderous. "I trusted you!" I cried out, and in return I heard his laugh . . . his cackle. Alvord had often talked about evil in his class; the reality of it, how it existed, how it was as real as the spinning globe to which we clung.

Days later, in a frenzy, I began calling hospitals, halfway houses, rehab clinics, trying to find the place where Ricky's son lived—if indeed he had a son.

"Don't do this to yourself," Danny said. He saw me on the phone, sweating, asking questions, shaking with anger, trembling with outrage.

But one day I actually located the boy. He was in a hospital in a city only a half hour's drive from my house. I named his name, Bobby, with Ricky's last name, and someone asked me to wait, they would call him to the phone. And a man picked up the phone and said "Yes? This is Bobby."

I told him I was a friend of his father, that his father had my typewriter.

"Oh sure, I know about that. You're his old friend. He left the typewriter here with me. You can come and get it." His voice had the same tones as Ricky's voice. The same seductive sound—the "Oh sure" a kind of promise, the "come and get it" the serpent's invitation.

"His landlady said he went to sea . . .?" I felt I must have another piece of the puzzle, at least one more piece.

"Yeah—he got a job teaching English on a Navy ship. I told him he better take it, he wasn't going to freeload off me the rest of his life."

"I'm sorry," I said to the boy. "I'm sorry about your accident . . . and about your troubles with your father."

"Hey, don't worry about it. It's nothing new. But if you want his address on the ship I could give it to you."

"No—thank you," I said. "I don't want it. I think your father and I have come to a parting of the ways. Good-bye, Bobby, I wish you good luck."

"You, too," Bobby said. "Anyone who knows my father needs it."

Then, two years after I talked to his son, I got the third phone call. "This is a voice out of your fucking past."

"Hello, Ricky." My heart was banging so hard I had to sit down.

"I heard from my son you want your goddamned typewriter back."

"No, no—"

"You'll have it back. It's in little pieces. I'll be on your doorstep with it in twenty minutes."

"I don't want it, Ricky. *Don't come here!* Keep it."

"I said you'll have it back. I *always* keep my word, you fucking . . ."

"Please, keep it. I don't need it! Keep it and write your book on it!"

"Just expect me," Ricky said. "I'll be there, you can count on it. Watch out your window for me."

And so I did. For a week. For a month. I keep watching and sometimes, when the phone rings, I let it ring and don't answer it.

Tell Me Your Secret

The time was the fifties and everything we young women did was fraught with danger. We could get pregnant, we could get raped, we could get lost, we could get seduced, our boyfriends could beg us to iron all their shirts for a year and then not marry us after all. We couldn't get diaphragms without a doctor's appointment but couldn't ask to be fitted for one unless we were about to be married. If we, somehow—heaven forbid—became pregnant, we'd heard that Puerto Rico was the only place we could get an abortion that wouldn't kill us. We were suspected of lascivious behavior as a matter of fact: the campus dress code was rigid and demanded that we not wear shorts more than one inch above the knee, and then only under a non-transparent raincoat, and only for essential sporting events. The dorm mothers rushed around the lounges where we met our young men, ordering us to keep "all four feet on the floor at all times." And of course no men, not even our fathers, were allowed into our dorm rooms.

Those of us who aspired to education learned soon enough that the college administrators at our Florida university were seriously unwilling to give graduate fellowships or teaching assistantships to women, convinced as they were that we'd run off and get married and that men were better risks and more deserving in every case.

Our mothers let us know they hoped for the best, especially that we would be engaged before graduation since afterward, because we'd all be elementary school teachers, the chances of our meeting marriageable men would be negligible. Our fathers, knowing how men are, feared the worst, that we would lose our virginity before being spoken for, but none of them—being men themselves—ever talked to us face-to-face about their concerns.

In spite of all this, I kept humming along in a little cocoon of self-direction, certain that none of society's prescriptions for me were going to affect the outcome of my future. I would get a fellowship if I wanted one, a husband and babies in the right order if I wanted them, and no one I didn't want to get my virginity would get it. I would stay as innocent as I wanted to be for as long as I wanted to be.

An event that upset my grip on this blind certainty happened on a Saturday in the month of May, just before final exams of my junior year. I was in my dorm room ironing a dotted-Swiss pink party dress with fitted bodice and scoop neck and a little white bow at its center. I had just come back from town where I'd bought pink leather flats to go with my dress, and I'd also had my hair cut short so that—with just a toss of my fingers—curls would shimmer all over my head. I was twenty years old and as pretty as I would ever be in this life.

Tonight, in the woods at the edge of town, there would be a party at the home of my psychology professor—Barton Flack, a bearded and attractive man, who—in the classroom—sat on the edge of his desk, tapping his shined loafers against the wooden desk-edge as he lectured. He was famous for inventing a board game that was selling out all over the country and making him a millionaire. With the proceeds, Barton (as he asked us to address him in the interests of equality) had built a modern glass and wood house deep in a forest of Florida pines, with bedrooms separate from the house and ringing the living area like a circle of motel rooms. (He raised his brows suggestively when he described these rooms to the girls who hung around his desk after class.)

He had intimated all semester that when school was out, he'd throw a party like none other and a couple of his selected favorites would be invited to meet some mystery guests, friends of his from the intellectual and art worlds who would surely raise a few hairs on our heads.

Iconoclast that he was, he still had to get around authoritarian rule: girls had to be back in the dorms by curfew. He had to figure out how we could spend the night at his place. We told him we lived under a microscope: each time we left for the evening we were required to sign out on a card kept in a box at the reception desk. We had to state our destination, the name of our companion(s), and our expected time of return. When we came back (if we had the good fortune not to get seduced and left for dead in the lime quarry) we had to certify and initial our time of return.

Barton arranged a deception for me and another student of his by inveigling a couple of his women friends to pretend they were our "aunts" who would appear before the dorm mothers and testify in writing that they were our relatives and were taking us off campus for a night of wholesome and purely educational activities. The opera, perhaps. The other girl, Diane Weinberger, who also lived in my dorm, had agreed to cooperate in the plot. She was not my friend, this short, plain, ordinary-looking girl who never wore makeup, who wore glasses, who was a math major, and who had the distinct look of a lesbian about her (or so some said. I had no experience with lesbians, so left it to those who knew better). Barton seemed to admire her serious demeanor, her powerful mind, and her indifferent dress—she seemed an iconoclast also—at a time when there weren't many around who were girls.

As I prepared for the party, ironing my dress and packing a small overnight case with clothes for the next day, my roommate, Flora Lu Matterfield, sat like a hippopotamus on her bed wearing her elastic chin-lift device, and watched me with a look of despair on her face.

"Honey bun, I'm worried about you, going to that man's house for the night, with God knows what's going to happen out there in the woods. You know that man has a reputation! He knows female psychology, he's famous for it, so that's why he can convince you you're going out there for some so-called party when he could be planning to sell you down the river into white slavery. Otherwise why wouldn't he want to get you back here safe and sound by curfew?" Her mouth, held in an unnatural position by the elastic straps, caused her to speak as if she were under water.

"Parties in the real world don't even get *started* till around midnight, Flora Lu. How can I expect him—*the host*—to deliver me back here by curfew?"

"Well, if they find your body in the swamp," Flora Lu said lugubriously, "I refuse to testify in court and say I warned you. I won't muddy your name. I'll just pretend I never saw you pack your little pink lacy nightgown in that little case. I didn't see a thing."

"It's not lace. It's cotton-flannel, Flora Lu."

"In the dark, who will know the difference?"

Flora Lu was frowning and mumbling to herself and leafing through Bride's Magazine and I was putting the finishing touches on my dress when the room buzzer sounded. I went to the intercom and buzzed back.

"Special Delivery for Franny at the front desk."

"I'll be right down." I tried to imagine who would send me a Special Delivery. Maybe I was being notified that I'd won a poetry contest I'd entered. Maybe it was from Ted, a young man with whom I'd been pen pals for years. He liked to shock me by sending bizarre packages. Once, after he visited Italy, he sent me little sealed bottles of polluted water from the Venetian Canals.

The girl at the desk handed me a blue airmail envelope, with scrawls all over it that said: "RUSH! PRIVATE! URGENT! PERSONAL!" The return address was from Billy Carp, a childhood friend of mine who still lived in Brooklyn, where I'd grown up. I took the letter upstairs and read the first sentence: "*Dear Franny, I saw your grandmother this morning and I will see her again this afternoon.*" This puzzled me. Why would Billy see her in any case? She was 87 years old; I hadn't seen her in several years, myself. She was in a nursing home, paralyzed by a stroke. My aunt lived nearby and visited her daily. My aunt and Billy's mother were friends, but Billy was at Brooklyn College and wouldn't normally be seeing my grandmother. "*No one here wanted to tell you this, but I feel it's my duty as your friend to be sure you know the truth. Your parents have always protected you from the realities of life, whereas my mother always let me have it right up front, from the day my father died when I was twelve to the lovers my mother brought home when I was in high school.*"

Feeling alarmed, I turned the page over and read the end of the letter.

"She was old anyway, and her life wasn't worth much. Don't lose too much sleep over this. It's the way of the world. Love from your good friend, Billy." Now I scanned the letter in panic, looking for the operational phrase, which finally I found. *"Your grandmother died today of massive blood loss from bleeding ulcers. Your folks didn't plan to tell you this till after you finished your final exams. I went with my mother and your aunt to the hospital this morning, and we'll be going to the Jewish Funeral Home this afternoon."*

I sat down on my bed.

"Honey, you're white as a ghost. Tell Flora Lu what's wrong."

"My grandmother died."

"Lord a mercy," she said. She put down her magazine. "Well, I guess you can just forget your little party now." She stared at my face and then pulled off her chin-lift device. "Honey, you stay here with me and I'll take good care of you. We'll light a little candle and pray together for her precious soul that just passed on."

I left my room, walked out the back door of the dorm and followed the path out to the miniature golf course. I looked up: trees, sky. The great glory of Nature. Death. Death was part of Nature. I knew I wasn't feeling the proper emotions. This was bad news. My mother's mother dead. Someday it would be my mother, then me. I kept pushing myself into different slots, trying to know what to feel. Where were my tears? Where was my heart? Why wasn't I crying? Why, in fact, was I thinking about my pink dress and worrying that now I probably wouldn't get to wear it tonight? I suddenly remembered my father's older sister, my aunt who had committed a terrible crime in our family. I'd heard her black heart cursed many times: *"Did you know that the night her mother died your Aunt Ruth actually went to a party?"* It was the worst that could be said about her—this horror she had committed, this taint she had brought down on the family. Privately I had always thought it wasn't such a bad thing to do: if you had a party to go to and someone died, why not go to your party? The dead wouldn't particularly care, would they? If they loved you, they'd want you to go on having your life.

I definitely wanted to have my life. In fact, I had a feeling that some part of it was actually going to start tonight, at the party. My anger swung toward Billy. Why hadn't he minded his own business? Now I had an obligation to feel bad. I'd have to call home and argue with my parents, blaming them for treating me like a child. I would get upset, I might cry, I'd lose my dreamy party rhythm (I was losing it already), and I'd be too far gone to think of going anywhere.

Maybe I could just pretend the letter hadn't arrived. It was just a matter of information. Why not imagine I simply didn't know about this death and continue to feel happy? I could go back upstairs and choose which necklace to wear to decorate the scoop neckline of the dress—a small, final act of grace I had been looking forward to all day. If only I hadn't told Flora Lu!

I looked up at the dorm windows and I felt that, against my will, the entire landscape of my world had changed. I was now obligated to think about the meaning of death, the short span of man's life, how life was, as we had learned in Shakespeare class, "a walking shadow, a poor player that struts and frets his hour upon the stage and then is heard no more . . . a tale told by an idiot, full of sound and fury, signifying nothing . . ."

Right now I was supposed to be shedding tears, trying to remember little things about my grandmother and starting to miss her. I also should probably be thinking about God and his role in all this, if there was a God and if he had a role. This was all very far from my present interests. Light years away. The deeper meanings of life seemed totally irrelevant to me. Why should I waste my time on such useless pondering?

At 8 p.m., as soon as the buzzer rang in my room, I hurried out with my little suitcase despite Flora Lu's pronouncement that I was bound to go to hell for this. The "aunt" who came to sign me out at the front desk wore an emerald-green satin dress, gold earrings shaped like serpents, and sling-back suede high-heels. As I came down the ramp into the lobby, she teetered toward me in little mincing steps because of the narrowness of her dress and held her arms out to embrace me. As she hugged me to her visibly pointed breasts, waves of her perfume blazed into my eyes and made them tear. Since she apparently had already completed her paperwork with the dorm mother, she put her arm around me, took my overnight case in her free hand, and walked me toward the door. Just then Diane Weinberger arrived in the lobby and I saw a woman in a navy blue suit—carrying an alligator handbag—rise from a chair and walk toward her. Another embrace took place: Diane stood like a stick of concrete while the woman exclaimed about how pretty she looked. (Diane was dressed in brown corduroy pants and a man's plaid shirt.)

"Shall we go?" my new friend advised. She led me out the door. I gave myself up to her, let her put me into her red sports car, let her speed away into the night with me, and allowed her to deliver me into the labyrinth of the professor's dark woods.

All of the guests at the party, standing in the circular, brightly lit living room, holding drinks and paper plates of food, were reflected back upon themselves from the great panes of glass that looked into the black forest. It seemed a scene from a horror movie: while they were all blindly chattering away and eating hors d'oeuvres, the woods were closing in on them like an iron trap and would shortly devour them.

I would surely be afraid to live here myself, walking alone through the house at night, reading unprotected in the glare of the bright lights, while outside, surrounding me, the mysterious woods hid whatever eyes might be looking in at me.

Barton had furnished his new house with orange furniture—strangely-shaped plastic orange tables, orange canvas cloth laid over black metal chair frames, orange Chinese paper lanterns, orange ash trays. My professor circulated among his guests; he was smoking a cigar. His shoes were especially highly polished, his beard neatly trimmed, pointed and giving him a little air of the devil. He put his arm around me and told me I looked beautiful.

Leading me around the circular room, he introduced me to his friends: a South American diplomat (a tall, hairy, bearlike man with a sweet smile), an actress (the woman in green satin who was my "aunt"), a poet, a playwright, the owner of an alligator farm, a professor of philosophy.

Diane Weinberger stood under an orange paper lantern talking to the diplomat; her hands hung at her sides, holding neither cup nor plate. The man kept offering his plate to her, and finally he picked up a shrimp wrapped in bacon and popped it into her mouth. When she had swallowed, she opened her mouth for another.

Music was playing: Yma Sumac singing one of her weird and unearthly songs—she was a woman whose voice had an uncanny range, from bass to highest soprano. I'd heard her on the radio—she gave me the feeling that if I listened to her too long I would be driven insane.

I told myself that I was finally at the professor's party, the party I had so badly wanted to attend and for which I had prepared for days. The party that promised so much and for which I had betrayed the moral teachings of my upbringing and made an enemy of my roommate. Since I was here, I was duty-bound to enjoy myself. And if Diane Weinberger—a girl as Jewish as I was—could eat shrimp and bacon, so could I. I piled my plate high. I ate at least a dozen of these delicacies; they were delicious, the white chewy forbidden shrimp circled by the fried, crisp, salty, flesh of pig.

There was dancing and drinking long into the night. No one danced with me, but I sat in an orange chair and watched those who did. Barton and the actress-in-satin moved their bodies together in ways I didn't know was possible. At some point, during a lull in the music, my professor brought out his board game and we all sat down on the orange rug in a circle to play his invention: "Tell Me Your Secret."

There was the traditional gameboard and the conventional die to throw. Unlike Monopoly that frequently sent you to jail, this game had instructions on the board to "Go Back To Your Mother's Womb" or "Confess In The Palace of Dreams" or "Take A Card From The Treasure Cave."

The cards were dangerous as quicksand: they required that each player tell a secret. "Tell your most embarrassing memory." "Tell about the time you stole something from a store." "Tell about the night you saw your parents in bed together." "Tell about the first time you played doctor as a child." Each time a member of the party hesitated, Barton would pour his guest another glass of champagne, and the others would urge him on. There was much laughter and then, eventually—a secret was blurted out, after which there was even more laughter. The things I heard were shocking to me; I felt I needed a long time to think about each confession, to understand what its impact on the person might have been. Everyone else, though, would listen to a confession, laugh knowingly, and then look up, ready and waiting for the next revelation.

My turn was coming up soon. The South American diplomat told of how, when he was fourteen, he had had sex with his cousin, a woman of twenty-five. Diane Weinberger revealed that her older brother used to read dirty stories to her and then gave her a nickel to rub his penis "till it popped and the scum came out." She stated this with cool satisfaction. Then she admitted she didn't think any man could ever excite her as much as her brother had in their youth.

How could I play this game? What comparable thing could I say—that I had once read a scene in a novel called "God's Little

Acre" about a girl getting spanked with a hairbrush and it interested me unduly so that I read it over several times and still remembered it? Or that I had taken a quarter from the dresser of one of my girlfriends and hid it in my sock when I was eleven years old? I began to think of Flora Lu with longing; oh to be back in my dorm room, safe under the blankets, the lights long out after the more-than-reasonable curfew, which was designed for my own good!

Now some truth would be extracted from me and transform me in the minds of others—and even my own—into a different person. In the next few moments, I would lose my privacy forever.

The die were put in my hands by my professor. "Have courage!" he whispered to me. "The truth will set you free."

I cast the die. I moved my game piece. I chose my card and read it.

"Tell the thing you are most ashamed of."

I looked around the circle at the faces of the guests who now seemed to wait in judgement for my confession. Everyone's eyes were upon me, everyone's mouths seemed loose and limp, hanging open with lascivious hunger.

"I came to this party . . ." I said, "even though I just learned today . . . I came here even though . . . my grandmother died." I waited for the glass walls of the professor's house to implode, for one of the glass shards to pierce my heart. I thought of my mother, broken-hearted at home, and of my father, who would die of grief to see me here, besotted with champagne and fattened to bursting with bacon and shrimp.

"How old was she?" the actress asked.

"She was 87."

"Oh well. That doesn't count then, you can't be guilty about *that*!" she said. "She lived long enough. It has to be something you're really ashamed of."

"It counts." Barton defended me. He came and knelt beside me and put his arm around my shoulder. "She *is* ashamed. That's what Franny has to tell you. That's what you have to accept. The rules of the game are that you can't challenge what someone feels is her truth."

I passed the die to the next person in the circle. She tossed them and I was forgotten. I excused myself and went to find the orange bathroom where all the little orange soaps were in the shapes of women's breasts. I wanted to cry, but I had had too much champagne to be able to get near the place where my tears resided.

It was nearly dawn and I was half-asleep in a chair when the actress offered to lead me to my guest room for the night. Just as we had heard, the bedrooms were separate from the house, arranged in a row of motel-like rooms, their walls, like those in the house, made entirely of glass that looked into the woods on two sides. I went into the bathroom which adjoined the guest room on the other side and locked both doors in order to get undressed out of view of the windows, to put on my cotton-flannel nightgown and brush my teeth, like a good girl. Through the door I could hear the voices of Diane Weinberger and the South American diplomat. He had a deep booming laugh, like rolling thunder. Her laugh was high and whiny, but full of a strange, giddy joy. Soon they stopped talking and began gasping and guffawing breathlessly as if they were tickling one another.

I got into bed and shut off the bedside lamp as fast as possible. With the light off, I could see a few feet into the woods by the glow of light coming from the next room. The pine trees were enormous, weighted down by Spanish Moss that waved in the wind like witches' hair.

From the other side of the wall I could hear the noises of Diane Weinberger and the hairy man. I could hear the bedsprings rumble, I could hear her high cries and his low groans. I listened, totally alert, for a very long time. Holding onto the sides of my bed, I traveled with them on their ride, their slow, deliberate journey over the twists and turns of the tracks, inching up the roller coaster to the screaming, blinding pitch of sensation. After their last screams, someone turned off the light in their room, plunging the woods into darkness.

I lay there, hot in my bed under the sheet, smelling the scent of sawdust from the new wood flooring. Heat lightning flashed in the sky and the rumble of thunder vibrated through the room. With every flash of light, I thought I saw a face looking in the huge window. I begged myself to go to sleep.

Through the glass I watched the full moon riding under and over the blowing storm clouds till it was buried in blackness. Again I saw a face at my window. The door, which had no lock on it, opened slowly and Barton Flack's voice whispered my name.

"Franny? Are you awake? There's a big storm blowing in. It can get pretty fierce out here; I didn't want you to be afraid."

"I'm not afraid," I said.

My professor came and sat down on the edge of my bed. He was wearing some kind of loose caftan; he found my hand and began to stroke my arm.

"This has been a very strange night for you, Franny," he said. "I know you've been very, very careful in your life so far. I just want to tell you—there's no prize for being careful." He reached up and touched my face. Then he leaned forward, cupped my head in his hands and kissed my lips very gently. "You could come into bed with me and my friend," he said. "We could ride out the storm together. It could be one of our secrets."

He waited for my answer. After a great burst of lightning, the moon appeared again in the sky. My white-haired grandmother was by now deep under the ground, cold as stone, still as stone, giving up her soft flesh to the history of the earth. "The sun shall not smite her by day, nor the moon by night," I heard in my mind. My own history was just beginning. How short a time lay ahead to be under sun and moon.

My professor was standing now beside my bed, his hand extended to me. "Come," he invited me. "We will enjoy the night."

After a moment, I let him pull me to my feet.

How Love Came to Grandmother

My elder daughter has long outgrown "The Three Bears," "Rumpelstiltskin," and even "Rapunzel"—and these days when she is in bed with the flu or a cold (today it is a strep throat), and when she has tired of her current jigsaw puzzle, her movie magazines, and the uninventive guppies in the stringy bowl on the night table, she asks me to tell her a story "from the old days."

"Tell me again how you met Daddy," she says. We always have a little furtive smile together when she says that, because the story is a secret between us, and one Daddy is never allowed to hear. If he ever comes into the room during the telling, Mattie expires in giggles, and little Clara, who is usually busy in the middle of the floor with her dominoes or Rubber Robots, laughs her little baby laugh as though she is more in on the joke than anyone, and poor Daddy goes away puzzled, but always in good-humored indignation. At the moment, Clara is napping and Daddy is at work.

So I begin. "In the old days, when I was a young girl, your grandfather, who is my daddy, had a little clock shop in downtown Brooklyn."

Mattie snuggles down under the blankets with a delighted smile now that she has captured my attention for probably the rest of the morning, because we both know what this story leads to: how Grandmother met Grandfather, and how Great-grandmother met Great-grandfather.

But it is fun for all of us, I don't mind, there is something deeply satisfying about pouring our very unimportant family history into these eager little ears, and to imagine Mattie telling it sweetly to her children, and they to their children in the generations to come.

So I automatically touch Mattie's forehead with my lips, disregarding her impatient shrug, and, noting that her temperature is, if not normal, at least no higher than it was, I go on with the love story I have told so often, remembering the sound of the story now better than the events of it.

"The clock shop was on Hanson Place, just down from the Long Island Railroad Station, and you always knew when you were getting near the shop because right on the corner was the Williamsburg Savings Bank, with a great round clock on its steeple. Your grandfather always set the clocks in his shop by the bank clock. On Saturdays, when there was no school, I went along with him to work to help in the store. My job was to wind all the clocks and watches in the window, and set them all at the right time, and dust out the showcase and sweep the floor. Most of the time your grandfather sat at the back of the store over a little wooden table, repairing watches. A great bright bulb shone down on the table, and Father wore big black magnifying glasses up around his forehead, which he slid down over his eyes when he had to look at a very tiny watch part.

"One day your daddy came along, and looked in the window. He was very young and handsome (and very skinny then, too—though you'd never believe it), and he carried some music books with him. He was on his way to his piano teacher's house for his lesson, which he took every Saturday morning. He looked in the window for a long time, and I looked at him, my heart beating very fast, and finally, with a very puzzled expression on his face, he came into the store and said to me: 'Excuse me, but could you tell me what time it is? I'm on the way to a music lesson, and I'm afraid I'm late.' I thought it was just a big excuse, because there were more watches in one square foot of that window than in half of Switzerland, and I thought your daddy, seeing me through the window, had been unable to resist my charms, and had to come in and meet me.

"But just then your grandfather's voice boomed out from the back—'Young man, Eastern Standard Time is written on the face of every clock in that window!' 'Yes sir,' said your daddy, 'but every clock says something different.'

"Father and I both ran out in front and looked in the window, and sure enough, every single clock told a different time. 'Ruthie,' your grandfather said to me, severely, 'didn't you wind the clocks this morning?' And of course I hadn't, because I was too busy mooning around and dreaming of a handsome man like your daddy, and wishing he would come along and carry me off on his white horse."

Mattie giggles. "You mean they didn't have cars, it was so long ago?" I make a face at her, and she sticks out her tongue at me, and then goes on to finish the story in her little singsong. "And then Daddy stopped in to see you every Saturday when he went to his piano lesson because he was sorry he had gotten you in trouble, and then he fell in love with you, and when you finished school he married you."

"Something like that."

"Boy, it's a good thing he did," Mattie says,"—else where would *I* be?"

"You might be someone else," I tell her. "A movie actress, or a famous ice-skating star . . ."

". . . or a ditch digger," she adds. After a minute she says, "Mother, how do you suppose I'll meet my husband?"

"Oh, you never know. It doesn't matter really. It's always nice, however you do."

"Maybe I'll never get married," she says. "I'm going on twelve and I've never even had a date."

"I wouldn't give yourself up for lost yet, sweetie. Most people get married if they want to."

"Aunt Jenny wanted to. What about her?"

Aunt Jenny is my mother's sister, actually Mattie's *great*-aunt, who is now seventy-three, living out her lonely, petty life in a co-operative apartment building for old people in Coney Island.

"Aunt Jenny is another story. She never tried to meet men. She stayed cooped up in the house all the time like a nun. Even when the family was desperate for money after your great-grandfather died, she wouldn't budge out of the house to get a job."

"She seemed very nice when she was here Christmas," Mattie remarks.

"Well, she's nice when she wants to be," I say, hearing my voice take on a defensive tone, "but how do you explain the way she acted when Great-grandfather died, and your grandmother had to go out and support the whole family, while Aunt Jenny wouldn't lift a finger? You know that story, don't you?"

"I know that story," Mattie says. Her voice is flat, and she is twisting a ringlet around her finger, not looking at me.

"Well, was that a nice thing to do?" I say. "She was perfectly capable. She could have helped carry the load a little. Instead my mother had to do it all."

"Aunt Jenny had very bad pimples. She was embarrassed to go out of the house."

"How do you know?"

"She told me that at Christmas. She told me her face was so awful, she cried about it every day."

"It wasn't that bad at all, Mattie. My mother told me it was all in Jenny's mind."

"Well, I like her," Mattie says.

We are both silent, and the friendly morning seems rather ruined, somehow.

Finally I say, "Time for your medicine. Do you want a little orange juice?"

"No medicine yet," Mattie states. "First tell me again about how Great-grandmother met Great-grandfather. I like that one."

She is cheery again, so I try to be.

"Well, my grandmother who is Great-grandmother to you was born in Poland. That's a little country across the ocean—"

"I know where it is," Mattie interrupts. "We had it in Geography."

"Anyway, she wanted to come to America—everyone did in those days—so from the time she was twelve years old, just a bit older than you, she worked as a housekeeper for a lady in Poland, and saved all her money for boat fare."

"And she didn't have to go to school because in those days only the men went to school to study the Torah, right?"

"Right."

"And her mother didn't mind that she went to work because things were different in those days. Right?"

"Right."

"Would you let *me* quit school and go to work?"

"No. Things are different these days."

Mattie smiles crookedly. "Okay, tell me about the herring."

"When your great-grandmother was eighteen, she had finally saved up enough money to come to this country, so she collected her few clothes, and her mother (that's your great-*great*-grandmother) packed her enough food for the trip, and she left for America."

"Do you know how my great-great-grandmother met *her* husband?" Mattie asks.

"No," I say. "Things get lost that far back."

"Okay, go on."

"She went steerage class, because that's the way you had to go if you had very little money, and she had to travel in the bottom of the ship, under the deck, and they had no beds or bunks and had to sleep on blankets on the floor. A lot of the passengers were dirty and had lice on their bodies, and Great-grandmother wore a *babushka* on her head, hoping it would protect her hair from the lice, because she knew if any got on her, she would have to pour kerosene in her hair and then have her head shaved when the ship landed in America.

"They had a very rough crossing, and the ship rolled for days and days, and Great-grandmother got very seasick. She couldn't eat any of the food her mother had packed for her, and she got weaker and weaker, but every time she unwrapped a cracker or a piece of cheese, she just got more nauseous, and had to stuff it right back in the bag before she threw up.

"On the third day of not eating anything, she fainted, and a young man, also traveling steerage, helped her to sit up, and asked her if there were anything he could do to help. 'I haven't eaten in three days,' she said, 'and the only thing I can imagine swallowing is a piece of lox. That's the only thing in the world that I think I could eat.' 'Would herring do?' said the young man. *'Herring!'* cried Great-grandmother. 'A whole ocean full of fish, and the nearest herring is in Poland.' 'The nearest herring is in my pocket,' said the young man—and he pulled it out, and fed it to her, and she gave him all her crackers and cheese and fruit, and he gave her the rest of his herrings, and they ate together all the way to America."

"And got married when they got here," said Mattie.

"Correct."

"And then they had your mother, and your mother married your father and they had you, and you married Daddy and had me."

"Correct again. How about your medicine now?"

"Okay, but only if you promise to tell me the story of Grandmother right afterward."

"It's a deal." I go into the kitchen for the capsule, and check Clara in her crib on the way back. Mattie swallows the pill with a terrible face and a shudder.

This telling of tales seems less delightful today than it has ever been. Mattie is not listening to me the way she used to. She is interrupting more, and being too critical. She is watching my face peculiarly, with the same expression she had one night a few years ago when I had finished telling her "Snow White and the Seven Dwarfs" for about the millionth time. With that funny look on her face, she had turned her head up to me and said, "That's all a bunch of hogwash, isn't it, Mother?"

Now she settles down under the blankets again, and says, "This one used to be my favorite one of all—about the long hair."

"Isn't it your favorite any more?" I ask.

"We'll have to see," she says cryptically.

"Well—" I begin. "This is the story of how my mother met my father, which is the story of how your grandmother met your grandfather. As you know, your great-grandfather died when Grandmother was a very young girl."

"That's the man with the herring," says Mattie.

"And your great-grandmother was not very well—"

"From eating all that lox," says the child.

"So Grandmother had to go out and work to support Aunt Jenny and Great-grandmother."

"And Aunt Jenny stayed home and wouldn't work because she was lazy," says Mattie in the tone she uses to reel off the timetables.

"That's right. She was very lazy. She would stay in bed till noon, and Grandmother got up at six and went to work all the way to Manhattan on the subway, and Aunt Jenny stayed at home reading love poems and taking valentines."

"For who?"

"How should I know for who? For the man-in-the-moon, I suppose. When Grandmother asked her if she would wash and iron some clothes because she had to wear a clean dress to work every day, Jenny complained and grumbled all week. One night, during the summer, Jenny decided to have a party, although she hardly knew a soul because she never set foot out of the house. She called up a few girls she knew and asked one of them if her boyfriend could bring along an extra boy for her.

"When Grandmother came home from work that night, the party was going on, even though it was very late. Grandmother had worked overtime, and was tired, and a friend of hers had been kind enough to drive her home from work. She said goodnight to him outside, and came into the house. She walked through the bright living room where everyone was, then through the kitchen and up the backstairs to her bedroom. She put on her nightgown, took all the pins out of her mane of brown hair, and brushed it one hundred strokes over each shoulder. Then she decided to sneak down to the kitchen to have a glass of milk before she went to sleep. She went down the backstairs into the kitchen, and pouring the milk in a glass, stepped outside onto the dark back porch to sit on the wicker glider and drink it.

"And there was Grandfather. Sitting on the old rocker, smoking his pipe in the dark—the smell of summer roses coming up from the backyard. Grandmother said 'Excuse me' because she hadn't meant to come out and scare him like that, and Grandfather said to excuse *him*, he really should be in there with all the people, but he didn't like parties much, and he had been dragged along as an extra man, and he didn't feel very extra. He just wanted to sit by himself till his friend was ready to go home.

"Even though he was shy, he told Grandmother she had the prettiest, softest hair he'd ever seen, and she laughed and said how could he see in the dark—and he laughed too, and soon they were laughing so hard together that Grandmother spilled milk down the front of her nightgown, and just as Grandfather was leaning over to offer her his handkerchief, Aunt Jenny came out on the porch and Grandmother decided she had better go up to bed. And the next evening Grandfather came by and took Grandmother walking, and soon they had set the date."

I take a deep breath and look at Mattie. "The end," I say.

She looks neither amused nor delighted. She is making an odd face. Finally she says, "Poor Aunt Jenny."

"What has Aunt Jenny got to do with it?"

"No one ever married her. She never had any fun. If Clara ever does to me what Grandmother did to Aunt Jenny, I'll kill her."

"What on earth are you talking about, Mattie?"

"That's not what happened at all. All that stuff about just coming down for a glass of milk."

"What do you mean?" We eye each other as enemies.

"Aunt Jenny at Christmas told me the same story. Only it wasn't the same. I said to her 'Tell me the story about how Grandma met Grandpa' and she told me something, but it sure wasn't what *you* always tell me."

"What was it?"

"Well, first of all, Aunt Jenny had all these pimples, and she cried every time she looked in the mirror, she was so miserable. And Grandmother was beautiful. Aunt Jenny said she was the most beautiful girl anyone could imagine, with a skin like lilies and hair like a waterfall. Aunt Jenny had to stay home all the time with Great-grandmother, while Grandmother went out to work every day and wore pretty clothes, and met different people, and had lots of boyfriends. All Aunt Jenny did was take out the garbage and do Grandmother's dirty laundry, and cry her eyes out. Once she tried to get a job working in a bakery, and the lady there told her that with a face like hers no one would buy the bread she touched."

Mattie stops, and reaches for a Kleenex on the night table. "What a lousy life she has," says the child.

"What *else* did she have to tell you?"

"Well, about this party. Aunt Jenny was so lonely she couldn't stand it anymore, and she thought maybe if she could meet a nice boy and let him get to know her, he would see she wasn't as awful as she looked. So she called up three of the girls she knew who all had boyfriends, and invited them to a party, and asked one of them if her boyfriend could bring along a boy for Aunt Jenny to meet. So they had this party, and someone brought along Grandfather for her to meet, and he was very nice to her and polite and she almost thought he liked her, until Grandmother came home from a date, her lipstick all smeared up and everything. She marched right through the living room on her high heels, showing off her pretty legs, and with her nose in the air, too stuck up even to say hello to anyone. And she had this big wavy bun of hair that caught the light, Aunt Jenny said, and shined like silk. And Grandfather kept staring at her.

"As soon as Grandmother disappeared, Grandfather just left Aunt Jenny flat, and went out on the back porch by himself. In a little while Grandmother came downstairs, in her nightgown. Imagine," says Mattie, ". . . in her *nightgown!*"

"*I* told you that," I say, in shock both at my child and at what she has to say to me.

"You didn't say a *sheer* nightgown."

"Is that what Aunt Jenny told you?"

"Yes. Anyway, Grandmother walked around in this nightgown, with her hair hanging down past her waist and swinging every which way, and everyone stopped and looked at her. She went into the kitchen and the light shined right through her nightgown."

"Mattie, that's my *mother* you're talking about."

"Yes," she says. "Thank God you're not that way."

She pulls another Kleenex and blows her nose.

"Then Grandmother went out on the porch where Aunt *Jenny's* date was, and she was half-naked nearly, and she stayed and talked to him most of the night, and when Aunt Jenny finally got the courage to go out there, they were pawing each other."

"Where did you get that *language*?" I cry.

"All the kids say that."

"Well, you are not to speak that way."

"What's a word that means the same thing, then?"

"Never mind. No such thing ever happened. Aunt Jenny was filling you up with a lot of fairy tales. She's just a malicious, jealous old woman."

"Well, she has a right to be, having a sexy, stinky sister like that, who had all the fun."

"You *believe* her?"

"Well, if Grandmother stole Aunt Jenny's only chance for a husband when *she* could have married anyone else in the world, that's pretty crummy."

"It's not true."

"If Clara ever does that to me, I'll kill her. I already get pimples on my face, sometimes, and Clara's hair is much prettier than mine. No one will marry me and I'll end up going crazy."

"You leave Clara alone. If your grandmother were alive, you could ask her yourself. It's easy for Jenny to spread her lies with my mother not here to dispute them."

"I like her. She's my favorite aunt."

"She'll never set foot in this house again!"

"Then I'll go see her when I grow up."

"Go ahead then. Do what you please."

I find in amazement I am about to cry, and worse, have visions of slapping my daughter senseless for what she is saying, and how she is saying it.

"Mattie," I say very quietly after a minute. "I loved my mother very much. Do you understand that?"

"I'm tired of all these stories," Mattie says. "I think my hair is falling out from this disease I have. If I'm ever going to get married, I better take a nap and try to get well."

The Cost Depends on What You Reckon It In

THREE TIMES a day I ran to Sherman's Rest Home on Ocean Parkway where my mother was put away. I brought her whitefish and borscht and pickled herring, foods that would hasten her death, the doctor said, but he didn't know they were the only things that could quicken her into life for a minute.

When I came in, my mother rolled her head toward me and looked at the brown paper bag in my hands.

"Boiled flanken," I would say. "With horseradish." And my mother would blink blandly at me and wait for me to unwrap the prize and feed her.

"It's against regulations," said Isaac Sherman, the man who ran the Home. "The others get jealous. They don't like your mother already, you visit her too much. Them, their children never visit. Only once in a while."

"I can't help that," I told Mr. Sherman. "And you shouldn't worry so much. I'm saving you money."

"Money, money," he said, rolling his eyes as if money were the last thing on earth he was concerned with under such circumstances. But he didn't press his objections. The more food I brought my mother, the less of his own he had to supply.

I fed my mother, the food dribbling down her chin, and the other old ladies watched the spoon as it moved from my lap to my mother's mouth, back to the plastic container in my lap again. Once, when my mother could not even be tempted by her favorite—gefilte fish—I turned to the other ladies and asked them if they would like some. There was enough for each of them to have a little piece, I said. But of one accord, out of hate or envy or what I do not know, they all averted their eyes from me as though they had not been following every word and movement exchanged between my mother and myself, and pretended indifference.

So I took the gefilte fish home with me and ate it for lunch myself.

My visits to Sherman's Rest Home were so skillfully planned that my family was hardly aware of my triple disappearances each day. The first trip took place directly after the children and my husband were gone for the day, the second—at lunchtime—no one was home to witness, and the third, after dinner, always occurred under some pretense—that I was running out to pick up a loaf of bread, or that we needed a quart of milk, or that I was just going for a walk and would stop and look in on my mother just as though it were a coincidence that I was going in that direction.

My mother was so completely removed from the lives of my children and husband that she was already dead to them. I did not take my children to visit my mother at the Home—I told them children were not allowed there—and my husband could not bring himself to go. His own mother had been in one for too long, and it had taken its toll on him, in guilt and in agony. So on Sundays, when I spent the entire afternoon at the Home, my husband took the children to Prospect Park.

One afternoon when I came into the Home, I found my mother in bed with a red straw hat on her white hair.

"What on earth, Mama?"

My mother smiled. "They gave it mir."

I had never learned Yiddish very well, so my mother always spoke it to me in combination with English. It came out sounding something like English words do when you add on German endings.

"*Who* gave it to you?" I asked, looking at the red paper rose.

Then my mother, who cried very easily these days, began to cry.

"What's wrong, Mama?"

My mother pointed across the room with her good hand. The bed was empty.

The young colored girl who tended the old women said, "That lady, she die this morning ma'am. Her daughter, she come and give the other ladies her things."

I took the hat off my mother's head and put it on the table beside the bed.

"Well," I said cheerfully, "I have rice pudding today."

"Gib mir mine slippers," my mother said, shaking her head at the food. "Ich vil geh for a valk."

"She been sayin' that all day ma'am," the colored girl said. "Ever since this morning."

"You can't walk, Mama," I said. "You can't stand up."

"Ich kann stehen," my mother said, nodding her white head up and down. "Gib mir mine slippers. Unter der bed."

"You can't stand, Mama," I said again. "You're getting better, but you're not well enough to stand yet."

My mother nodded, smiling, her false teeth very white and even. "Ich bin besser," she said. "Ich bin besser now."

"If you feel better, I'll ask Mr. Sherman to have the nurse put you in a wheel chair. But you can't stand up."

"Ich *kann!*" she said, and tears of frustration began to run down her cheeks.

An old lady in a private room across the hall began to scream like a witch, and my mother closed her eyes. "I'm in a crazy house," she said.

I left the rice pudding with the colored maid and told her to feed it to my mother. I went home, and when my children got in from school I was baking them a chocolate cake.

When I went back at suppertime, Mr. Sherman was at my mother's bedside. He was arguing with her.

"Try to understand, Mrs. Weissberg. Your leg is paralyzed from the stroke. If you try to stand *up*, you fall down and break your head."

"So I'll break it," my mother said. "A broken head isn't better than *this?"*

"If you continue making such a disturbance your daughter will have to take you away. We can't have such scenes."

"So she'll take me away. Home I would rather be anyway. Home she would rather *have* me than in this far-shtunkener place."

I came up to the bed. My mother saw me. "Gib mir mine slippers," she said. "Ich vil valken a little. I'll walk home with you."

"Mrs. Shapiro," Mr. Sherman said to me. "Your mother has been crying all afternoon. She wants to get up and walk."

"Mine tochter," my mother said to me, nodding.

We had been through all this when I had her at home. There was only one way to make her understand.

"Get my mother's slippers," I said to the colored girl. My mother watched me, her face bright with gratitude.

I took the slippers from the girl and put them on my mother's paralyzed feet. "Help me," I said to Mr. Sherman. "She has to learn."

Together we sat my mother upright and swung her legs over the side of the hospital bed. Together we lifted her and lowered her slowly to the floor. Her feet, in their loose slippers, touched bottom. Then we let go of her.

She fell on her face.

We caught her before she hit, and when we got her back into bed, I said, "Now you understand, Mama. You're paralyzed. You can't walk."

"Tomorrow ich kann," my mother said, and the look she gave me made me turn and shout at Mr. Sherman. "Tomorrow she can. Maybe *tomorrow* she can!"

And then I had to leave, because my mother was killing me.

It began to get worse when she found out Papa was dead. She'd been calling his name in her sleep for about two months before Mr. Sherman told me about it.

He said to me one day when *I* was spooning chicken soup into my mother's mouth: "Who is Sam?"

"Sam is my father," I said. "Why?"

"Your mother wants him. She calls for him."

"He's been dead for twenty-three years," I said.

My mother coughed and then began to choke on the soup in her throat. "Sam is dead?" she said to me, incredulous.

"Papa was very sick," I explained. "A long time ago, when I was young, he died. Don't you remember?"

My mother began to sob, the chicken soup running out of her mouth down her chin. I wiped her face with the towel that was around her neck as a bib.

"Please, Mama," I said softly. "Try to behave yourself."

"Ich bin all alein," she said. "All alone."

"Don't you have me?" I said. "Don't I come to see you every day? Here. Try to eat some more soup."

"Soup. What do I need soup for? To make me live longer?"

"What kind of talk is that?" I said severely. "Don't you want to live?"

My mother stared at me, her blue eyes blazing, and then put the question to me: "This is living?"

That night I asked my husband about the possibility of bringing my mother home again.

"I think maybe I can manage it now," I told him. "In the beginning it was too much, but now I think I could manage."

"In the beginning," my husband said, "I found you locked in the bathroom every ten minutes crying your eyes out."

"I'm all right now," I said. "I don't cry any more."

"No," he said. "It's too much for you."

"We have to pay Sherman seventy dollars a week," I said. "It would be cheaper to have her home."

"Only cheaper if you reckon all costs in money," my husband said. "The money will manage to hold out as long as your mother does."

"In a way," I said, trying to concede with reluctance, "it really *is* better at the Home, because they get her into a wheel chair once in a while. I could never lift her myself."

"Of course," my husband said quickly. "And there are people her own age there."

"Yes," I agreed, almost happily, "and they have a doctor who comes every day."

"Certainly," my husband said. "She's much better off there."

"And I go to see her three times every day."

"Yes," my husband said. "She's *much* better off there," and then he took his pipe from the ledge over the stove and went into the living room.

But she *hates* it there, I screamed silently at his retreating back. My mother hates the Home and she is dying full of hate. But I never said a word aloud. Instead I began wildly to grate potatoes so I could surprise my mother with potato latkes tomorrow.

The complaints about the pain started the next day.

"A burning," my mother said. "A burning here." She pointed to her stomach.

"Like heartburn?" I said.

"No. Heiss. Like fire."

"Did they give you a new medicine?"

"Vus far a new medicine? Medicine helps?"

I called the colored girl over. "Did you feed her anything different? Did they give her any new medicine?"

"No ma'am."

"Is the doctor here today?"

"He doesn't come till the afternoon, ma'am—on the days he come."

"The doctor will look at you this afternoon, Mama," I said.

"What do I need a doctor for? He'll make a miracle? I'll get better?"

"You *are* getting better," I said. "Mr. Sherman told me you can move your fingers a little."

I picked up her paralyzed arm that lay swollen and puffy on the sheet and unbent the rolled fingers. "Soon maybe you'll be able to move your whole arm."

"Sherman should geh in der'erd!" My mother spat the words.

"Sherman is a bad man?" I asked.

"Ich kann nicht moven mine fingers," my mother said.

In the afternoon my mother could not eat the potato pancakes I brought and began to cry.

"Es brennt like fire," she said, pointing to her stomach. "It hurts."

"Did you move your bowels today?" I asked.

"Farshtunkener moogen," she said.

"No good?"

"Broken," she said. "Everything's broken."

I had the nurse give her an enema. The pain did not subside. At three o'clock the doctor still had not come.

I called Mr. Sherman. "Where is the doctor?"

"Maybe he isn't coming today," Sherman said.

"I thought he comes every day."

Sherman shrugged. "Sometimes he does, sometimes he doesn't. He has emergencies maybe."

"That's what I pay you for," I said. "I pay you for having the doctor come every day. I want him to look at my mother."

Mr. Sherman patted my arm. "Please, Mrs. Shapiro," he said. "The doctor comes right away if we need him. Only today everyone seemed well. I told him not to bother."

"My mother isn't well. She has a pain."

"Ach!" he said. "A pain. Who doesn't have a pain? Me, I have one in my chest right now. Every time I breathe."

"I'm sorry about your pain," I said, "but I want the doctor to look at my mother. I know her. She doesn't make up pains."

"At that age," Sherman said, "what can you expect. They all have pains. They come. They go away."

We talked across my mother's bed as though she didn't exist. I looked at my watch. My children were getting out of school. They would be home soon.

"Look," I said, "I have to go now. But I want the doctor to look at my mother."

"All right, all right," Sherman said. "I'll call him. He'll come."

"Mama," I said, looking down at her little face on the pillow. "The doctor will take care of the pain this afternoon. And I'll be back right after supper. I'll bring you some lox."

My mother closed her eyes against me with her opinion of lox at this stage. I had not the strength to convince her otherwise.

In the evening the pain was worse.

"The doctor didn't help it?" I asked my mother.

"Doctor, doctor," she said. "What doctor?"

"He didn't come?" I asked. "After I left he didn't come?"

My mother shook her head.

I went to Sherman's office. "Why didn't you call the doctor?" I said. "I pay you seventy dollars a week."

"Can I help it, Mrs. Shapiro, if he was out?"

"Where is he now?"

"They can't reach him."

"You don't know another doctor you could call?"

"Please, Mrs. Shapiro, calm yourself. You think it's something terrible. It's only a pain. Believe me, they all have pains. They only want attention. It's nothing serious."

You should roast in hell, Mr. Sherman, I felt myself thinking, but I turned and went back to my mother.

"The doctor will come tomorrow," I said. "Can you wait?"

My mother nodded.

"Is the pain any better?"

"It's only a pain," my mother said, and when I left, walking through the halls smelling of urine and unwashed hair, I almost believed Mr. Sherman. At that age, who didn't have pains?

In the morning there was a red stain on my mother's nightgown. She opened her eyes only after I spoke her name.

"Is it worse, Mama?" I whispered.

"Es brennt und es brennt," she said to me.

"Did you tell the nurse?"

"A schwartza," my mother said. "What does she know?"

"Did you have anything like tomato juice this morning?" I asked, knowing better. "Or borscht?"

My mother started to cry. "Ich kann nicht reden," she said. "No koyech."

My mother was too weak to talk.

I sat beside her all morning, and stroked her white hair. It was gray against the pillow. At noon, when some of the other ladies were being fed, my mother began to moan.

"What's the matter?" I asked, bending over her.

"The pain," she said. And then she vomited blood.

I ran to Sherman's office. "Goddamnit!" I screamed. "I need a doctor for my mother. She's bleeding. She's in terrible pain."

Sherman looked at me and started to say something. Then he changed his mind and picked up the phone. In ten minutes the doctor was at my mother's bed.

"She has a perforated intestine," he said and then he went into Sherman's office to call an ambulance.

My mother lay there weakly, crying without sound. "We're taking you to the hospital, Mama," I said, holding her hand. "They'll fix the pain there. They'll make you all better."

"Bessie, Bessie," my mother said. "Don't leave me."

I bent and kissed my mother fiercely and held on to her with all my might. I didn't let go of her hand till they took her into the operating room at the hospital.

At three a doctor came into the waiting room to speak to me. "Your mother has come through the operation very well," he said.

"She's very old," I said, looking into his young face.

"You may see her tonight," he said, "during visiting hours."

I stayed at the hospital all afternoon, phoning my husband after I had dinner in a drugstore alone. At seven o'clock I went in to see my mother.

She was being fed intravenously through the arm. Her eyes were open.

"How are you, Mama?"

She shook her head.

"The pain will be better soon," I said. "They fixed it."

"Worse," she said.

I could not look into her eyes. "No. Better. It will take a few days."

"Ich vil Sam," she said to me.

I shook my head. "Don't talk, Mama. Rest."

My mother closed her eyes. I went out to speak with the doctor.

"She is doing very well for her age," he said. "She is recovering remarkably well."

"When can she leave the hospital?" I asked.

"Two weeks, maybe three."

"Back to the Home?" I asked him, and when he widened his eyes to mean *How should I know?* I shook my head to say *My God I didn't mean to ask you*, and then I went back to my mother's bedside to ask it of myself.

At nine the nurse told me to go home. My mother was fine, she said. If they needed me, they would call right away. I kissed my mother's taut white forehead and felt a blue vein beating under my lips.

"I'll be back in the morning, Mama," I whispered.

"Nem araus the needle from my arm," she said.

"Why? Does it hurt?"

"I don't want any more medicine," she said. "I'm tired."

"It's food," I said. "Not medicine."

She shook her head. "No more," she said. "Please. No more."

The nurse came out of the shadows of the room and seemed to wink at me. She gave my mother an injection. My mother closed her eyes and did not complain further.

I took the trolley home and stayed up till midnight, waiting. At two the phone rang.

"Your mother is very weak," the nurse said. "The doctor suggests that you come."

I went into the bathroom to dress, and when I came out my husband was already in his coat, waiting to take me to the hospital.

As we closed the front door, the phone rang again. I did not have to answer it to know what it was.

"Yes?" I said.

"Your mother has just died," the doctor said.

"I know," I said. "Do you want me to come?"

"There is no need," the doctor said. "We can't make any arrangements till the morning."

"Where will you put her for the night?" I asked.

"In the basement," the doctor said.

"Thank you," I said.

In the morning, he approached me about my mother's body. He wanted it. "We don't know what went wrong," he said. "The operation was successful."

"But the patient died," I said wryly.

He smiled politely. "We would like to perform an autopsy," he went on. "We want to know what happened. It might have been that her heart gave out, or something else. But the operation was amazingly successful for a person of that age. We want to know what the final cause of death was."

"She was old," I said. "Worn out."

The doctor smiled again. "We need more details than that," he said.

"No," I told him. "You can't have my mother."

"It may save others," the doctor said, "if we find the cause."

"I'm sorry," I said. "You can't have my mother to cut up."

The doctor nodded, turned on his heel, and left me alone.

On the day of the funeral there were twenty people at the chapel. I didn't know my mother had been known to so many people. There were a few relatives and neighbors, but mostly there were friends, old women I had never seen before.

My children stood looking into the casket for a long time. My daughter came over to me and took my hand.

When it came time to close the coffin I went over and placed my hand on my mother's chest. The material of her dress sank three inches under my hand. There was no body that I could feel. Then I stood back and let them screw down the lid. I held my breath till they were finished and exhaled only when I realized that I was blacking out.

It was raining that day. The mourners drove to the cemetery with the sound of windshield wipers beating in their ears.

The rabbi said a prayer at the open grave and one of the old ladies began to cry. I stood looking at the box in which my mother lay. Then they lowered the coffin into the earth.

Only once before in my life had I watched that happen, and I had screamed. "Please," I had screamed, "don't let them cover my father."

Then I realized what was wrong.

"This is the wrong grave," I said aloud.

The rabbi looked up startled. The old lady who was crying closed her mouth.

"My mother's plot is next to my father's. This is the wrong grave."

"Are you not mistaken?" my husband said.

"No," I said stubbornly, raising my voice. "My mother has to be buried next to my father, and my father is not here. He's somewhere else in this place."

A cemetery attendant went to call the manager. The manager came and looked at the grave with the coffin already in it, and ran back to the main office to check further. The funeral party stood around, silent, and the rain kept coming down. It wet the surface of the coffin, making it shine brightly. The manager came back with the news that there had been a terrible mistake.

The rabbi, getting wet, said, "Surely it does not matter where your mother is put to rest. Her soul is already with your father's."

"Yes," the manager said hurriedly. "What does it matter now?"

I looked at all the people who had come to see a funeral. "It matters," I said. "How long will it take to dig another grave?"

The manager came up to me. "Mrs. Shapiro, may I suggest that we bury your mother here, in *this grave*, now. Then, tomorrow, we will transfer her to the proper plot, next to your father."

"No," I said. "I don't trust you."

"The new grave cannot be dug immediately," he said, "and all these people are waiting."

"I don't care about the people," I said. "She's my mother, and she's got to be buried next to my father."

The manager drew himself up sharply. "There is no one to dig a grave until tomorrow," he announced.

I turned to all the people. "My mother is not going to be buried till tomorrow," I told them. "Thank you all for coming." Then I saw to it that they put my mother in a vault for the night and arranged to come back the next day.

The rabbi asked, "Will you want me again?"

"No," I said. "I think your prayer will hold until tomorrow."

Then we all drove home in the rain.

The next day I took a taxi to the cemetery by myself. I watched while the colored men dug out the grave next to my father's and went with them when they went to get the coffin out of the vault. They carried it back to the grave and slid it in.

I picked up a handful of dirt, after the custom, and threw it on my mother's coffin. I heard it land softly on the wood.

Then I watched while the men covered the coffin with dirt. When they were through I thanked them and tipped them.

After they left I knelt beside the newly filled grave and placed my hand on the soft mound.

Please God, I said to myself, let her rest in peace.

And then I surrendered my mother up to the earth, and went home to my children.

We Know That Your Hearts Are Heavy

PIGEONS are crowding the window sill to keep out of the rain. The drizzle has just turned to downpour, and the birds have flown up from Boston Common. They are stepping on each other's toes to find a footing on the two-inch ledge. The victims of missteps do not fall six stories and spatter their blood on the pavement; they merely hang in midair, flutter a hundred wet black feathers, and immediately land back on the ledge, dancing a wild two-step to get dry.

The phone rings, and I spin around. Before I quite realize it is the phone and not my employer coming in the door, I have hidden in my lap certain papers from the top of my desk that are obviously not the work I am supposed to be doing, and have picked up a pencil, which I poise professionally over nothing. I compose myself enough to lift the receiver.

"One moment, please," says the operator, and then I hear my mother's voice coming to me from Miami.

"Mother!" I cry.

"Janet, darling, how are you?"

"Is anything the matter?"

Long-distance calls always frighten me. My family is neither rich nor sophisticated enough to call merely to talk. There is always a reason. The last call from home came because my mother heard that a hurricane was approaching Boston, and she wanted Danny and me to move out of our rickety attic apartment in Cambridge and go to a sturdy hotel until it was over.

Since my mother does not answer me immediately, I say, "Are you and Daddy all right? Is Carol all right?"

"We're fine," she says. "How are you? How's Danny?"

"We're fine," I say. "Is anything new?"

"How's the weather up there in the North Pole? I thought it's supposed to be *spring*, and the low was eighteen yesterday." My mother studies the Boston highs and lows and reports to us in every letter how much better off we'd be in Miami. She cannot understand why the University of Miami would not be just as good a place for Danny to do his graduate work as Harvard.

"We had a hailstorm last night," I add, for no sensible reason.

"And how is your job?"

"It's fine, it's fine."

I wait, and then it comes. "Janet, Daddy is flying to New York this afternoon. Uncle Benny has had a heart attack."

"Oh, no," I say. "Poor Celia."

Celia is my cousin who is four days younger than I am, and who looks like Elizabeth Taylor. She is due to have her baby any day. I say this to my mother.

"She's due *today,*" my mother says. "The poor child."

"Is it very serious?"

"He died, darling. Uncle Benny died."

I am silent for a moment, digesting this. My Uncle Benny is my father's elder brother. He looks just like my father (though I in no way resemble Elizabeth Taylor), and he is very rich and lives on Park Avenue in Manhattan. He has always been my favorite uncle, even though most of the relatives do not like him because of all his money. I think he has always loved me because I look so much like him.

"How is Daddy taking it?" I say. Outside, the pigeons are now standing on each other's heads.

While my mother is saying that he is as all right as can be expected, it occurs to me that I will go to New York to see my father, whom I have not seen in a year. I tell my mother that, and she says she doesn't want me to go, and I say I will, and she puts my father on to argue with me, and suddenly I say something frightful. I tell my father that I want to come because I have never been to a funeral and I want to see what one is like.

He is angry, I am sure. I see him thinking, Do you imagine a funeral is a *show?* And I am thinking, in self-defense, it was very unfair of all of you to conceal Grandma's death from me when I was in college and not tell me till after the funeral, so that I still can't believe she is dead because I was not *there.* I have never seen anyone dead, and I am twenty-two, and I think I must not grow one day older till I do.

But my father is too preoccupied to get angry. He simply says there is nothing much to see at a funeral; he is going to fly back to Miami as soon as it is over, and in just two months, in June, he and Mother and Carol will all drive up to Boston to see us, and there's no need for me to go to any funeral, especially if the weather is bad. He does not sound very convincing or stern, though, which is strange, because those are the things my father usually is.

Finally, I say what one of us always says on long-distance calls, "This is costing a fortune," and my mother gets back on the line to tell me to keep warm, and then I remember that my Aunt Beth, Celia's mother, died less than a year ago, and I ask my mother if Uncle Benny might not have died of just being sad.

"On Park Avenue," my mother says, "a heart attack and too many sleeping pills can be the same thing," and the call is over and I am left with all kinds of terrible thoughts.

I lean forward to stare out over the Common, and the papers in my lap slide to the floor. I pick them up and set them back on the desk. They are greeting-card verses. Someone has told me that you can sell greeting-card verse for two dollars a line. If I can sell one eight-line verse a day, I will be able to quit this job, which I hate, and stay at home and not have to go on the hideous subway every day. The money from the verses will help put Danny through graduate school just as surely as the money from this job in the publishing house.

Today I have been doing Bereavements. In the last week, I have written a number of Birthdays, Get Wells, Mother's Days, Wedding Days, Baby Arrivals, and Valentines. Today, a gloomy April day, seemed appropriate for Bereavements. I think of Uncle Benny, and then I read the verse I composed this very morning:

> We know that your hearts are heavy
> And your sorrow is very deep,
> But remember: The Lord loves all his lambs
> Who rest in Eternal Sleep.

Obviously, it is not quite right. It is not, as my title says, "A Comforting Thought During Your Time of Bereavement." But then, I have never been bereaved; it is no wonder I cannot write sincere Bereavement verses.

I decide I am going to New York despite my parents' wishes. And right now I am getting out of this office; I can't stand it here any more. I put my verses into my purse and go down the hall to tell Mr. Cowper that I have to go to New York to a funeral, and I say it so fast and sadly that he perhaps thinks it is my father and not my uncle who has died.

I take the subway to Harvard Square and walk home from there. Danny has the hi-fi on; he is playing the sad songs of Schubert again—the rain has affected him, too—and when I get to the top of the third flight of stairs I knock on our door. He opens it and I say without looking into his eyes, "I have to go to New York to see my father. My Uncle Benny just died, and my father is flying to New York this afternoon."

"What?" says Danny, and to my horror I find myself smiling as I repeat the words.

Danny does not see. He helps me peel off my raincoat, and throws it across the back of a chair. He turns off the phonograph, and then closes the book he has been reading.

"I have to call the bus station and see when a bus leaves," I say, and at the same instant Danny is saying, "It's a bad day for such a long trip, but I think we can make it O.K. if we drive slowly."

I am shocked. It has not occurred to me that Danny will come. I have been imagining this as a private family affair. Danny does not like families, and he will not like mine. None of them are the kind of people we would have for friends, but I feel for them something akin to love, which makes them bearable, while Danny has no reason at all (except that I am his wife) to be tolerant of their crudities and illiteracies. I fear that he will be impatient, then offended, then angry, and finally will insist that I leave with him, which I will not want to do. I shall see this through to the end, even if it means disregarding Danny's wishes.

However, none of this can be explained. Danny is already saying he will have to miss his advanced seminar, but it is more important that I go to New York.

In less than twenty minutes, we are ready. We leave the attic in a mess—the bed unmade, crumbs under the kitchen table. By one o'clock, we are on the Massachusetts Turnpike. At the Connecticut state line, the rain turns into snow, and we now have to go thirty miles an hour instead of forty.

Before I understand that something has happened, Danny has stopped the car suddenly and is pulling out his wallet. In a moment, a highway patrolman is looking in my window.

"Open it!" Danny says, nearly shouting at me.

The patrolman takes Danny's license and reads it. "Are you going to a fire?" he says.

I wait for Danny to say we are going to a funeral. He says nothing. It seems he has changed lanes unsafely. The patrolman talks across me. He is very young; wet snow is clinging to his hat and to the tip of his nose. He is lecturing Danny about reckless driving, and I keep wanting to say, Please don't yell at us—it is snowing so hard, and my Uncle Benny is dead, and my father has to come thirteen hundred miles in an airplane this afternoon to see his dead brother, and my cousin has a baby in her, which is about to be born any minute.

The patrolman is now writing out a ticket, and is asking Danny if he is a student. He talks on and on, and I could kill Danny for not telling him. I want to tell everyone that someone has died whom I love. It is so important—how can anyone give us a *ticket?*

Finally, we are driving again, very slowly. Danny is chastened. His lips are tightly closed, he is trembling slightly, and I do not say anything.

We get into New York at eight-thirty, and, by calling several relatives, we learn the whereabouts of my father. He is at the Lakeview Chapel, where Uncle Benny is laid out. It takes Danny nearly another hour to find the chapel. Though we were both born in Brooklyn, neither of us knows Manhattan. I walk a few feet in front of Danny as we approach the funeral parlor. My heart is beating very fast. In the lobby, which is very much like a hotel lobby, a man at a desk asks us which "party" we are with. "We are with the Goldman party," I say, and Danny and I look at each other.

Danny has met my Uncle Benny once, just after the death of Aunt Beth. On our honeymoon, we stopped in New York and had dinner with him. His two children were there—Celia and Fred—and Celia's husband, Glen, and Fred's wife, Melissa. Melissa was obviously pregnant, and Celia was also pregnant, though we did not know it. My Aunt Beth had always had a delicate heart, and the relatives attributed her death mainly to the fact that Melissa was a Catholic.

The night we visited, my Uncle Benny spoke very softly and sadly. He said he was getting along—he was trying to keep busy, the children came to dinner once a week, he would get used to being alone in time. After dinner, he took us aside and said, "Look, children, if you ever need anything—money, *any*thing—you know it's here waiting for you. Just call me collect. Please remember that. You know you don't have to be bashful with me." He put one arm around me and one hand on Danny's shoulder. "You never have to worry as long as I can help you out."

Danny thanked him, and I kissed him, and for a minute he covered his eyes with his hand. Then Fred came in to show us his wedding pictures. Fred's wedding had been an immense affair, at which it was said my Uncle Benny got drunk and cried, and in nearly every picture was my Aunt Beth—a large woman, with a lovely straight nose and her hair pulled back in a chignon. None of Uncle Benny's brothers or sisters had been invited to the wedding. Only his Park Avenue friends had that honor. The youngest of the three brothers, my Uncle Sol, had said, "Benny didn't want his poor relatives from Brooklyn there. God will punish him for such a sin."

The punishment having now been visited upon Uncle Benny, Danny and I walk across the soft, deep carpet of the lobby to the elevator, and are taken to the fourth floor. There is a great commotion coming from the end of the hall. We advance, and enter an anteroom where there is a coat rack. I glance through an open door into a larger room and get the impression that everyone is standing there holding a highball. For one instant, I see my father—tall, beloved, hunched over slightly, his arms crossed over his chest as though he is cold—talking to some person I do not know. I look away, pretending I have not seen him, and Danny takes my coat and hangs it up. I stand there, looking down at my shoes, and suddenly my father is hugging me, his suit jacket scratching my cheek. I kiss him, and turn my face away, feeling tears rise and then subside. Then I look at him and say, "Oh, Daddy." He hugs me again, and, remembering, releases me and shakes Danny's hand. Danny is already uncomfortable, but there is nothing I can do. I must think about other things right now. I forget about Danny, and later see him sitting alone in a corner at the far end of the room, his chin in his hand, his eyes staring at nothing.

My father, holding me tightly by the hand, does not reprimand me for coming. I understand that he is glad. We weave around groups of standing people; no one, of course, is holding a highball, but that impression is still with me. I see the faces of aunts, uncles, cousins—all of them from the same neighborhood in Brooklyn, all of them together for the first time in probably thirty years. Most of them have not seen me since I was "so high." A few stop us to tell me that, and to marvel at the fact that I am now married. "Where is the husband?" they say, and I point to Danny, in the corner, who looks as though he might be Uncle Benny's son, the way he is sitting so quietly, staring so sadly at the rug. "Imagine!" they say. *"Married!"* Mostly, they are marvelling at how old they have grown. An occasion such as this moves them to philosophy. There is talk of dying everywhere. After all, Uncle Benny was only fifty-four—it could happen to anyone.

My Aunt Ida comes over to us. She is a widow. My Uncle Benny has been supporting her and her nine-year-old daughter Charlotte for the past six years. "Janet dear," she says, "what a stunning suit you are wearing!"

I stare at her. Her brother is dead, and she is telling me I am wearing a stunning suit. Suddenly I am struck by a horrible thought—this is *Celia's* suit I am wearing! Over the years, since Celia and I were children, my Aunt Beth used to make up a package of Celia's outgrown clothes every few months and send them to my mother for me. The last package had been sent about a year ago. It contained the suit I am wearing. Fred's clothes went to my Uncle Sol's son Bill. Even though both my father and my Uncle Sol now lived in Miami, my Aunt Beth, I am sure, had continued to think of them as the poor Brooklyn relatives.

In a moment, my Aunt Ida wanders off, and my father leads me firmly down the length of the room. He says softly, "Have you seen Uncle Ben?"

"No," I say. "Where is he?" at the same moment understanding that he is right in this room with us.

My father puts both hands on my shoulders and gently turns me around, and there, in front of me, is the dead man.

What, when I first came into the room, I thought was a display of flowers is not merely that. Sunk deep into hundreds of expensive blooms is a beautiful coffin. The upper half is open; the lower half is closed and covered with roses. In it lies my Uncle Ben in a navy-blue suit. He is wearing a tie. In his pocket is a handkerchief with the initials "B.G." I cannot look at his face. There is a feeling in my body I have never had before, of something stopping or freezing. My father is beside me, but I know that when I look at the face of the dead man I will see the face of my father—it does not matter that *now* it is my Uncle Ben. I look at the face. It is not my father. It is not my uncle. It is the face of someone who is not there. There are my uncle's cheeks, and his nose, which is shaped exactly like my nose, and his lips, but the color of life is gone. The feeling I have is as real as my heartbeat: he has gone out.

But where has he gone? I become hysterical and turn to my father.

My father steadies me, and leads me out into the hall. Near the elevator, where it is quiet, he sets me down on a bench. "Janet," he says.

I cannot control myself; it is more terrible than I can stand. My father's dear flesh, which I am touching, cannot stay forever. My mother cannot stay, Danny cannot stay, my sister Carol cannot stay. *I* cannot stay! It is too much to explain. I am able only to cry against my father's sleeve. Danny, who has come out after us, is holding one of my hands, and I kiss his fingers, and I kiss my father's sleeve, and then I take a deep breath and stand up.

In a few minutes, we all go back to the filled room. People are looking at me. They are probably thinking, Why is *she* so upset? It is not *her* father.

I speak to no one, and find myself, finally, beside Celia. She is in a low chair, dressed in a black maternity dress, her belly swollen so large it does not seem part of her. She is pale, but she is wearing lipstick, and her hair is fashionably combed. I feel as though she is twenty years my elder. In one year's time, she has had two deaths and a conception happen to her. Nothing has ever happened to me. I don't know what to say.

Celia says, "I'm so happy for you. It must be wonderful to see your father."

"Oh, no!" I say, but she is going on.

"It is *so* nice you could see him after so long. I'm glad someone is getting some pleasure from this."

She means to be polite—she is showing her good breeding—but what can she mean? Her finishing school has not taught her that you do not have to offer your father's life in politeness.

I say, "I'm very sorry, Celia," and she smiles at me. She is very beautiful.

Then I leave her and go to the corner in which Danny has been sitting all evening. He and I sit there together, and I watch my father go back to the coffin and stand before it with his head bowed. What is he thinking? What is he remembering? What is he feeling? "Danny," I say, "I can't stand it. I can't *under*stand it."

"Sh-h-h," he says, squeezing my hand, and that is all the help he can give me.

Just then, a little gray-haired man comes into the room. He shakes slightly from a palsy, and he makes an announcement. "Will the immediate family of the deceased view the body once again if they wish to, as the coffin must be closed in a half hour and cannot be opened tomorrow before the funeral."

He leaves as quickly as he has come, and my father moves away, to give Celia and Fred the last half hour.

Fred walks toward the coffin and looks into it, and then walks away, squeezing his eyes shut as though he has a pain in his head that he cannot endure. Celia and her husband approach it, holding hands, and stand before it for a long time. Celia's arm is now around her husband's waist, and I see her clench her hand into a fist and bang it against the small of his back in a tiny futile gesture. I am ashamed of my outburst. She is a braver person than I am.

The little palsied man comes back into the room, and Celia and Glen back away from the coffin. She does not see, but from where I am *I* see the little man take a comb out of his breast pocket, lean into the coffin, and comb my Uncle Ben's hair neatly back off his forehead. Then he lowers the top half of the coffin and seals my Uncle Ben inside.

People are getting their coats. There is some difficulty about where Danny and I will spend the night. My father is staying with my Aunt Pearl and Uncle Carl in Brooklyn. My Uncle Sol, who has flown from Miami with my father, and my Aunt Ida, who lives all the way out on Long Beach, are also staying with them. My Aunt Pearl and Uncle Carl say *we* should come home with them, too, but I know they live in a one-bedroom apartment and have no place to sleep so many people. They will manage, they say, but Danny is doubtful. He would rather we stayed at a hotel. I cannot explain to him that we *can't* stay at a hotel—this is not a night one leaves the family. He should not have come along if he cannot do what has to be done.

Fred comes up and says why don't we stay in Uncle Ben's apartment. There are three large bedrooms (he means we do not have to sleep in the bed that Uncle Ben died in); no one is using them.

Danny is willing, but my father wants me with him. He feels what I am feeling. "I haven't seen her in a year," he explains to Fred. "We'll manage somehow."

Danny and my father and I all get into our car, and we follow my Uncle Carl's car back to Brooklyn. Everyone will meet at the synagogue the next morning at eleven.

Seven people are to sleep in an apartment that has only two single beds—Danny and I, my father, my Uncle Sol, my Aunt Ida, and my Aunt Pearl and Uncle Carl. My Aunt Pearl is trying to arrange things. It seems it is a very delicate question, the delicacy lying in the fact that Danny and I are newlyweds. We are to sleep together, and yet we cannot be given a room to ourselves. Do older people think that newlyweds make love even on the eves of funerals? From their whispering and arguing, it seems so. The conclusion is that we will have to take the consequences of this death. So Danny and I are assigned one of the single beds, my Aunt Pearl and Aunt Ida, who are sisters, the other, and a beach chair is set up at the foot of our bed for my Uncle Carl to sleep on. In the living room, my Uncle Sol will sleep on the couch and my father on another beach chair.

Danny is hating this—he will not sleep in a room filled with strangers; he will not be subject to their curious opinions on young love; he will not be the object of ridiculous imaginings—but he says nothing, because he is afraid to upset me further, and I am grateful.

It is bedtime. To be done with it, Danny undresses and is the first in bed. I am next. We both feign immediate sleep. It is frightfully hot. I am wearing a high-necked flannel nightgown, packed because it was so cold in Boston when we left. It must be ninety-five degrees in the apartment. My Aunt Ida crawls into the second twin bed, which is less than a foot from our bed. She sighs. She says, to no one in particular, "Isn't it wonderful how fast the young can fall asleep?" My Uncle Carl, who weighs over two hundred pounds, gingerly lets himself down on the beach chair, which creaks terrifyingly. "Oh, God," he says.

My Aunt Ida's head is toward me, and she is breathing in my face. I am choking. I cannot move, because I am supposed to be asleep. Danny seems actually to be sleeping. It is the only sensible way out of this ridiculous situation.

For a while, there is nothing but creaks and sighs. I imagine my Uncle Sol and my father already asleep in the living room. The conferences about the sleeping arrangements have embarrassed my father, too—we did not even say good night. My Aunt Pearl comes into the dark room and sits down on the edge of the bed in which Aunt Ida is sleeping. Suddenly a flashlight beam illuminates the ceiling.

"For God's sake, Pearl, what are you doing?" says Uncle Carl from his beach chair.

"Sh-h-h," she says. "Setting my hair."

On the ceiling I can see the giant corkscrew of a ringlet.

"Aw, come on," Uncle Carl says. "Go to sleep, Pearl. It's nearly three o'clock."

"Shut up," she whispers. "I'll look enough like a witch already from crying." There is the clink of bobby pins. *"How* could Benny have killed himself?" she says into the dark.

"Who says that?" says Uncle Carl. "The maid found him dead in bed. A heart attack."

"Don't tell me," says Aunt Pearl. "He was living death all the time since Beth died. His heart was broken. He was a broken man."

"With all his millions?"

"Oh, shut up. Money isn't everything."

"You'll wake the children."

"They're not such children. They're married to each other."

I see on the ceiling a giant corkscrew subdued to a circle. The flashlight must be in her lap, shining up through her hair.

"I once told him to drop dead," my Aunt Pearl says. "God forgive me. I was eighteen and I wanted to go to the roller-skating rink at the Greek's. My father was dead already, and Benny was the head of the family. He said I couldn't go—it was a cheap place; he didn't want me picking up boys. I said too bad, I'm going anyway, so he grabbed me and put me over his knee and spanked me. I told him to drop dead. Heaven helped me, Carl—he's dead."

"Yeah, thirty years later," says Uncle Carl. "Look, Pearl, go to sleep. Don't make yourself suffer."

"Suffer, suffer," my Aunt Pearl says. "To be alive is to suffer." She is crying now. The beach chair creaks, and Uncle Carl's head looms on the ceiling. Then the flashlight is shut off.

"Carly, Carly," Aunt Pearl is whispering. "We should only go together. God should be good to us. I don't want to be without you—we should go at the same time."

Uncle Carl is whispering and Aunt Pearl is crying, and, finally, gratefully, I fall asleep.

I wake, and the night is not yet over. There is the sound of breathing all around me. From the living room comes the grating sound of someone snoring. Could it be my father? When I lived at home, he did not snore. But that was years ago, before I went away to college. Danny's knee is in my back and I cannot change position without falling out of bed. I hold back the blanket and step onto the floor. I tiptoe into the bathroom, where I wash my stinging eyes with cold water and comb my hair with someone's green comb. I do not know what to do. I cannot return to the narrow, stifling bed, but neither can I leave Danny there alone. What would happen if he should wake and find himself alone in the midst of all my breathing relatives?

But I will only be gone a little while. In the living room, my father is pressed into a narrow beach chair. He is snoring. I stand above him, wanting to kiss him. "Daddy," I whisper, but he does not waken.

Finally, I put my coat on over my nightgown and go outside. It is windy and cloudy, but there is a faint suggestion of dawn. My Uncle Carl's apartment is only two blocks from the house in which I spent my childhood, and I walk there. Perhaps *it* will tell me something about where the years go.

The house is smaller and meaner and uglier than I ever imagined. The front yard, which had been like a hundred acres to me, is not more than fifteen feet long. I feel cold and foolish; my nightgown is sticking out from under my coat. I go back and crawl into bed with Danny. I am grateful for his warm body, because I am shivering. The next time I wake up, it is morning.

In the living room, they are finally talking about what they have all been thinking of: the will. Uncle Sol says solemnly, "Ida, I hope you have been provided for."

Aunt Ida says, a little shortly, "There is nothing to worry about."

Uncle Ben has been supporting her for six years, and she evidently does not wish to discuss it. She sits on the couch between Uncle Sol and my father, and ruffles her short black hair with her fingers. She does not wash her hair more than once a month. She vacuums it. She uses a drapery attachment from her old Electrolux, believing that it stimulates the brain. Aunt Ida has been very superstitious since the night Uncle George died; he had a convulsive seizure on the night of a full moon, and Aunt Ida believes he was under a spell. She swears he bared his teeth at her, like a wolf, before he passed out of this life. He was not "lost" to her, though, since she felt his life force pass into her body, and she believes she has the strength to live and raise her child alone because she has two life forces bouncing about within her. For the last few years, she has been a health faddist. In her purse, she carries a dozen pill bottles.

Presently, Uncle Sol says, "We are not worried, Ida—we only hope Ben had the foresight to make a will." The brothers of the Goldman family have always looked with suspicion on wills and insurance policies. They seem like asking for trouble. "A man like Ben," says Uncle Sol, reflecting rather desperately, "a man with such a business mind must have had the foresight." Uncle Sol leans back, a frown on his forehead. It is known that Uncle Ben, in order to avoid certain income taxes, years ago put one of his corporations in Uncle Sol's name. As a return for this favor, Uncle Ben has been paying Uncle Sol's income tax every year, in addition to paying him a token salary of fifty-five dollars a week. Uncle Ben promised Uncle Sol's son, my cousin Bill, a new car on his eighteenth birthday. Bill is now seventeen. Uncle Sol's meager earnings from his fabric store will never afford Bill a new car. Neither will those earnings support Uncle Sol's family if the store is his only income. Uncle Sol sighs. "Ach," he says, "an ugly business."

"I wonder," says fat Uncle Carl, sitting on the edge of the beach chair my father slept in, "whether there was fancy paper business—accountants and lawyers, things like that."

"Sure there was," says Aunt Pearl. "A man like Ben doesn't keep his money in a piggy bank."

"I was just thinking maybe he arranged with his lawyer or someone that Ida should be taken care of if anything happened."

"There's nothing to worry about," says Aunt Ida.

Aunt Pearl says, "Carl, run out and get something for breakfast. Bagels and lox."

Carl rises. My father goes to him and presses a bill into his hand. "Buy it with this," he says.

"Don't be a big shot," Uncle Carl says, shoving it back. "I got plenty of money."

Uncle Carl has not got plenty of money. Five years ago, he sent Aunt Pearl to her brother to ask for a loan. Uncle Ben loaned them five thousand dollars to start a dry-cleaning store with. The store failed. Uncle Carl now works as a cutter in a dress factory. It is clear that Uncle Carl is wondering if Uncle Ben tore up that IOU, or if accountants will unearth it and force payment from him. He leaves to get the bagels and lox.

"What about you, Abram?" says Uncle Sol.

"What about me?" says my father.

"What do you think about a will?"

"I think we shouldn't worry about it. There are other things to think about this morning."

Uncle Sol is silenced. He and my father look down at their laps.

Aunt Pearl goes into the kitchen to prepare for breakfast. In a minute, she calls, "Ida, come help me."

Aunt Ida sighs, gets up from the couch, and goes into the kitchen. In a few minutes, Uncle Carl comes back with two brown paper bags. He sets them in the kitchen, and puts up two card tables in the living room. Aunt Ida returns from the kitchen, carrying one empty plate. She places it in the center of one of the card tables, and sits back down on the couch between her brothers.

We hear a cry from the kitchen. "Damn her, damn her, damn her!" Aunt Pearl is sobbing.

Carl runs to the kitchen. "Pearl! What's the matter?"

"My God-damned sister," she sobs, coming to lean against the wall of the living room and point at Ida. "I ask her to help and she carries in one lousy dish. I'm up all night, and I have to cook for everyone, and my husband sleeps on a beach chair in his own house, and she sits on her fat behind."

"Pearl," my father says, getting up and going to her. "There's no need to fight like this today. Everyone is upset. Try to calm down."

"Oh, shut up!" she screams. "Who do you think you are—big brother Ben, bossing me all over the place?"

"Stop that," my father says. *"Stop that!"*

"Just like old times," Aunt Pearl goes on, wildly. "Ida gets away with everything and I get stuck with the dirty work. Where was Ida when Mama died? Do you know where she was? She was at a *party!* That's where devoted Ida was."

"Pearl, Pearl!" cries Uncle Sol. "What's the *sense?"*

Aunt Ida is still sitting on the couch, twisting her fingers together.

"Don't *you* talk!" Aunt Pearl shouts at him. "Who do you think it was who almost *killed* Mama? You, with that *shiksa* you nearly married!"

"ENOUGH!" My father, now the eldest brother, now the head of the family, gives the sternest order I have ever heard. "THERE WILL BE NO MORE OF THIS."

Everyone is silent.

Finally, Uncle Carl says, "Come on. Let's have breakfast."

Little by little, the air calms; we all settle down at the table. Danny has come in from the bedroom, all dressed and shaven. He looks embarrassed because he has heard the fighting. "Good morning," he says.

Aunt Ida smiles at him. She is in the midst of lining up her dozen pill bottles on the table. She offers pills to each. "Sol? Abram? Carl? Janet?" We shake our heads. She says softly, "Pearl, you?" Another no. Then, hesitantly, "Danny?"

Danny accepts. Aunt Ida beams. Into his palm she pours pills of many colors, shapes, contents. This is for good blood, this is for the circulation, this is for the liver. One is more mysterious—it is for life force. Danny doesn't wince. He swallows them seriously, one by one. Aunt Ida loves him. She smiles at my father—Your daughter has married a fine boy. She smiles at me—You have a fine husband. Everyone feels a little better.

On the table are onion rolls, bagels, rye bread. There is butter and cream cheese. There is whitefish and lox and sour cream and bananas and pickled herring. There is coffee and cream and sugar.

Everyone begins to talk about what a good man Ben has always been. It cannot be denied that he has been very generous to all of them. If he did not mingle with them socially, it has to be understood. After all, his friends were a different type; Beth was a different type. But Ben never forgot his family. They were never in need. Ben always believed blood ties were the strongest ties on earth.

Uncle Sol bursts out, "But why should *he* have been the only one to go to college? Why did the rest of us have to work in the clothing factory? Why was *he* the only one who was Bar-Mitzvahed? It wasn't fair." He seems close to tears.

Now they are bringing up old grievances. Ben had everything; they had nothing. Ben had an education, Ben had a car, Ben had a *chance*. They had no chance. They are all failures.

My father nods. He is agreeing that he is a failure. It is not possible for me to stand in front of all these people and tell him he is not a failure. I love him. He has done everything for me and for Mother and for Carol. He has worked like a dog in fifteen different businesses and sent me through college; he will send Carol through college. He has taught us to think, he has given us strength to cope with pain and fear, he has taught us to be honest and fair.

Aunt Pearl, who has been silent since the fight, now says, "It's ironical. Don't envy. He's dead, this brother of ours who had everything. His Beth is dead, his children are orphans, his grandchildren he will never see. Such good fortune, such luck is that?"

They are silent, considering. Indeed, the tables have been turned. Here they all sit in Brooklyn, eating bagels and lox, while Ben is in a coffin on his way to the synagogue.

"May he rest in peace," my father says. "No more talk now."

They observe that it is late, it is time to get started. The service is being held at eleven. The table is cleared quietly.

My father tells me to wear something warm. It is windy and rainy again, the worst kind of day for putting away in the earth. Again something is stopping, freezing in me.

We drive through Brooklyn, through Prospect Park, through downtown, across the East River into Manhattan. Somewhere, on the busiest parkway, we have a flat tire. We *can't* have one; we are already late. "Don't worry," says Uncle Carl. "They can't go ahead without us. They will wait." He must be thinking, but not saying, that Benny will wait, too.

My father is out of the car, kneeling on the road. His face is red with the strain of taking off the tire. "Danny!" I cry. "Help him!" He is only two years younger than Uncle Benny.

The flat tire is fixed; we go on. We are aware of how risky the world is.

At the synagogue, I feel dizzy and weak from lack of sleep. Downstairs is a ladies' room. My Aunt Pearl is there before me; she is powdering under her eyes. "Janet," she says to me, "life is worse than you know," and she is gone. I stay there and try to quiet my stomach. I am afraid for my father. I have never seen him cry, but I am afraid I will see him cry today.

When I come up the stairs, an attendant stops me and says I am too late—I will have to wait outside.

"Wait outside?" I cry.

"Are you related to the deceased?" he asks.

"I am his niece," I say, and push past him. I am at least as important to this service as the Wall Street cronies who are here. They cannot keep me out. My father is waiting for me.

All the relatives are in a long line at the back of the room. The front three rows of seats are empty; the rest of the temple is filled. This is the Park Avenue congregation. These are all Uncle Benny's rich friends. We walk down the aisle. My father is holding my arm as he did at my wedding. Danny is walking behind us, alone. The line files into the front row. My father takes the last seat, and there is no room for me next to him. I have to sit in the second row, diagonally behind him.

Celia is also in the front row, looking as though she has not slept at all. She is wearing a black hat with a thin veil that covers her eyes.

The rabbi begins to speak. With a shock I see the coffin, not two feet from my father, right under the platform on which the rabbi stands. The top is completely covered with roses. It is so magnificent a box you can almost see the congregation reflected in its polished sides.

The rabbi is saying what a good man Uncle Ben was, that all of us know what an honor it is for a man's remains to be brought under the sacred roof of the shul. This good man was president of the Men's Club. No matter how busy he was, he never missed a Friday-night service. He was religious and pious and honorable. Sometimes, on a weekday morning, he would come into the temple alone and sit at the back, staring at the Ark of the Covenant. Ben Goldman was a fine man. Ben Goldman loved all his children.

When he says that, he looks at the front row, where Melissa sits next to Fred, and he repeats, "He loved *all* his children." The Catholic daughter-in-law is included. This is a generous rabbi.

What the rabbi cannot mention—and what perhaps is Uncle Ben's greatest achievement—is that Uncle Ben has just been given a larger writeup in a new book called *Moneymakers* than anyone else in the country has been given. He has been described as the shrewdest chemical man in America in this book. A photograph shows him watching a ticker tape, a far from pious expression on his face.

The rabbi says, "And now this good soul has gone to join his beloved Beth," and I see my father cover his eyes, and I begin to cry. Danny takes my hand, but I gather momentum and am shaking so hard I cannot breathe.

Men come forward and lift the coffin. Very slowly, they walk toward the back of the shul, rose petals slipping off the coffin to fall under their feet. My father is the first to follow the coffin out. I drop Danny's arm and run ahead to hold my father's. He averts his face, and from deep in his chest I hear a ripping sound that I know is the sound of a man crying who has not cried in forty years.

Outside, in the wind, he is in control again. There are seven black limousines lined up to take the mourners to the cemetery. My father opens the door of the third limousine. "Get inside. I don't want you to catch cold."

"Where are you going?"

He points to the second car.

"I want to go with you," I say.

"I have to go with the brothers and sisters."

He won't let me argue. I get into the third limousine. In the second are the brothers and sisters, in the first the children of Ben and their mates, and in front of that the hearse, with Uncle Ben under his roses.

Danny leans back uncomfortably in one of the seats that have been pulled up from the floor—the most uncomfortable in the car. There are six strangers with us in the car. The driver is a pock-marked, yellow-skinned, unpleasant-looking man. Beside him are a couple with bored faces. In back of us are two middle-aged women and one very old woman.

The car moves slowly away from the curb. It is daytime, but the headlights of the cars in the procession are on. The yellow-faced driver maneuvers skillfully in the heavy traffic. This is just another working day for him.

One of the middle-aged women leans forward and taps me on the shoulder. "Are you related to Benny?" she asks in a rasping, masculine voice.

"His niece," I say.

"Are you Abie's girl?"

"Yes."

"I thought so. You look like him. I lived next door to your father in Bensonhurst. I was his first girl. My name is Mickey."

I am repelled. My father has as much as betrayed my mother with this vulgar woman.

"I didn't use to talk this way," she explains. "I had part of my voice box removed. Cancer."

The little old lady now taps me on the shoulder. "You want I should show you the pictures of my grandchildren? I'm your father's Aunt Sadie."

So this is Aunt Sadie, the aunt my father dislikes most. I do not know why, exactly, but I do know her husband owned a clothing warehouse and gave my father—then a boy of eleven—the night watchman's job in it. My father used to sit shivering in the dark, hearing rats run across the floor and imagining horrors he can hardly explain. For this he was paid twenty-five cents a night, while the same uncle sent Benny to Hebrew school.

The old lady is showing me snapshots. "This is Ruthie, she had a birthmark big as an apple, the biggest doctor in New York took it off, she's a beauty now, you could never know."

I nod wearily.

"They kicked me out from the family," she says. "Last winter, I was in Miami Beach, I called your father, he should come to see me at my hotel, he never came. Same with Sol. Probably the wives didn't let. I never liked your mother."

"Look," I say, "we're going to a funeral. Maybe we should all be a little quiet."

She sits back, silent.

We are out of the city at last. It can't be much longer. The couple in the front seat light cigarettes. The pockmarked driver then lights a cigarette for himself. We are coming into open country. The old lady taps me again. "Here," she says. She stuffs something folded into my hand. "That boy next to you must be your husband. I know you had a wedding. I was never invited, but I don't hold no grudge. Just because I was never invited is no reason I can't give a present."

It is a five-dollar bill. "Look, Aunt Sadie," I say. "I don't want it. It's not necessary."

"I have nothing against you," she says. "It's your mother who didn't invite me. Buy yourself something."

We are pulling into the cemetery. My heart pounds and I see a blackness before my eyes for an instant.

The wound of my Aunt Beth's grave is not yet healed, and beside it a new one is open. They are sliding the coffin out of the hearse and carrying it toward the grave. A green rug is placed over the hole, a board across the rug, and the coffin upon the board. This is done very quickly, even before all the limousines are empty.

There is a canopy covering both graves. No tombstone marks Beth's grave; it is not yet a year. A chair is brought forward for Celia. She declines it with a shake of her head.

The canopy flaps in the wind, and the rabbi steps under it, carrying a closed black umbrella. The relatives gather in, and once again the gray-haired, palsied undertaker appears, now distributing long-stemmed red roses, one to each person. His expression is as blank as if he were dealing out a deck of cards.

I try to see past Celia's face into her thoughts. What if that were my father, locked in that coffin? What if his face were being put away from me forever? And then I ask myself a question against all knowledge. How do they know the dead are dead? What if, tonight, Uncle Ben opens his eyes and calls to be freed? Is Aunt Beth lying beneath this very earth, listening? Is she thinking, Finally, Ben, you are coming to sleep?

It seems against all things human, to bury someone under the earth who has breathed in light and air from the instant of birth. Why not lay the dead among green trees, in the open woods? Are not the ants and beetles better than the lead-sealed, waterproof, airtight, thousand-dollar mahogany casket?

My head is spinning in the pain of its own inadequacy. What does it *mean* for Uncle Benny to be dead?

The rabbi is reading the service in Hebrew. I do not understand it. At the end, at a signal of the rabbi's hand, Celia and Fred step forward. Celia steps too far, upon the unsupported part of the green rug, and lunges forward, nearly falling into the grave underneath. She is caught by my father and Fred, who hold her until she can balance herself again. Fred takes her hand, and the brother and sister say the Mourner's Kaddish: *"Yisgaddl veyiskadash Sh'may rabbo be'olmo . . .*" They say it well—they have said it often for their mother. For a moment, I believe in the prayer; I believe there is God, this is His language, He is there, and Uncle Ben is all right. But my disbelief is suspended only until Celia steps back, nearly staggering, her face gray with anguish.

"Throw the rose," says the rabbi. Celia tosses the rose upon the coffin. Fred does the same. We all toss our roses forward, as though we are playing a game of quoits, and it is over. They are hurrying the pregnant girl out of the wind and back into the limousine.

But it is not quite over. The brothers and sisters of Uncle Ben remain behind. The four of them are crying, facing in the world's four directions, away from each other. Privately, each one is accepting the finality of his brother's death. It seems they are ashamed to look at each other, for when they are done with whatever each has had to do in his heart, they still do not draw together.

We pile back in the cars, in the same distribution as before, and we drive away.

There. I have seen a funeral—I have seen it all, and what do I know? I have understood nothing.

It is silent all the way back to Manhattan. The funeral party meets in Uncle Ben's apartment, where his maid, the colored woman who discovered his body, serves us corned-beef sandwiches and potato salad.

It is announced that the family will sit *Shiva* in two places—the brothers and sisters at Aunt Pearl's house, the children at Celia's house. But it is understood that Celia and Fred will not serve out the week of mourning, sitting on boxes on the floor, barefooted, the men unshaven, the women without color, the mirrors covered with sheets. They are of the modern generation; they have obligations; one of them has got to get a child born, the other has to learn the chemical business. Let the old folks sit *Shiva.*

Pleading his wife's tiredness, Celia's husband takes her away. Melissa and Fred leave with them. The strangers go, and the rest of us are left in Uncle Ben's house.

"There was no will," Uncle Sol says. "Fred told me."

So. All the money is to go to the children. No car for Sol's son, no rent for Aunt Ida. And do even I feel a little disappointed?

Nothing matters. I am sick of it all. I want to go home with Danny to our rickety attic where we bang our heads on the ceiling every time we get out of bed. I want to go back to my tiny office and watch the pigeons strutting on my windowsill, which overlooks the Common. There are things to do—many things to do—and I understand that that is the only answer I shall have to all my questions.

A Daughter of My Own

Every girl I know who has ever had a baby has had her mother come and stay with her for two weeks—or her mother and a nurse—and each one tells me how wonderful it was, and how she never could have survived without her mother's advice and help and soothing presence.

I just don't know. I think I love my mother as much as any girl loves hers, and I think I have always gotten along better with my mother, on the average, than most girls do with theirs. But if I never have another baby it won't be because I didn't like being pregnant or being in labor or losing six-months' worth of sleep—it will be because I won't know what to do about my mother.

When I found out I was pregnant in September, and told my mother I was due to have the baby in April, she immediately began making plans to fly up "in February or March, whenever you want me." It had never occurred to me that I would want her at all—I mean, it was my baby, and we were very far away from my parents and they didn't have the money to toss away on airplane trips, and my husband was a student at the time and at home nearly all day to give me any help I might need, and there just wasn't room for anyone. There was hardly room for the baby. Bill and I lived in a three-room apartment near the University, and had figured that by gouging out the shelves from a built-in-the-wall living room bookcase, we could just manage to squeeze in a tiny crib for the baby. We hadn't exactly planned on enlarging our family just yet, and there was quite a bit of arranging and arithmetic to do in those early months. Not that we were unhappy about it—far from it—it just took some adjusting.

My husband was happy to adjust to a baby, but not to a mother-in-law. What bothered him most, to begin with, was that if she came up *before* I had the baby, he would be left alone with her for five days in the house while I was in the hospital. I could see what he meant: my mother wasn't one to discuss Aristotle, and Bill wasn't one to discuss the upbringing of children, at least not with my mother and not the upbringing of *his* child, and that seemed to be all she thought about these days, as far as we could judge from her letters.

It was hard to tell her not to come before the event, because I knew what was on her mind. To put it rather simply, she wanted to hold my hand. My mother had always held my hand through crises—I had been a very sick child: four pneumonias, one broken arm, a heart murmur, an infected appendix, crooked teeth, crossed eyes, and nosebleeds. I'm quite sure I couldn't have survived any of those blights without my mother's five fingers around mine—while they were giving me oxygen, while setting my arm, while taking an electrocardiogram (which she ruined the results of because she interfered in some way with the electrical current by touching me), while I was being put under ether, while the braces were being tightened, and so on. I think that in those frightening years when doctors loomed everywhere, the grip of my mother's fingers when needles were piercing my very soul was all that sustained me.

Now I was having a baby. People died in childbirth, I knew, and even if you made it through it it was bound to be pretty rough. My mother nearly died having me, and I knew how worried she was, and why she wanted to be around to whisper encouragement at the hardest moments. The only difference, I felt, was that this was not a *crisis.* I was not sick, I was not frightened, I was not even worried. I was in perfect health, I liked and trusted my doctor, and I loved the little thumps I was beginning to feel low down where my appendix had once been. Most important of all, though, was that I *had* someone to hold my hand if necessary, someone who would fill the bill very well in the absence of my mother: my husband.

I don't suppose my mother gave him much credit for being useful in any situation. After all, here we had been married for three years and I had been supporting *him*, while all he did, as far as my mother could tell, was lounge around in unpressed pants all day reading big musty books that left yellow crumbs of paper everywhere on the floor. Which her daughter then had to vacuum!

I tried to show my mother how calm and unworried I was. I sent her clippings of the foetus in different stages of development with long technical explanations about its growth. I recommended books on childbirth for her to read, which told how simple and safe the procedure was these days. I wrote her with the gain of every new ounce, knowing that she believed gaining weight meant being healthy, since I had always been a very skinny, unhealthy child. I had Bill take pictures of me in different smiling poses, my immense belly foremost, my jolly wave saying "See how fine I am? Nothing is wrong with *me.*"

Finally I was able to persuade my mother to come right *after* the baby was born. When she agreed, though reluctant and somewhat hurt, I was finally able to relax and enjoy the remainder of my pregnancy. I saw every old Tarzan movie on TV that had ever been made. I sat at the window on gray afternoons with all the lights off and watched the snow come down, eating from a plate on my lap that usually held green olives and grapefruit halves. I spent long hours staring up at the ceiling from my bed, imagining my baby, and imagining *me* with my baby.

Bill was home nearly all that winter, studying for his comprehensives, and we talked to each other mostly at dinnertime, usually about what names we would like the baby to have, and how we wouldn't do to him the bad things that we thought had been done to us. It was a fine snowy happy winter—wet and icy outside, warm and steamy inside. I bought eight-dozen diapers in my ninth month, and washed them all three times, by hand, so they would be soft for the baby. Bill bought a used crib and we painted it and got a new mattress. We read Dr. Spock, we read *Childbirth Without Fear*, we read Gesell. We were ready.

The baby started to come on the very day he was scheduled to come, which made us think that he had a very reliable character. We saw the doctor in the afternoon and he told us to go home and call him when there was "some real action." So we went home and Bill fed me strained chicken soup, and we timed all the warming-up pains, and soon it was dark out and I was warming up a little faster. We played all six Brandenburg Concertos while I lay on the living-room couch, and Bill sat on the floor next to me with a pencil and paper and his wristwatch in his lap. At eleven we called the doctor who said "This sounds like it, come on down."

The snow had changed to rain, and it was a very appropriate, dramatic night for racing to the hospital. I knew though, from the hospital brochure I had, that if we arrived before midnight we would be charged for the entire day, so I cautioned Bill to drive as slowly as he could, and we meandered to the hospital—even circling a few extra blocks to kill time—until the baby made it known we had better meander no more, and we covered the last five miles in about thirty seconds.

We parked in the hospital lot at four minutes to midnight. I was game to sit it out till twelve, but Bill was beginning to get glassy-eyed and I was not as confident as I sounded, so we went in and signed the admittance form and they wrapped adhesive tape around my wedding ring.

Bill was permitted to stay with me as long as I wanted to be awake, and we stayed together till nearly dawn, having a very sweet dreamy time, holding hands in fact, and making faces at each other every time a nurse came in to listen to the baby's heartbeat, or time a contraction.

When he went away, I was floated into an elevator on a very soft high bed, and in the morning I had a little girl, six pounds, two ounces.

I had truly never felt better. It was a bright sunny morning, and I was cranked up on my neat white bed and the light was coming in right on my knees, making them warm and comfortable. I had just seen my baby in a tiny plexiglass cart, pink and perfect, asleep, and more beautiful than any beautiful thing I had ever seen in the world. They wouldn't let me hold her because I was still rather groggy. In fact, no one would believe me later when I told them I had seen a nurse come into my room a few minutes before, and take a swig of whisky straight from a bottle she kept in her deep white pocket.

I drifted about in the bright sunlight for a while and then Bill peeked his head into the room, grinning like mad, and we had a big kiss and a tremendous long smile together and then I sent him off to see his daughter.

He was with me all afternoon, but occasionally went out into the hall when a nurse came in to poke my stomach and take my pulse and temperature.

He came back one time with roses for me, and I felt like a queen there in the sunshine, all loved and loving, and I thought we had just begun to get happier than we had ever been.

When they came in with my dinner, Bill got up to leave, and I remembered that he hadn't called my mother. I told him to do that right away, and he said he would, but it seems he drove home first and had dinner and fell asleep, and it wasn't till about ten at night that he remembered to call, and the baby had been alive nearly twelve hours by then.

Everything started falling apart. My mother called me the next day at the hospital when I could walk to the phone, and the first thing she said was "Why didn't Bill call me right away?" So I made up something about his wanting to make sure I was all right before he called, but it wasn't very pleasant to argue and to come out of that gentle haze I'd been in, and I resisted it. I said I had to hang up and go back to bed, I was getting dizzy, but my mother managed to mention that she was coming in two days, when I would be ready to go home.

I spent the rest of the afternoon worrying about her coming and feeling very helpless and unhappy. They brought the baby to me only twice for the first two days, to get her used to me, and me to her. There was no sense in her coming oftener, since she wanted mostly to sleep, and my milk hadn't come in yet. It was very fine to hold her, and each time the nurse left I would unbutton her little kimono and examine her tiny body and count all her toes and fingers.

After they took her back to the nursery I'd get worried again about my mother, and feel bad till the next time they brought the baby to me. When I told Bill my mother was really coming, that she had bought her plane ticket, tears came to my eyes, and he tried to cheer me up by saying that as long as she *had* to come, she would be a great help and not to worry a bit, but he didn't sound very convinced himself.

My mother arrived the evening of my fourth day at the hospital. I was to leave the next morning. Bill had a night class, so no one met her at the airport, and she took a taxi to the hospital, and dragged her suitcase by herself, and when she came up to the desk they told her it was final feeding time and no visitors allowed now till morning. She told them she hadn't seen me for a year, and some kind lady let her up, and she came into my room just as the baby finished nursing, and without a word, I held out the baby to her and she took her, and we both were crying, because it had been so long and we loved each other so much, and now I had a daughter of my own.

But even though I was so happy to see her, that perfect moment couldn't last very long, and it didn't, because immediately she was asking me if we could pay the hospital bill, since Bill was obviously not earning any money, and then asking again why Bill had waited so long to call her, and asking if I had had "too terrible a time." Nothing had seemed wrong till then, and suddenly I was worrying about the hospital bill, and feeling very sorry for myself because it was hard to sit down and my breasts ached while they were getting used to the baby's nursing schedule. I didn't want to feel bad, I wanted to stay feeling like that queen in the sunshine for a while, but it was too complicated, we were talking all about practical things and old rifts were coming up, and I wished I had someplace to go back into like where my baby had been all those months.

When my mother left to meet Bill downstairs and go home with him, she said "Do you want me to come with Bill in the morning when he picks you and the baby up?" and I said "Whatever you like," hoping that she would understand I really meant This Is A Private Time And It Would Be Nicer For The Three Of Us To Be Alone.

But the next morning she was there, very proud and pleased, giving directions to everyone. "Bill, you go down to the cashier, and I'll stay here and help Molly pack up all her things and then we'll have the nurse dress the baby," and then she asked me if I had a nursing brassiere and I said no, so she went down to the gift shop and bought me two for five dollars each, and I knew she couldn't afford it and neither could we, and everyone was bustling around so that I could hardly think of what time in my life it was—the time that I was taking my little baby to her home where I would be her mother for the rest of my life.

We drove home, my mother sitting in the back seat, leaning over my shoulder all the way, looking at the sleeping baby in my lap and touching her little curled fingers, and saying how beautiful she was, which was true, but somehow seemed false with my mother saying it aloud like that. Bill didn't speak all the way home, and when we got to the house, he took my suitcase and went inside and my mother and I sat in the car waiting for him to come out and open the door for me, which he didn't do. After five foolish minutes, I had to open the car door myself, nearly dropping the baby and nearly crying, and my mother gave me a look which said all she had always thought of Bill, and it nearly broke my heart, to have everything ruined when it could have been so nice at a time like this.

I went inside and put the baby in her crib, and didn't know what to do then. Bill had gone into the kitchen with a book, and was sitting at the table reading. I wanted to see him so badly, but he hardly looked at me. I wanted him to admire the baby and tell me what a fine child I had made and what a good brave girl I was, but he never raised his eyes. It seemed as though I had not seen him in years, and I was missing him because I had been away from him for five days in the hospital and, in a way, for all the months before that when, if he so much as gave me a warm kiss, my already overburdened heart would begin to palpitate and shudder to remind me that warm kisses would have to wait till the baby did not demand so much blood and energy of it.

And now we were further apart than ever.

My mother took over. "You get into bed," she said, "I'll take care of the baby. You need to rest."

"But I want to look at her," I protested.

"You'll look later—you just got out of the hospital"—and she took off my coat and led me into the bedroom she'd never even seen and tucked me into bed and closed the door to leave me aching and open-eyed and missing my baby and my husband.

The baby, because she was small, had to nurse every two and a half hours, and each feeding lasted nearly an hour, so I was never able to sleep for much more than an hour at a time. The nursing which I had loved so much in the hospital became a terrible ordeal at home, because neither Bill nor my mother could be in the room together with me and the baby at that time without becoming very embarrassed. If one was in the room and the other inadvertently came in, they would both avert their eyes from me, as though neither would acknowledge to the other his intimate relation with me. The baby and I had done beautifully in the hospital, but now with *everyone* avoiding everyone in our three rooms, and doors being closed as they went in or out, and me being so exhausted and tense, the baby sucked less and cried more, and made me desperate for relief of some kind, sleep at least, or a little privacy and quiet. Privacy was what we lacked most—I wanted to be alone with my baby, I wanted to be alone with Bill, and I wanted the three of us, so newly a family, to have some time alone. My mother, though, was everywhere. If Bill came over to the crib to look at the infant, my mother would appear and look too—and look at Bill to see his reaction, and he would mumble and walk away.

On the third day home my mother said, "I've never seen Bill kiss the baby . . . doesn't he like her?" and what could I answer? "You haven't seen him kiss me either"—or—"He'd kiss her if you weren't watching all the time"? So I just sighed and asked my mother to bring me a drink of water. "Nursing makes you very thirsty," I told her.

That week, my mother prepared all the meals and called us in to eat when they were ready. She washed the baby's diapers every day and hung them up outside. She rocked the baby so I could sleep, she bought me a rubber ring to sit on so I would be more comfortable, she cleaned the apartment from ceiling to floor, she baked my favorite kind of chocolate cake, she sewed hems on my skirts that needed them, she let out the waist of everything that no longer fit me, she ironed, she mended, she labored like ten mules.

And it was horrible. One night, in bed (my mother was sleeping on the couch in the living room), Bill whispered to me, "I'm sorry, Molly, if I seem so awful to her and to you, but I can't stand this. I don't feel as though this is my home anymore. I feel as though I were courting you again and calling for you at your mother's house—the way she calls us in to meals and is so polite, and the way she just goes into our closets and drawers as if it were her own house. I feel like I don't belong here."

I took his head in my arms and held him, but he said, "I really can't stand it, Molly," and then he asked me to please do some of the cooking and dishwashing so my mother would remember it was she who was visiting us and not us visiting her. "I know you're tired and still a little sick, but she won't even let me into the kitchen, and you have to show her what she's doing to us."

So the next day I started to wash the dishes after breakfast though I hadn't slept three hours in twenty-four, and my mother asked me if I were crazy, to get back into bed this minute, and I said no, I felt fine, I was getting stronger every day, and then I fainted.

Which made Bill even sadder than he had been, and soon he just left the house in the morning and went to the library and didn't come back till suppertime. He had yet to hold the baby.

So I stayed in bed, and my mother brought my meals in to me, and brought the baby in for me to nurse, and did the changing and dressing, and soon she would not even wake me if it were feeding time, but would make up a formula bottle and give it to the baby, so as not to disturb me, and soon I wasn't having enough milk because she had destroyed the pattern and the breasts didn't think they needed to make any more.

One night when the baby started crying, I leaped out of bed and lifted her from her crib, and carried her back to my bed with me, where I was going to wake Bill and tell him to look at his daughter finally. But suddenly my mother was right in our bedroom, white and disheveled in her nightgown, her eyes not yet focused, her gray hair disordered from sleep, her arms out for the baby—"Give her to me, Molly, I'll get her quiet, you go back to sleep."

I couldn't help what I said, and it was wrong of me, but I said "Why on earth do you have to come poking around every minute? Why can't you leave us alone?" and my mother, horrified, went right out of our bedroom, and I heard her walking around in the living room in the dark all the rest of the night, while I sat in the bedroom with the baby in my lap till the sun rose.

In the morning my mother's eyes were red, and she said it was because she had a cold, and she was going to fly home because she didn't want the baby to catch anything from her. It was only the end of the first week, and she had planned to stay two. I knew all I had to do was ask her to please stay, and she needed me to, her eyes were on my face so pitifully, but all I did was say that I was surely much stronger now and could manage alone easily, and Bill spoke for the first time in days, to volunteer to take her to the airport any moment she wanted to be there.

My mother and I couldn't look at each other, both of us had tears on our cheeks all morning, and she packed and I pretended to be busy in my bedroom.

On the way to the airport she said from the back seat, "I had to borrow on Daddy's life insurance policy to get enough money for plane fare. I suppose I should have stayed home. You didn't need me."

"I did, oh I *did*, mother," I cried, and then recognizing the lie exposed by this solemn, unhappy trip to the airport, I fell silent, while my mother fumbled in her purse for a handkerchief.

"I thought you would need me," she said, and the grief in her voice was so deep, I reached back for her hand, to hold it, but she pulled it away and looked out the window. "A good day for a flight," she said, making her voice steady.

My hand dropped to my lap, where my daughter lay asleep wrapped in a blanket, and I touched her little cheek, thinking, Will You And I Ever Come To This?

At the airport, Bill wanted to go up on the Observation Deck because it was early, and he paid three dimes to get us through the turnstile. As soon as we got there, my mother said "It's too windy here for the baby. Let's go down," and Bill said, "A little wind can't hurt her," and my mother said, "Wind is the worst thing for an infant, not even two weeks old yet," and Bill said "It's a warm wind," and my mother said to me "Are you going to let her catch pneumonia because of him?" and I said "Oh please, let's not fight, it *is* a warm wind, Mother," and she said "Have it your way. I have to get on the plane."

She went down, and in about two minutes we went down, too, and she had checked her luggage and was ready to leave.

"Goodbye, Mother," I said. "Thank you for coming."

She stood stiffly, looking at my face as though she didn't know me, and then she began to walk toward the gate. I ran after her and threw my arms around her and hugged her, crying "I love you, Mother, I love you," and we embraced desperately, as though this were the last time we could ever express our love, and then she went through the gate, her head down, her hand to her eyes.

I went back to Bill who stood to the side with the baby, and shouted at him, *"Why couldn't you have let her kiss the baby goodbye? Why couldn't you? Why did you have to carry her away like that?"* and he didn't answer me, just put the baby in my arms and then put his arm around my shoulder, and began to lead me to the car. When we got outside, I did not even look at the big plane my mother was flying away in. We walked to the car, and the wind blew the baby's cap off, and I yelled at Bill, "It *is* too windy for the baby. My mother was right! Don't you see? She was *right!*"

The cap, filling with wind, flew and bumped across the parking lot, and Bill and I watched it until it got tangled under the wheel of a car, and then we just left it there and drove home.

Honeymoon

On their way out of the Bun Boy coffee shop in Baker, Rand gave Cheryl a quarter to buy a Bio-Rhythm fortune card from a vending machine. She stood in the hot desert wind, her skirt lashing about her legs like a whip, strands of hair flying into her mouth, while she laughingly read him the news that the biograph rated her low on luck, low on sex, and low on leisure plans, while it rated her high on health, endurance, and driving.

"So can I drive the rest of the way to Vegas now?" she asked. "It's so boring just to look out the window. There's no scenery."

"Get in the car, please," Rand said, his pants legs flapping like banners in a used-car lot, ". . . and don't put another ding in my door."

"I didn't put the first ding in," she said, getting into his red Corvette. She automatically took a sip of water from the insulated cup hanging in a holder on the dash and made a face. "Yuck—hot."

"You just had a milkshake," Rand said. "Why do you have to drink old water?"

"I don't know," she said, shrugging. "I just saw it there. Don't worry about it."

He pulled onto the road, and up ahead of them Cheryl saw white pom-poms on a car. "I wish *we* could have a 'Just Married' sign," she said. "Then everyone would look in *our* car when they passed us."

Rand accelerated, and Cheryl peered into the car with the pom-poms. The girl, a blonde like her, turned her head the other way when she saw Cheryl staring. The boy, who looked about the age of Rand's son, gave her a zany grin, friendly and lewd at the same time. Cheryl waved, giggling out loud. She turned to Rand, seeing his handsome profile against the twisted joshua trees in the distance. "How could I be low on sex and leisure plans if this is my honeymoon?" she asked. She reached over and stroked his thigh. "Anyway, I've *never* been low on sex."

"How do you rate on money?" Rand asked.

"They don't have money on the chart," Cheryl said, consulting the card. "But it says that today is a triple-critical day for me."

"Then stay away from the slots."

"Are you kidding? Last time we went to Vegas I got three bars twice!"

"Play blackjack," he said, "the odds are better."

"Sure, the way *you* do it. If I could count cards, I'd walk away with a few thousand dollars every time, too."

"Even without counting," Rand said, "the game gives you better odds than the slots."

"I always do something wrong," she said. "I hit when I should stand, I stand when I should hit . . ."

"Memorize the chart I gave you. It tells you exactly what to do."

"It's too hard," she said. "I can't memorize the chart. I'd rather play the slots."

"Well—at least stick around for the first hour or two to play for me. They know me in most places, but they don't know you yet."

"Do I have to play even on my honeymoon?"

"Of course," Rand said. "You don't want them to give me trouble, do you?"

They had a system. If Rand placed his chips to the left side of the circle, it meant Cheryl should hit. (Cheryl remembered this by thinking that if she was left back a grade, she was bad and should be hit.) The chips placed to the right meant she should stand and not take any cards. (She remembered this by thinking that when her answer was right, she would stand at the front of the class and everyone would applaud.) If Rand put his elbow on the table she was supposed to double down on her bet. If he reached into his pocket for his handkerchief, it meant she should bet a hundred dollars. If he took out his wallet and looked inside it, she was to bet *five hundred dollars.*

She felt important, having hundred-dollar chips on the table in front of her, and she loved it when he didn't make errors and they won big. Afterward he'd be so energetic and high, swinging her around in their room, making good love instead of letting her do all the work, later taking her to Spice on Ice, or some other flashy midnight show, both of them all dressed up. She adored the glitter—the massive headdresses, the pastel doves flying across the room, the seminude ice-skating—the glory and pageantry of it all. Rand wasn't interested in the dancers—even with their breasts hanging out of the costumes with cut-out fronts. He said he didn't think women marching around in circles on a stage were erotic. What he liked were the really dirty movies, which turned Cheryl on but made her feel slightly sick. She didn't need sick movies to be turned on, she was only nineteen and her blood pulsed at the slightest invitation, her dreams were lush with limbs and lips and loving whispers. But Rand said the movies were good for him; he needed to get a little charge now and then.

When she'd called home with the news, her mother had been hurt and angry. Cheryl was really surprised because her mother was tough and had always made fun of big affairs with strolling violinists and airplanes that flew by with flashing bulbs which spelled out "Congratulations on your marriage." She'd phoned from outside the Van Nuys courthouse to tell her parents she'd just been married, and her mother had said, "That's nice, I suppose," and then was absolutely silent. Cheryl almost said, You didn't really want to be there, did you? but thought better of it. Her mother didn't ask her a single question—like who was there, or what kind of ring he gave her, or which dress did she wear—so Cheryl finally volunteered into the silence that they were going to Las Vegas for their honeymoon.

"A work-play vacation?" her mother said. "How convenient for him."

"Can you put Daddy on?" Cheryl asked, wobbling in the phone booth on four-inch-high black heels. In the courthouse, she had turned her ankle coming up the stairs, wearing those heels. Rand liked her to wear that kind of shoe—he had bought her half a dozen pairs.

"Daddy's busy," her mother had said.

"Well—wish us luck," Cheryl said, wishing she didn't have to beg.

"In Vegas . . . or for life?" her mother asked.

"Fuck it," Cheryl had answered, hanging up the phone. Maybe she hung up the phone first and then said it, she couldn't remember, with Rand standing there impatiently in his striped suit, his hair—still thick but at least half-gray—riffling in the breeze. She didn't bother to cry. Rand had no patience with her when she acted like a baby.

"Well, that takes care of your folks. They give you a bad time?" he asked, seeing her face.

"That's okay," she said, "it doesn't matter. Don't you want to call your son now?"

"Not really," Rand said.

"Well, he's the one that had a fit that we were living together."
"He'll find out," Rand said. "Let's just forget about them all right now and get this show on the road."

"Look what I got in the rest room of the coffee shop," Cheryl said as they drove along. "Mr. Hiram's Super Funbook with three free meals."

"Just what we need," Rand said. "Sirens in your ears, hookers bumping asses with you, and sexy Chinese girls patting the dollar slots, whispering 'Try this one, it's hot.' "

"At Mr. Hiram's they give you a free color photo," Cheryl said. "On one of our trips I went in there without you, and I got a picture of my face on a fake dollar bill, and a free phone call home."

"I can give you all the change you need," Rand said, "assuming you want to call home again."

"I don't. Believe me, I don't. But maybe it would be nice to get the free picture. Sort of a wedding picture."

"I've had enough of those already," Rand said. "Don't you think three is enough?"

"How about later on, maybe we can ask someone to take just one snapshot of us with my Polaroid?"

"Maybe," Rand said. "We'll see."

Cheryl stared for a while out the window at the spiky yucca plants and the knobby dwarfed trees. "I wonder if we'll have a room with a mirror this time," she said. "I wonder if we'll have fun."

"Don't we always?" Rand said.

Her best girlfriend had a job now doing word processing for ten dollars an hour. In high school they had talked about going on to junior college and studying computers, but in the end her friend got on-the-job training on a Wang and now worked in downtown LA for an engineering company.

Cheryl had taken a summer job at Saks, gift wrapping, and in the fall decided to stay with it a while until she had a clearer idea of what she wanted to do. Her mother and father seemed relieved that they weren't going to have to fork over five thousand a year to send her to some fancy college, and as long as she was paying her own gas and insurance on the '71 Ford they let her use, they didn't bother her. That is, until she met Rand—he was having a birthday present gift-wrapped for his third wife—and started seeing him every night. Then her parents started babbling all the usual stuff: "more than twice your age, after you because you're a gorgeous young girl, you ought to be dating his sons!"

What did they know? The guys her own age were nothing, invisible, scarecrows on hangers. They glugged beer and walked to some drumbeat in their heads; she was sick of faded jeans and running shoes and guys who couldn't wait to turn you on with grass or with their own throbbing bodies. They had no money, and never would. Times were getting so crazy that they all had to live with their parents, no one could afford the rent on an apartment, even sharing with two or three guys. Half of the guys she knew thought they would be famous rock stars; they couldn't even carry a tune.

Rand was a real person. He had a science degree, he had been an engineer or something for many years till he got sick of it. His kids, from his different wives, were all grown up, and he was sending his youngest son through college now. He really knew where it was at. He never told dumb jokes. He didn't play games. He said what he wanted and she liked that. Do this, do that—and she did it, because usually it was a better idea than anything she could think of herself.

Now with their luggage carried in, he tipped the bellboy and locked the door of their room.

"Call room service and order us each a big shrimp cocktail," Rand said, his body reflected a dozen times in the mirrored room as he hung up his clothes in the alcove.

"I don't know if I want that," Cheryl said. "Maybe I want a hamburger."

"Call! Call!" he said. "Hurry up. When I get out of the shower I want it to be here."

And when it came, big white shrimp with pink tails and pink veins arched in a goblet over a snowball of ice, heads swimming in luscious red cocktail sauce, she knew he was right. It was exactly what she wanted. She chewed in a luxury of wanting the shrimp, grateful to him. When he came out of the shower she had eaten half of his shrimp, too—and he looked at the bloody plate and laughed, and peeled off his damp towel and swatted her. "That's what I love about you," he said. "Your healthy appetites. All of them."

By the time they got to the casino, she was quite satisfied, and chewed her lip comfortably while she adored him. She sat two stools down from him at the blackjack table, and felt his concentration burning toward her, his eyes counting the cards, figuring out when a ten-card would come up, knowing how many aces were left to fall at his—or the dealer's—place. The dealer was "Nancy from Indiana"—a sweet-faced, red-headed girl with heavy black eye makeup. He was joking with her, and tilting his toes, and counting cards at the same time. He was really brilliant. He won three forty-dollar bets in a row and bantered with the dealer: "It's not how you play the game, but whether you win or lose." The girl didn't get it. Cheryl hadn't gotten it the first time he'd said it either, but later he explained it to her and now she thought it was a funny joke. He took his handkerchief out of his pocket now, and Cheryl bet one hundred dollars on the next hand. It came up a ten and a jack, and she didn't even watch for his signal as he slid his chips to the right; she was catching on, she knew she had to stand with a twenty, it didn't matter what the dealer had.

Bad luck! The dealer had blackjack. Nancy-from-Indiana swept the chips away, click, click, click, just like that, not caring for the narrowness of his eyes, the ugly clenching of his jaw muscles. This was what Cheryl hated, when it didn't go his way and his temper got foul.

She played the next three hands at his instruction, and twice he was wrong again. He had lost his concentration. He scooped up his remaining chips, raised an eyebrow at her, and walked to the keno lounge. After playing two token hands to establish that she was separate from him, in case the pit boss was watching, Cheryl met him there. He was adding some figures on a keno sheet, writing with thick black crayon.

"Why don't you ever play bingo with me?" she said. "I think that would be fun." The kind of look he gave her made her want to race away, to run all the way back to LA, to see her mother, even to go to junior college. She abruptly left him, saying she was going to the rest room.

A black woman in a uniform was mopping up leaks from the faucets with hotel towels. "You know how the engineers make these hotels," she said to Cheryl. "Every minute this place don't go up in flames, I thank God."

But the mirrors were perfect. They had the right kind of pink light coming down that always made her skin look especially creamy and smooth. She smiled at herself, a flash of a smile that was brilliant. Sometimes she really *was* gorgeous and she felt proud. When she stood at bus stops, her thick blonde hair blowing around her face, she impressed the traffic, she knew that.

"You winning, honey?" the black lady asked. Cheryl saw her white plate waiting, empty of tips.

"Yeah, I'm really lucky tonight," she said, digging in her big red nylon purse and putting a twenty-five-dollar chip on the plate. "This is my honeymoon."

"No kidding," the lady said. "How about that?"

Cheryl went out into the casino again, into the smoke and the clatter of silver dollars and the raucous shouts coming from the craps table. She saw Rand's rounded back hunched at another table; he was playing again. She wandered around to the slot carousel, got twenty silver dollars, and idly put them in a machine, three at a time, to buy all three payoff lines. The last pull she only had two to put in, and son of a gun, the three bars showed up on the bottom line and she hadn't paid for them. Shit, she hated that. It happened once before and she didn't get three hundred quarters. Things like that could make her cry. She couldn't believe she would cry over something like that. Yet she was filling up, her nose and eyes, and she wanted to say to God, How come not me? How come everyone else is so lucky, only not me? Right next to her a young couple, maybe twenty-two or twenty-three, had two ice buckets filled with silver dollars. As she watched they hit another jackpot and the girl yelled, "*'O-kay!*" and the guy gave her a big hug. Cheryl checked to see if the girl had a wedding ring. She did, and an engagement ring, too. Cheryl looked at her own wedding band. Already she didn't like it;

she had picked the wrong one this morning. They had been in too much of a hurry, trying to squeeze in a wedding and a trip to Vegas in the same day. Rand had said he would buy her a diamond if they had a big hit this weekend. The high rollers all bought their women jewelry. Sometimes the wives took half the winnings right off the table, cashed in the chips, and went straight to the jewelry store to buy gold bracelets. Cheryl would never have the nerve to scoop up half of Rand's winnings. Maybe she just hadn't been married long enough.

Now an old man on her other side hit three oranges and stood back, chewing on a cigar, while thirty coins clanged down into the tin bowl. He put three more dollars in the slot, and three bars turned up, giving him a hundred more. He looked around for something to do while the bells rang and the money arrived, and said to Cheryl, "You using this machine?"

"No, you can have it," she said, stepping back, and she felt a few tears wash over the edge of her eye.

"Hey, hey," the old man said. "You lose everything?"

She nodded.

"Then take a handful of mine. Go ahead, I won't feel it. I have oil wells."

"I don't think so," Cheryl said. "I have to quit now."

"Here," he insisted. "Just fill up a bucket."

"It doesn't work that way," Cheryl said. "I don't think you can use someone else's luck." She went out to the lobby to look at the waterfall. A new bride was standing there, a young Mexican girl with flowers on her wrist. Her husband, a handsome Latino with a pencil mustache, wearing a white jacket, came over to Cheryl and said, "Could you take a picture of us, please?" He handed her his camera. "Just push here."

They were both children, Cheryl thought. Men her own age were really children, weren't they? She took a picture they would keep forever, but they would never remember her standing there, taking it. She knew she would always remember them.

"We appreciate it," the girl said, the water crashing down behind her, sending up a rainbow spray of dots against the rocks. To their retreating backs Cheryl said, "I wish I had a wedding picture. I just got married, too."

Deciding to go back to the hotel room, she crossed the pool area and saw a Hawaiian luau in progress. Four black-haired girls in flowered red dresses were dancing a hula on a wooden platform. The music was very serene and dreamy; the girls' hands were as delicate as birds. Their hips slid slowly back and forth under their long dresses as if they were under water. Cheryl knew she would never be that peaceful. She stood on the damp grass and watched, feeling the tears come again. Then she took the elevator up to their room and fell asleep.

"Butterflies, Love-Lites, roses, cigars . . ." The cigar girl passed their table in the coffee shop and Cheryl tapped her on the back. The girl swung around, her long stockinged legs seeming to take up most of her body.

"Are those Love-Lites you're wearing?" Cheryl asked. "How do they work?" The girl wore flashing red lantern earrings, a blinking red pendant, and a blinking butterfly pin.

"Little hearing-aid batteries," the girl said. "They last forever."

"Could you get me one, Rand?" Cheryl asked, smiling at him.

"Sure," he said. He was composed again, shaved and smelling of Brut. "If you like . . ." He took out his wallet. "How much?"

"Twenty-five," the girl said, "if you want the Love-Lite earrings."

Cheryl imagined that if she were ever in a dark tunnel, the Love-Lites would light her way to safety. She took off her little ivory elephant earrings and attached the new ones to her ears.

They finished eating their breakfast. She and Rand were in the hotel with a huge gold-colored pot outside—about fifty feet high with a fake ugly rainbow coming up to it.

"Cheap," Cheryl had remarked as they turned into the parking lot. "It makes the whole idea cheap. Now whenever I see a rainbow I'll be reminded of this brassy pot and this ugly rainbow. And when I hear 'Over the Rainbow' I'll think of smoky rooms and bad bets."

"Maybe you'll think of mirrored rooms and piles of money."

"Same thing," Cheryl said.

"Well, let's get going. I could use you to play for me this morning."

"I don't really want to," she said. "I want to do something else. You're safe. They don't know you here, do they? It's a new hotel."

"I suppose I could get along without you for a while. But not tonight."

"I'll play for you tonight, then."

"And do what all day?"

"Who knows?" she said. "Go to Hoover Dam maybe."

As soon as she got on the tour bus she felt a little better. The casinos always seemed like churches to her, with people praying for grace all over the place. You could feel it when you passed a bingo room, the hush, the living prayer, as they all waited to be chosen. In Vegas, to pray and to play was the same thing: you could get saved, you could get lucky. Only the difference was, if God gave you grace, no one lost. In Vegas, if you won, you were just ruining the next guy.

Cheryl leaned her face into the air-conditioning slit under the window. The bus was filling up with lots of elderly ladies. She never wanted to be one of them, with their bluish hair and their pointy eyeglasses. They looked like old birds, all the same. How did they ever have any fun? Sometimes Rand looked like an old bird with his skinny shins, the way the skin on his legs seemed scaly. She was glad he was cooped up in some casino, in the dark daytime inside of those places. She was going out into the sun . . . where she could thaw out.

She was definitely feeling better. She looked out the window as the bus crossed the desert and she decided there *was* scenery out there. She saw pinkish clay rock formations, and long sandy stretches of browns and beiges and pinks. It looked like a painting. Some clouds were lining up overhead, so it didn't seem quite as hot or bright. Sometimes she thought she had seen everything, thought everything she was ever going to see or think, and the next eighty years of her life were going to be exactly the same as the first twenty. But once in a while she saw something new and got a different feeling, and when that happened, it gave her hope again. At first, being with Rand had given her a thousand new thoughts and feelings, but now she was having no new ones. Like everything else, it had gotten old—and she had only married him yesterday. If, as her mother said, the marriage—considering his record—was sure to be a short-term thing, then *that* was rotten. And if it was to be forever, till death did they part, that seemed rotten, too.

When she first started living with Rand, her mother had said, "Just don't come back home to us with a baby for me to take care of for you." It never occurred to her that she might have a baby with Rand. One of his sons' wives was pregnant. He didn't seem like the type of husband you'd want to have a baby with, a man who already was going to be a grandfather.

"Hoover Dam up ahead," the bus driver announced. "When we park, please line up at the second tower on the Nevada side."

As soon as she got out of the bus, Cheryl found herself behind a young couple in black motorcycle jackets. They each had one hand stuck in the butt pocket of the other's jeans. The girl, curvy and very cute, had long fuzzy black hair, while the guy was tall and good-looking, and wore pointy lizard-skin boots. Cheryl admired his dark wavy hair. When he turned to look down at the river, Cheryl saw a toothpick in his mouth. He made her heart leap, giving out that kind of raw sexiness that did something to her. She wished she were his girl. For a minute, she would have given anything to be that girl.

Blocks of tourists, maybe twenty at a time, were allowed to board the elevator. For five minutes at a time the line came to a stop. Every time it stopped, the guy took the toothpick out of his mouth and kissed his girl, bending her backward passionately. Once the girl looked behind her, embarrassed, and smiled apologetically at Cheryl.

"That's okay," Cheryl said, "I don't mind. I think love is great." She walked behind them as they inched toward the elevator, and looked down the vast sloping side of the dam, which curved downward to the Colorado River, a greenish strip far below them. Tiny dots—birds—flew and lifted against the concrete curve. Cheryl realized that a person could easily kill himself by jumping off here. She had also noticed that it would be easy from the parking garage of The Mint, seventh level, and filed away the information in her head. Most public places tried to keep you from killing yourself, putting up high fences or barbed wire, but then there were other places that didn't seem to worry about the possibility. Right here, at Hoover Dam, you could just get up on the waist-high railing and jump down into the curving concrete side of the dam. If she ever really needed to do it, it would be a long ride from LA.

The motorcycle couple moved along with the line. Now the guy, wearing a black T-shirt under his leather jacket with the words "Harley-Davidson, Denver, Colo, USA" on it, had his hand under his girl's belt line and was pressing down to bare skin, as far as he could get under the tight jeans.

"Hey," the girl whispered to him, peeking over her shoulder at Cheryl, "don't do that." The guy turned around and winked at Cheryl. "Hey, you come here too, sweetheart. I have two hands; I can do you both at once." Cheryl laughed and took a step forward, and then the guy had his arm around her, too. The girl laughed and he laughed and the line began to move forward quickly, so she crowded into the elevator with them, and the three of them descended into the mountain, 528 feet down, clinging together.

They walked through a long tiled tunnel behind their guide, a short man with a booming voice who assured them the tunnel did not leak. It was cold in the tunnel and the lights above them were very dim. Now and then the bulbs would black out for a few seconds. Cheryl could feel the thrumming vibration of machinery all around her. "The walls of the dam are 107 feet thick," the guide said. "It is 726 feet high." She was still wrapped in the arm of the guy in the motorcycle jacket. "If you've heard rumors that men were trapped in the concrete, put your minds at ease. The cement here was poured eighteen inches at a time, so it could cure, and you can't lose a man in eighteen inches of concrete. *However*, it *is* true that ninety-six workers were killed between 1931 and 1937: twenty-four fell to their deaths, three drowned, ten were killed by explosions, five were electrocuted, twenty-six were struck by falling debris, twenty-six were struck by machinery, one died in the elevator, and one in a cableway accident."

The girl who was sharing her guy with Cheryl shivered. "How creepy," she said. "What if we get stuck down here?"

"Don't worry," Cheryl offered. "I have my Love-Lites." She held back her hair and showed the girl the glowing lanterns swinging from her ears. "If anything goes wrong, they'll light our way out of here." The girl reached over and took her hand tightly. "How neat," she said. "We're so lucky to have you. This place spooks me."

Cheryl changed places with the guy so that she was between him and the girl; she held hands with both of them going down the long tunnel. In the powerhouse they saw the row of immense electric generators which took the river water and turned it into electricity. The guide gave them a thousand figures, and while he told them how many acres the lake covered, how many kilowatts the power plant produced, Cheryl noticed some little metal machines that resembled robots, funny round tubs with bleeping antennae. She pointed them out to the girl, who squeezed her hand tighter and giggled. "This is so much fun," she said. "I'm so glad we found you."

"Want me to take a picture of you two with my Polaroid?" Cheryl asked, hunting in her nylon bag for her camera. They were being led now through a diversion tunnel, a long dark passage made of volcanic rock ten to fifteen million years old, through which water had run while the dam was being built. The three of them let the tour group pass by them, and then stood alone in the black tunnel. The rocky sides dripped moisture from condensation, and as in a subway train, the lights flickered and went out. From far down the passageway they could hear the gasps and delighted fright of the tourists, and the guide's reassuring voice. Cheryl stood secure in the pinkish glow of her Love-Lites, her new friends gathered close to her. She arranged them against the jagged wall and let her flash explode.

"Want us to take a picture of you?" the girl asked.

"That would be real nice," Cheryl said. "This is sort of a special occasion for me—I've been wishing someone would take a picture of me all day."

"Couldn't you ask anyone?" the girl said.

"Not really," Cheryl said. "I'm out here by myself." Just as she tore the finished picture from the camera and handed it over to them, the lights flashed on, illuminating the three of them in a ring of whiteness. "Look," she said to the guy, "I even got your boots in the picture."

He laughed. "I guess you know what counts," he said. "Here, let me take you now." He posed her against the rock, and she tossed her hair back to let her lanterns shine out. While they were waiting for the print, her friends told Cheryl that they were staying in a camper parked at some strip hotel, and were heading for Zion in the morning.

"Say," the guy said, "if you're traveling alone, maybe you'd like to come along with us for a while." He put his hand on his girl's shoulder and said, "How's that for an idea?"

The girl looked at him. "Well, I guess we could squeeze her in."

"Sure," he said, "the more the merrier."

Cheryl, her back against the rough wall, felt as if the gates of the dam had just been opened, and she was being swept out to sea on the emerald waters.

"Will you do it?" he asked. The girl had taken out an Afro comb and was picking at her fuzzy curls, standing a little away from them.

"Yeah . . . sure. I will! It sounds great."

"Where are you staying?" he asked. "We'll have to come by and get your luggage."

But just then there was a last warning call for the elevator going up, and because she couldn't run fast on her high heels, they got way ahead of her making a dash down the tunnel. Dancing with impatience, Cheryl had to wait for the second trip up. When she got to the surface they were gone. She walked frantically from the tower on the Nevada side to the tower on the Arizona side, and searched for them in the crowd near the statues of the Winged Figures of the Republic at the entrance to the dam. She heard a faint buzz reverberating off the canyon walls, and in the distance saw the little ant of their motorcycle climbing the hairpin road toward the desert.

Finally she joined the crowd of old ladies going back to the tour bus, and when she found a seat she settled down to study her wedding picture. It was just her luck, she thought, that even the Love-Lites didn't shine out in it. They hung there, like charred corks, from her ears.

At the Fence

She is standing on her neighbors' doorstep, seeing herself as they will see her in a second: a cranky, middle-aged lady with a complaint. For an instant she is *them* seeing herself come up the walk in a polyester dress, her hair going gray, peering into their screen door, into their private life, prepared to introduce some petty irritation into their newly-wed bliss.

She can see the young man lounging on the floor, his back against the couch cushions, watching the end of the Yankee-Dodger game. He has just come home from work and is drinking a beer. At first she thinks he might be wearing his underwear, but sees with relief as she puts her eyes to the screen that his shorts are of the jogging or swim-suit variety. His wife is in the kitchen, heating another frozen pizza. Anna believes—because of the nightly odor of oregano and sizzling mushrooms—that the young couple must eat pizza for every dinner during the week; on weekends it must be steak because then Anna can smell the fire-starter burning on their outdoor barbecue grill.

"Uh, yes?" the young man answers to her unwelcome knock, getting up reluctantly and glancing back at the TV screen. He shakes a long lock of black hair out of his eyes.

"Excuse me," Anna says, "I'm sorry to bother you, but I'm your neighbor, Mrs. Mazer, I live next door, and your dog was barking as he often does till after two o'clock in the morning. He has a very loud bark."

The young man looks behind him, and there comes the dog—a sleek black Doberman trotting right to the door, his long snout coming up against the screen, his stubby tail wagging.

"Yeah, he does, doesn't he?" the young man says, and bends protectively to pet his dog.

To show her good will, Anna says sincerely, "He's really a beautiful animal." Just then the man's wife swings into view, wiping her hands on her blue jeans. She is perhaps a year or two younger than her husband, about nineteen, the age of Anna's oldest daughter, Karen, yet she comes to the door as if she owns not only this rented house, but also the world with Anna in it. She puts her hand on her husband's bare shoulder; only then is Anna aware of the thick black hair on his chest, the private hole of his navel looking at her eye. The girl has cornsilk blonde hair, long and thick, and she twists it, ropelike, over one shoulder as she stands there looking out. Her breasts are heavy and loose inside a blue T-shirt.

"Hi, I'm Liz," she says conversationally.

"The dog—" Anna continues. "I realize it's a new place for him here, but I would like you to be aware that he whines and howls all day when you're both at work, and last night—I guess you were out late—he was really frantic, running from one end of the yard to the other, barking hysterically. Even if you *are* home he tends to bark in the middle of the night, but it's worse when you're gone. I guess he stopped barking when you came home, around two."

"Yeah," he says, "that's when we came home, around two."

Anna wonders where they went, and what could be more enticing than this new little house, their bedroom at the back with a glass door to the garden, the kitchen so handy to warm up frozen foods in. The husband looks over his shoulder at the TV.

"I don't mean to disturb you, really," Anna says, "but it's agonizing to be trying to sleep and to have that bark never stopping. It makes me feel desperate, as if I have no control over my life."

Too melodramatic, I'm telling them too much, she thinks, moving away from the screen and down a step, to show she is going, won't take any more of their time.

"Yeah, well, we hope he quiets down." He scratches his thigh, and adds, "But he's not going to be sleeping in the house—we got a new rug."

"Look—" Anna says, suddenly thinking of how her heart pounded last night as she listened to that piercing, perpetual racket and of how she considered calling the police, then realized they could do nothing more than some official preliminary paperwork, "the thing is I work at home, I do calligraphy, and I often work outside on the patio, or in my bedroom, and I just can't concentrate with all that noise. Even when it's quiet, I know he's going to start in a minute again, or *could*, and I just can't function." To her surprise, she hears her voice crack and feels tears heat her eyes. She didn't know she could act this well; at least she thinks she's acting because she didn't know she felt this badly.

The young man is bored now. She can see him wondering how this crying woman got here just when the Dodgers were going up to bat. But she can't leave without saying just a few more things. "The point is, I can't *do* anything to control what's happening to me," she begs in spite of herself. "I can't stop your dog from barking and there's no room in my house where I can hide. I hear him *everywhere*—even in the closet! If only I could contact you during the day to tell you about it! It's been going on for a whole month now, since the day you moved in."

"Well, I guess he's lonely," the wife says suddenly. "What he needs is another dog to play with." She snickers. "But *it'd* probably bark, too."

"I don't understand why you have a pet, just to leave him alone all day. Why do you need a dog? You both work!"

"Hey!" the husband says with a flare of anger. "That's *why* he's here. I mean, if we were both here all day, why would we need a watchdog?"

"Well, I'm home all day," Anna says, backtracking with a weak smile, believing for an instant she can convince them to give their dog away and make her their watchdog. "I could watch out for you.

I mean, I always look out my windows. If I saw anything funny going on, if I saw a truck in your driveway, I could call you. Is there someplace I could reach you during the day?"

Her voice is reedy with guile: she really wants to be able to call them up and scream, "Come home and shut him up! I can't listen to that noise another second!"

"If she saw a truck in the driveway," the wife says, "it'd probably be one of your buddies." She elbows her husband and laughs.

"Well, me," he says, keeping to the point. "I'm a housepainter, so I can't be reached, and she—well, she works in a store and you can't call her there." His voice is protective and mean now, he's had enough of this, and to show it he bends down and pats the dog again, lovingly. "Good boy, Fletch, yeah, we'll get you some of that good food soon."

Anna feels worse than she did in the middle of the night. It's gone wrong. The young man is really hostile now, and she's gotten nowhere, just a crank on his doorstep.

"You know, I like animals, I really love them," Anna says in a last effort to set it right, show them that she's a fair, nice person. "I mean, I'm all for pets. I have two cats myself—."

"Yeah," he says. *"They're* probably what makes my dog bark. One of them was in my yard. I even fed it. I sure won't do *that* again." Now he's holding the dog by its red leather collar as if to keep it from springing at her throat. She suddenly remembers a half-dozen movies in which Dobermans were killers, one in which Rock Hudson is a mad scientist who discovers a way to age a human embryo to an old woman in a few short weeks. Anna thinks that it was just yesterday she was newly married, and now she's old. She doesn't believe the problems she's thinking about these days could really be her problems. She hasn't had enough of starting out, she's just getting used to being grownup, being married.

"We also have a little aviary—maybe you've seen my daughter's birds when your dog gets out the door and you come up between the houses to get him."

"He don't ever get out," the husband says threateningly, stepping back, his hand on the door now, ready to close it on her.

"But he does!" Anna says. "You were in my yard just yesterday morning."

"Not me," he says. "Sorry—we got to eat now," and he closes the door.

Anna's husband is doing a crossword puzzle at the kitchen table; her oldest daughter has her book bag over her shoulder and the keys to Anna's car in her hand.

"I'm going over to Ben's," she says. "See you—"

Anna wants to ask, Aren't you going to have dinner with us? When will you be home? Do you have a sweater? but those are old records that spin soundlessly around her children's ears.

"What if I need to use my car?" she says instead, meanly, striking a bull's-eye.

"Do you?" Karen asks.

"No, I don't," Anna says, "but what if I did?"

"Then Ben would come and get me," Karen says reasonably.

"On his motorcycle," Anna says. "Well . . . go"—waving her away—"go see Ben."

Ben, her daughter's lover, is the wrong man for her daughter, but Karen says she will marry him very soon. Not *live* with him, which Anna often prays will happen, but *marry* him. Anna would much prefer the new arrangement for them so when Karen grows up and finds out how off-center he is, how insincere, superficial, humorless, stupid, the break won't be as complex as divorce. Anna also reasons that if Karen moved in with Ben, she would be out of her way, out of the house where now Anna has to witness her in her adolescent turbulence, its ugly, heavy, despairing side. She doesn't even want to look up from her desk these days when Karen comes in sullenly from classes at the junior college, doesn't want to say, How was school? as she said it, gladly, when Karen (bright and darling and lovable) was in second grade but going daily to do reading with the sixth graders. Karen has given notice that she is going to quit school to get a job so she can marry Ben. Ben has no plans, no interests right now, and even that isn't the trouble. It isn't his motorcycle, either—Anna is not that dense or backward. It's just that her heart hurts when she considers Karen's giving her life to that dull boy, a boy who makes rat-tat-tat sounds like a six-year-old playing soldier whenever he describes some fantasy film he's seen in which lasers shoot out of spacecrafts.

As she sets dinner plates on the table, her husband, Lou, absently raises the newspaper to let her get one under it. *His* mother was convinced Anna was the wrong girl for *him* more than twenty years ago, and she fought Anna like a banshee, with threats, scenes, blackmail, insults, curses. To no avail, of course—here they are, not having half the fun his mother was afraid they were going to have, and not anywhere as ruined as his mother predicted. But ruined enough, by normal attrition, repetition, the insidious deadening of responses. At least at the beginning there was that spark arcing over them, between them, encircling them, which clearly Karen has not got with Ben—there *is* no current as far as Anna can see, but Karen, in her dullness, doesn't even seem to know there's that to hope for.

The other children, old teenagers, come dragging into the kitchen for dinner; they used to set the table for her, used to check a wheel-chart on the refrigerator for their weekly chores, used to vacuum, straighten up the bathroom, take out the garbage. Now they do nothing but wait to be waited on, and Anna hasn't the strength to fight back anymore. Arguing takes more energy than doing everything herself, though her energy level, in general, is very low, and losing sleep every night hasn't helped.

"That black dog," she says to Lou, "you heard him last night, didn't you?"

"Well, yeah, I suppose, maybe I did."

"Don't say that just for my sake," Anna says. "Did you hear that horrible barking or didn't you?" "I think I was sleeping," Lou says.

God, she thinks, *heavy and impenetrable, like his daughter Karen. Hardly conscious sometimes.* Maybe if his mother had tried just a little harder, Anna would have been saved from him, from this life of servicing him and his children. Sometimes she says it aloud, that she doesn't feel she has her own life, and Lou or one of the children will say complacently, "Well, you have your calligraphy."

But she can't even do her calligraphy with the dog howling. Sometimes a distant fire engine or police siren will start the dog going, and he begins a thin wailing, less eerie than the coyotes' wailing she hears at night from the hills, but burdened enough, an outward-spiraling tornado of loneliness and misery. Then it will pause briefly before turning into an explosion of staccato barks, getting shriller and more panicky, till finally the animal is running from one end of the yard to the other, rattling the fence, clawing at the spaces between the boards, yipping and yapping in a frenzy that can go on, easily, for several hours without pause.

"They should require every person who owns a dog to have the dog's larynx removed," Anna says, dropping silverware onto the table. "No one has a right to do this, to destroy a person's peace, just because he likes the idea of having a dog. A man and his dog!—what a dumb, romantic notion."

At the same moment she is thinking that she would like Karen to marry a young man like the one next door. A man who has a dog—a man, who, with his woman and his beer and his ballgame, seems like the sort of man a woman should have, a man who protects his rights, who doesn't back down, who stands firm. She thinks of his hairy chest, and to her surprise something clutches low down in her abdomen, in the place where the estrogen is running low.

She wishes all her children would move out tomorrow and end it right there. She wishes Lou were really her father and she could live in the house with him but still go out in the world for adventure and romance, and then he'd be there to hold her warmly when she came in from her excursions in the shimmering night world.

Of course, it could never happen. Sometimes she feels she will never go anywhere again, and if she does, it won't matter where, she'll be bored and tired at any spot in the universe. As far as her success as a mother goes, if she has raised such a perfect child, her firstborn, Karen, who knew the names of all the dinosaurs at three, how come a girl like that dopey blonde next door can figure out how to set up such a neat arrangement for herself, a handsome man, a bed, an endless supply of pizzas, while Karen falls in with a young man of no redeeming charm or beauty or intelligence whatsoever? Do all parents feel this about their children? Is it her duty to intervene and *forbid!* Or at least try to? At first she thought interfering was against her principles, but now she realizes she just hasn't the energy to do it. What difference can it make? In the end she will have to recognize that her children aren't perfect people, no matter how much of herself she handed over to them—they're just ordinary, mixed-up kids who have all the predictable problems.

Besides, how can she know if her instincts are correct? What if she insists that Karen never see Ben again . . . and then Karen never in her life meets another man who wants her? Then she'll live forever with Lou and Anna—she'll be a spinster of fifty and Lou and Anna will be seventy-five, and she'll be taking Anna's car out to the cotton-spool factory where her job will be to spin cotton onto plastic spools. Who will do Karen's laundry when Anna and Lou have died? No one; she'll never wear clean underpants again, and won't care, either.

It's getting away from her. Anna serves dinner. Later, when she goes to bed, she watches the cold computerized numbers of the digital clock and thinks how buttons are taking over the world, video games and phones and microwave ovens and food processors and word processors and machines on which you can play carnal movies in your bedroom. Warmth has gone out of everything. She shivers with a chill, and at that moment the dog starts to bark and her body flares with anger or sorrow or with a vindictive hormonal flush, and then she feels as if she is burning in hell.

Judge, she says to herself, getting her case in order, *do you think it's fair? Don't dogs belong in big country spaces where they can roam and explore? Isn't it a true crime to lock an animal in a yard and then leave it alone all day, and long into the night? And isn't my home my castle? Shouldn't I be able to take a nap, or read a book, or make love* (as long as we're envisioning the ideal life) *without either the threat of sudden barking or its actual occurrence? Is there no way justice can be done in my favor?*

She will not tell the judge her other fantasies: how the young couple shake the little house with the force of their passion (a young wife does not have soft swinging breasts for nothing), how, after the beer and the pizza and the ballgame, the young man takes his other satisfactions before he has to go out into the cold morning world to smooth fresh new paint over old walls.

And is it the appearance of this dog in her life which is really the greatest injustice that has been done to her? And what about the moral wrong done to the black dog with his long moist snout as he daily runs from one end of the yard to the other—hardly a watchdog, hardly a man's best friend, just a whimpering, crazed abandoned creature, without a mate, without a friend.

On the next weekend night, long after the coals in the barbecue grill on the other side of the fence have died out and the couple has roared away in their pickup truck, when the full moon is overhead, Anna gets her two biggest pot covers and takes them out into the backyard. She holds them poised like a cymbal player waiting for her cue in the pit of a great orchestra. In the house her remaining daughters are sprawled on unchanged bedsheets, sleeping in old sweatshirts and torn cords. Karen has not come home from Ben's yet—she often does not arrive till three or four o'clock in the morning. Lou is posed in bed like a marble statue on a sarcophagus. On Anna's desk are a hundred blank sheets of beige bond paper on which she is to hand-letter wedding invitations for a high school friend of Karen's, a girl who is marrying a twenty-seven-year-old astronomer, handsome and highly placed in a government job.

Anna waits, counting the beats, as breathless as if the stars are her vast audience and this is her debut. And when it comes, first the whine, then the howl, then the full-fledged bass and treble of the mad dog's great range, she runs in her nightgown, barefoot, across the damp grass of the yard, runs to the fence and crashes the pot covers together in a series of clashes, bangs and shrieks till the night sky shakes with the lightning and thunder of her fury.

Then . . . silence. She has terrified him. She feels her lip curl. Hah, good. She imagines the dog to be like a native in the jungle who witnesses a meteorite fall. He will be cowering now under the oleanders, his ordinary restless anguish changed to full terror. Well, this is only the beginning. She will teach him.

Back in the house, she sees that she has actually awakened her sleeping daughters. They are stumbling, bleary-eyed, down the hall. What happened, they wonder. A car crash? Only her husband still sleeps: no kiss, no catastrophe, no symphony can wake him.

Anna replaces the pot covers in the cabinet under the stove, but not before a sliver of silver metal, shredded from the edge of one of the covers by her wild banging, pierces her finger, drawing bright blood.

The next day she buys a pair of ear plugs, little cylinders of wax and foam, and at night jams them into her ears as if she is corking up her vital fluids. After she inserts them and lies down under the covers she hears only the pounding of her heart, each beat pushing the ear plugs, little by little, out of her, as when her husband, that last, long-ago time, fell asleep during lovemaking and in slow pulsing degrees slipped from her body.

She tries to sink down to sleep, but now anxieties of what she cannot hear reach her consciousness—the phone (her old mother, stricken, or Karen on the night streets in the old car, stranded, raped); the creaking of a door (a burglar); the whispering of passionate noises in her ear by her husband (he is not ninety; he is only facing in his way what she is facing in hers).

But then, as though through deep water, the dog's barking reaches her mind, blurred but stirring, a call to her energies: she is needed out there at the fence, she is wanted. This time she carries the tape recorder into the yard and carefully, like a technician fully versed in the uses of the buttons of destruction, presses "RECORD," gathering evidence for the judge in her case against the young couple, those lucky folks, so obliviously licking oregano from each other's lips, or peacefully, deeply sleeping.

The next day she writes the newlyweds a letter on a piece of the beige wedding-invitation stationery, taking a risk. Her daughter's friend probably will not count them, will never know Anna has only sold them ninety-nine sheets and taken pay for one hundred.

> *Dear Neighbors*— [she writes in her best italic script]
>
> *I am not well due to the barking of your dog. Please put him in the house or take him with you wherever you go. You have brought chaos into my life by moving to this quiet block, and I will have no recourse but to call the police if you do not take proper measures.*
>
> *Anna Mazer*

It has taken her almost thirty minutes to write this, using her finest, most graceful golden nib. She ought to send them a bill for her services. They probably have more money than she has—after all, they eat steak, which Anna never buys, and they haven't got three sullen children to buy clothes and educations for. *Someone* ought to pay her!

Making sure they have left for work (both cars gone), she strides out past her walk and along the street to their mailbox, where she leaves the letter. Then, thinking better of it, she takes it out and carries it by hand to their kitchen door, where they enter every night after the day's work. She slides it under the door. As she does so, the dog comes trotting into view from the backyard, and she is within a foot of him as he pushes his snout against the space between the boards in the side gate.

It occurs to her that she will poison the dog if his owners don't fix up the trouble in her life. The dog yips, and absently she pats him through the fence as she plans what she will do. Valium in a hot dog, perhaps. But it probably won't kill, just sedate. If necessary she will go into the city and find a real drug pusher on a street corner. (She could probably ask Ben; no doubt he would know the right people.) A calculated number of barbiturates would do it. She wishes she were more knowledgeable in this seamier side of life.

The dog is licking her hand, dancing with pleasure at her company, his rear end wiggling in rippling convulsions. No one has been that happy to see her in a long time. She kneels and begins to croon to him, "You hate them for the way they leave you alone, and *I* hate them for the way they leave you alone. We should join forces, you know. Why don't you kill them, like the dog tries to do in the Rock Hudson movie?" She laughs. This is all very silly. She feels suddenly happy, not having laughed in some time.

"So long, kid," she says to the dog. "Try to have a nice day. Try meditation. Don't get so tense about everything."

Back in her house, she sits down at her desk and begins work on the wedding invitations. If Karen were to marry Ben, would she have to be personally responsible for a big party? For wedding invitations, dinners, a band, liquor? Would she have to make hors d'oeuvres and pass them around on little trays to Ben's friends who are wearing Star Trek T-shirts?

His parents are divorced and living on different continents. She thinks of his short stubby fingers and his brash thighs, riding her daughter. Perhaps—who knows about such things?—even sluggish, dull daughters might feel something.

When the dog begins to cry, she goes out in the yard and gives him a hot dog through the fence—to get him used to the idea, she tells herself, but he comes so fast to the fence, looks at her with his liquid brown eyes so longingly, that she feels her heart leap with gladness. She goes back into the house and brings out the whole package of hot dogs, feeding them to him one by one, watching with satisfaction as he devours them with pleasure.

Yet late that night, when the barking begins just as she has fallen asleep, she flails out in frustration, groaning, and strikes her husband in the center of his soft stomach.

"What? What?" he says, sitting bolt upright, and then he hears the sound. "The dog again, eh?" he says. "Are they home?"

"They don't hear *anything,*" Anna says.

"Well, now *I* hear it." He looks to his wife for approval; finally now, after so long, he hears it. He once again has something in common with her.

"What do you want me to do?" he asks. "Call them?"

"Why don't you?" Anna says. She feels suddenly excited, her husband is going to stand up for her, like the young man with the beer and the dog stands up for *his* wife, doesn't let anyone call her at work.

"Look up their number," he says, but she already is pushing buttons on the bedside phone; she has known their number by heart from the beginning. The digital clock reads 3:33. When her husband takes the phone from her as it begins to ring, she dashes into the kitchen and lifts the extension.

"Hullo?" finally comes the dull voice of the young man, heavy with sleep or sex. She can imagine him standing somewhere in that honeymoon cottage, naked, hairy, hot with the beating of his young blood.

"This is your neighbor," her husband says in a deep voice. "We're having trouble sleeping because of your dog. Could you do something about it?"

"God damn!" the young husband says. "Get the fuck off our backs, will you? We don't want fancy letters from your wife, either. You're just a couple of fucking old farts,"—and Anna hears him hang up the phone.

She comes back to the bedroom, her face flushed, her blood pounding in her head. Already her husband is calling the police, his anger causing his fingers to tremble as they search among the buttons. She listens while he tells the police the story, gives the address, hangs up. "They're coming over to talk to the guy," her husband says. "I won't be treated that way. I'll go to court! If necessary I'll go over there and kill it!"

Kill it. For her. She is overwhelmed. She turns the lamp off and gets into bed beside her husband. She embraces him, turning on her side toward his stretched-out body. They lay tensely, waiting for the lights of the police car, which finally come washing up over the ceiling.

They can hear the policeman knocking on the front door of the little house next door. There is a low interchange of polite voices. Her interests are being protected, she is going to be taken care of. They hear the door close, the police car backing out of the driveway, driving away.

"Well, maybe now we can get some sleep." Her husband pats her shoulder, moves her arm off his stomach, and seems instantly to be breathing softly, drifting into sound sleep. All the breath goes out of her. Now she is filled with fear. The young man is the type who probably has a gun in his house. A real man has a dog and a gun. He will blast her children in the yard. Or strangle her cats. Or slash the aviary wire and let out her daughter's precious birds—she can see the flutter of finches and doves as they ascend over the house and fly away forever. It will end as a headline in a tabloid newspaper. Her husband will kill the black Doberman with his bare hands and the young man will get out his gun and shoot her husband. Karen will marry Ben. Her other daughters will run off to a commune. The wind will blow away her wedding invitations, and the ink will come out of her pen nib in blots.

She imagines the young man right now stroking the polished barrel of his shotgun, and she feels herself arc out of bed and land on her toes like a ballet dancer. She hurries into the backyard. The stars are as sharp as at the beginning of creation. A tall palm at the far end of the yard is fanned out against the moon. There is a rustling in the brush on the other side of the fence as she approaches it.

She whispers, "Here boy, come here," and the beautiful black dog with his princely face comes to the fence and thrusts his warm nose through the crack till it is cupped in her fingers.

"Listen . . ." she says. "Just wait here and be very quiet." She walks on the sharp, damp blades of grass to the door at the back of the garage and returns with a hammer. By the light of the moon she pulls and pries at a board in the fence until she wrenches it from the bottom rail. Making a tiny kissing sound with her lips she holds it aside and the dog pours through like a waterfall, shimmering and coursing down the length of her leg. She kneels and puts both arms around him, long enough to feel his hot breath on her face.

"Come with me," she says, standing and leading him by his red collar up the patio steps, into the house, and across the soft carpeting of the living room. He follows her out the front door and into the wide street where they both stand in silence, panting in the cool air. His ears are up, his hind legs spread slightly apart. She bends quickly and gives him a sharp rap on his rump.

"Go!" she commands. "Go!"

He starts forward like a thoroughbred, like a whippet, a black arrow flying into the dewy night. She watches him gallop till his image begins to fade against the slurry blacktop. She doesn't breathe as she sees him pause, tense, and then leap in a single bound over the horizon. At that moment she realizes she has forgotten to climb upon his back.

Someone Should Know This Story

I had no interest at all in spending the weekend with Carolyn, especially on such short notice, and also because Carolyn communicated most of her ideas to me by pushing, shoving, and jolting me about.

She was not really a friend of mine, but a girl of fourteen, my own age, who happened to be the daughter of my Aunt Ava, who was not really an aunt of mine, but the wife of a man who once asked my mother to marry him when he was just out of law school and she was a legal secretary in a firm where he applied for a job.

I could tell my mother wanted me to accept Ava's spur-of-the-moment invitation—it had something to do with being very civilized about her relationship with Ava, and it seemed important to Ava, too, that I "dump my nightie and a toothbrush in a bag and come right along."

Ava had driven into Brooklyn to visit her old mother who was in a rest home on Ocean Parkway, and she had dropped in to see us "for old times' sake." When she arrived, my mother had just come up from the basement with a heavy wicker basket full of wet laundry. By the time I had led Ava and Carolyn through the length of the house to the back porch, my mother was already leaning out over the railing, pushing the clothesline across the yard. They talked over the squeaking of the pulley.

Although I rarely liked to help with the wash (it was only in the winter I enjoyed being there when it was pulled in, every shirt and pajama frozen stiff by the cold), I stood beside my mother and shook out towels, getting them ready to hand to her with two clothespins for hanging.

"We send our clothes out to the laundry," Carolyn said, poking me fiercely in the ribs and laughing. She had buck teeth, but even so she was attractive because she had large breasts and a small waist like her mother, and brilliant straight dark black hair. Ava wore her black hair pulled back in a perfect chignon, with a string of colored stones woven somehow through the bun.

My mother's short wavy hair was nearly white—even though she was only in her early forties, she was often taken by my schoolfriends to be my grandmother—and I experienced a queer loyalty toward her just then, as she stood pushing the clothesline across the yard, wearing flat straw shoes and a seersucker housedress.

Ava wore high-heeled pumps and carried a shoulder bag made out of a whole alligator—I could count the teeth in the alligator's mouth as she stood talking to my mother.

"Herbert would be so pleased to have Janet stay with us. He's so fond of her."

I liked Herbert very much myself, but it was a feeling I never mentioned. Years before, he had come to our house on the pretext of some legal service he was doing for my grandmother, and he had seen me standing in the doorway beside my mother. As if I were not present, he said to her, sadly, "You know, Anna, she could have been mine."

"Why don't you go, Janet?" my mother asked me. "It will be a nice change."

I thought about my plans for the weekend: on Saturday I was going to take my grandmother to the movies, where we would get another flowered china cup to add to our growing set of dishes, and on Sunday several of my friends were going to come over to play canasta on the back porch. I looked about the backyard, where my dog was sleeping in his doghouse, where the lilacs were just starting to bud on the tree, where my little sister was sitting on the grass, coloring in her coloring book, and I thought of spending a weekend being shoved about by Carolyn.

"I can't go," I said. "My piano recital is June 10th, and I have to practice."

"Nonsense," Ava said. "We have the Steinway and no one ever touches it. Carolyn took lessons for six weeks and that was the end of that. We'll close you in the living room whenever you want to practice and you'll have perfect privacy."

If my father had been home he would have helped me out of it. He had no use for this occasional but continuing friendship with Herbert and Ava, and took no part in it. He considered Herbert to be a weak, scrawny asthmatic, and as far as reckoning with the visibly great material rewards Herbert lavished on his family as a result of his education, ambition, and successful legal practice—well, my mother had always been a free agent, and could have married anyone she chose. My father, who dealt in antiques, was not about to bow his head in shame.

I packed my clothes, and the blue sheet-music edition of "Claire de Lune," and drove back to Manhattan with Carolyn and Ava, my eyes tearing all the while from the smoke of Ava's cigarette filling the interior of the black Buick.

I was introduced first to the doorman and then to the elevator man. Several women with packages were coming into the building just then, and we were packed against the walls of the elevator with hardly room to breathe. No one said hello to Ava, and she stared ahead haughtily, taller than anyone in the car.

As soon as we got into the carpeted hallway of the sixth floor, I noticed the absence of air. It was springtime and there was no air on Park Avenue. No backyard, no grass, no flowers, no pets. How did they live here?

But in a moment I saw there were cut flowers in a silver vase on the dining room table, and I was shown the house pet from a distance: "His name is Malachi, and he will not hurt you unless he is provoked." Ava smiled briefly at me, and went down the hall into her bedroom.

"What provokes him?" I asked Carolyn. The dog was a huge, unattractive collie; he lay under the piano, staring at us and breathing heavily.

"Just don't go near him," Carolyn said, punching my shoulder for emphasis. "Come on, follow me."

In the kitchen I met Suellen, a black woman who scowled at Carolyn and said, "Don't you ask me what's for dinner. Whatever it is, it'll have to suit you."

"What's that?" I asked, pointing at a machine screwed into the wall.

"An ice crusher," Carolyn said. "Don't you have one?"

"No, we don't." I felt suddenly very frightened and trapped. There was nothing here I wanted to do, no one I wanted to be with or even liked. Herbert was kind, but I knew he would have very little to do with me.

I considered for a moment phoning my father at his store, and begging him to come and get me. I knew he would—he would come in an instant. But just the thought of him calmed me; the way he loved me was so tremendous that I could survive anything as long as I remembered him. My mother sometimes said she thought she had been destined for some other life, with a man of breeding, education, money. Of all her boyfriends, most of whom had been young lawyers, only my father was working in the pajama department of Loeser's when she met him. It never occurred to me to ask her why she actually married him, a man with an eighth-grade education, since it seemed obvious to me he would have been the best possible choice in the world—for anyone.

And yet, sometimes I saw her watching him work with his huge powerful hands, with dirt that was as permanent as his skin embedded under his nails, watching him move some heavy oak chifforobe he had just bought, his face red with the strain of the labor (once he cracked two ribs and did not know it for days), or watching him peer through a loupe at pieces of old jewelry he kept in a cigar box—and I saw on her face a certain distance, maybe distaste or self-pity, maybe regret that she had come to spend her days with a man who had never read Shakespeare's sonnets. I knew that in our bookcase we had the sonnets, given to my mother by Herbert, and inscribed by him to her. If my father had seen it there, or minded it, I never knew.

Ava came out of her bedroom, dressed in a long silk robe, and went down the hall into another room. Even though this was an apartment, it seemed to have more rooms than our whole house did. There were antiques on all the polished surfaces of the furniture, and I could tell they existed here in a different sense than did the ones in my father's store. Here they were works of art, carefully dusted and displayed, while in my father's shop antiques were piece goods, merchandise, to be traded and sold, with profit the only goal in mind. In our own home we had no antiques. My mother could not stand them. To her they were just "old things" that belonged to "other people."

Carolyn threw her arms around me and bear-hugged me from behind. I gasped, and stood trying to catch my breath. "I just can't believe you're here," she said. She dragged me by the hand to where her mother was in a little alcove, talking on the phone. "Get bonbons," she whispered, and her mother made an impatient gesture with her hand for Carolyn to be quiet. Ava was ordering cuts of beef, fruit, vegetables, rolls and pastries.

"If your mother shops on the phone," I asked Carolyn in a whisper, "how can she be certain they won't send her rotten tomatoes and bad meat?"

"Simple," Carolyn said, so sure of herself. "We'd never call that grocer again."

I thought of the way my mother shopped, pushing our old black-wicker baby stroller to the Avenue, stopping at each store to stand in line—the fish market, the bakery, the drugstore, the delicatessen. And what exactly were bonbons?

When Herbert came home he was carrying a sheaf of papers. He saw me sitting on the couch and smiled gently at me. "Is your mother here?" he asked softly, eyebrows raised.

"No. Aunt Ava was in Brooklyn today, and she brought me back to spend the night."

"Oh, Brooklyn, yes," Herbert said. He wheezed badly. He wore glasses and was going bald.

"Ava?" he called. He looked at Carolyn. "She's not in with Ravi, is she?"

"Of course not," Carolyn said. Something hard passed between them. "She's steaming her face." When her father had gone down the hall to his room, Carolyn mumbled, "She's not a fool, you know."

When we were all seated around the dinner table, Ava rang a silver bell and the maid came in with the first course. Dinner took a very long time, and there was no conversation. After each course was finished, Ava rang the bell and the maid appeared. Everyone seemed quite miserable, waiting and waiting while each place was cleared and the next dish brought. Finally Herbert cleared his throat and said, "Well, Janet, how do you like it in this neck of the woods?"

"It's fine, Uncle Herbert," I said. "It's very interesting."

After dessert I asked Carolyn which room was the bathroom. She pointed down the hall, and when I opened the door I thought she meant, I saw a dark young man sitting at a desk, wearing a turban on his head.

He stood up slowly. "How do you do?" he said with great significance. His teeth were brilliantly white in his dark face, and I experienced a kind of thrill that I had never felt before. He was evaluating me as if I were a grown woman.

"Excuse me," I said. "I didn't mean to open your door. I didn't know anyone else lived here."

"They try to keep it a secret," he said, with some soft laughter. "It would be embarrassing for anyone to know they were down on their luck and had to take in a boarder."

I knew I could not stand in the doorway and engage in conversation. "Pardon me," I said again, "I'm sorry," and I backed out quickly and closed the door. I was breathless when I came back into the dining room; I was reminded of the days, not so long ago, when I used to read Nancy Drew mystery stories, in which just such discoveries were commonplace.

"Why don't you two girls do something?" Ava suggested. "What do you do with your friends at home, Janet?"

"We like to play canasta," I said.

Ava said, "Carolyn has a nice puppet collection in her room. Why don't you both go in there and play for a while?"

In the morning when I awoke, Carolyn was not in her bed. I put on my skirt and blouse and went down the hall to the kitchen. Suellen said to me, "She has a riding lesson every Sunday morning. She said she forgot to tell you, but she'll be back by noon. The riding school comes and gets her at 8:30, and she didn't want to wake you. She said you should wait for her and practice the piano."

"Where is my aunt?"

"Asleep. But she's got a lady coming here in a little while, and we got to clear the kitchen. What do you like to eat? There's some French toast left."

She served it to me covered with maple syrup; at home my mother sprinkled a little sugar and cinnamon on it, and that was the way I liked it. I had never realized that life for other people could be so different in so many ways.

As I passed down the hall I could hear Herbert wheezing in his room. I heard the whoosh-whoosh of his rubber atomizer. I got "Claire de Lune" from my suitcase and went into the living room, where the dog was lying under the piano. He growled softly as I pulled out the bench. I hoped that French piano music would not provoke him.

I practiced for at least an hour, for the first time really happy to have a reason to work out the hardest passages. I simply could think of nothing as acceptable to pass the time as playing my music. I hoped that at least one good result of this visit would be that I might do nicely at my recital.

I wondered when they were going to take me home. Since no one talked very much here, I felt it would be impolite to ask anything outright. I had had trouble sleeping, and my stomach hurt during the night. I considered trying to find the bathroom in the dark, but I wasn't absolutely sure which room belonged to the dark young man, and I couldn't take a chance. Just before we went to bed, I had asked Carolyn about him.

"Oh, Ravi," she said. "He's an Indian prince or something. He's a student at the university and he lives with us because we have so much extra room. My father hates him, but my mother likes him."

"Do you like him?"

"It doesn't matter," she answered. "He has no use for me."

When I was through practicing I went into the kitchen for a glass of water. Ava was lying naked on a towel on the kitchen table, and a woman was slapping her back with both hands. I stood in the doorway watching. The woman, who was dressed in a white uniform just like Suellen, hit Ava's back with the sides of her hands, and then the flat of them. The smacks were hard enough for me to hear. There were bottles of lotions and powders on the counter. Ava's head, wrapped in a towel, rested on her arms. Her eyes were closed.

I went quickly down the hall past Herbert's bedroom, where he was wheezing more loudly than before. I didn't know where to go—in the living room was the unfriendly dog, the maid had disappeared, and at the end of the hall was the Indian prince. There was no outside to go to, and Carolyn had no books of the kind I liked to read. Her parents seemed to buy her only games and books that were suitable for an eight-year-old.

The door at the end of the hall opened suddenly and the prince came out. "Good morning," he said, bowing. "May I ask if you are a cousin of the family's?"

"I'm not related," I said. "My mother once almost married Carolyn's father, but I don't think that makes me anything here."

"What a shame," he said.

"That I'm not related?"

"That Herbert didn't marry your mother. No doubt he could have been a much happier man." "How do you know?" I asked.

"I live here, my dear," he said, smiling. We stood very close together in the hall. He must have been on his way out, for he was holding a briefcase in his hand.

"That is a strange noise," he said. We could hear the slaps resounding down the hall.

"My aunt has some woman . . . working on her in the kitchen."

"On Sunday?" the prince said. "How unusual." He set his briefcase down on the floor. "I won't go out after all," he said.

He remained there, looking at me and smiling. My heart pounded. I thought of the puppets, which suddenly seemed something attractive I wanted to play with.

"You have extraordinary blue eyes," the prince said. "You also play the piano with dedication. One day you will be an interesting and beautiful woman."

"Excuse me," I said. I turned around and rushed to Herbert's door. I knocked on it.

"Come in," he said. He was in an armchair by the window, reading the newspaper. On the table beside him were his atomizer, his medicine, and a cup of coffee.

"Do you think you could take me home early, Uncle Herbert?" I asked him. "I'm really not feeling very well."

"I think Ava was planning to take you home this afternoon," he said.

"But couldn't you? Now?"

"Let me tell you the truth about this, Janet. Ava doesn't like me to see your mother very much. You know, in the old days I was very fond of your mother, and Ava is still jealous."

I wondered if I should tell him that I thought my father was also jealous of him.

Herbert said, "I wonder—do you know that I once asked your mother to marry me?"

"Yes, of course I know that."

"Do you know the circumstances? Did she ever tell you about it? How we went to a Chinese restaurant that night?"

I shook my head.

"Someone should know this story," he said.

I sat down.

"We'd been going out for a long time. Your mother was not a passionate person, it was never easy to know her feelings. We went to plays and concerts and she seemed to enjoy my company. Your grandmother liked me a great deal—in fact, I think she even began to love me like a son—and I was very optimistic. I bought your mother a diamond engagement ring. We went to dinner that night, and when she reached for a fortune cookie, I stopped her hand and said, 'Here, your future is in this little box.' She looked at the ring and she refused it. I insisted she take it, that it was for her and that I didn't want it back even if she didn't accept my proposal. She handed it to me, and I handed it back to her, and finally she just dropped it on the table. When we got up to leave, we each thought the other would feel he must go back and get it, but neither of us did. We left it on the white tablecloth."

"Forever?" I asked.

"Forever."

"My mother has no diamond rings now," I told Herbert.

He finished his coffee and then said he would check with Ava about taking me home. I followed him down the hall. Ava was no longer lying naked on the kitchen table. The woman in white was packing up her bottles of lotions and powders. The sound of Ava's laughter came from the prince's room.

"Come! Come!" Herbert said suddenly. "*I'll* take you home. Quickly . . . get your things."

I didn't wait to say good-bye to Carolyn, nor did I ever thank Ava. Herbert drove me all the way back to Brooklyn without speaking to me. He wasn't angry or distant, he was just thoughtful, and I began to relax and let my guard down. I put my head back against the seat and almost fell asleep.

When we pulled up to my house, no one was in the front garden, but my dog was asleep under the beach chair and my father's pipe rested on its wooden arm. Just then my mother came to the front door to shake out the dry mop, and she saw us. She smiled and waved. Her white hair shone in the sun.

Herbert and I got out of the car, and he carried my small suitcase to the bottom of the front stoop. He looked up at my mother, who stood on the top step.

"Daddy's in the backyard," she said to me quickly. "Run around to the back and tell him Herbert's here and to come and say hello."

I skipped up the alley and burst into the backyard, and into my father's arms. He hugged me so hard I almost cried. He was bare to the waist, cutting dead branches off the peach tree. Drops of sweat ran down through the curls of dark hair on his chest.

"Mommy says to come and say hello to Herbert."

I pulled my father forward by the hand; he came slowly, letting me drag him toward the front of the house.

My mother had come down from the steps and was standing close beside Herbert. She seemed to stop talking suddenly as we came into view, and Herbert extended his hand to my father.

"You have no idea what a great pleasure it was to have your daughter with us this weekend."

My father shook Herbert's hand briefly, and my mother swayed to and fro, leaning on the pole of her dry mop. Herbert, hot and nervous in his tweed suit-jacket, shifted from one foot to another, saying his awkward good-byes. My father, who had bits of leaves and twigs in his thick black hair, looked around the yard, taking stock of the gardening he still needed to do. I saw that while I had been away, the popcorn-ball bush had bloomed into color.

When Herbert had driven off, my mother kissed me on the forehead and took my suitcase inside. I followed my father up the alley into the backyard and sat on the swing while he clipped branches off the peach tree with the rusted shears. My dog ran in circles around the yard like a maniac.

Once my father paused and looked over his shoulder at me.

"Glad to be home?"

In answer, I began to swing, grinning, and he stopped what he was doing to give me a magnificent push skyward.

Memorial Service

A POSTER of Superman hung in the boys' room, the last remnant of their tenancy after my sister Carol had cleaned out their drawers and closets in a burst of manic energy. It was the day before Bard's "funeral." Although the cremation had already taken place, a service had been arranged by Bard's mother and sister. Carol was sick with a bad case of bronchitis which had been hanging on for weeks. She had said to me she didn't see why it was necessary to have some elaborate ritual to mourn her husband's passage from life when he had elected to kill himself.

I held back the flaps of a large carton for her as she tore shirts and jackets out of his closet in their bedroom and threw them into the box, letting the hangers clang on one another in a fierce racket. She was giving most of his clothes to the Salvation Army, saving only a few things—his London Fog raincoat and his Shetland wool sweater—because my daughter Myra had asked her to save them for her. The house was already listed for sale with a realtor; in two days it would be open to prospective buyers. She wanted to sell it fast, for money, so she would have something to live on while she figured out what to do.

Early this morning we had gone to an equipment-rental company near my house and walked among the tillers, backhoes, and earth movers till we found a white Ford van which seemed to be the right size. Two bearded young men behind the counter tried to flirt with Carol, one of them asking if she needed help moving, the other asking if she had any use whatsoever for an able-bodied man. She leaned her thin elbows on the counter beside a crinkled piece of black carbon paper and held her head in her hands. Her dark hair fell forward like a curtain around her face. Then she looked up at them and said, "Please, I don't have the strength for these games now."

"She has the flu," I explained, and, picking up the key to the van, took her arm and led her out to the parking lot.

She insisted on driving. She said she was too restless to sit still. In the back, her two boys slid about on the ridged metal floor, trying to anchor themselves. Our plan was to go through the house, take back to my garage what she wanted to keep, throw away the junk, and put price stickers on everything else she wanted to sell tomorrow morning at the yard sale, before the service. She had already placed an ad in the Sunday paper.

"Don't you think you're trying to do too much at once?" I had asked her as she drove the rattling van too fast along the freeway. She kept trying to take deep breaths. The boys were complaining that the floor of the van was dirty, that they had no soft place to rest their backs, that the smell of the exhaust was making them sick. I had a notebook on my lap; we were making lists of what she had to do. There were five pages of lists, having to do with the furniture sale, with the closing of utilities and bank accounts, with paying off debts and bills. One page was a reminder to call the crematorium to make sure the ashes would be scattered at sea as specified the following Thursday. Another page had been set aside to list the kinds of work Carol thought she was qualified to do to support her family. The notations on that page read: "#1, Waitress; #2, Typist." I had idly scribbled Carol's remark when she couldn't think of a #3: *"God help me, I'm not prepared for this."*

"How could I be doing too much?" she asked. "I mean, after this last week, what could be too much? If I could live through that, I can live through anything." She tried to breathe. "I think I'm hyperventilating," she said. "I hope I don't faint and kill us all." She laughed. "Or maybe that would make it convenient. After all, his mother and sister reserved the church already, his mother is flying down, and Mom and Aunt Gert and Uncle Harry will be there, and Bard's two friends, Clint, the junkie, and his buddy the drug dealer, so we could get it all over with at once." She changed lanes without signaling, cutting the wheels sharply, so that the boys rolled against each other in the back. "To make it a real party I could have invited all the women from the shelter. They'd arrive with balloons and little party hats to celebrate."

"Are you that bitter?"

"No, I'm not bitter. I'm grateful to them, I think. But you know their policy, no sympathy for the batterer. A dead husband is one less crazy man in the world to deal with. They don't believe in crying over it. They say it's sometimes a blessing in disguise." She gave the van more gas. "I never got as tough as they wanted me to get. I just could never say good riddance and walk away. I loved him too much. They couldn't indoctrinate me quite to that point."

"Hey Mom, will you *watch* it?" Abram, the oldest boy, called in alarm. "You just cut off that BMW."

"Can you believe it?" Carol said to me. "His mother and sister arranged for the church, the minister, the organist, they probably ordered flowers, and they're billing *me!*"

"As far as they're concerned, you owe them an eternal debt because Regina picked up Bard's car from the police station. At least, that's how it sounded that afternoon when Regina finally called me. She made it clear that it was the worst ordeal of her life, driving Bard's car back to your house, having to breathe in the fumes that were left in it."

"Ugh," Carol said, and shuddered. "The Volvo. I never want to see that car again. He kept the vacuum cleaner hose in it all the time. I never understood why. How could I have guessed what he was planning to do with it?"

"You'll want to sell the car, too," I said, adding it as an item on the list of things for sale.

"Make a new list," she said. "Title it *Memorial Service.*" She turned her head and called above the noise of the engine to her sons: "Think of some things you want to say about Daddy. You'll need to say some things about him at the funeral tomorrow. Janet will write them down. Tell her how you feel about all this."

"I don't want to say *anything,*" Abram said.

"*I'll* tell you how I feel!" David, her younger son, screamed from the back. "I hate everything. I hate this truck; it's hard as a rock and noisy and it stinks here."

"And *I* don't want to move away! What about our backyard?" Abram demanded. "What about my treehouse, and my fort? What about Mike and my other friends?"

"We'll all have to make adjustments," Carol called to him over her shoulder. "Some things we just won't have from now on. And we won't make a fuss about it, either. Do you understand me? We aren't going to make any fusses."

Superman stood six-feet tall on the boys' bedroom wall, which was smudged with fingerprints and crayon lines. In his red cape and blue tights, his yellow belt and jockey shorts, he stood guard—his fists clenched, a single lock of hair falling forward on his handsome forehead—beside a window that looked out onto the foliage of the backyard. Strawberry plants with their red fat berries were creeping out of the pots in which Bard had planted them. Oleanders were in bloom under the window. Bard had made himself a tea of oleander leaves one day a little more than a month ago. Carol had come home from the store and seen the stew of leaves bubbling on the stove. Bard sat at the kitchen table he'd built into the wall, stirring some of the mixture in a cup. He had been trying all that morning to convince Carol to agree to something (she couldn't remember what—one of his plans to sell the house and grow kiwi fruit in the desert, or open a worm farm in the mountains and raise bait-worms for fishing), and she had repeated her usual rational arguments. When she came home with her bags of groceries he was ready for her. He raised the cup and gulped down some of the tea.

"I don't believe you're doing this! Did you swallow the whole cup? Was it full?" she had demanded of him. The children had come in from the yard and were watching.

"What do you care?" he'd said. "Here—want some?"

She had taken him, then, to the emergency room of the hospital. He had seemed rather pleased with all the excitement.

"Just watch him," the doctor had said. "He probably hasn't had enough to do him much harm."

A few days after that, Bard tore that same kitchen table from its moorings, broke the legs from it, and threw it out into the backyard. Then he had bashed his head through the wall and bit his youngest son on the scalp.

While Carol was working in another part of the house, I knelt on my hands and knees and pulled the last of the coloring-book pages and toys from under the boys' beds. I found, among the dust puffs, two of the boys' metal hot cars, odd socks, pennies, jacks, and a red plastic death's head ring. I put them all into a yellow sand pail with a little painted shovel on it—as well as a rubber snake, a ball, and a set of red wax vampire's teeth.

"Jesus Christ!" Carol called, stomping down the hall toward me. "All Bard's things are gone from the garage! His fishing rods and his camping gear, his drills and saws, his Coleman stove, all his stuff!"

"Do you think he sold them or pawned them for food money those last few days?"

"No, I think his sister stole them."

Bard's sister Regina lived in Venice, a block from the beach, in a little wooden house that was splintered and battered by ocean wind. She had been an aspiring actress. Long ago she had had her nose and breasts improved to increase her chances at stardom, but now she was selling suitcases and imitation designer jeans imported from Taiwan at a little sidewalk booth on the Venice promenade.

"Oh Carol, *sweetie,*" she sighed as she opened the door for us, but she had trouble embracing Carol with her drink in one hand and her cigarette in the other.

Carol stepped back. "Would you mind putting that out?" she said. "I'm having trouble breathing as it is."

"Oh, you poor baby," she said. She took another long drag and threw her cigarette out the door, behind us. Then she came down the steps and ground it out with the toe of her wooden clog. Her legs, in cut-offs, were muscular and aggressive-looking.

"You have no idea what a nightmare it was," Regina said, pushing a hairpin into place in her blonde, messy bun, ". . . driving that car that he died in, sitting in that seat where he took his last breaths, my poor crazy brother, thinking his . . ."

Carol cut her off. "I can't find his fishing rods. They weren't in the garage. Do you know where they are?"

"It was just lucky that he had my number in his wallet," Regina went on. "If he hadn't, God knows, he could have been just one more missing person in the morgue. Of course, if you hadn't been hiding away in that shelter for battered women, the police would have called *you*, which would have been the best thing. In fact, if you want to get right down to the nitty-gritty, if you hadn't been in the shelter he probably wouldn't have done it. But what's the difference? Maybe it was meant to be that I got the bad news first. That's how it worked out, and I didn't shirk my duty. You know *that*, Carol. And I couldn't sleep all that night. God, did I cry."

"You didn't call my sister till two days later," Carol said coldly.

"Well, the first night, I thought, like Mom always taught us, never tell anyone bad news at night, then they have the whole dark night to think about it. Never tell bad news till the sun is shining . . ."

"That was the *first* night."

"Well, then the next day I called Mom, you know, and she nearly had a breakdown on the phone, so I had to keep her from killing herself—she's not the strongest person, you know. None of us are." Regina laughed a little wildly. "By the time I got her calmed down it was night again. You know how it is."

"He killed himself on Saturday, Regina," Carol said. "I didn't learn about it till Monday afternoon. You didn't call my sister till Monday afternoon."

"What's the difference?" Regina said. "Dead is dead. Are you all coming in?"

"Where are Bard's fishing rods?"

"You're just lucky they weren't stolen," Regina said, leading us into her living room, motioning for us to sit on her tattered couch. "Hey, boys, you want some grape juice or something? Just help yourselves in the kitchen."

"They don't need anything," Carol said. "Not only the fishing rods are gone, along with Bard's drills and his camping gear. A coatrack we bought at Bamboo Imports a few months ago, it was right inside the front door. That's gone."

David, who had disappeared down the hall, called out, "Hey, it's in here, in the bedroom, Mom."

Regina and Carol looked at each other.

"Look, Carol," Regina said, "Bard told us you were gone for good, that's what he told Mom and me. He said they were teaching you how to hate him in that shelter, that they were brainwashing you and he didn't have a chance, and anything we wanted we could have because he wasn't going to need it."

"He told you that? To come into the house and take our things?"

"Well, he said if he took off we could have anything we needed."

"Took off?"

"He said he might take off for good, to the Kentucky hills or somewhere, that he just couldn't live around here anymore without you and the boys."

"You *needed* his drills and his fishing rods?"

"Well, Mom wanted those. I shipped them up to her."

"You took them out of my house? When? The instant you got the call from the police?"

"I didn't think you were coming back."

"How did you get in?"

"How? Through the door, that's how! Because when my poor brother ran out to kill himself he didn't bother to lock the door. Maybe he wasn't thinking about your coatrack just then. He just left the front door wide open. He left his note to you on the floor, just inside the door."

"HIS NOTE?"

Regina took a cigarette from the box on the coffee table and lit it with trembling fingers.

Carol's voice was wild with threat. *"What note did he leave? Where is it? Why wasn't I told about it?"*

"It was nothing," Regina said. "All it said, more or less, was I can't live without you and the boys.' That's all."

"Get it for me," Carol said. "I want it."

"Mom has it. I sent it up to her with the other stuff I shipped up. After all, he was her only son."

"I don't believe this," Carol said. She swayed toward me, leaned against the wall, tried to take a deep breath. She coughed, a rough, rattling sound that curled up through her lungs. She had trouble catching her breath.

"Get Mommy a drink from the kitchen," I said to Abram, who was standing at his mother's side. "Water."

"Oh, hey," Regina said, "let's not fight at a time like this. You can have anything back that you want. I just brought a lot of stuff over here for safekeeping so no one would steal it, and I sent some of it up to Mom in case she could find some consolation in having his things around. You know how she worshiped him."

"When is she arriving? It has to be soon, doesn't it, if the funeral service is tomorrow?"

"I'm meeting her tomorrow morning at the airport," Regina said.

"Then call her tonight and tell her to bring me his note. I haven't seen it. I didn't even know that he left me a note. It belongs to me and I want it."

"Call her? Tomorrow is Mother's Day, Carol. I hate to upset her any further. She's suffering enough. Couldn't it wait?"

Abram came into the living room. "Aunt Regina has our oak candlesticks, Mom," he said. "And our folding stepladder. And she has our wine glasses that Daddy bought in Mexico. They're in her cabinet." He held out a glass of water to Carol. "Here, I brought you your drink in one of them, so you can feel at home."

"Let's see if there's anything here I can't live without," said a big red-faced man in a cowboy hat, stepping among the objects for sale on Carol's front lawn.

"Can you use a car? . . . cheap?" Carol asked.

The Volvo was parked at the curb, where Regina had left it the Saturday night she had picked it up from the police station. Bard had been found in it, dead. Earlier that Saturday he had called me to say that if Carol didn't call him back from the shelter in ten minutes, he was checking out forever. He had driven the Volvo into the parking structure of a big singles complex, apparently in obedience to Carol's request that if he had to kill himself, to please not do it in the house where she might come in and find him. A tenant had discovered him on the upper level of the parking structure, near some stored sailboats, slumped over in his seat, the vacuum cleaner hose connected from the exhaust pipe to just inside the back window.

"How cheap?"

"Oh, God, I don't know. Five hundred dollars? My husband just put in a new motor and transmission that cost over fifteen hundred."
"So why doesn't he want to keep it?"

"They're getting a divorce," I said to the man, moving over the grass toward the car. "Do you want to look at it?"

He opened the driver's door and leaned in. "Smells funny," he said. "Looks dusty. What is all this soot on the windows, anyway?"

"It's a good car," I said. I began to cough. I wondered what they had done with the vacuum cleaner hose. There was still a towel in the back seat. Had he used that to plug the window opening where the hose came in?

"Naah," the man said, backing out. "I don't think so."

Out on the lawn, Carol was leaning on one of the four posters from the frame of her waterbed, talking to a young couple. She was talking very fast, her cheeks flushed. She had hired some neighborhood teenagers early this morning to move everything that she wanted to sell out to the lawn. "I don't want to keep any of this stuff," she said to me. "I don't want to sit on that couch again, touch that lamp again. It's over. It all goes."

She was coughing heavily.

"Are you okay?" I asked.

"Nothing that a little hemlock wouldn't cure," she said. She moved off, rushing around on the lawn, asking the Sunday morning buyers, "Do you like it? How much will you give me for it? I'll take anything reasonable. Even unreasonable. Just make me an offer." Now she came back and said to the couple, "You can have the waterbed for fifty dollars; we paid four hundred. It's in perfect condition. Go around to the backyard with my sister. The mattress is draining back there. She'll show it to you."

The couple followed me to the back. A translucent green hose, attached to the waterbed in the house and coming out through the sliding glass door, lay gleaming like an emerald snake in the sunlight on the wooden patio deck. A stream of water came flowing from it in irregular bursts. The water puddled in a dingy pool in the grass.

"Why is she selling it?" the girl said to me. Her hair was in braids; she was pregnant.

"Domestic difficulties," I said.

"Yeah, I know how that is. Well, we'll think about it, thank you," she said. "Sometimes, you know, for a bed, you'd like to start brand new."

"Well, good luck then," I said. When they had left, I went into the garage and began putting things in boxes—half-empty cans of paint, machine oil, screws, masking tape. Carol had said I should take home anything my husband might be able to use. I accidentally tipped a little bottle of gold glitter from the workbench; it scattered through the air like a sun exploding and clung to my black skirt and my black shoes. I had forgotten that I was dressed for a funeral. An aluminum film canister seemed about to tip off the shelf. I caught it in my hand and opened it. Inside, a thousand little seeds rattled against one another. Then I found a hundred-pound bag of pinto beans in the dark, cobwebby corner under the workbench. I put the film canister in my suit pocket and dragged the burlap sack to the front lawn.

"Look at this," I said to Carol. She was counting out a wad of bills.

"I sold everything," she said smiling. "They cheated me blind, but I don't care. What do I care? I'm rid of it. They're coming back in a truck to get it all in a half-hour. We're lucky, you know. We could have sold none of it." She coughed, holding her breasts. When she caught her breath she said, "Don't worry about me. It sounds bad but I'm actually getting better, it's breaking up."

"Look in here," I said, opening the burlap sack and letting her see the spotted beans, curled upon one another like nesting animals.

"Oh, yeah," she said. "*That* was going to save us when doomsday came. One day, when we didn't even have enough money to buy milk for the boys, he came in and said to me, 'How come we don't have an emergency supply of food? I feel like killing.' So he went out and bought that crap. It's probably still on his credit card. I'll probably get the bill for it next month."

"I think we ought to take it home in the van. It's good food. You could live on it for a year."

"God!" she said, turning on me angrily. "Who *knows* what kind of poison he sprayed on that? Who knows what he might have put into it? Maybe he was counting on my eating it. Then I would join him, just like he wanted me to, me and the boys. No, just *throw* it out, throw out all the food in the house!" She kicked the heavy bag of beans.

"Do you know what this is?" I asked, reaching into my pocket and holding out to her the canister of tiny seeds.

"Oh, that," she said. "That's probably the most valuable thing he owned, *prime sensimilla*, the best. His pride and joy. Do me a favor. Take all these seeds out in the back yard and scatter them to the winds. Give the birds something to be happy about. Let them have the peace he never could get from that stuff. Let someone have peace, because he sure couldn't. I sure can't."

Regina and her mother, both of them wiry women with bleached hair, entered the church uncertainly and then went to sit by themselves in an empty pew a few rows from the altar. Bard's mother took a large, flowered handkerchief from her purse and wiped her eyes. My mother and aunt, followed by my uncle, entered the church, their elbows linked, and looked over at the two blonde women, then took seats in the same row but at the opposite end, across the aisle. Our relatives had arrived separately, in two cars. My husband, my children, and Carol's sons in our car, and our mother, aunt, and uncle in Uncle Harry's car. As Carol had predicted, Bard's two friends, the junkie and the drug pusher, slouched in and sat in the back. ("I had to call them," Carol had explained to me. "You can't have a memorial service with no one there. It wouldn't be fair to Bard.")

The boys came to stand at their mother's side. They were dressed in sport jackets and dress shoes much too small for them, the best Carol had been able to unearth from the cartons we had brought back to my house in the van. The boys wore around their necks little silver sneakers on chains which they had been given by the art therapist at the battered women's shelter when they had lived there with their mother. Last night, before they went to sleep, we had finally composed a list of things they wanted to say about their father. They didn't want to say them aloud, so I promised that I would do it for them. Carol, holding each son by the hand, went to sit in the front pew. I sat in the row behind her with my family. My daughters, in their lacy, unfamiliar dresses, looked frozen. My husband took my hand and said, "Soon this will all be over and we'll try to get back to some normal kind of life."

Carol, in front of me in her dark blue suit, shook with a violent chill every few seconds. Behind me I could hear the whispers of my mother and aunt. I thought they were relieved that Bard had killed himself, since in their view he had never offered Carol anything but trouble and danger.

I remembered how he had sounded on that last day, begging me to have her call him. I remembered the letter he had sent me for her, which began, *Dear Carol, Oh please, Carol, give me strength, give me courage, give me love, give me light. I am so scared being so alone. I am not violent. I am ashamed, lonely and unhappy with my lot. Losing you is too much, nothing I could have done could deserve that punishment . . ..*

The organist began to play; a minister in a white robe came and stood behind the lectern. My Jewish mother and aunt whispered to one another, uneasy about being in a church. When I glanced back at them once, they were staring at Christ impaled on his cross of wood, a dark figure against the beacon of muted afternoon light coming through the stained-glass window.

The minister spoke about tortured souls, about peace which could be obtained only in heaven, about forgiveness and love. Carol's face was rapt, colored by the rainbow of light coming through the window. I had the sense that the empty church had filled, that a great throng of witnesses had arrived to take part. The minister promised that Bard was now free from earthly pain. I felt a tap on my shoulder, and reaching back, felt my mother take my hand and press it hard. I thought I should reach forward, for Carol's hand, but her attention was perfect and private. Even her children did not touch her. Then I heard my name called. I rose and walked carefully up the carpeted steps.

I unfolded my page of notebook paper on the lectern. "Here are some things," I said, "that Bard's sons said about him." I found myself looking at Bard's mother and sister. I was surprised that they did not look like villains or criminals. They were both crying. My mother was crying. My aunt and my daughters were crying. My husband looked somber and shocked.

"This is what Abram said about his father:

'He gave me happy feelings.

'He figured out hard things.

'Some of the things he liked to do with me were fishing, wrestling, and visiting. I wish he never had an illness. I wish I could have had him longer. I miss him a lot. I will always love him.'

"Here are some things David said about his father:

'He was a good dad to me.

'He took me fishing, he taught me how to build things out of wood, how to fix things, how to work on my bike; he taught me many things, like the times tables. I wish he had been a happier person and not so sick. I am sad that he will not see me grow up.' "

"I stepped down from the altar, moved down along the carpeted stairs, and found that I was passing Bard's mother as she made her way up them.

"It's a terrible thing for a mother to outlive her son," she said. "My son was just too sensitive for this life. He couldn't take it like most of us do. I loved him, I adored him. And since he won't be around to see his sons grow up, I'll try to hang on as long as God lets me and be here if they ever need me." She glanced down at Carol. "I hope their mother will let me visit them sometimes." She paused for a long time, and looked at each one of us. "Well," she said finally, "I know Bard can hear me, so I'll say, 'Good-bye, son, no, not good-bye, just so long."

Outside, the ocean wind was cold. Carol was shivering. We all surrounded her, circled her, in our dark suits. Regina and Bard's mother stood hesitantly outside the circle till my mother stepped back and, putting her arms around their waists, drew them in. Bard's friend, Clint, said, "Hey, listen, let me buy you all some coffee." There was some murmuring about what to do. My husband suggested that we all go back to the house; he pointed out his car and invited everyone to follow him.

The furniture that had been on the lawn was all gone. A few boxes waited for pickup by the Salvation Army. Carol entered the empty house. She sat down on the green rug in front of the cold fireplace. Charcoal-black streaks stained the white brick mantel and a swirl of ashes blew up in a flurry of wind which came in the open front door.

Bard's friend Clint arrived with two dozen doughnuts and styrofoam cups full of steaming black coffee. For the children he had bought little wax cartons of milk. He had remembered straws and napkins. The doughnuts were incredibly sweet; flakes of sugar stuck to everyone's lips and fingers.

Bard's mother asked Carol if she could speak to her privately. Carol had trouble standing, so I helped her to raise herself to her feet and she walked with Bard's mother down the hall. From the living room I could see them standing in Carol and Bard's old bedroom, standing in the square on the rug where the four bedposts had made their indentations. Bard's mother produced a little box and handed it to Carol. I saw Carol accept the box. The two women whispered together. Carol put out her arms and the older woman stepped forward and came into them. They hugged awkwardly. Then, blowing her nose on her flowered handkerchief, Bard's mother hurried into the bathroom and closed the door.

I went back to join Carol. "She brought the note," Carol said. "And I'm giving her the Volvo. She wants it. She told me she always knew he'd do it someday. That he had a thin skin; that he wasn't tough enough for this world."

The boys ran through the bedroom and out the sliding glass door to the backyard for a final climb up to their tree house. Carol left me and wandered down the hall. When I went to look for her a little while later, I found her in the boys' room, standing before the poster of Superman, shaking like a pneumatic drill.

In the hospital emergency room, a nurse sat Carol in a wheelchair and said there would be a wait, they had a bad case coming in. Carol, vibrating in her monumental chill, tried to nod. I protested to the nurse that this, too, was an emergency, that my sister's fever was very high, that she had just come from her husband's funeral. When this special pleading did not move her, I whispered, "A suicide's funeral!"

But just then the automatic glass doors parted and three police officers in black uniforms helped two orderlies rush a gurney with a man on it through the waiting room.

"Motorcycle accident," someone said, in fearful awe. It was the nurse, standing beside me.

In a moment we heard screams coming from a distant room, the strangled sounds of a man crying, "Ma! Ma!"

Carol took my hand. At last she cried. "God," she said, "I hope he lives."

"I Don't Believe This"

After it was all over, one final detail emerged, so bizarre that my sister laughed crazily, holding both hands over her ears as she read the long article in the newspaper. I had brought it across the street to show it to her; now that she was my neighbor, I came to see her and the boys several times a day. The article said that the crematorium to which her husband's body had been entrusted for cremation, had been burning six bodies at a time, and dumping most of the bone and ash into plastic garbage bags which went directly into their dumpsters. A disgruntled employee had tattled.

"Can you imagine?" Carol said, laughing. "Even that! Oh, his poor mother! His poor *father!*" She began to cry. "I don't believe this," she said. That was what she had said on the day of the cremation when she sat in my backyard in a beach chair at the far end of the garden, holding on to a washcloth. I think she was prepared to cry so hard that an ordinary handkerchief would not do. But she remained dry-eyed. When I came outside after a while, she said, "I think of his beautiful face burning, of his eyes burning." She looked up at the blank blue sky and said, "I just don't believe this. I try to think of what he was feeling when he gulped in that stinking gas. What could he have been thinking? I know he was blaming me."

She rattled the newspaper. "A dumpster! Oh, Bard would have loved that. Even at the end, he couldn't get it right. Nothing ever went right for him, did it? And all along I've been thinking that I won't ever be able to swim in the ocean again, because his ashes are floating in it! Can you believe it? How that woman at the mortuary promised they would play Pachelbel's *Canon* on the little boat, and the remains would be scattered with 'dignity and taste'? His *mother* even came all the way down with that jar of his father's ashes that she had saved for thirty years, so father and son could be mixed together for all eternity. Plastic garbage baggies! You know," she said, looking at me, "life is just a joke, a bad joke, isn't it?"

Bard had not believed me when I'd told him that my sister was in a shelter for battered women. Afraid of *him?* Running away from *him?* The world was full of dangers from which only *he* could protect her! He had accused me of hiding her in my house. "Would I be so foolish?" I had said. "She knows it's the first place you'd look."

"You better put me in touch with her," he had said menacingly. "You both know I can't handle this for long."

It had gone on for weeks. On the last day he called me three times, demanding to be put in touch with her. "Do you understand me?" he threatened me. "If she doesn't call here in ten minutes, I'm checking out. Do you believe me?"

"I believe you," I said. "But you know she can't call you. She can't be reached in the shelter. They don't want the women there to be manipulated by their men. They want them to have space and time to think."

"Manipulated?" He was incredulous. "I'm checking *out*, this is *IT*. Goodbye forever!"

He hung up. It wasn't true that Carol couldn't be reached. I had the number. I had not only been calling her, but I had also been playing tapes for her of his conversations over the phone during the past weeks. This one I hadn't taped. The tape recorder was in a different room.

"Should I call her and tell her?" I asked my husband.

"Why bother?" he said. He and the children were eating dinner; he was becoming annoyed by this continual disruption in our lives. "He calls every day and says he's killing himself and he never does. Why should this call be any different?"

Then the phone rang. It was my sister. She had a fever and bronchitis. I could barely recognize her voice.

"Could you bring me some cough syrup with codeine tomorrow?" she asked.

"Is your cough very bad?"

"No, it's not too bad, but maybe the codeine will help me get to sleep. I can't sleep here at all. I just can't sleep."

"He just called."

"Really," she said. "What a surprise!" But the sarcasm didn't hide her fear. "What this time?"

"He's going to kill himself in ten minutes unless you call him."

"So what else is new?" She made a funny sound. I was frightened of her these days. I couldn't read her thoughts. I didn't know if the sound was a cough or a sob.

"Do you want to call him?" I suggested. I was afraid to be responsible. "I know you're not supposed to."

"I don't know," she said. "I'm breaking all the rules anyway."

The rules were very strict. No contact with the batterer, no news of him, no worrying about him. Forget him. Only female relatives could call, and they were not to relay any news of him—not how sorry he was, not how desperate he was, not how he had promised to reform and never do it again, not how he was going to kill himself if she didn't come home. Once I had called the shelter for advice, saying that I thought he was serious this time, that he was going to do it. The counselor there—a deep-voiced woman named Katherine—said to me, very calmly, "It might just be the best thing; it might be a blessing in disguise."

My sister blew her nose. "I'll call him," she said. "I'll tell him I'm sick and to leave you alone and to leave me alone."

I hung up and sat down to try to eat my dinner. My children's faces were full of fear. I could not possibly reassure them about any of this. Then the phone rang again. It was my sister.

"Oh, God," she said. "I called him. I told him to stop bothering you, and he said, *'I have to ask you one thing, just one thing, I have to know this. Do you love me?'*" My sister gasped for breath. "I shouted *No*— what else could I say? That's how I *felt*, I'm so sick, this is such a nightmare, and then he just hung up. A minute later I tried to call him back to tell him that I didn't mean it, that I did love him, that I *do*, but he was gone." She began to cry. "He was gone."

"There's nothing you can do," I said. My teeth were chattering as I spoke. "He's done this before. He'll call me tomorrow morning full of remorse for worrying you."

"I can hardly breathe," she said. "I have a high fever and the boys are going mad cooped up here." She paused to blow her nose. "I don't believe any of this. I really don't."

Afterward she moved right across the street from me. At first she rented the little house, but then it was put up for sale and my mother and aunt found enough money to make a down payment so she could be near me and I could take care of her till she got her strength back. I could see her bedroom window from my bedroom window—we were that close. I often thought of her trying to sleep in that house, alone there with her sons and the new, big watchdog. She told me that the dog barked at every tiny sound and frightened her when there was nothing to be frightened of. She was sorry she had gotten him. I could hear his barking from my house, at strange hours, often in the middle of the night.

I remembered when she and I had shared a bedroom as children. We giggled every night in our beds and made our father furious. He would come in and threaten to smack us. How could he sleep, how could he go to work in the morning, if we were going to giggle all night? That made us laugh even harder. Each time he went back to his room, we would throw the quilts over our heads and laugh till we nearly suffocated. One night our father came to quiet us four times. I remember the angry hunch of his back as he walked, barefooted, back to his bedroom. When he returned the last time, stomping like a giant, he smacked us, each once, very hard, on our upper thighs. That made us quiet. We were stunned. When he was gone, Carol turned on the light and pulled down her pajama bottoms to show me the marks of his violence. I showed her mine. Each of us had our father's handprint, five red fingers, on the white skin of her thigh. She had crept into my bed, where we clung to each other till the burning, stinging shock subsided and we could sleep.

Carol's sons, living on our quiet adult street, complained to her that they missed the shelter. They rarely asked about their father and occasionally said they wished they could see their old friends and their old school. For a few weeks they had gone to a school near the shelter; all the children had to go to school. But one day Bard had called me and told me he was trying to find the children. He said he wanted to take them out to lunch. He knew they had to be at some school. He was going to go to every school in the district and look in every classroom, ask everyone he saw if any of the children there looked like his children. He would find them. "You can't keep them from me," he said, his voice breaking. "They belong to me. They love me."

Carol had taken them out of school at once. An art therapist at the shelter held a workshop with the children every day. He was a gentle, soft-spoken man named Ned, who had the children draw domestic scenes and was never once surprised at the knives, bloody wounds, or broken windows that they drew. He gave each of them a special present, a necklace with a silver running-shoe charm, which only children at the shelter were entitled to wear. It made them special, he said. It made them part of a club to which no one else could belong.

While the children played with crayons, their mothers were indoctrinated by women who had survived, who taught the arts of survival. The essential rule was: *Forget him, he's on his own, the only person you have to worry about is yourself.* A woman who was in the shelter at the same time Carol was had had her throat slashed. Her husband had cut her vocal cords. She could only speak in a grating whisper. Her husband had done it in the bathroom with her son watching. Yet each night she sneaked out and called her husband from a nearby shopping center. She was discovered and disciplined by the administration; they threatened to put her out of the shelter if she called him again. Each woman was allowed space at the shelter for a month while she got legal help and made new living arrangements. Hard cases were allowed to stay a little longer. She said she was sorry, but he was the sweetest man, and when he loved her up, it was the only time she knew heaven.

Carol felt humiliated. Once each week the women lined up and were given their food: three very small whole frozen chickens, a package of pork hot dogs, some plain-wrap cans of baked beans, eggs, milk, margarine, white bread. The children were happy with the food. Carol's sons played in the courtyard with the other children. Carol had difficulty relating to the other mothers. One had ten children. Two had black eyes. Several were pregnant. She began to have doubts that what Bard had done had been violent enough to cause her to run away. Did mental violence or violence done to furniture really count as battering? She wondered if she had been too hard on her husband. She wondered if she hadn't been wrong to come here. All he had done—he said so himself, on the taped conversations, dozens of times—was to break a lousy hundred-dollar table. He had broken it before; he had fixed it before. Why was this time different from any of the others? She had pushed all his buttons, that's all, and he had gotten mad, and he had pulled the table away from the wall and smashed off its legs and thrown the whole thing outside into the yard. Then he had put his head through the wall, using the top of his head as a battering ram. He had knocked open a hole to the other side. Then he had bitten his youngest son on the scalp. What was so terrible about that? It was just a momentary thing. He didn't mean anything by it. When his son had begun to cry in fear and pain, hadn't he picked the child up and told him it was nothing? If she would just come home he would never get angry again. They'd have their sweet life. They'd go to a picnic, a movie, the beach. They'd have it better than ever before. He had just started going to a new church that was helping him to become a kinder and more sensitive man. He was a better person than he had ever been; he now knew the true meaning of love. Wouldn't she come back?

One day Bard called me and said, "Hey, the cops are here. You didn't send them, did you?"

"Me?" I said. I turned on the tape recorder. "What did you do?"

"Nothing. I busted up some public property. Can you come down and bail me out?"

"How can I?" I said. "My children . . ."

"How can you *not?*"

I hung up and called Carol at the shelter. I told her, "I think he's being arrested."

"Pick me up," she said, "and take me to the house. I have to get some things. I'm sure they'll let me out of the shelter if they know he's in jail. I'll check to make sure he's really there. I have to get us some clean clothes, and some toys for the boys. I want to get my picture albums. He threatened to burn them."

"You want to go to the house?"

"Why not? At least we know he's not going to be there. At least we know we won't find him hanging from a beam in the living room."

We stopped at a drugstore a few blocks away and called the house. No one was there. We called the jail. They said their records showed that he had been booked but they didn't know for sure whether he'd been bailed out. "Is there any way he can bail out this fast?" Carol asked.

"Only if he uses his own credit card," the man answered.

"I *have his* credit card," Carol said to me after she hung up. "We're so much in debt that I had to take it away from him. Let's just hurry. I hate this! I hate sneaking into my own house this way."

I drove to the house and we held hands going up the walk. "I feel his presence is here, that he's right here seeing me do this," she said, in the dusty, eerie silence of the living room. "Why do I give him so much power? It's as if he knows whatever I'm thinking, whatever I'm doing. When he was trying to find the children, I thought he had eyes like God, and he would go directly to the school where they were and kidnap them. I had to warn them, 'If you see your father anywhere, run and hide. Don't let him get near you!' Can you imagine telling your children that about their father? Oh, God, let's hurry."

She ran from room to room, pulling open drawers, stuffing clothes into paper bags. I stood in the doorway of their bedroom, my heart pounding as I looked at their bed with its tossed covers, at the phone he used to call me. Books were everywhere on the bed—books about how to love better, how to live better, books on the occult, on meditation, books on self-hypnosis for peace of mind. Carol picked up an open book and looked at some words underlined in red. *"You can always create your own experience of life in a beautiful and enjoyable way if you keep your love turned on within you—regardless of what other people say or do,"* she read aloud. She tossed it down in disgust. "He's paying good money for these," she said. She kept blowing her nose.

"Are you crying?"

"No!" she said. "I'm allergic to all this dust."

I walked to the front door, checked the street for his car, and went into the kitchen.

"Look at this," I called to her. On the counter was a row of packages, gift-wrapped. A card was slipped under one of them. Carol opened it and read it aloud: "I have been a brute and I don't deserve you. But I can't live without you and the boys. Don't take that away from me. Try to forgive me." She picked up one of the boxes and then set it down. "I don't believe this," she said. "God, where are the children's picture albums! I can't *find* them." She went running down the hall. In the bathroom, I saw the boys' fish bowl, with their two goldfish swimming in it. The water was clear. Beside the bowl was a piece of notebook paper. Written on it in his hand were the words, *Don't give up, hang on, you have the spirit within you to prevail.*

Two days later he came to my house, bailed out of jail with money his mother had wired. He banged on my front door. He had discovered that Carol had been to the house. "Did *you* take her there?" he demanded. "*You* wouldn't do that to me, would you?" He stood on the doorstep, gaunt, hands shaking.

"Was she at the house?" I asked. "I haven't been in touch with her lately."

"Please," he said, his words slurred, his hands out for help. "Look at this." He showed me his arms; the veins in his forearms were black-and-blue. "When I saw that Carol had been home, I took the money my mother sent me for food and bought three packets of heroin. I wanted to OD. But it was lousy stuff, it didn't kill me. It's not so easy to die, even if you want to. I'm a tough bird. But please, can't you treat me like regular old me; can't you ask me to come in and have dinner with you? I'm not a monster. Can't anyone, *anyone*, be nice to me?"

My children were hiding at the far end of the hall, listening. "Wait here," I said. I went and got him a whole ham I had. I handed it to him where he stood on the doorstep and stepped back with distaste. Ask him in? Let my children see *this?* Who knew what a crazy man would do? He must have suspected that I knew Carol's exact whereabouts. Whenever I went to visit her at the shelter I took a circuitous route, always watching in my rearview mirror for his blue car. Now I had my tear gas in my pocket; I carried it with me all the time, kept it beside my bed when I slept. I thought of the things in my kitchen: knives, electric cords, mixers, graters, elements which could become white-hot and sear off a person's flesh.

He stood there like a supplicant, palms up, eyebrows raised in hope, waiting for a sign of humanity from me. I gave him what I could—a ham and a weak, pathetic little smile. I said, dishonestly, "Go home, maybe I can reach her today, maybe she will call you once you get home." He ran to his car, jumped in it, sped off, and I thought, coldly, *Good, I'm rid of him. For now we're safe.* I locked the door with three locks.

Later, Carol found among his many notes to her one which said, "At least your sister smiled at me, the only human thing that happened in this terrible time. I always knew she loved me and was my friend."

He became more persistent. He staked out my house, not believing I wasn't hiding her. "How could I possibly hide her?" I said to him on the phone. "You know I wouldn't lie to you."

"I know you wouldn't," he said. "I trust you." But on certain days I saw his blue car parked behind a hedge a block away, saw him hunched down like a private eye, watching my front door. One day my husband drove away with one of our daughters beside him, and an instant later the blue car tore by. I got a look at him then, curved over the wheel, a madman, everything at stake, nothing to lose, and I felt he would kill, kidnap, hold my husband and child as hostages till he got my sister back. I cried out. As long as he lived he would search for her, and if she hid, he would plague me. He had once said to her (she told me this), "You love your family? You want them alive? Then you'd better do as I say."

On the day he broke the table, after his son's face crumpled in terror, Carol told him to leave. He ran from the house. Ten minutes later he called my sister and said, in the voice of a wild creature, "I'm watching some men building a house, Carol. I'm never going to build a house for you now. Do you know that?" He was panting like an animal. "And I'm coming back for you. You're going to be with me one way or the other. You know I can't go on without you."

She hung up and called me. "I think he's coming back to hurt us."

"Then get out of there," I cried, miles away and helpless. "Run!"

By the time she called me again I had the number of the shelter for her. She was at a gas station with her children. Outside were two phone booths—she hid her children in one; she called the shelter from the other. I called the boys at the number in their booth and I read to them from a book called *Silly Riddles* while she made arrangements to be taken in. She talked for almost an hour to a counselor at the shelter. All the time I was sweating and reading riddles. When it was settled, she came into the children's phone booth and we made a date to meet in forty-five minutes at Sears so she could buy herself some underwear and her children some blue jeans. They were still in their pajamas.

Under the bright fluorescent lights in the department store, we looked at price tags, considered quality and style, while her teeth chattered. Our eyes met over the racks, and she asked me, "What do you think he's planning now?"

My husband got a restraining order to keep him from our doorstep, to keep him from dialing our number. Yet he dialed it, and I answered the phone, almost passionately, each time I heard it ringing, having run to the room where I had the tape recorder hooked up. "Why is she so afraid of me? Let her come to see me without bodyguards! What can happen? The worst I could do is kill her, and how bad could that be, compared with what we're going through now?"

I played her that tape. "You must never go back," I said. She agreed; she had to. I brought clean nightgowns to her at the shelter; I brought her fresh vegetables, and bread that had substance.

Bard had hired a psychic that last week, and had gone to Las Vegas to confer with him, bringing along a $500 money order. When he got home, he sent a parcel to Las Vegas, containing clothing of Carol's and a small gold ring which she often wore. A circular that Carol found later under the bed promised immediate results: *Gold has the strongest psychic power—you can work a love spell by burning a red candle and reciting, "In this ring I place my spell of love to make you return to me," This will also prevent your loved one from being unfaithful.*

Carol moved across the street from my house just before Halloween. We devised a signal so she could call me for help in case some maniac cut her phone lines. She would use the antique gas alarm which our father had given to me. It was a loud wooden clacker which had been used in the war. She would open her window and spin it. I could hear it easily. I promised her that I would look out of my window often and watch for suspicious shadows near the bushes under her windows. Somehow, neither of us believed he was really gone. Even though she had picked up his wallet at the morgue, the wallet he'd had with him while he breathed his car's exhaust through a vacuum cleaner hose, thought his thoughts, told himself she didn't love him and so he had to do this and do it now, even though his ashes were in the dumpster, we felt that he was still out there, still looking for her.

Her sons built a six-foot-high spider web out of heavy white yarn for a decoration, and nailed it to the tree in her front yard. They built a graveyard around the tree, with wooden crosses. At their front door they rigged a noose, and hung a dummy from it. The dummy, in their father's old blue sweatshirt with a hood, swung from the rope. It was still there long after Halloween, still swaying in the wind.

Carol said to me, "I don't like it, but I don't want to say anything to them. I don't think they're thinking about him. I think they just made it for Halloween, and they still like to look at it."

Chicken Skin Sandwiches

In 1950 my father met a man named Jim Bucks who had a little money and wanted to finance my father's inventions. My father thought he knew of a way to get maple syrup to run out of trees faster than anyone had ever done before, and Jim Bucks was working on getting access to a forest of maple trees on which they could experiment. Although my mother was usually suspicious of the men my father befriended, she went out of her way to impress Jim Bucks by playing the Minute Waltz for him on our Knabe grand piano. When she finished performing for him one night after dinner as my father and Aunt Hilda and my grandmother sat listening, Jim Bucks, in his striped shirt with gold cufflinks, applauded so loudly with the pink, thick palms of his hands that I had to cover my ears.

This was a time of relative peace in our household; the war had finally ended and its repercussions, at least as far as we were concerned, were fading away. My mother had conceived and borne another child, my fat-cheeked sister Carol, whose arrival soothed her grief, in part, over the baby she had lost during the war when she and my father had been in Florida. She had miscarried on a troop train coming back to Brooklyn after my father was notified that he had to get a defense job at home or be drafted.

Although the trip to Miami Beach had been intended as a winter vacation, a period of privacy long promised to my mother, it was there that my father first put into action his talent for inventiveness. He had been struck with the idea of a business tailored to the needs of the war while sitting in the lobby of our hotel, the Mellow Vista, which was mainly occupied by soldiers. Daily he observed the soldiers struggling to write letters on hotel stationery, which was pale pink and had two brown palm trees on it. I often sat at the long table in the lobby with the soldiers, drawing on a piece of stationery while they sat with their heads in their hands, thinking of what to write in their letters home.

My father believed he could solve their problems. He did some scouting around in Miami and brought back a machine which cut phonograph records, its thick needle designed to carve spiral springs of black plastic thread as it turned round and round on coated paper discs. He rented a tiny store on Collins Avenue and had a sign painted which read: *SEND YOUR VOICE HOME TO YOUR MOM! TO YOUR BEST GIRL!* He furnished the store with a desk and chair; he set up a small, cozy booth with a brown curtain for privacy in which a soldier could sit or stand as he spoke his thoughts into the microphone before he was shipped out to fight in the war.

My father let me sit on a stool in the store, collecting plastic thread as it spun off the records. It sprung about in my hands as if it had a life of its own. My mother, who had always been skeptical of my father's inventions, developed a new respect for him as the little business began reaping profits. She, with her musical bent, suggested that my father buy a ukulele in order that soldiers who found it too hard to think of something to say might instead strum a little tune or sing a song on the record. My mother and father had begun to whisper together about staying in Florida and not going home at all, but buying a second recording machine and a piano which my mother could play while the soldiers sang to their sweethearts in the privacy of the curtained booth.

My mother gave herself freely to her music—she played the piano with surprising gentleness and emotion. I was grateful for a chance to see her in this soft submission because in our real life together she was nervous and defensive and distant. In Brooklyn my father had loved to sing while she played his favorite songs: "I'll Take You Home Again, Kathleen," and "Danny Boy." To me he liked to sing "You Are My Sunshine." For herself she preferred Beethoven, Schubert, and Chopin.

My mother was passionate about privacy, never having had any during her marriage except for the vacation trip to Florida in the midst of the war. At home in Brooklyn we lived with my unmarried Aunt Hilda and my grandmother. We all shared a little house with a lilac tree in the front yard and a peach tree in the back. I found the arrangement quite agreeable; my grandmother had infinite patience with me and was anxious to teach me the complicated procedures involved in cooking *kreplach* and *tzimmes*, while Aunt Hilda, who earned money by running a beauty parlor in our closed-in sunporch, always made me welcome when she did a manicure or a permanent. I loved the variety of life in that house; if my mother was irritable or having a migraine, I would join my grandmother for a cooking lesson, or plunk myself down in the beauty parlor and watch Aunt Hilda's competent fingers push at the cuticles of one of her lady customers with a smooth wooden stick, making a little pale moon appear at the base of each nail. Sometimes while she was giving a permanent she allowed me to dip the chemical paper rolls, which looked like small cigars, into a bowl of hot water, then took them from me quickly as they began to sizzle lest I get burned. When she did haircuts, I marveled at the way she could select her comb or scissors or thinning shears from the pocket of her apron without looking down. She bent backwards like a dancer while she gave haircuts, sighting in some magical way at her customer's hairline, intent on making every hair even with the one beside it.

My mother thought it was not healthy for me to be breathing in the smell of nail polish every day. She hated the sight of the women's dark hairs which lay twisted and wet in the upstairs bathroom sink after Aunt Hilda gave shampoos; my mother also feared that the gossip I listened to in the beauty shop—amazing tales of childbirth and evil-hearted men—would warp my mind. She wanted my father's inventions to make us rich so we could move away, buy a new house of our own, and have privacy.

My father didn't seem to mind our living arrangements as much as she did; he kidded a lot with my grandmother and complimented her on her snow-white hair and her delicious honey cake. He gave her a pair of heart-shaped diamond earrings from his antique shop and said she looked in them like the Queen of England. He teased Aunt Hilda about her tiny waist, her graceful collar bones, her delicate hands, and ignored the fact that her skin was very bad. When my mother began to enter one of her moods, which could escalate from a complaint about my not eating to a tantrum during which she threatened to lock herself in the bathroom and take iodine, my father would dip his head at me to indicate *Go, Scram, Vamoose* and I would knock back my chair and run to Aunt Hilda's side and let her take me upstairs and keep me out of danger till my mother got tired of yelling and lay down in her bed with a cold cloth on her head.

Jim Bucks wanted to take my father away to New Hampshire for ten days. He had arranged to borrow the maple woods of a friend, and he wanted my father to apply his ingenuity and concentration to the syrup project without interruption. My mother, who hated to let him go far, was agreeable this time. She was busy with the new baby and seemed to think that Jim Bucks was legitimate. He was a short, dapper man with a neat blond mustache and alligator shoes. He had wandered into my father's antique shop and offered my father a twenty-dollar bill for the contents of the teacup of loose change my father kept on the counter. My father warned him he'd lose money, but Jim Bucks had just laughed and insisted he wanted to take a chance. After the deal was made, Jim Bucks counted out the quarters and half-dollars and nickels and dimes, and found that he had made himself a five-dollar profit.

After that he and my father were good friends. He came to eat at our house, bringing me boxes of spearmint Chiclets, and he flirted with Aunt Hilda, just enough to please her, but not enough to threaten her. We all knew she wouldn't be interested in him anyway because he wasn't Jewish. She often told me she was content not to be married; that living in the house with me and my sister made her feel as if she had children of her own, and living in the house with my sweet father made her feel as if she had a husband of her own.

My mother was very charming to Jim Bucks; she laughed a lot in his presence, perhaps believing that he was her ticket to a house of her own. The antique store made a bare living, but only that, nothing more. The trip to Florida during the war had been her only time alone with my father and me, without having my grandmother and aunt hovering in the background.

In the summer of 1950, even though we were still as crowded in the house as ever, even though my grandmother infuriated my mother by opening her bedroom door every morning to collect laundry from under the bed, my mother had other things to think about besides privacy—the new baby and polio.

Polio was a wide green bug with dancing red eyes. It lurked in the water fountain at the playground and on the handlebars of other children's bicycles. It was on the wing-tips of the seagulls at the beach, on the armrests of the dentist's chair, and in the Good Humor Man's ice-cream bars. I was not allowed to go anywhere other than our front yard and backyard during the summer of 1950. My Girl Scout troop was taking a boat trip to Bear Mountain; my best friend Harriet went, but I was not allowed to go. I hung around the house, annoyed at my sister, who woke from her naps in a fierce temper and cried for an hour or two afterward. I was bored. I was tired of making *kreplach*, and I wished something exciting would happen. My mother intimated that soon something very exciting would happen. She had let my father go to New Hampshire to contemplate speeding the maple syrup out of the trees. She seemed almost lighthearted.

Harriet brought me back a pine cone from Bear Mountain, but my mother would not let me touch it, fearing it had some foreign germs on it. She made Harriet leave it on the railing of the wooden gate to the yard. Harriet, who had the happiest, most infectious laugh I had ever heard, was my only friend who could beat me at playing jacks; she had beautiful red hair and freckles; she talked to me through the screen door (as my mother held the handle to keep it firmly closed) and told me that our troop hadn't had a very good time on the trip and that I shouldn't feel too bad about having missed it. Mrs. Gargano, our leader, had cut herself on her Girl Scout knife, showing the troop how to carve chopsticks out of twigs. And Eleanor Weiss had caught poison oak. When Harriet left, my mother hugged me and told me that I was lucky not to have gone.

She talked about luck all the time. Women who lived with their families in houses of their own were lucky. Harriet's mother, who lived in a house across the street with her husband and Harriet, was an example of a lucky woman. My mother (my mother felt) was an example of an unlucky woman. If only she could be free of my aunt and my grandmother! If only my grandfather had not died; if only Aunt Hilda had married.

My sister was always screaming, her red mouth open and her tongue flailing. It was a long summer. My father came back, not having solved the mystery of slow-flowing maple syrup. But he had invented something else during the long hours in the car with Jim Bucks. His new idea would be a ride called the Merry-Go-Bob, which he hoped they could build at Coney Island next to the Parachute Jump. People who rode it would stand on little wedge-shaped pies on a circular floor which revolved like a merry-go-round. Above them would hang an immense arrow. It would be like a human wheel-of-fortune. The ride would end suddenly. Whichever wedge the arrow clicked to rest above would be the winning wedge. The lucky riders on that section of the pie would win prizes.

Jim Bucks and my father often sat at the dining room table till late at night, drawing pictures and making plans. My grandmother, coming around the table with her silver crumb catcher tray and her little sable brush, would cluck at them and tell them that getting rich was not everything in life. Aunt Hilda, sitting on the couch, knitting a sweater, would smile in the warm cone of light from the standing brass lamp. My mother would pace back and forth in the kitchen, her heels clicking on the linoleum, her face alert. Upstairs, alone in the bedroom I shared with her, the baby would yell, demanding attention. I loved having Jim Bucks visit our house; my mother never once in that period threatened to take iodine.

One night Jim Bucks and my father invented chicken skin sandwiches. When my grandmother rendered chicken fat in a heavy pan over a low heat, with a bit of onion in it, the pieces of chicken skin would brown and turn crispy like bacon (which we were not allowed by my grandmother to have in the house). The fried skins, which my grandmother called *grevens*, were so delicious that Jim Bucks and my father decided they would open a food stand in Coney Island next to the Merry-Go-Bob. They laughed as they discussed what to call their chicken skin sandwiches; Jim Bucks thought Fakin'-Bacon would be a good name. They imagined themselves becoming as famous as Nathan's Hot Dogs. For several nights they rendered the fat from chicken skins in our kitchen till the yellow smell of chicken fat hung over my hair like a pall. They made sample sandwiches and went around the neighborhood offering them to our neighbors who were sitting out on their stoops to get a breath of cool evening air. Jim Bucks and my father were like jolly madmen. An evening hardly went by without their inventing a new item.

Soon they were down in the basement, building a hockey game in a wooden box with carved players whose movements could be controlled by wooden knobs on the outside of the box. By spinning the knobs, my father and Jim Bucks would make the players holding hockey sticks swing and hit a wooden puck. Jim Bucks said he was definitely going to put this one into production. My grandmother wanted to know where he got his money—was he a bank robber? My father said he had never asked. The two men were together every night, murmuring and talking long after I had gone to bed. My mother suffered her lonely state very well; she was comforted by dreams of the future. She held the new baby on her shoulder and pulled me to her side, promising us a private playground in the backyard of the new house we would soon be buying.

My father's next inspiration was a device he named Stand-A-Plate; it was a flat rectangle of plastic with ridges in it designed to hold dinner plates in a standing position in a kitchen cabinet. He thought it was his greatest genius-stroke of all. Jim Bucks was wild about the idea; during dinner he clapped my father on the back and told him they were going to be on Easy Street from now on. He began making plans to get it patented and arrange for a factory to make a mold and produce it. My father went to see the president of Woolworth's, and by some miracle the man agreed to stock it in all their stores. The project was expedited with lightning speed. My mother began secretly reading the real estate ads in the newspaper. One day, breaking the rule of not letting me go far from the house because of the danger of polio, she took me with her to three Woolworth's stores, proudly pointing out to me and the salesgirls that the gleaming rows of brightly colored plastic Stand-A-Plates were my father's invention.

It didn't take long before we learned that returns had started coming in. Customers were complaining to Wool-worth's that the Stand-A-Plates tipped over, breaking their precious dishes. My grandmother, who had been given a dozen of them in yellow plastic by my father, said she could have told him that herself, but she didn't want to hurt his feelings.

My mother got migraines nearly every day after this happened. Aunt Hilda seemed serene. She kept me close to her when she could and taught me all she knew about cutting hair. She gave me a little tortoise-shell box containing a nail file with a mother-of-pearl handle, a nail buffer made of ivory and suede, and some emery boards. She enclosed a card that said: *Be good sweet maid and let who will be clever. Stay as sweet and dainty as you are. You are the darling of my life.*

The Stand-A-Plates were tipping over all over America, and they came back to my father from Woolworth's in daily shipments.

Railway Express trucks stopped at our house every morning. Crates of Stand-A-Plates were piling up to the ceiling in our basement. Then—more trouble: my father learned from the toy stores which were selling the hockey game that the wooden knobs came off the box or got stuck and wouldn't turn; they were sorry, but they would stick to stocking Monopoly.

My father, who still took the subway every day to downtown Brooklyn to his antique store, began to work on one last idea. Jim Bucks had stopped coming to dinner, so my father talked to the rest of us about it. His face looked a little weary, but his blue-green eyes were lively. My mother played with her food and was not so attentive to him as she used to be. He was sure this new one was a winner. He was thinking about all the time people wasted waiting for the train. He was going to write to Sears Roebuck suggesting they install their mail-order catalogs in every subway station in America—on long tables, with chained-on pencils and piles of order forms. People waiting for the trains would browse and order millions of dollars' worth of goods.

A few nights later, the same night my father finished drafting his letter to Sears, my mother presented to us *her* invention. We were sitting in the living room after dinner; my grandmother was sewing up a hem on one of my mother's dresses, and Aunt Hilda was pressing flowers in her scrapbook, letting me help her. My father, smoking his pipe which smelled deliciously of cream soda and cocoa, was reading the paper. My mother came waltzing down the stairs wearing a white feather boa around her neck and a red-sequined evening gown.

We all watched her as she slithered toward the piano and slid her slim red bottom onto the black bench. She began to play a waltz that we had all heard her play a thousand times. But this time she sang to the music in a fine, high, sweet voice:

All the world shines with a golden glow
Because you love me,
And the very clouds are bowing low

Because you love me,
Every little flower, every tree,
Seems to join me in my ecstasy,
Because you've told them I'm the one,
I'm the one, alone.

The moon is beaming down on us tonight
Because you love me,
The stars are dancing in its silvery light
Because you love me,
The heavens and the earth
Smile and rejoice,
The bells ring out in lilting happy voice,
Because you've told them I'm your choice,
I'm your choice alone.

She swayed back and forth on the piano bench, the low-cut gown exposing the delicate bones of her spine. I had never seen her in that red dress before. She made the piano sing as I never could when I banged out my Bach inventions and my Bartok exercises. My father stared in admiration. My Aunt Hilda's mouth was a thin line.

"I'm sending this song in to a contest," my mother announced when she had played the last triumphant chords. "I heard about it on the radio. If they choose my song, they will send me and my family out to Hollywood, California."

My father, looking worshipful, applauded loudly with his big powerful hands. Upstairs, my little sister started to scream from her crib. My mother had high color on her face; she was radiant with excitement.

"*Then* we'll move," my mother announced to my Aunt Hilda. I laid my head down in Aunt Hilda's lap, and she stroked my hair gently.

"Go up, Hilda," my grandmother said, "and get the baby quiet."

"*I'll* go up," my mother said.

"Let Hilda go," my grandmother said. "She's the only one who knows how to soothe her."

Aunt Hilda sat paralyzed, holding me. My mother tossed her feather boa and smiled. She went upstairs, her hips swinging, to quiet the baby.

The next morning I was chosen to be the one to mail off my mother's song and my father's proposal letter to Sears. I walked proudly to the mailbox on the corner and pulled open the metal door. Making sure no one was looking, I quickly kissed both envelopes and dropped them into the mailbox, together, one on top of the other.

When I got back to the house, I found my mother and Aunt Hilda sitting together at the kitchen table, their faces frozen. They had just learned, from a neighbor's phone call, that Harriet had caught polio. Her first symptom had been the dreaded stiff neck. She was in the hospital, burning with a high fever.

We waited all day for news. Toward evening we learned that Harriet's legs had become paralyzed. Very late that night my friend died. The next day Mrs. Gargano went from house to house so that everyone in our Girl Scout troop could sign a sympathy card addressed to Harriet's parents. I wasn't allowed to sign it—my mother said she didn't want me touching a card everyone else had touched.

She kept me in the house for the rest of the summer, watching me all the time. She and Aunt Hilda whispered together, thinking up ways to entertain me so I would not try to go out in the dangerous air on the stoop, or play jacks in the alley, or attempt Russian Seven with my pink Spalding ball against the brick wall of the house next-door.

When the summer ended, my mother reluctantly allowed me to go back to school, but each day when I came home she felt my forehead anxiously and asked me if I could bend my neck forward. Just after Christmas, a man who collected statues of elephants came into the antique store and priced the most impressive and valuable object my father owned. It stood in the window on a red velvet cloth—a four-foot-tall bronze elephant with a gleaming ruby in its forehead and real ivory tusks. When my father learned that the man was a carpenter, a trade was arranged—the elephant in exchange for the conversion of our one-family house to a two-family house. By springtime, my Aunt Hilda and my grandmother had moved upstairs into their own apartment, which had a specially built bathroom sink in it designed for giving shampoos. The staircase between the upstairs and downstairs now had doors with locks at both ends. The closed-in sunporch became the bedroom my sister and I had to share. Each morning the sun exploded through its nine windows, shocking us awake.

Tabu

Although Mrs. Marcus frequently came across the street to our house saying she needed to borrow sugar or margarine, I knew she really came to report to my mother on the progress of Ruthie's freakish chest development. First she would sigh with exasperation. "Can you imagine? I have to *shlep* all the way downtown to Macy's again to get her another brassiere. That child grows a cup size every week!" Another sigh, barely concealing her proud astonishment. Then a sideways glance at me, having my milk and cookies at the kitchen table.

My mother didn't have to look at me. She knew every inch of me. When I looked at her, there was no mistaking the mortification on her face: we came from a family of flat-chested women. I could tell she was thinking that if evolution continued on its present course, women like us would soon be extinct.

My father, sensitive to the leaden gloom left behind in the wake of one of these visits, was hard-pressed to know just how to comfort me. He reminded me that I was still the champion jacks player on our block—a position Ruthie had aspired to since fourth grade. He suggested I might even have hidden talents I hadn't fully explored. My long, dextrous fingers, for example. Would it not be wise for me to resume piano lessons again? When I showed no gratitude, he added, puffing on his pipe, letting out clouds of butterscotch-scented smoke, "You do know, I hope, that you have lovely hair."

Lovely hair! I had wild curls which popped out each morning from my scalp like powerful springs! (Ruthie had straight black shining hair, which hung down her back like a curtain. Her mother once said to mine, "I think a Chinaman must have crept through my window one night!" My mother had replied, "Knowing you, I can believe it!")

Claus Mueller, the third of my many piano teachers, was hired that winter. This time I promised to apply myself. It was becoming evident, now that I was soon to turn fourteen, that I had better look to my future in earnest. I acknowledged to myself with regret that great beauty would not be my forte; therefore other avenues had to be developed . . . quickly! As if it were not absolutely evident, my mother pointed out to me that Clans Mueller, who would be coming weekly to the house to instruct me, was a *man*. This in itself suggested the importance of my talent, as nearly all my friends took piano lessons from women. Mr. Mueller, a bachelor of about thirty, was six feet four inches tall. During my lessons, as I played and replayed the measures he requested, he paced back and forth through our living room wearing his overcoat and a long wool muffler. He tossed his turbulent, bushy hair and signaled his approval of a well-done passage by a snort through his large nose. At certain moments I found him to be almost handsome. To distract myself from the endless repetition of scales which he required of me, I imagined the ad for Tabu—imagined my mother ceasing her endless pairing of socks on the couch, imagined her going down to the basement to stare at the clothes revolving in the Bendix, imagined Mr. Mueller unwrapping his long muffler and lassoing my shoulders with it, imagined him sliding me off the smooth black piano bench and into his arms, where he would kiss me with the passion of a Beethoven gone wild.

Ruthie also started taking lessons from him. Her mother had the eye of a buzzard when it came to Ruthie's advancement; Mrs. Marcus told my mother she felt Ruthie needed to develop some ladylike skills, which I thought was a laugh. I feared her fingers might become so strengthened by playing scales that she'd eventually be able to bypass me in "eightsies" at jacks. In truth, she'd stopped playing jacks with me at the end of last summer, never being able to get much past "fivesies." Thinking of Claus Mueller pacing in

Ruthie's living room gave me grief. Knowing Ruthie, her craftiness, and the way she could pop out with new talents, I worried that she might emerge as the next José Iturbi.

We were in the first year of high school that winter. Ruthie had begun traveling with a different crowd. Dark, handsome Italian boys, who wore the top three buttons of their shirts undone and sported large crucifixes which gleamed aggressively from the swirls of their black chest hair, circled about her in the lunchroom. As if witnessing a miracle, they hopped about and genuflected as she delicately dipped potato chips into a swirl of mustard which she had dabbed onto the center of the cellophane bag. Potato chips and mustard—I, too, was awed by so inspired an innovation. Each day I dutifully ate a tuna salad sandwich and an overripe banana for my lunch. Ruthie began wearing the collar of her blouse turned up in back—but always was careful to smooth it down on the bus on the way home after school.

I continued to associate with my old friends from grammar school—whiny girls with thick ankles who aspired to gain ever more badges to sew on their Girl Scout uniforms. Some of them were also scheduled to give piano recitals which I was obliged to attend. At these performances my friends wore starched cotton dresses with puffed sleeves. I thanked heaven that Claus Mueller had not once suggested a recital might be looming in the future for me.

In theory, Ruthie was still in my Girl Scout troop, but she rarely came to meetings. During the last meeting she attended, we were shown a film on menstruation. On the screen little butterflies circled around a flower while a sugary voice told us that with proper hygiene, no one would ever know we were having our "delicate condition."

"That's not true," Ruthie announced. "I smell different then, even to myself." We all stared at her, astonished at the implications of her knowledge, her crudity, her daring.

Mrs. Marcus continued to borrow sugar and margarine from my mother, but the news about her trips to Macy's was no longer so remarkable; Ruthie apparently had reached her upper limit, a C cup, and Mrs. Marcus could only announce, when she felt the need to use impressive numbers, how many (and not how big) were the brassieres she had to buy for her daughter.

"Practice your scales!" my mother urged me as the afternoons turned dark early. She buttoned her sweater against the chill. "I hear that Ruthie is up to 'Für Elise' already."

I shrugged. I was doing the sonatinas of Diabelli. I was doing *theory* in my music notebook. "Für Elise" was like onesies in jacks.

News of the party came from my mother, not from Ruthie. "We have to get you a pretty new dress," my mother announced one evening, as she was frying liver on the stove. I noticed how shapeless her housedress was; I realized that my lack of style was largely due to her insufficiencies.

"What for?" I was really most interested in my father's big shirts these days; I wore them over my dungarees and they hid the exact size of my chest. No one seeing me in one of his shirts could know if I was an A, a B, or a C.

"So you'll look nice for Ruthie's party."

"What party?"

"Her birthday party."

"When is it?"

"You know when her birthday is. January 12."

"She didn't mention any party to me."

"Well, you'll be getting an invitation, don't worry."

"Ruthie and I hardly talk to each other anymore."

"Well, you've been friends for years. Her mother says Ruthie wouldn't *dream* of having a party without inviting you." When she saw the look on my face, she added, "Besides, you don't have all that many parties to go to these days, do you?"

Invitations to two major events came in one day's mail. One was to Ruthie's party:

We're having a little shindig,
The donkey's on the wall—
The dartboard's on the table,
We're going to have a ball!

The other was to a fashion show at Abraham and Straus department store:

Dear Scout Family,

Girl Scout Troop #383 is proud to announce their participation in a fashion show of spring and summer delights, all modeled by our own scouts. Each girl will model the fashion best suited to her looks, and best news of all—each girl will get a 50 percent discount to buy the outfit she models! Don't miss it! See you there!"

"I'm not a model," I told my mother at once. "My leaders didn't even ask my permission for this."

"No one else is a model either," my mother said. "You'll do it; you'll see, you'll have fun, you'll get a party dress at half-price just in time for Ruthie's party. You can surprise her in a beautiful new dress."

"Ruthie's in my troop, Ma. She'll get this letter. She'll probably get a new dress too."

"She won't come," my mother predicted. "Mrs. Marcus says Ruthie's way beyond Girl Scouts. She's a law unto herself."

A week before Ruthie's party, on the day of the fashion show, we bumped into Ruthie and her mother on the platform of the Avenue N train station. Snow was just beginning to fall. I was wearing a storm coat, a woolen stocking cap, and gloves.

"You're going downtown?" my mother asked.

"None other," Mrs. Marcus said.

Ruthie stood on the far side of her mother. Melting snowflakes were beginning to glitter like drops of mercury in the filaments of her black hair. She wore a sailor's pea jacket, the kind worn only by the tough girls at our high school.

"Ruthie is modeling?" my mother asked.

"She is."

"For the discount?"

"For the career experience," Mrs. Marcus said.

"She's going to be a *model?*" my mother asked, turning toward Ruthie.

Ruthie performed for my mother a little smirk she had been perfecting at school, a maneuver during which she made her red mouth into a tight line and flipped up the corners of her lips briefly.

"Just think of it," my mother said dreamily. "From the same block, two famous girls, friends since childhood. A beautiful model and a concert pianist."

Ruthie had walked away from us to study two dirty words written in black crayon on a Tabu ad. When the train came, we took seats—I with my mother, she with hers, we behind them. Once we were underground, rushing through the great subterranean tunnels, the evocative words bounced in front of my eyes each time the bulbs in the ceiling of the car dimmed or flickered out entirely.

The mothers sat in a small auditorium, and our Girl Scout leaders and the girls from my troop milled around in a tiny, freezing dressing room. An officious woman, wearing a pencil behind her ear, told us to strip down to our slips. The command in itself was an alarming challenge. Without storm coats, loose cotton dresses, big shirts belonging to our fathers, it was all out there for everyone to see; right under the slip—the bra and its obvious size: measure of our future happiness, indicator of our fortunes in the years to come.

The bossy woman slapped a tape measure around my chest, my waist, my hips. "30, 22, 30," she called out. "This one is hopeless."

Hopeless!

Suddenly, I missed my father desperately. *Daddy*, I implored him, *what about my pretty hair? What about my dexterity' at Diabelli sonatinas? Did my talents at jacks, my good grades count for nothing?*

An intake of breath from my fellow scouts caused me to look over my shoulder. Ruthie was emerging from behind a screen wearing the first bikini I had ever seen in person. I experienced a physical stab of pain in my throat, in my chest. Her breasts, which heretofore had been fabulous, were made real. Soft, velvety, creamy, they shimmered, they quivered. They protruded from her basic body in a way that seemed dangerous, fantastic, diabolical. I suddenly knew why males must adore her, why the young Italians circled her in the lunch room, why the neighborhood boys gathered on her stoop after school and begged her to come out and play stoop ball with them. I recognized with a fatalistic grief that, by nature of my sex, I was not destined to relish those unique extrusions personally, but at least I should *have* them!

The girls fluttered around Ruthie like the butterflies around the flower in the menstruation film. Her measurements were called out, announced, exclaimed over. Her little pink bikini glowed like the sun. "This one will sell like hotcakes," the officious woman announced. "For you, hon, you don't get 50 percent off, you get to keep it free."

"Free! Free!" Ruthie ran out to the stage of the auditorium and called the news down to her mother. I knew my mother was waiting for *my* news. Waiting to see *my* act.

On me they tried outfit after outfit. Time was getting short. Guests were arriving to fill the auditorium. A middy-blouse and skirt were lowered over my head, then a shirtwaist dress, then a circle skirt with a poodle embroidered on it, with matching sweater and scarf.

"Everything hangs on this one," the woman said. "Too bad we don't have a shower curtain for her to model."

I stood there, once again in my slip, glaring at her. She said loudly, in her cigarette-hoarse voice, "Sorry, we can't use you, kiddo, so you might as well go down and watch the show." When she turned her back, I took a straight pin out of a pin cushion I saw on a chair and stuck it in the seat of her dress, straight in. One of these hours she was going to have to sit down.

There was a blizzard the night of Ruthie's party.-Looking out my kitchen window at the black, freezing sky, I announced that I didn't think I would go.

"You have to, it's an obligation," my mother said. We had worked out some weird outfit—a gabardine skirt, borrowed from my aunt, pinned to fit at the waist; a blouse with gardenias on it, which my mother had worn on her honeymoon. Patent leather flats, real stockings, a garter belt that was killing me. Around my neck on a black velvet ribbon was my grandmother's cameo: it had the profile of a queenly woman on one side and lilies of the valley hand-painted on the other. Set in gold. Surrounded by seed pearls. The family heirloom. My mother dabbed perfume on my throat and behind my ears. I felt her linger, looking behind my ears to see if they were clean. If she had dared to say one word, I would have burst into tears, hut she didn't. She just kissed my forehead and said, "Do you want Daddy to walk you over?"

"No," I said, hut my father put his pipe down in a saucer on the kitchen table and began pulling on his galoshes.

"It's only across the street," I insisted.

"It's icy out there," my father said.

"It's dark," my mother warned.

"It's dangerous," my father added.

"I've crossed that street a million times."

"Not in a terrible storm."

I put on my storm coat. My mother had offered to lend me her skunk fur coat, perhaps to make up for the fact that I didn't get a new dress at half-price, but I declined, believing privately that it still smelled of skunk.

Once we were outside, my father took my elbow and guided me down the iced-over front steps. From there he walked ahead of me through the deepening snowdrifts.

"Step in my footsteps so you don't get your feet wet," he said. I tiptoed after him, my small feet fitting neatly in the outline of his huge ones. In the street, the snow was ridged in strange patterns by the tires of cars; I could see diamond shapes and parallel lines in the faint light coming from Ruthie's windows. I had made this trip to her house at *least* a million times: to play jacks, to have lunch, to run with her under the sprinkler, to pick cherries from the tree in her backyard, to sleep over, to play house.

My father waited while I rang the bell. He stood hunched in the cold wind, his coat open at the neck. I wondered why I had never bought him a muffler. I began to worry about his exposed throat. For the first time I thought that perhaps he could someday get sick, catch pneumonia, even die.

Finally we heard footsteps coming down the hall. My father bent and kissed the top of my head. "Call me when you're ready to come home."

"What if it's late?"

"Call me. It's just across the street. No trouble. It's slippery crossing alone."

He left me there, to cross alone himself. Mrs. Marcus opened the door wearing her coat, with Mr. Marcus all bundled up right behind her. "Come right in," Ruthie's mother said. "You kids will have all the privacy you need. Ruthie made us agree to go to the movies. She promised to be a little angel without us here—Scout's honor."

The door closed behind me like the gate of a prison. I adjusted the cameo around my neck and walked forward.

Five Italian boys I recognized from the lunchroom at school were there in Ruthie's living room, slouched on the couch and slumped in the two armchairs. They looked as if they didn't belong on furniture, but should instead be on leashes or in cages. Some girl I didn't know—she was dressed in the mode of a Spanish flamenco dancer—was playing "Chopsticks" very badly on the piano. She had a broken comb sticking out of her hair like a chicken bone.

"Hi," I greeted them because—before I had left the house—my mother had advised me that it never hurt to be friendly. I scanned the sunporch for signs of another familiar soul—praying for even a girl from my Girl Scout troop. *Where was the donkey? Where was the dartboard?* "Where's Ruthie?" I said finally, into the air. Then I stared at my feet. The glare from my patent leather shoes nearly blinded me.

"Getting ready," one of the animals on the couch growled mysteriously. He was chewing on a toothpick. I seriously doubted that his father had crossed any streets to get *him* here.

"I'll go get ready, too," the Spanish dancer said, and, with a little spin of her red gauzy skirt, she disappeared.

After a moment, I sat down primly on the piano bench, my back to the keys.

"You gonna give us a concert?" asked the one with the toothpick.

"Maybe Ruthie will, a little later," I suggested. "I'm told she's doing very well on 'Fur Elise.' And this *is* her party."

"A concert isn't what she's planning to give, you can be sure of that," he said. They all laughed very hard at this, and when the laughter died down, one of them started it up again, as if he were revving a motor in his throat. They kept this up, sounding like a herd of motorcycles. I stood up finally and chose a pretzel from a bowl on the table.

"Who are *you?*" one of them finally said to me. "You look like you wandered in here by mistake."

"I'm Lady Godiva!" I said nastily, shocking myself. "Who do I look like?"

At last Ruthie made her entrance, flanked by the Spanish dancer and three girls I recognized from my gym class as ones who were always getting detention notices. She sashayed in wearing a pink cashmere sweater which was decorated, on the rise of one of her extraordinary breasts, with a plastic pin shaped like a telephone. Ruthie's phone number was inscribed in the center of the dial in large black letters. She wore a black straight skirt, slit high at the sides. And she wore real high heels, sling backs, black suede, with little rhinestones set in a design at the toe. She glanced at me as if she had never seen me before and had no idea why I might be there.

"Happy birthday," I said, finally.

She ignored me. "We're ready," she announced to the boys.

"For what?" I asked.

"It's a party game," she said impatiently, shaking one shoulder as if an annoying fly had landed on it. Then the creatures lumbered off the couch and chairs and all nine of them disappeared into Ruthie's bedroom.

Ruthie's bedroom! Whose door they now closed in my face as I tried to follow them in! The room where we had played with our Sparkle Plenty dolls together, had scraped the polished floorboards raw with the metal spikes of our jacks.

I went back to the room and was alone so long I ate all the pretzels in the bowl. Then I started on the M&Ms. I was beginning to feel nauseated. I considered that they might be playing a game where I was "it"—as in hide-and-seek—and expected me to go after them and find them. But it didn't seem likely; by now I felt they would have called me if that were the case.

I looked for the pile of comic books Ruthie used to keep on a shelf under the coffee table, but all I found there was a *True Romance* which had on its cover a photograph of a woman wearing a slip with one strap torn. She was turning her head away from a man who was shouting at her.

For some reason, I began to wish Claus Mueller were here, seeing me all dressed up, sitting alone in Ruthie's living room while the party went on behind her closed bedroom door. I thought he should know about the way she was treating me, but it was not something I could ever tell him while I was taking a piano lesson; certainly not while my mother sat on the couch listening, darning my father's socks or folding laundry. I thought I might write Claus Mueller a letter and leave it, sealed and addressed to him, in Ruthie's *Classical Easy Favorites for Beginning Piano* book.

Having nothing else to do, I spread out my aunt's skirt on Ruthie's piano bench, changed the position of my cameo so it did not close off my windpipe, and commenced to play through the classical easy favorites, one after another. I was on "Country Gardens," conjuring at just what note, should I be giving Claus Mueller a private concert, he might slide me off the bench with his muffler and fold me in his arms, when I felt a flare of anger ride up me like an army of poisonous bugs.

I jumped off the bench and stomped to Ruthie's bedroom where I pounded very hard on the door.

"Who is it?" grunted one of the hulks, whose job, it seemed, was guard dog.

"Lady Godiva," I said. "What's going on in there?"

"That's for us to know and you to find out."

I banged on the door again. I heard a low rumble of laughter. Then mumblings, whisperings, a quick debate. I heard Ruthie's voice say "No! If my mother finds out . . ."

I examined the poster on Ruthie's door: Alice-in-Wonderland beginning to fade through the looking glass. I stroked the lines of Alice's hair and waited. The door opened a crack, then closed again. Ruthie's voice: "We have to let her in or my mother will kill me." Another long conference.

Why didn't I just leave? I didn't want to be here, did I? Then why did I so desire to set my patent leather shoes inside that room?

The door swung open. The guard dog stepped back. "You can come in now," he said. His crucifix swung as he bowed, mocking me, to invite me in. I stepped into the room, dimly illuminated by Ruthie's Mickey Mouse night-lamp. Mickey, with his white-gloved fingers held up in the air like fat white sausages, looked to me like a lunatic.

I entered further. A rank smell in the cave-like room seemed compounded of sweat, perfume, and rancid Pixie Pink lipstick. Ruthie—from a darkened corner—said to me, "You can play one round with us. You take my place."

"How do I play?" I asked. "What are the rules?" I had a fleeting thought that I could still get out.

"Do what you're told," Ruthie's voice—sinister, almost unrecognizable—instructed me. Just then one of the girls took my arm and pulled me over toward Ruthie's bed. I was positioned along its long edge and other girls were pushed into place on either side of me. I could feel the flounce of Ruthie's quilt against the back of my legs. I had always admired the flying unicorns on her quilt. The one on my bed had teddy bears on it.

"The rules are simple," Ruthie said. "When the Mickey Mouse light goes out, the boys kiss the girls. That's all."

I could discern some hulking forms across the room, each one with a foot forward, like runners about to begin a race.

"Here goes," Ruthie said. "One, two, three—GO!" The room went black. Huge shapes catapulted out of the darkness. One fell on me, throwing me across the width of Ruthie's bed. On either side of me I could feel the roiling, wrestling forms of others. A heavy, gasping face smeared saliva across my lips. A body ground me down, screwing me into the bed till I stopped breathing. A clawlike hand was squeezing around among the gardenias of my chest. When a tongue forced its way between my lips, I flung up my knee with all the force I could muster.

"Shit!"

"Moron!" I shouted, shoving him off.

"Jesus!"

"What did she do?"

"Kicked me in the balls! Jesus!"

The light came on, showing me Ruthie's savage face as it came right up against mine, almost nose-to-nose. "You said you wanted to play, you little fool," she hissed.

"I did want to," I said.

"Now I suppose you'll run home and tell your mother."

"That's for me to know and you to find out," I said right back to her, eyeball-to-eyeball.

The slobberer was getting up from his knees now, quickly recovered. "You better pay up, Marcus," he said. "A deal is a deal."

Ruthie scowled. "Okay," she said. "Get in the closet with me, right now." She followed him in; I heard her skate key fall off its hook and hit the floor.

"You can let me out of here now," I said to the guard dog, who was sitting on the floor beside the door. Sullenly he flicked it open.

"Lady Godiva," he said. "Who the hell is that?"

"You'd never know in a million years," I said.

"At least I'd never've sold out," he sneered. "Kiss you? Never! Not even to feel Marcus up."

"Down, boy," I said. "Chew on your bone."

Before I got my storm coat from the hall closet, I tore the Alice-in-Wonderland poster off Ruthie's door, letting it keel over onto the floor. Then, buttoning all my buttons, I went to stand at a window in Ruthie's sunporch, debating whether or not to call my father. I stared across Avenue O at my house.

The snow was still falling, falling softly, cushioning the points of the hedges, blunting the sharp edges of steps, stoops, sills. My house looked like a dollhouse—tiny, remote, the square bright windows quartered by the window supports. Shadows passed across the yellow squares: my mother, my father, doing their nightly dance, crossing, turning, moving, as if they had no awareness of the thrilling dramas being played out in the world just beyond the thin cold panes of glass.

The black street looked like a chasm. I let myself out into the snow. I examined the snowdrifts to see if I could locate my father's footsteps, but they were long gone. Although the street seemed endless, slippery, vast, I made my way, slipping, skimming, almost skating over the icy plain. I grasped the brass handle of my front door with pleasure and hung onto it for a long moment, surveying the distance I had come. I had found the crossing quite manageable, even agreeable.

HONEST MISTAKES

MY MOTHER wasn't talking to my father in Miami Beach in the summer of 1955. A man named Frank Stuart had conned my father into giving him our family's life savings: "Just for the payroll, just over the weekend, just till Monday." My father hadn't even asked my mother's permission; he couldn't conceive of dishonesty—at the very worst he believed in honest mistakes. He was still hoping it would get straightened out, that Stuart would turn up with the two thousand dollars, with an apology that he'd had to leave town for some emergency, that in fact he was back on the job in which my father was a new partner. Construction was big in Florida then. The whole world wanted to live in Florida, a paradise on earth. Hadn't we come here for that?

After a certain point, my mother did not engage in further discussion with him. In silence each morning she got dressed to leave for work: she'd had to take a job as a typist at Wimbush Realty to pay the rent. It wasn't enough—we were in trouble. My father spent the day reading the classified ads. He was still circling "Business Opportunities" in red pencil, though she'd told him, in one of their fights, to forget that crap and look for a *job*. He wanted to open his own small business—all he needed was a little capital again.

After she left, he and I were stuck together in our blistering one-bedroom, northwest-exposure apartment. (A southeast exposure got the ocean breeze—but those apartments cost *money*.) Slouched on the studio couch where he slept (my mother slept on the other one, catty-cornered), running his fingers through his wild, curly hair, he smiled at me from time to time, just a shadow of his old, sweet, reassuring smile, but I couldn't buy it. I was having problems of my own: a new high school, a new climate, and, worst of all, Lilijoy, a girl from my school who lived in the apartment right above ours and had boys honking for her at all hours from fancy convertibles (visible—if I *looked*— from my bedroom window).

"I'm going to think about a job, Daddy," I said to him one morning. "There's too much time on my hands." I lifted a section of the classifieds from his lap—and I got my own red pencil. My parents didn't expect me to get a summer job; boys got jobs. Boys had to buy gas for their cars and take girls out on dates, so boys got beachboy jobs at hotel pools, putting out towels, arranging cushions on chaise lounges, and catering, in general, to the wealthy women who rented cabanas. Once in a while a girl from school would invite me to her cabana, where we would change into bathing suits and then swim in the hotel pool. Most of the girls in my class were from rich families who owned houses on Indian Creek Drive or Alton Road and whose mothers kept cabanas. The others were like me, squashed into one-or two-bedroom apartments near the high school or in North Beach while their fathers tested the various business angles of paradise.

A stifling humid puff of air, sifting around the corner of the building, ruffled the pages of the newspaper. I had had my own dreams of paradise, hatched and embellished on the three-day-long car journey last fall from Brooklyn to Miami Beach. With a U-Haul trailer bouncing about behind us, my father, in high spirits, draped a towel on his head like an Arab and occasionally hooted like an Indian. I preferred to lay low in the backseat and think my own thoughts. I imagined myself, for one thing, wearing an aqua linen dress on the first day of school—it would complement my gorgeous suntan-to-be. I also imagined that we would live in a perky little house under a row of palm trees near the beach; it would have a hedge around it. On the other side of the hedge would be another house in which a handsome boy lived. I would walk through the hedge in my linen dress and sit with him on his front step. He would give me a coconut. That was as far as the fantasy went, but it was quite enough to set my heart pounding with hope.

From upstairs now, I could hear Lilijoy laughing in the hallway, then the thud of loud footsteps on the stairs, the slam of the outside door, the roar of a boy's car.

My father and I looked at each other. He knew. He raised his eyebrows at me and went back to the paper. We couldn't really help each other. I circled an ad: "Doctor's Assistant, No Experience Needed."

After my interview with Dr. Zucker, I went to a thrift shop in South Beach and bought a nurse's uniform. It was 100 percent nylon and zipped up the back, a little tight for me. The zipper pulled in my waist dramatically before the cascade of gathered pleats and big pockets fell over my hips. Nylon was hot in the Miami Beach sun, and I had to wait a long time on Lincoln Road for my bus home, but I felt happy. I had just got a job on the first try, and I had bumped into Roger Slavitt in front of Walgreen's and he'd asked me if I could spare some time to tutor him in English; he was a football player who had been on the front page of the *Beachcomber* every week during the schoolyear. *Slavitt Scores Winning Touchdown. Slavitt Escorts Homecoming Queen to Prom.* We'd arranged that he'd come over next Saturday afternoon and I'd explain Emily Dickinson to him. I wasn't wearing aqua linen when he saw me, but white nylon, and the effect, I felt, was dazzling. I thought, in fact, I looked a little like a bride.

The job promised to be easy. Dr. Zucker had two offices; while he was in the Miami office, I was to man the phones in the Miami Beach office and make appointments. When he was present, I was to funnel the patients into the examining rooms, set out the injection bottles, and later autoclave the syringes. He had outlined a few other duties: sorting sample medicines, ordering bottles of liver extract when they got low, sweeping the floor, wiping down the sinks, typing a few invoices. I had the feeling that he hadn't even looked at me during the interview. My impression of him was of a tall black-haired old man with a pencil-thin mustache.

From the window of the reception area, I could see down to the end of Lincoln Road to the ocean. The blur of blue sky blending into blue sea gave me a sense that the world was pillowed in a spongy, protective cushion. Being high up—the twelfth floor—made me feel powerful; the cold blast of the air conditioning was bracing. I was certainly much better off here than sitting in our apartment, glumly commiserating with my father. On my desk was *The Taming of the Shrew*. It was slow going, but I intended to better myself over the summer, which my mother thought was essential for me to do. She had assured me that I'd worked hard all year and deserved the summer to rest and read and get smart.

"Are you college-bound?" Dr. Zucker had asked me. "Or can I count on you to stay on here?"

"I can't possibly afford to go to college," I told him. "My father lost his fortune in a business investment. I have to help the family out. I think you should consider me a permanent employee." Dr. Zucker seemed to understand I had already graduated from high school. I let it stand. I feared that I might actually *not* be able to go back to high school—that I would keep this job forever, sitting on my reclining desk chair and looking out over the ocean.

The first two women who came for their appointments carried Saks purses and wore big diamonds on their fingers. Gold pendants hung around their sunburn-scorched, wrinkled necks. I realized very soon that all Dr. Zucker's patients were old; this surprised me because the sign on his door said he was a gynecologist. I'd had the idea the office would be full of pregnant women radiant with the glow of impending motherhood. Instead, his patients were fading and fairly desperate about it.

A few times Dr. Zucker warned me not to forget to put the liver extract back in the refrigerator or it would lose its potency. Occasionally he left it out overnight himself, then injected it into the ladies anyway. Once, when I began to tell him the extract was warm and useless, he winked at me, and I shut my mouth. Later I asked him what the liver extract was supposed to do, and he said, "It's the fountain of youth, honey," and he winked at me again.

While he was in his Miami office, two mornings a week, I passed the time by reading his medical texts. The pictures of diseased female genitalia caused my heart to skip beats; they were grossly magnified and no human connection was visible; just swollen parts, with tumors, or suppurating sores, or orifices with spéculums inserted in them. Occasionally I felt I must have some air, but Dr. Zucker had warned me never to open the windows; the building was old and the frames were rusted shut from the salt air.

Sometimes I browsed through his files of medical charts, but they were full of technical language, and his handwriting was difficult to decipher. I spun on my chair. I typed a few bills. I read a little Shakespeare. I daydreamed about Roger Slavitt. He was coming to my house every Saturday. Mr. Katz, our principal, had warned him that if he didn't improve his English grade, he would be forbidden to play on the team in his senior year.

Roger and I didn't stay two minutes in the apartment; the air was sour with hostility between my parents, who were still not speaking. Since the bedroom had been graciously assigned to me, my mother and father were careful to occupy only the living room, sitting on their respective studio couches unless my mother was silently making my father a meal. He hadn't yet "forgotten that crap" and found a job though he pretended to be looking for the right one. The truth was that he cruised around Miami Beach construction sites looking for Frank Stuart, bearing him no particular malice. He simply hoped he was back in business, and they could go on from where they had left off—with that promising deal.

Roger, who stood six foot four in his huge white sneakers, was disturbing to my mother. She had to support the back of her head with her hand in order to look up at him. While I was getting my books together, my father told Roger he was thinking about "going into upholstery on a shoestring—all you need are some tacks and a roll of cloth." Roger told my father that sounded good to him, that his father had started out in the used furniture business and now owned three factories. Then he smiled at my mother. She didn't respond. She had actually turned white-haired in the last months. She was working overtime for Wimbush Realty, where properties were sold for enormous profits while she was being paid a typist's wage. To cheer her up, and because I felt nervous about walking out the door with Roger, I whispered to her as we left that we ought to have lunch out together on Monday. She agreed it would be fun—but said she'd bring along a picnic and we could eat in the doctor's office. It would be cheaper.

Roger and I walked across the street to a little kids' playground, and I let him choose a bench. He wanted to keep his suntan, so I said I didn't mind sweating it out. The sun, coming off his white T-shirt and shorts, created dancing stars in my eyes. I handed him the book and told him to ask me about the things he didn't understand. He wanted to know why hope was the thing with feathers. He said how come the day undressed herself and wore gold garters. He said how come, if Emily was nobody, and she said so herself, we had to read her poetry.

I told him "There is no Frigate like a Book to take us Lands away," and he said, "Friggin' books," and laughed. I wanted to keep him there as long as I could. I hoped Lilijoy would come bounding down the stairs and out the door and see us sitting there on the bench: the big football player and me. I wanted to stay a long time watching the sun bead the perspiration on the golden hairs of Roger's thighs. Anything was better than going back into the apartment to sit there in the thick animosity of my parents' bitterness. Why was I so stuck? There were things going on in the world to which I had no access at all: parties, movies, pizza outings, nighttime barbecues at the beach. Roger talked about these things as if they were the stuff of life itself. He was dating Penny Bloom, the homecoming queen. He told me he loved to take her to Fun Fair, the hot-dog place on the causeway, where you could put anything on your hot dog for free, onions, pickles, ketchup, mustard, sauerkraut, and then play miniature golf till they closed down. After that, he'd drive only with Penny to Pelican's Island, where they'd "you-know-what" till the police swept the place with their flashlights. "God, me and Penny are so frustrated, if you know what I mean," Roger confided in me. "And the last thing we need is Trouble." He rolled his eyes. "Like Brenda." Brenda was the girl whose father caught her in the shower with her boyfriend and a few weeks later she turned out to be pregnant in the bargain. I looked over the playground to where some kids were on a jungle gym.

"Hey, did I insult you?" Roger said. "I didn't mean to talk dirty or off-color or anything. Listen—I never even asked you, what are *you* doing for fun this summer?"

"I'm working for a gynecologist," I said.

Suddenly he peered at me. I noticed that his face was enormous. He had very large slug-like lips, one on top of the other, like nesting primitive animals. They looked truly bizarre to me.

"Hey, you wouldn't be able to get hold of any stuff, would you, I mean, you know, one of those things, to prevent trouble like Brenda had?"

"One of what things?" I said, though I knew immediately what he meant.

"The thing the woman wears. You know? Penny says she can't get one unless she goes to a doctor and tells him she's getting married."

"I might be able to get you one," I told Roger. "The doctor has them in his office."

"Oh, if only you could get me one!" Roger said. "I mean get Penny one. I'd do anything for you! What do you want me to do for you?"

"Let's just go sit on the steps of my apartment building," I told him. "Or, better yet, could we sit in your car in front of my house?"

"Sure," he said. "But I don't get it."

"That's okay," I said. "You don't have to."

He had a two-tone blue Chevrolet, and I fiddled with the radio till "Hold Me, Thrill Me, Kiss Me" came blasting out. After a while Lilijoy came to her window and flashed her head back and forth, two or three times. Finally I knew she had seen us and taken it in. I went right on reading to Roger:

The Dying need but little, Dear,
A Glass of Water's All.

On Monday morning, Dr. Zucker was standing at the instrument table, looking in the mirror above it and trimming his mustache with scissors I had taken from the autoclave a few minutes before. When he was done, he laid the scissors back in place in the cabinet. No appointments were scheduled for this morning and only one patient was expected after lunch—Mrs. Greenbaum. Dr. Zucker stood looking out the window and talked to me. He confided that because things were slow he had been advised by a colleague about a new idea for business. He wanted me to do a little job for him this morning: would I mind taking a packet of special business cards around to a few nearby hotels. He held one out for me to examine. It showed the snakes of the caduceus wound around its winged staff and read: *Dr. Sidney Zucker, Specialist in Honeymoon Disorders.* He told me he had already made an arrangement with several hotel managers. This is how it would work: If a manager noticed that a honeymoon couple was not, for example, going up to their room for their mid-afternoon nap, if it was clear that they were not holding hands across their beachchairs, then the manager would tactfully place Dr. Zucker's card on the nightstand in their room. If, as a result, the doctor got a new patient, the manager would get his cut. Dr. Zucker let his lips smile at me. He reminded me of Roger, who had also asked me to do him a strange favor. "Vaginismus is common," he added. "It generally scares them to death."

He smiled again. "By the way, I can't be here this afternoon. When Mrs. Greenbaum comes by for her liver injection, will you give it to her?"

"Me? I'm not a nurse! I can't possibly."

"There's really nothing to it," he said. "You've seen me do it dozens of times by now. Just get the air out of the needle and have her flip up her skirt."

"No! No!" I could think of no other word to say.

"Well, don't get all excited. You can decide when she comes. For now, just lock up the office, jump on a bus, and go uptown to a few of the hotels on this list."

Dr. Zucker reached into his pocket and pulled out some change and a five-dollar bill. "Bus fare. And treat yourself to lunch, Jenny," he said. "You deserve a little bonus."

The Fountainebleau Hotel had terrazzo tile floors, sparkling with bits of marble. No one in my family had ever stayed in a hotel like this. I wandered through the lobby and then went into the coffee shop. The tinkle of silverware and glasses gave me the impression that we were all inside a music box. Everything was pink formica. Glancing at the menu, I considered bringing my mother back here to treat her to lunch with Dr. Zucker's five dollars. But the prices made my heart pound, something like the way it pounded when I examined the doctor's medical texts. To consider paying that much for a sandwich! Yet people did it. The place was full of people doing it right now! What if *I* did? What if I did everything I was afraid to do? What if I did what I wanted to do, without a million considerations? Kate, the shrew, didn't worry about considerations, and she certainly had won my admiration.

I got out of there and followed the arrows to the pool where I spent a half-hour on company time admiring the muscles of the lifeguard. Women with oiled skin were turning brown on their beachchairs like chickens under the broiler. When I finally had my fill of coconut-scented sun-tan lotion and salty sea air, I went inside, located the manager's office, and left him a handful of the doctor's new business cards.

Back on Lincoln Road, I went straight into Dr. Zucker's private office and sat at his enormous mahogany desk. I examined photographs of his children, two sons who were surgeons somewhere in California, and one of his mother, in a babushka, taken in a village in Russia. He had had three wives, but he had no pictures displayed of any of them.

I opened his desk drawer and took out handfuls of sample medications: acne creams, dandruff shampoos, antibiotics, antihistamines, remedies for bee stings and menstrual cramps, heartburn and seasickness, sleeping pills, tranquilizers, special vitamin supplements. Many were expired, but I knew that when he gave them to patients he tore off the labels so they wouldn't know. He didn't mind my watching him do this. He liked to wink at me as if all his actions were a cause for good humor.

I chose some samples of sleeping pills and put them, as well as a good supply of other medicines, into the wide pockets of my nurse's uniform. I might need them someday. I got up from the doctor's desk and opened the storage cabinet on the wall where he kept the diaphragms. Rows of them were packed in long cardboard boxes, ranked by size (65, 70, 75, 80), and each one was in a pink vinyl kit decorated with flowers. I admired them, awed by the possible circumstances in which those springy rings encircling those powder-white rubbery cups might be brought into action. These items, too, might be expired, for all I knew. I chose a medium size for Roger, and also one for myself, along with two tubes of pearly white spermicide cream, and put them in my pockets. A pile of little booklets that explained the diaphragm's use were also for the taking, so I took two of those.

"Yoo-hoo," called a fluttery voice from down the hall, and I ran to see who it was. My nervous system was sizzling; I was not accustomed to pillaging and theft. Mrs. Greenbaum was clattering along in her lucite high heels, her blonde hair bouncing, like a separate entity, on her head. "I'm early, darling. Will you tell Doctor I have mah-jongg this afternoon, and could he do me now?"

"He's not here, Mrs. Greenbaum."

"Then you do it for me, darling. I hate to miss my shot."

"But I'm not a real nurse," I said. "I just wear this dress."

"Sweetheart, you must know how to do it! You've watched Doctor do it to me many times."

"But would you want to take a chance?" I had to know if she valued herself so lightly.

"Honey, I've taken more chances than your sweet brain can imagine. What did my son say in the war? That he flew between the bullets? That's the story of my life."

For one second I hesitated. How did a person know in life where to draw the line? Where was it written that I had to follow all the laws? I already had stolen goods in my pockets. The liver extract bottles were *all* expired; I should tell her to go away and never come back and not waste her money. But she was reaching up to tighten a loose diamond earring: "You know—Dr. Zucker is my angel. He makes me feel like I'm eighteen every time I walk out of here. You're so lucky to work for him. He's a handsome devil, isn't he? Don't worry about it, sweetheart. I'll call and see if he can squeeze me in later in the week."

I walked her to the door and stood in the corridor till the elevator arrived. As she got into it, my mother got out, looking in her drab gray dress about fifteen years older than Mrs. Greenbaum. Maybe—I thought—I should consider giving *her* the liver extract!

She hugged me in a half-hearted way and opened her paper bag in which I saw tuna sandwiches and two prune Danishes, a special treat she bought from the Jewish bakery on Washington Avenue. She looked around and pursed her lips, letting me know she was impressed with my working conditions. She told me she worked in a room without a window and typed Wimbush's correspondence on an ancient manual machine. She'd heard—had *I* heard—about these new electric typewriters that went as fast as the wind with only a feather-touch of your fingertips. She wished that someday she could type on one of those. How nice it was to talk to my mother about something pleasant; how very nice not to have my father between us like a big sad bear.

We ate at my desk, spreading the food out on the green blotter and using the huge volume titled *Basic Gynecology Text* as a coaster for the pink and green Tupperware containers of iced tea she had brought along for us to drink. She admired my view. I asked her if someday she would like to buy a sailboat and sail away with me to some Caribbean island.

"No men?" she asked me.

"No men," I said, and she smiled and reached over to squeeze my hand.

After lunch I showed her how I autoclaved, scrubbing the glass syringes in hot soapy water with a miniature bottle brush, wrapping the glass and the hollow needles in squares of brown linen, and then inserting them into the cavern of the silver steam oven to be sterilized.

"Maybe you should think of going to medical school," she said to me.

"Why bother? I could do everything right now that Dr. Zucker does, without wasting all that time and spending all that money."

I took her into one of the examining rooms; she insisted on carrying her wooden basket handbag with her everywhere in the office. I showed her where we laid the used speculums, in a glass container full of formaldehyde. One speculum was still in the sink, so I brought it over and tried to open the metal lid of the container. It was stuck. I pulled harder and suddenly the entire glass box slid off the table and crashed at my mother's feet.

She jumped away, her dress already splattered with formaldehyde. Terrible fumes rose from the floor, searing our lungs. The linoleum began to melt before our eyes.

"Oh God," I cried. We were both choking.

My mother ran to the window and tried to open it.

"Don't do that!" I yelled, but she was struggling with a rusted lever midway up the tall pane, and, when she managed to raise it, she pushed the huge window outward. We both watched the enormous rectangular frame break off at the hinges and swing out over the street as she leaned out with it, holding it by one little lever. Its bottom edge teetered on the window sill.

"Hang on to it, Ma!" I cried.

"I'm trying," she gasped, holding it now with both hands. Her bag was still swinging on her arm, a ridiculous woven basket with a stiff wooden handle and fake red cherries on the two hinged lids.

"If it drops, you'll *kill* someone!"

My mother's eyes met mine. "I didn't do it on purpose," she informed me. Her neck was taut from the effort of holding on. I couldn't help her—there was no other place to grasp the window except from the handle in her hands.

"I may have to let it go," she told me. The window was swinging in a deep, slow arc. "Look down! Is anyone on the street?"

"I can't see the street," I moaned, pressing my face against the other window.

"Then run outside! Go down and warn people away. I'll try to hang on as long as I can. Hurry!"

"What if you drop it before I get down?" I was begging her. "What will I do if you *kill* a person?" I was already running down the hall.

"If I do," she called back, "tell him it was just an honest mistake."

Looking up from below, on Lincoln Road, I could see the glass pane a dozen floors above me, waving like a crystal flag in the sunlight. It swung and turned, glistened and sparkled. I jumped up and down and pointed skyward, yelling at everyone on the sidewalk. "Stand back, a window is going to fall out. Get back, move away!" People glanced up and then ran into the street. A man pulled me with him and a bus thundered to a stop in order not to hit us.

Then my mother gave up the window. It fell, floating and gleaming, almost in slow motion, gyrating gently on the way down, the sky as blue as ever through its turning pane. It bounced once, like a tree, and shattered into diamonds.

I looked around. No one lay dead or bleeding. But could I believe no damage was done? Upstairs the floor was melting away, thousands of expired pills were turning to dust, hot air was shooting into the windowless hole and blasting down the cold halls. Somewhere up there was my white-haired mother, lost among the diaphragms, her basket on her arm, as puzzled as a farm girl out to gather berries, but not a berry anywhere.

That night, long after the sun had gone down, it appeared my mother was still too shaken to cook. Staring at the ceiling, she lay on her studio couch and did not protest when I asked my father if he would take us to Fun Fair for dinner. The lights from the lines of cars on the causeway shimmered like a string of stars. We each ordered a mile-long hot dog and french fries and went to the table of free condiments to decorate our food. My father seemed to go mad, squirting on worms of ketchup and mustard, piling his hot dog with shards of onions and ropes of sauerkraut. My mother put only one long line of blood-red ketchup on her frankfurter.

We ate at an outdoor table, watching the high-school kids and family groups playing miniature golf. Everyone was so intense out there in the land of little castles with turrets, and windmills, and bridges over water. People hit their golf balls as if nothing else in the world counted. When they missed their targets, they moaned in pain.

My father apologized to me that we weren't going to play golf; he shrugged. It wasn't cheap to play. We could see he was still hungry. He stood up, looked around, and went back for more free sauerkraut, heaping it on his paper plate in a little gray mountain.

I chewed my fried potatoes, dipping the salted zigzag squares in ketchup, loving them and wishing there were more.

When we finished eating (we had water to drink, Cokes would have added another dollar to the bill), we got in the car. The door on my mother's side was tied shut with rope, so she had to slide in from my fathers side, squeezing past the steering wheel. I sat in the hack.

My father, instead of going straight home to Miami Beach, drove a short distance and then pulled off the causeway, turning down the dirt road to Pelican's Island.

"Oh, don't go there!" I cried out as we humped along the rutted car tracks.

"Why not?"

I tried to think of an answer, picturing the rows of cars with my high-school buddies in them, necking away.

"I need to go home and finish reading Shakespeare," I said.

My father considered this but continued down the dirt road. Because he had only been there before by day, to go fishing, he seemed surprised by the astonishing population of cars; it was like a parking lot at a drive-in movie.

I touched his shoulder. "Turn around, Daddy! Please turn around!"

"I want to see the moon," he said. "I'm entitled." I felt tears fill my eyes. I put my other hand around his neck and let my fingers cup his chin. But his body was immovable, like a rock.

"Turn the car around," my mother said to him, breaking her long silence. "Don't you know what this place is?" He looked at her. Their noses were sharp in the moonlight, like swords.

"We won't stay long." He pulled into a space and shut off the motor. We were between two cars from whose glued-together occupants I hid my face. He got out and walked down to the water's edge and took his rightful eyeful of moon. He had always told us the best things in life were free, and tonight he insisted on his fill.

His baggy pants fluttered in the soft wind. He bowed his head. When he got back into the car, he slammed the door and drove us home.

That night I considered swallowing all the expired sleeping pills, but I wasn't sure they would do the job. I thought of using the diaphragm, but with who? Instead, I washed my hair with stolen dandruff shampoo and formulated what I would say to Dr. Zucker when I called him the next morning to quit.

Getting a different job turned out not to be a problem. Mr. Wimbush put me in touch with Kirschner Mortgage Company, and they hired me on the spot to post mortgage payments on a huge NCR machine with a thousand buttons. A basket of mail was given to me, and I used a razor-sharp knife to slit the envelopes. The checks went in one pile and the invoices in another. I entered the amount of payment on a square yellow card that I pulled from and then returned to a metal file cabinet. I worked very quickly, in a little cubicle without a window. All down one long row were women in cubicles doing the same thing. Kirschner and his partner worked across the room in separate, elegant, handsomely furnished and carpeted offices.

On my third day there I posted a payment to the account of a man named Frank Stuart. The property was a motel in Hallandale, and twice it had been threatened with foreclosure. I wrote down the name and address of Frank Stuart, taken from his check (he lived in Little River, a suburb of Miami, near the Hialeah Race Track), and I gave it to my father as soon as I got home.

He hugged me so passionately he almost broke my ribs. Then he told my mother what I'd learned and did everything she told him to do, called the police, called the Better Business Bureau, went through the proper channels. My mother, praising him warmly for coming to his senses, helped him by writing all the official letters. It took months. When they finally traced Stuart, they learned he had filed for bankruptcy and left the state. But we were past all that by then. My father had opened a tiny watch-repair shop on Flagler Street, and my mother was now working as an executive secretary for an important lawyer in a big modern office. I was back in school, a senior, and busy sending away for applications to colleges.

One Saturday my mother invited me to her office to fill out the forms there. I was wearing my new aqua cotton shirtwaist dress (my mother had a new black plastic shoulder bag), and we rode the bus together down Collins Avenue, watching the lines of palm trees fanning out along the oceanfront. Walking up Lincoln Road, we both glanced upward at the same instant. Dr. Zucker's window was still boarded up, blank as a blind eye.

In her office, my mother proudly unveiled her electric typewriter for me. I smoothed my skirt and sat down. I turned on the power. Neatly and professionally, my fingers flying like winged angels over the keyboard, I filled out those blessed applications, line by glorious line.

Night Stalker

Night Stalker. *Night Walker.*

The anchormen outdo themselves giving the murderer poetic names. One news reporter calls him *The Valley Intruder.* No one can agree on his essence other than to warn that he is dangerous. "Light up and lock up," the police chief advises. "And get yourself a big barking dog."

That's her trouble—Berry still has Sylvie's dogs at his house and won't give them back to her. Her mistake was to let Berry train them for quail hunting and now he says he has too much invested in them to give them back to her. "If you just want to rub up against something soft—or is it something hard?—you can get that anywhere, as you have demonstrated so well," he said last week in a flat, ugly tone of voice. "But the dogs and me—we share an art form."

Sylvie buys a cowbell at the flea market in the Rose Bowl and hangs it inside the back door of the house she rented when she moved out of Berry's house. She forgets it's there, though, and every time she goes out to feed her cats, the big square bell swings against the door with a wild dissonant clang and shocks her.

She keeps a piece of paper on her refrigerator, fastened to the door with a magnet shaped like a pair of kissing lips, and whenever she thinks of a killer's descriptive name, she writes it down. "Son of Sam," "Zodiac Killer," "Skid Row Slasher," "Hillside Strangler."

The reason the media can't settle on a name for the Stalker is that he doesn't seem to have any special needs—he kills everyone, men and women, young and old. The other psychos had had definite preferences: girls with dark hair parted down the middle, derelicts clutching wine bottles, hookers, hitchhikers. The Night

Stalker/Walker doesn't give Sylvie a chance to wrap her fear around anything specific. He seems to want to be democratic in providing his services.

At the beginning of his rampage, the police announced he was out to get women living alone. They said his mode of entry was through open windows in dimly lit yellow houses without fenced yards. They said there were indications that he liked to observe women watching television late at night before he struck. Sylvie decides the police are talking about her on the news, and in a minute will give out her name and address. That's her exactly, down to the "dimly lit." She now lives in a little rented yellow house which has no outside light, no fenced yard (if she had one, she'd have bought a German shepherd and a Doberman right away—to make up for Franco and Chumley, her dogs which Berry won't give back to her).

And she always watches television late at night. With no one to talk to, the television is her main human connection. It doesn't matter what comes on the screen—David Letterman giving people coins to put in the candy machines, Rumpole of the Bailey mumbling under his breath, the moose on the wall at Fawlty Towers coming off the hook and hitting John Cleese on the head. Even Captain Kirk, in his straight-backed moral certainty, is oddly reassuring. When finally she has to go to bed, when her eyes won't stay open, she locks the doors and windows and says goodbye to her cats, just in case. "I surrender myself into the arms of Jesus," she tells them, kissing them both between the ears. She thinks anyone's arms would be comforting, under the circumstances.

Driving to work she hears on the radio that one of the Stalker's surviving victims has revealed an important fact: the killer has discolored and rotted teeth, widely spaced. Perfect, she thinks, imagining the man leaning over her in bed. She knows just which side he'll be standing on when he comes to her, how he'll blot out the red light from the neon-bright display on her clock. Berry used to keep a shotgun under the bed. She longs not for him but for the highly developed muscles in his arms and for his perfect aim.

On the freeway, on her way to the hospital, she looks into each car that passes her. She believes that if any man glances out the window of his car and smiles at her, she will see at once his rotted, discolored, gapped teeth.

She had just wanted to be easy on herself during the winter. She was the one with the forty-hour job, she was the one tied down, while Berry was off in the woods with her dogs, hopping from one state to another, elk hunting, quail hunting, visiting his Vietnam buddies, hunkering down somewhere for a month while she drove her little Toyota to the lab, put on her lab coat, stuck needles in the tender stomachs of mice, made notations, cleaned up, drove home again, fed the cats and ate alone. Her dogs' big stainless-steel bowls, dented and empty, rolling in the wind against each other outside the back door, caused her more misery than the vacant side of Berry's waterbed. Now and then she'd get a call from Berry, from some honky-tonk bar in the north, telling her he was making good money acting as a guide to elk-hunters, winning a lot of cash at poker, telling her that the dogs were doing just fine. Several times she was aware he had covered the mouthpiece to say something to someone else. For a long time after she hung up, the sound of pounding music remained in her ears.

Being easy on herself meant giving herself permission to jog with Richard—Dr. Richard Gomber, the man for whom she conducted experiments and did research. Before lunch every day the two of them jogged together around the hospital. They took a convenient path—it made a loop around the cafeteria, the motel-village where families of dying patients lived, the catastrophic illness wing, and the medical records building. Whenever they passed the famous fountain at the entrance to the hospital, droplets of cool water hit her in the face like a vaccine. Sacred water: it flew into the air above the blessed dancing family—a mother, father and child, hands joined in celebration. Health and joy and love—reminders, should anyone passing by forget, of the reasons for wanting to remain alive.

Her chest heaving, her heart pounding, she would forget what was coming till they were right at the hospital entrance where the fountain made its dramatic statement, and then she saw them—sitting on its cold stone rim—a mother and child. Though the people were never the same, they always had the same look about them. The mother sat holding the hand of her bald little son, or her bald little daughter, the two of them taking the air, getting buoyed up, finding courage for going into chemotherapy, or for going home to deal with its effects. Not once did Sylvie ever see a father sitting on the edge of the fountain.

Having children was not something she had thought about much before, but whenever she saw the little five-year-olds sitting on the rounded, mica-sparkled rim of the fountain, she wanted to caress their bald heads, stroke their frightened faces, and rock them in her arms. She began to understand why she didn't care for Berry: he was not a carrier of fine genetic material. She wished she had considered that when she was younger. She would have looked for a man like Richard, whose intelligence illuminated and enlarged all that he touched. A pediatrician for children with leukemia, his job, when he wasn't inserting huge hollow needles into the breastbones of children, was to kill the laboratory mice and see what was going on inside. Her job was to shoot leukemic cells into the mice.

One day in winter, though it was raining, Richard wanted to run. He said he felt unable to face the afternoon's work without his run. He took Sylvie's hand briefly and pulled her into the corridor. They began to run in their white coats through the halls of the hospital. No one suspected an emergency because everything was an emergency here. Their casual hospital had abandoned the idiotic rules of regular hospitals, rules which fussed about children visiting, worried about the spread of germs, detailed to the minute the permitted hours of socializing. At this place there was only one thought beating in the veins of every patient, nurse, doctor, and lab worker: nothing silly mattered, there was no time for silliness.

Therefore the older children were permitted to play music on their tape decks till all hours—the songs of their rock heroes who had energy to spare and whose cries and shouts magically, temporarily, revivified. On that rainy winter afternoon, Sylvie and Richard ran past a room where two spirits were gyrating in their hospital robes, a bald teenage boy and a bald teenage girl, their bony buttocks showing through the openings in their white cotton gowns, their toothpick legs vibrating as they danced.

That night, Richard came home with Sylvie although at his house his wife was keeping his dinner warm, and two children waited for him. It was the same night that Berry's friend Judson came by to borrow some tools and the next time Berry called home, he told Sylvie he didn't want her there when he got back. She tried to explain that she was being easy on herself, that it had been a terrible, lonely winter, but Berry wasn't interested. Actually, she didn't really care that she had to move out. Berry had floated so far away from her, he was like a feathery seed pod; she could hardly focus on him. Besides, she'd always disliked his waterbed. She could never get still in it; it never let her become peaceful and perfectly still while she slept, but always nagged her back to some guarded alertness by its insistent churning restless tides.

Once Sylvie has moved out of Berry's house she imagines she has changed. At the lab, she finds herself staring at her image reflected in the stainless-steel sides of the autoclave, looking like an angel in her white lab coat, injecting the underbellies of the mice that struggle in her hand. She doesn't look like an evil woman. She wonders why people who do what they have to do are considered evil. Is the Night Stalker more evil than she?

When she and Richard jog, whenever they pass a mother and her bald child resting on the rim of the fountain, Richard makes a strange sound—it's almost like a sob. It could be merely an exhalation of exertion, but it recurs each time they see a little child sitting in the rainbow spray of the fountain, and Sylvie understands it's involuntary. He doesn't know he makes the sound. It comes from his soul.

The radio hints that the Stalker does indescribable deeds in the homes of his victims. He enacts rituals; he writes on the walls with blood, he mutilates, sings, chants, hops on one foot like a beheaded chicken while speaking in tongues. The morning paper features a composite drawing of him—a curly-headed, pointy-chinned boy with large, liquid brown eyes. His eyes are like the eyes on paintings of waifs done by commercial artists: grieved and suffering eyes. The police haven't much to go on; they're alerted by a dentist who remembers that such a man has been in his office—a man with stained, rotted, widely gapped teeth. Copies of the man's dental records are sent to thousands of dentists in the city. Sylvie imagines the killer sitting in an air-conditioned office aromatic with peppermint mouthwash; he is racked with pain and is watching a clock (like the one her dentist has in his office) made of silver ball bearings; as each minute passes, a silver ball falls with a noise like a gunshot from one wooden tray into another.

In her yellow unfenced dimly lit house, she gives the killer a better name than anyone has thought of yet. *Night Talker.* He comes at night and he talks. He talks to women and men, to old dying people and young dying children. He tells them dramatic, descriptive, passionate tales of what he has seen on his street, in his home, on his ward, in his ghetto, barrio, town house, mansion. He confides that he considers himself not a murderer but a deliverer from pain. When he finally visits Sylvie with his gun or hatchet or knife, he will want her to remember that he has walked through the halls of her hospital and has seen the sweet skeletal teenagers dancing to Bruce Springsteen's hoarse throbbing encouragements.

Sylvie suspects she is beginning to let go. One of Richard's children, his five-year-old son, has been getting small black and blue marks all over his body. Petechiae. The *sign.* Richard is in bed with her in the yellow house when he tells her this. He tells her this and then leaps out of bed. He finds the cowbell on her kitchen door and rings it over his head. In a fury, he asks her, "Why is the Night Stalker any different from the Stalker in my lab, in my house? Why are you so afraid *here* but not in the lab? Do you think your white coat protects you from anything? Do you think mine protects *me?*" He runs through the house naked, ringing the cowbell. She sees the heavy knob of the ringer shaking in time to his trembling penis.

In the morning, she discovers the teenaged boy, the bald dancing boy, in her lab in his wheelchair. The radio on her shelf is playing loud music and he is watching the mice in their silver cages. With the long thin fingers of his right hand, he is offering a tidbit through the wire grid.

"What's this?" she says, in mock fierceness. "Didn't you see the sign? No feeding the animals in this zoo!"

"Why not?" the boy asks her, turning upon her face his huge blue eyes, radiant and blue as heaven.

Why not? She asks herself. She wonders if he wants to know about the experiments, how some mice are being deprived of Vitamin E, how others are being given an all-protein diet.

"They deserve a little fun," he says. He looks like a hundred-year-old man, his bald skull is almost pointy at the top. "Don't you think they ought to have a taste of fudge brownie before they die?" He's not pleading for special favors; there's no hint of self-pity in his remark.

"By all means," she says. "Go right ahead." She takes her grease pencil and makes a mark on the card on the cage where the brownie crumbs are being pushed through the grating. These mice will be unusable in Richard's experiment. They will have to be killed sooner then others, because of their chocolate treat.

A news bulletin on the radio announces the murder of an old woman living alone. The Stalker is suspected.

"Where do you live?" the boy asks her, putting his hand on her white lab coat, just on her hip. She feels a throb in her belly, low down, almost sexual.

"You mean what street?"

"No, I mean, is it a safe place?"

"Well, I hope so. It's just a little yellow house, shaped like a box. I keep the doors locked."

"Do you live alone?"

"Yes, usually."

"You don't think he'd try to come into the hospital, do you?"

"Does that worry you?"

"Sometimes it does," the boy says. "But not much. Do you have a dog?"

"I have two cats. I used to have two dogs, Chumley and Franco, but I don't have them anymore."

"What happened to them?"

"Someone thought he deserved them more than me."

"Did he?"

"I don't think so."

"That's not fair, is it?"

"I guess not," Sylvie says.

"My folks are getting me a dog when I get out of here. If I ever get out."

"Are you counting on that?"

"Not really. How can I?"

Sylvie motions to the cages, full of scrambling white mice, and lets her hand fall. There are no promises here, either.

"They're going to be looking for me soon," says the boy. "Another bone marrow today. I hate them."

"Is Dr. Gomber your doctor?"

"You mean Richard?"

"Yes. He's really gentle," Sylvie says.

"It doesn't matter," the boy says. "It hurts like hell anyway." He wheels his chair around, expertly, and waves at Sylvie as he rolls into the corridor.

"Come back anytime," she offers. "Bring me a brownie, too."

The Stalker has killed again. This time he shot the man in the house and raped the woman. Having a man in the house is no guarantee of anything. Sylvie locks her doors at night and kisses her cats goodbye, as usual. Instead of imagining Berry's strong muscles, or Richard's pained sweet face, she begins to imagine the boy in the wheelchair sitting beside her bed all night, keeping vigil. He is so serene, so resigned, so death-like, his head so much like a skull already, that he seems to pave the way for her, prepare her for the transition to being one of the Stalker's victims. She imagines the three of them could have a little visit first. They'd talk about suffering. Fear, panic, anger, neglect, unfairness. It would be quite a night. The boy in the wheelchair could talk about tolerating pain, the tricks he has learned, and reassure the Stalker that the dentist isn't so bad, nothing there coming even close to a bone marrow. And even a bone marrow passes, and you live through it. You live through everything till finally you quit, and when you quit nothing hurts anymore.

It's almost a jolly thought, and helps her to go to sleep. Richard's son hasn't got leukemia; it's something else, which can be fixed. Sylvie is ashamed of her disappointment. Somehow she'd painted for herself a delicious scene, in one of those sleepless cavernous nights of listening for noises outside the window—Richard's son would die, his wife would throw herself from the roof of the catastrophic illness wing, and Richard would marry Sylvie. They would have a child, and the three of them would dance for joy like the figures in the sculpture on the stone fountain.

The identity of the Stalker is made known at the exact end of summer, on Labor Day weekend. His face is in the Saturday morning paper, front page, he has been identified by fingerprints and soon they hope to catch him. He is not who she thought he was. His face is wrong; he is not a waif, he is not a sufferer, he is not a deliverer. He is an inflictor of horror, and has darkness written all over him. She is horrified that she imagined it would be interesting to talk to him.

It's been a long, hot weekend, full of the deadness that comes with holidays during which there is no formal activity. No work, no mail delivery, nothing to do. Richard is in Santa Barbara with his family. The smog is heavy, Sylvie's eyes burn. She can barely keep her eyes open as she reads the newspaper. She is so bored that she reads through all the want ads: business opportunities, personals, lost birds, dogs for sale. Sylvie decides to buy a dog. She makes a quick phone call to a man in the Valley who raises basset hounds. "I'm coming," she tells him, and her blood is up. She's grateful for purpose. While she puts on lip gloss in the bathroom, she turns on the radio and hears the triumphant voice of the newsman with his bulletin: someone has hit the Stalker on the head with a pipe and subdued him. He's caught! They've got him! She sinks down on the edge of the bathtub, feeling tearful. She realizes that she doesn't need the bother of a dog now, the house-training, the puppy cries, the barking, the fleas. But she's counting on going out the door, getting into the car, turning the key in the ignition.

As Sylvie unlocks her car, a woman from the house next door, who is standing in the street, runs up to her and hugs her.

"Thank God!" she cries. "Now we can open our windows! Now we can sleep at night!" Several children pour out of another small house and begin lighting fireworks. A celebration of the strangest sort begins to develop. Men come out into the street, some carrying beer cans, and gather, talking about the details of the capture, the arrest. The sound of an electric guitar bursts forth from a garage, filling the air with music. Strangers are congratulating one another as if the angel of death has passed over all of them.

The basset hound she chooses has ears which sweep the ground, and huge flat splayed feet. He has the kind of eyes she wants to see: sweet, limpid, loving. She holds him against her breast as if he is an infant. He comes with everything—shots, collar, leash, bag of puppy food, a huge plastic dish with a family of basset hounds painted on it.

She drives to the hospital with the puppy on her lap, overriding the sense of cliché she feels. The puppy won't stay in the carton. She laughs aloud at the feel of his paws dancing on her lap, tickling her thighs through her skirt.

Hardly anyone is on duty today. She parks in the visitors' lot and walks the dog to the fountain. Sitting on the stone rim with him, she holds him into the rainbow spray, and he bites at the droplets of water, barking hysterically.

Then she carries the puppy into the catastrophic illness wing, where she looks into each room till she finds the dancing boy who brought brownies to the mice. "Hi, I have a surprise for you," she says.

Slowly, he moves himself to a sitting position with the controls of the electric bed. He takes his headphones off his ears.

"I can't keep him here, you know," he says regretfully, taking the puppy in his thin arms and closing his eyes as the dog licks his face. "You can't really do this, you know. Even here there are rules."

"I need him for protection, I'm not giving him to you," Sylvie says. "I know the rules. This is just a visit."

"It's been a boring weekend," the boy says, stroking the puppy's ears.

"It's been deadly," Sylvie agrees.

GOOD-BYE, ARNY GOLDSTONE

"YOU REALIZE this could be the saddest day of your life, don't you?" Donna asked, maneuvering the car along the curves of Prospect Park on their way from Manhattan. "You can't go home again and all that?"

Janet's eyes were fastened on two women in bright red jump suits, standing on a hill.

"Hookers," Donna said. "Did they have them here when you lived in Brooklyn?"

"I don't think so," Janet said. "At least they didn't—well parade around like that."

"The first of many surprises," Donna said, leaning over and patting her knee. "Just hang on and be prepared."

"Why are you so *negative?"* Janet said. "Why shouldn't this be wonderful? Going back to the house I grew up in, seeing my old neighborhood, my old street . . ."

"Because it isn't going to be your old anything," Donna said. "Because twenty years is a long time. Nothing will be the same. The nice old people you knew when you were a little girl are dead, and the young people have married and gone, and the middle-aged people have moved to Florida or Long Island or—like you—to California."

"But I was so happy there," Janet said. "I spent the first twelve years of my life in that one place. I knew everyone in every house, and I knew their mothers and fathers and sisters and brothers, and their grandmothers and grandfathers, and they knew me and my sister and my mother and father . . ."

"All right, all right," Donna said. "I get the gist of it. But I went back to Philadelphia a few years ago to where I knew everybody's grandmother, and instead of my house I found a condominium, and instead of old Mrs. Esposito next door I found a pool hall, and instead of my elementary school I found a factory that makes paper cups."

"Oh, that reminds me," Janet said. "Could we drive by my old elementary school too? P.S. 238? I get a chill just thinking about how I had my first proposal of marriage there, when I was eleven."

"Tell me about it," Donna said.

"Well, it was during a fire drill. We were all standing out on the street by someone's hedge and Arny was stripping leaves off the bush by the handful, and then suddenly he stuck his face next to mine and said, 'Janet, you're not the prettiest girl in seventh grade, but there's something about you that makes me crazy and I hope I can marry you someday." '

Donna laughed. "Ah," she said. *"Now* I know why you wanted to come back to Brooklyn. You want to look him up!"

"Look up Arnold?" Janet said. "That's ridiculous. He wouldn't be here anyway. You just said all the middle-aged people have moved to Florida or California. He probably lives in L.A., a ten-minute drive from me."

"What's his last name?" Donna asked.

"Goldstone," Janet said. "Arnold Goldstone."

"Perfect!" Donna said. "It's just right. I love it."

They were driving down Ocean Parkway now. Janet's heart leaped at the familiar sight of the benches, the leafy trees, the pipe fence separating the bicycle path from the promenade.

"But where's the bridle path? And I don't see any bicycles either. And the fence—it used to have little pointy knobs on every post. God, I had never even heard of phallic symbols then!

I can almost feel how smooth they used to be. Gold—the knobs were gold."

"You're really thinking about Arnold Goldstone," Donna said. "Confess."

Janet laughed. She was delighted. The trip *was* going to be worth it all—the expense, leaving Danny and the girls for two weeks, coming back here to visit after so long. It was a trip with a practical purpose too; she was going to attend the eighty-fifth birthday celebration of a favorite aunt of hers.

When the invitation came, Danny had urged her to go. "It will be good for you to have a change," he said. "Get away from the children for a while, have a little vacation."

"But I'll *miss* you," she had said. "It's scary to think of going away from you for so long. It seems *risky.*"

"If you don't take a risk now and then," Danny had said, "you won't have any new experiences."

But now she was remembering an old experience; Arnold Goldstone at her twelfth birthday party; how, during a kissing game, he wouldn't let her out of the dark sun porch where they were playing Post Office, how he blocked the door with his long arms and held her there, demanding yet one more kiss, his body heat making her limp, confused.

"One more kiss, Janet—I have to have one more. I dream about you every night, you know."

"I thought you probably dreamed about Wendy," she said, for it was true that Wendy, who let boys do anything to her, had often been seen in the playground, behind the rest rooms, with Arnold.

"What has she got to do with it? You know about *her*," he said. "She's nobody. The only kisses I want are yours."

But she wasn't sure she could handle another kiss. The first one, given formally—it was, after all, part of the game—had been of a different quality from the wet, awkward, hurried smacks she had experienced at parties. Arnold's kiss was rough and hard; she thought she felt the knuckles of his fist pressing into her back; her knees lost their tension, went watery; and she felt a kind of swooning surrender swirl through her head, something delicious, scary, uncontrolled and possibly very dangerous.

"Tough," she said. "You can't have a second kiss, Arnold." She had pushed past him into the party room, blinking at the bright light, feeling a cold chill now that she had stepped out of the aura of his passion for her, realizing with sorrow that she had made the first of many practical, sensible choices in her life.

In school on Monday he had humiliated her. On the blackboard in his spidery handwriting was the terse message: "Anyone can see inside Janet's dress." She was wearing a loose, sleeveless pinafore on that hot spring day, no bra under it. She had sat all day with her arms pressed against her sides, trying to control her tears and anger.

She had never talked to Arnold after that. And then at some point her parents had moved away from Brooklyn. But every now and then, unexpectedly, as she moved through her happy domestic life, the image of his face would come to her, those wild, sexy eyes, his hoarse, nasal voice, his desire for her, his thrilling demands. The first was always the best. Her husband Danny was handsome, tender, totally suited to her. But no one except Arnold had ever demanded kisses of her like that—"the only kisses I want."

"Avenue O," Donna announced. "It's coming right up."

"Oh, look!" Janet cried. "There's the apartment house where the bad man lurked in the basement. On snowy days I liked to cut through the basement on my way home from school—the hot-water pipes were so nice and warm. But my grandmother warned me about the bad man who would get little girls and do bad things to them."

"So of course you didn't take the short cut," Donna said.

"I didn't—no, of course I didn't. I was a good girl," Janet said. "Always have been—a good girl."

"So you froze your butt off."

"I froze it off," Janet said. "Turn right here. Oh, God, this is *my street!*"

The trees were lacy, beautiful, just as she remembered them. She felt lightheaded, buoyant. When she actually saw her house, dappled sunlight coming down upon it, she began to laugh and cry at the same time. "Look! The stoop where I played stoopball. The sewer where all my balls went—"

"They're probably still there," Donna said.

"The lilac tree! Oh, my God. That bench. It's the same bench my grandmother used to sit on. She would sit there, knitting, and say to me, 'Don't run so much. Rest—you'll live longer." '

Obediently Donna was looking at the little house, as if she were trying to see the young Janet running, puffing, red in the face; playing stoopball, catching the flies as they came off the points of the brick steps.

"And there's Myron's house next door! Myron—we used to play Monopoly all the time on his back porch. His mother hit him at every meal because he wouldn't eat enough. Once she swung at him and he ducked and she broke her wrist!"

Janet was nearly levitating in her seat as Donna parked the car. "Look. There—across the street. That's where Rachel lived—she was this unbelievably sexy girl. She outgrew her bras every week; her mother kept complaining how she had to buy her so many new ones. And she was a champion jacks player, better even than me. Do you think that was fair, to have a shape like that and to beat me at jacks, too?"

Donna was laughing. "Do you want to walk around a little, or shall I just tie a string to you and you can float?"

"The tree! My wishbone tree!" Janet cried. "When I was four or five I used to sit in the vee of it. And now look how huge it is."

The front door of the house opened and a little old lady wearing a blue apron looked out. "Hello, girls," she said. "Could I do something for you?"

"Oh . . ." Janet said. "I used to live here when I was a little girl. This used to be my house. Is it all right if we just—well, stand here for a while and look at it?"

"Isn't that wonderful!" the old lady said. With her white hair, she looked the way Janet's grandmother had looked. But her grandmother had been dead fifteen years now. "Maybe you'd like to come in and look around?"

Donna gave Janet a warning glance, meaning, so far so good; but what if you go inside and it's all different, all wrong?

"I'd love to look inside, if you really wouldn't mind," Janet said. "I have a little camera. Do you think I could take a few pictures?"

"Darling," the old lady said, "do anything you like. Make yourself at home. It's a wonderful house. As soon as we saw it, we bought it right away for the basement. My son liked to build models, so we wanted him to have a basement."

"The basement terrified me," Janet said. "The furnace—the way the pipes clanked every morning when the heat came up. I used to think it would explode. Once I looked inside at the roaring fire . . . my father said I must never open the door of it." Her father been dead ten years.

"So come in, come in already," the old woman said.

Janet walked, knees shaking, up the front steps and Donna followed. Janet had a photograph of herself at the age of two climbing these steps. This was like stepping into another world, another existence. The numbers on the door, (her address—405—), were the same. The stained-glass porthole in the heavy door—it was all the same; the same sun sending light through the colored glass, making the same colored patterns on the floor of the sun porch where she had slept for twelve years. It was unbelievable that she was here. All those years in between—she had finished college, got married, lost her father, had three children . . .

"Go wherever you like, sweetheart," the old woman said. "I'm Mrs. Berkovsky. Would you like a cup of tea? Some honeycake, maybe?"

"No, no, thank you," Donna said. "But tell me a little about your son. What does he do now?" She nodded at Janet, meaning, Go, do what you have to, we don't have too long.

Janet traversed the three rooms downstairs, the continent of her childhood. Upstairs, tenants had lived. There in that corner had been the old GE radio; there under the window, her dog Spotty. The rooms were their old shape; Mrs. Berkovsky's polished furniture vanished under her hungry eyes and in its place she saw *her* things, her precious memories. Her mother broiling lamb chops between two wire grates on top of the stove, flames leaping upward toward the ceiling; in the back yard; her father pruning the peach tree, shirtless, his bare chest strong and tanned. Herself on the glider on the back porch, reading, writing in her diary, preparing for life, dreaming of the adventures to come.

Going down the cellar steps, her camera ready, she felt the chill of the dark, her fear of the roaring furnace and of the open hole under the house where the bogeyman lived and waited to strike. The green wooden storage benches were still there, exactly as they had been. That was where she'd kept Halloween costumes, games, puzzles.

"I don't believe this," Janet heard herself whisper, clicking her camera at everything, at anything. She was in a time machine; she was eleven years old. It smelled the same. The cracks in the cement in the alley were the same. The tiles in the bathroom were the same; when she had had stomachaches, she had sat in the bathroom, doubled over, counting the tiles.

Finally she emerged from the cellar into the kitchen. Donna, sitting with Mrs. Berkovsky, was leafing through the phone book. "Guess what?" she said, handing the book out to Janet and pointing. "Look at that."

"Arnold Goldstone!"

"None other."

"It can't be the same one," Janet said. "Impossible."

"Call," Donna suggested.

"Call?"

Mrs. Berkovsky said, "Use the phone, if you like, darling. It's in the front room."

Janet followed Mrs. Berkovsky into the front room, her old bedroom, the sun porch where Arnold had come toward her with his long arms, where he had demanded her kisses. On that night the street light had barely filtered through the Venetian blinds into the blackness of the room. The same blinds were open now, letting in the sun.

"So you'll have privacy," Mrs. Berkovsky said, shutting the door behind her.

Sitting on the day bed, she dialed the number. Her throat closed when a man answered the phone.

"Is this Arnold Goldstone?" she said at last, her voice trembling. "My name is Janet. I used to go to school with a boy named Arnold Goldstone . . ."

"Janet!" the man said. "Oh my God, Janet. I was just thinking about you today. In fact, I think about you all the time. I pass your house and I remember you. I remember your grandmother and her white hair. And your father, and all the junk in the cellar. Your mother used to make us milk shakes after school."

His voice was unmistakably the same, a little whiny, nasal; Brooklynese, marvelous. She felt herself smiling ridiculously, her mouth stretched wide, joy welling up within her.

"You *remember* me?"

"Remember you! Janet, you were my first *love.* You were the only girl I really loved. Oh, yeah, I had other girls for fooling around, but you were really something. You I could just sit and talk to for hours."

"Yes, I remember," Janet said.

"Are you still cute?"

"Am *I still cute?*"

"You know . . . you were the sexiest thing," he said. "I always dreamed about going to bed with you."

"With me? I was such a skinny kid."

"That's the way I liked 'em," he said with a low laugh.

"My God, Arny, if only you'd told me this twenty years ago, my whole self-image, my whole life, might have been different!"

"But I want to apologize for something while I have the chance," he said, his voice going to a whisper. "I've always regretted this one thing."

"*What?*"

"Just a minute—let me close the door here in my office."

"Oh, hurry," she said.

"Okay, I'm back. Do you remember once, it was a summery day, you weren't wearing a bra, maybe some of the girls were by then, and maybe your dress was slightly too big, or something . . ."

Do I remember?

". . . and all the guys were making remarks, you know, and I wanted to stop them, but I didn't have an adult mind then so I just went along with it . . ."

"Went along! You wrote that awful thing on the blackboard, Arny."

"Not me, Janet. Pinhead wrote it. You remember that moron in our class, Alvin Pinetta, we all called him Pinhead? He wrote it."

"I always thought you wrote it."

"I would never do that to you, Janet. When you love a girl, you don't want everyone looking in her dress, you know. I wish I had punched every one of those guys in the face. It's funny, but I think of that pretty often and I still feel bad about it."

In a mirror on the sun-porch wall, Janet could see from her reflection that she was crying.

"So how long are you in town?"

She took a breath. "Just this afternoon, Arny. A friend from Manhattan drove me in. I live in California now. I have three girls. My husband . . ."

"Yeah, I figured that would happen," he said. "I always wondered, but in my heart I knew. What else could it be? A husband, kids . . ."

"And you?"

"A wife, kids. What could you expect?"

"But is it okay?"

"Yeah, it's okay. And I made a lot of money. What do you think of that, Janet? That dumb kid, he got rich."

"You were never dumb, Arny."

"And I'm still pretty good-looking. My daughter tells me I'm really handsome. I work out every day."

"I can imagine."

"So maybe you could drop by with your friend. I have this restaurant on Avenue P now, Arnold's Salami Palace. That's where I am now, that's the number you called me at. Don't laugh at the name, Janet. It's a real good business. Remember my father—he had Irving's Appetizer Store? It's the same building. Modernized."

"I don't know, Arny. I think my friend has to get back to the city."

"Well, leave it open," he said. "If you come, you come. But, hey, I'm so happy you called. You have no idea how happy I am, I'm smiling all over the place."

"Me too. I'm happy too."

"So listen, try to drop by. It would really be something to see you."

"I'll try," she said. "Good-bye, Arny Goldstone."

"Hey, kid, I still love you . . ."

She hung up softly, sobbing with such exquisite pain and joy that the light coming in the stained-glass porthole of the front door swam before her eyes in swirls of fiery, brilliant colors.

She fell back on the day bed and recognized the light fixture on the ceiling of her room. This *was* her room. Of all the rooms in all the places she had lived or would live, this was her room.

It took her ten minutes to compose herself, to set her face straight, to open the door and walk to the kitchen, where Donna, with her sweet patience, was still talking to Mrs. Berkovsky.

"So," Donna said, "was it really your old friend Arnold?"

"Yes, it was," Janet said, smiling. "And would you believe he actually remembered me? In fact, he runs a restaurant right on Avenue P, a block away."

"Do you want me to take you over there?" Donna asked, watching her face carefully.

"Oh . . . I don't know, let me think about it," Janet said.

Donna took Mrs. Berkovsky's hand. "I do think we've taken enough of your time. You've been wonderful. Thank you so much."

"You're such sweet girls, come back any time," Mrs. Berkovsky said, hugging them.

As soon as they were in the car, Donna glanced sideways at Janet. "So shall I swing around to Avenue P?"

"Okay—why not?" Janet said, her heart roaring.

"It's a little risky, no?"

"This hasn't been the saddest day of my life so far," Janet said.

"Well, let's keep it that way. But if you want me to, I'll drive down to Avenue P and you think about what you really want to do.

And there, next door to the place where Janet once took ballet lessons, where Irving's Appetizer Store had been, stood Arnold's Salami Palace. Janet could almost smell the mustard out on the street. It was so pungent, beads of perspiration stood on her forehead.

"Stop or go?" Donna asked.

"I didn't say for sure I'd stop by. I told him I'd leave it open."

"And?" She slowed the car.

"No, go on. Just keep going. I think it's better to leave it open."

Mozart You Can't Give Them

In the downstairs apartment the young Mexican boy began to knock his head against the wall. Sometimes Anna thought it was just the low bass beat of some tenant's stereo, but as soon as she realized it wasn't regular, she knew it was the boy starting his morning tantrum. At least if he had some sense of rhythm—a little drummer boy. But he wasn't musical, only crazy. At almost the same instant the Russian lady across the courtyard began playing violent streaks of dissonance on her cello. Immediately Anna pictured a blackboard, wide and colorless as Russia, and across it came the shrieking chalk, an empty train scraping and grinding its way over the bleak plains. The woman should have stayed in Russia where there was more space, and not moved here to live ten feet from Anna and give her a headache every day.

As if all that weren't enough, Anna heard the clatter of the barbecue lid being lifted outside, and she rushed to lock her windows. On the tiny balcony next to Anna's, the father of the Armenian family was lighting the barbecue starter again. What was wrong with these people that they had to cook three times a day over charcoal? Didn't they know how to use a stove? If they were civil human beings in the first place, she would tell them that this kind of cooking could give them cancer. But when she slammed the sliding glass door shut, the man always sneered at her, looking like a walrus with his hanging mustache, and threw more lighter on the coals, for spite.

Charred edges of meat, which tasted like heaven itself, could kill you. What couldn't kill you? Pickled herring could kill you, lox could kill you, everything was full of nitrites. Anna heard plenty of lectures at the Senior Citizens' Center, she was an informed woman.

Chicken fat could kill you, cream cheese, sour cream, bacon; for years these foods had tempted her to stay alive. When her sister Gert had come with her to the Center for the lecture by the nutritionist, bacon had been the day's main subject. The old man Bernie, who was at the Center all the time, announced that if you drank orange juice when you ate bacon, something in the juice would cancel out the cancer. Gert had poked Anna and muttered, "Jews—all of these Jews—they have no business eating bacon anyway. No business even *talking* about it!"

"Look, get modern, will you?" Anna had said to her. "Get with the twentieth century. You're still living back in the horse-and-buggy age."

"At least people were decent then," Gert had insisted. "Not like this sewer we live in now. Don't invite me to any more lectures. I'm better off at home."

The fumes from the Armenians patio were filling Anna's apartment, choking her. "Who needs the Gestapo when you have this?" She dragged her kitchen chair into the walk-in pantry closet and closed the door, sitting there in the dark with the matzo meal boxes and the cans of soup. The stink of the charcoal lighter filled every crevice. "What should I do?" she said aloud into the darkness. "Run away three times a day to walk up and down Santa Monica Boulevard till they finish their steaks? Get myself mugged while they eat like horses on my tax money? They should only choke." She hoped the charred meat would work fast on them.

What had *happened* to America, anyway? After seventy-five years of running away from the East Side of New York with all those barbarians, here she was again with *these*. No progress. All that culture she thought was out there in the world, that she had tried to absorb, came to nothing—to this. What did the world care that Anna Goldman lived in two rooms, and in each room she had a piano!

There was a thud against the wall of the closet. She felt she had been hit in the kidneys.

"Wally, I swear—I'll bite off your little finger if you ever do that again!"

Another thud. The gay young men next door. She knew their pattern. A loud yelling fight, full of accusations. Dishes breaking. Furniture sliding around. Then the lengthy reconciliation, with those noises! Worse than cats in heat. Wasn't it embarrassing for them to meet her at the trash bin after they had carried on like that? Howls, gasps, shrieks, moans! "*Oh my God, oh my God, oh my God,*" one of them always screamed a hundred times. They should only do it in a church where God could hear them, Anna thought, and give me some peace. But when she met one or the other of them at the garbage bin, so well-groomed in his pink silk shirt, or his net underwear, he'd always graciously lift the lid for her, toss her garbage into the back, where she couldn't reach, wish her a good day. At least those boys had manners. They were raised in good American families. But she wouldn't go so far as to let them pull her grocery cart up the steps to her apartment. The last thing she needed was AIDS. She had read in the *LA Times* about the bathhouses in San Francisco, the catwalks where men would stand so others could do a specialized activity on them. Well, that was their business. She was modern, live and let live. Not like Gert, out of the dark ages. But did she have to listen to it all day? She had stopped eating out altogether except for the Center because so many of those gay boys worked in the restaurants. They had a knack for cooking. But did she want them laying lettuce on her tuna sandwiches? Not after where those hands had been!

She opened the closet door; the fumes enclosed her and she could almost feel the flames on her skin, crisping it like bacon.

"Bastards," she whispered. In her old age she should come to this, locked in a closet, instead of revered, respected, with her children gathered round. "They have their own lives to live," she corrected herself. They were loving and loyal, her daughters called her every day. She didn't want to live near them, the way Gert urged her to do—live in the suburbs with a church on every corner and listen to the leaf-blowers blast out her eardrums. The expert on high blood pressure at the Center had lectured on how noise raises the blood pressure of rats within two hours. He should only be here today listening to the racket from the Russian's apartment—he would have a stroke in five minutes.

"Enough of the dark," she said. She stepped out of the closet and heard her doorbell shrilling.

"Who is it?" she yelled, standing ten feet back from the door.

"It's only your landlady, darling, it's not a mugger. Open the door, Mrs. Goldman—we have something to talk about here."

Bitch face Anna thought. *I am not in the mood for this now.* She unlocked her three locks and drew the chain back. "I was just going out, Mrs. Blungman. I give a concert today. Can you make it fast?"

"At our age you shouldn't be in such a hurry," she said, "or it could kill you one-two-three." Mrs. Blungman was short and fat, like a matzo ball. Her face was a lump of dough, with a nose plopped on, two eyes gouged out, and cold blue marbles pressed in the holes. Her hair was thin, like white cotton thread pasted on a child's pink rubber ball.

"I have a complaint against you."

"Who made it?" Anna demanded.

"My sources are confidential. By the way, could it be it was you picked a lemon from my lemon tree?"

"Of course not! Why would I take one of your precious lemons?"

"Lemons are very expensive now in the stores."

"For your information, Mrs. Blungman, I could afford to pay a *dollar* for a lemon if I had to."

"So it wasn't you?"

"So I said."

"So, now to the complaint."

"That wasn't the complaint?"

"The complaint is coming, don't worry, it's right here on my tongue."

"Make it fast please. I'm on my way out."

"Alone? You of all people should know how dangerous these streets are. Where's your head after being held up at gunpoint in your store! You take big risks, Mrs. Goldman."

"When I'm in the tomb I won't take risks," Anna said.

"You don't sweep your patio," said Mrs. Blungman.

"I don't sweep my patio? You send spies up to my patio? It's two feet by two feet—I never go out there. No one can see it. The sun never shines there. It stinks from the Armenians' barbecue. I pay rent for my privacy. My patio is my kingdom just like my bathroom."

"So—since you raised the subject yourself, I wasn't going to discuss that today—I would like to know how come there are scratches in your toilet bowl? You clean it with Brillo? We don't allow that."

Anna felt her blood bubble up through her veins.

"You go snooping in my toilet? That's illegal. I could sue you."

"It's legal, darling, for a landlord to have a key to every apartment, in case of fire, to paint, to fix the air conditioner."

"You haven't painted in five years. The air conditioner has been broken since I moved in . . ."

Mrs. Blungman cut her off. "And we could evict you, Mrs. Goldman, if you don't keep your windows open from now on. Because for some crazy reason you keep them all locked up when you go out, and that causes termites in the building."

"*That's ridiculous! That's insane! You're the one who's crazy! Termites if I close my windows!*" Anna began to close the door. Mrs. Blungman stopped her with a heavy hand.

"I didn't get to the main complaint yet, darling."

"Your time is up. I have to go somewhere."

"They don't like your piano playing in the next building."

"Who says so?"

"I got sources. Not every apartment would allow two pianos for one tenant. You have twenty fingers?"

"I told you—one is from the antique store. When I had to give it up, I took the piano from the store here. But I only play one piano at a time. And with the soft pedal, always."

"The people in the next building don't like what you play."

"*What?* You want me to submit a program to them for approval?"

"You play too gloomy. If they have to listen they would like a few show tunes, a patriotic march, something from Barbra Streisand. Not what you give them."

"Mozart you can't give them," Anna said. "Of this I am aware."

"You live on a high horse, Mrs. Goldman. Relax a little, enjoy."

"As long as I sweep my patio and clean my toilet."

"You got it, darling."

Anna walked toward the Senior Citizens' Center. The streets swarmed with foreigners. She could be anywhere—Korea, Israel, Mexico, China. English was no longer the main language of this country. Even on Fairfax Avenue, Yiddish was getting buried. She would go into a bakery, and the women working there were wearing babushkas and jabbering in Russian. She would go to the doctor's office, and the technicians told jokes in Spanish. On top of this, the respectful separation of the sexes was gone—to have a cardiogram she had to submit to a black man snapping his fingers as he plopped rubber suction cups around the edges of her breasts. Her poor misled father, with his dreams of coming to America where the streets were paved with gold. Where anyone could become president (but not a Jew, he realized before he died young). He worked so hard, sewing all day in the factories, bringing home piecework at night. But here the foreigners came with jewelry hidden in their underwear, took their doles from the government, and broiled steaks on their barbecues while Anna choked. The foreigners thought life was a big joke—they were always laughing on the streets. Israeli men wearing gold chains in layers around their hairy necks pushed their dark-eyed, round-nosed babies up and down the streets in fancy strollers. In the city college where Anna took classes, the students with their slanty eyes or their gold-toned skin or their peasant faces all seemed slack, tired, indifferent. Their grades were barely C's.

None of them were like the immigrants she was descended from. *They* had worked like demons, learning the language, learning the ways of the new world. These people came and had it handed to them. They came to America poor, but they wouldn't work hard. They wouldn't learn English.

A few years ago when Anna had had her surgery, the Filipino nurses in the hospital had joked in their jabbering tongue, right over her head as if she were nothing more than a tree trunk in the bed, completely ignored her as they wired her into the transfusion machinery; they gossiped nonstop, joked—didn't have the proper respect for their work, for life and death, and for patients who were fighting for one over the other. They thought it was just a big party over here, that's all.

Anna didn't care, as Gert did, about morals, wasn't horrified by the prostitutes strutting up and down Hollywood Boulevard, or by the gay men screaming *oh my God* at their heights of passion. Sex was one thing. She could live with it if she had to, as long as no one was seducing her. But laziness, pure greed and laziness, that was something else.

"Where you been keeping yourself all my life, Sweet Lips?"

"I have no patience for you today, Bernie," Anna said, taking her tray, and moving along the lunch line. She only came to the Center because if she ate a real meal at lunchtime (and who could deny that seventy-five cents was a good price?) she wouldn't have to worry about cooking anything for her dinner. She weighed just under a hundred pounds—a fact which was both a source of pride and worry. If she should catch the flu, and not be able to eat for a week, she had no margin to depend on, she would turn into a skeleton. But compared to the matzo-ball ladies all over the place, she had the edge—a certain grace, a swing of her skirt. Bernie wasn't the only one after her. She could see herself in the mirror behind the cafeteria workers—her white hair perfectly short, clipped in a clean, even line. Not a single curl, a pompadour, a frizz; not a bleached mop, not a wig, not a movie-star's head of hair on the face of a crone. Integrity was what she stood for. She was a lost soul, one of a kind, and no one cared about what she stood for.

"White meat of the chicken, please," Anna said.

"Take what's on the plate or leave it, darling," the woman said. "You don't get special privileges."

"Listen, you *know* me," Anna said. "I volunteer my time at this Center just like you, I play a concert here every week. Today in fact."

The woman shoved the plate at her. Diamonds sparkled on her fingers. "A leg and a wing, darling—that's what's on this plate. Take it or leave it."

Bitch face Anna thought. Give them a little authority and they become like prison wardens. Mrs. Blungmans were everywhere. Sadistic. Vicious. The human race was too far gone. This woman was one of the worst, with her airs and her Zsa-Zsa accent.

Bernie sat next to her. His hands shook as he spread his napkin across his stained gray pants-legs. "My offer is still good, Angel Face," he said, beginning to lift a forkful of peas to his mouth. By the time he got the fork halfway up, most of the peas had spilled off. Anna brushed a pea angrily from her skirt.

"We'll take a cruise to Europe, just you and me, first-class, we'll dance the night away, Emerald Eyes."

She'd been through this before. She'd had a vision of herself in the middle of the ocean, with his corpse on the bed and the band playing "God Bless America" in the grand ballroom. ("A millionaire wants to marry me," Anna had told her daughters. "He has no children—you girls could be rich." "Don't sell your soul for us," the girls had advised her. "Don't worry," Anna had replied. "I wouldn't dream of it.")

The creamed corn was like glue. The chicken leg had a bone showing through, jagged, with black blood clotted in its marrow. Anna reached for her milk carton; her thumbs pressed the edges back and pain shot into both her elbows. She clamped her teeth and waited for it to pass. She didn't need reminders from her nerve endings of what was going on inside her.

"You're doing the wrong end," Bernie said, grease on his chin. "Here, I'll do it for you, Sweet Lips."

She pushed the carton toward him. Bernie couldn't open the milk container either. He was struggling intently, his tongue showing, breathing loudly, pulling at the cardboard with his gnarled fingers. Anna felt her mouth turn down, and tears, like burning acid rising too high from her empty stomach, seared her eyes.

She stood up. Her lunch lay congealing on the paper plate. She touched Bernie on the shoulder, gently.

He didn't turn his head to look up at her; he had arthritis of the neck bones. "I'll be down at the rec room at your concert, Gorgeous," he said. "I'll be there in ten minutes, front row, center. You'll know me by the red rose in my lapel."

In the bathroom Anna combed her hair and saw in the mirror her father's dream—the girl with long sugar-water curls, the girl raised up in the land of opportunity who could play so beautifully the piano he had worked for years to buy her. He wouldn't know her now if he saw her. The skin of her face was an accordion of the days of her life, folded one upon the other. This was what was left of her. What counted was inside, invisible.

Carrying her music, swinging her skirt, she went down the long empty hall to the rec room. The piano keys had only half their ivories. The keyboard welcomed her with its toothless grin.

She knew what they liked, her ten or twelve regulars and the four or five other poor souls who wandered into the rec room, passing time till the free blood pressure test or the cholesterol lecture. They liked "Fiddler on the Roof," "The Entertainer," "Roll Out the Barrel." She knew: *Mozart you can't give them*—but this was her show. It might do them some good. She opened her music book and warmed up her fingers.

Comes an Earthquake

Anna—who never once played a card game in her adult life—leaned back in one of the red metal chairs furnished for the guests of the Colby Plaza and watched her sister Ava hunched over her cards. Anna had been in Miami Beach five days already and was still at a loss to understand Ava and her friends. Furred in mink stoles and intent on their hands, they expertly slid new cards into their fans, closing and opening them like magic. What Anna couldn't understand was how these old ladies—women who'd lived through the Depression, who'd lost sons in the war (Ava's son went down over New Guinea and her youngest boy was peppered with shrapnel in France), women who'd lost a husband or two—could just sit on their behinds eight hours a day on a porch in Miami Beach and play poker!

"I'm wondering . . ." Anna said, "how is it that no one around here ever walks to the beach, only a block away? Where I live, in Los Angeles, you could give your right arm for a breath of air like this."

"So why not move here?" asked one of the ladies. No one raised her head from over her cards; Anna wasn't sure if the voice belonged to Ida (whose husband, Herman, was upstairs with Alzheimer's) or Sadie (emphysema—she smoked four packs a day) or Ava's best friend, Mickey (her husband had had a fatal heart attack when he tripped on two gay boys, naked on the beach at night, a year ago).

"Why should anyone move to a morgue?"

A man's voice. At first Anna thought it came from Collins Avenue, from the sidewalk five feet in front of her chair where a trickle of old folks passed by in the deepening dusk. The women, dragged down by their diamonds and mink, promenaded, as if along a hospital corridor, on the arms of old men wearing jackets and bow ties. Anna glanced along the row of metal chairs till she made out what looked like a dark balloon floating against the pink stucco of the hotel wall. She tried to focus her eyes. Glaucoma was working its way through her retina; one of these days the sights of the world would go black on her. (Amazing, how this morning, Ava, needing to sew a button on her housecoat, threaded the needle in just one pass; eyes like an eagle and she was ninety to Anna's seventy-eight.)

"Irving bubbie, light of my life, go back upstairs or go across to the Crown and see the show but do us a favor and shut up," said Sadie.

"Aah, they die like flies here," Irving said. "What's the point? Tell me," he leaned forward and addressed Anna. "What is the point of it all?"

Anna squinted, trying to see him better. She made out a pair of white suede loafers with red rubber soles, some skinny knees.

"There *is* no point," Anna said in his direction. "You're right—it's all a big nothing."

"Look around you," he said. "We all come to the last stop like lemmings running to the ocean. We run to Miami Beach and play cards with our last breaths. We're dying and playing cards at the edge of the cliff till we get shoved off."

"You're a sick man?" Anna asked.

"I have AIDS," he said.

"AIDS?" Anna said, shocked. She shut her mouth tightly. He didn't look like the type, but you could never tell. A snort came from Ava at the card table.

"Tell her, Irving, what kind of AIDS you have."

"You want to know?" He addressed Anna.

"Don't feel you have to talk about it," she said, trying to breathe very shallowly.

"I'm happy to tell you. I'm able to talk very freely about this." He paused. "I got hearing aids!"

It took a moment for Anna to digest this information. Then she felt taken. She wished fervently she were home in her dark apartment in Los Angeles where the Armenians next door choked her with their barbecue fumes. She had come on this trip to Florida to see Ava one last time before one of them died. Sisters were sisters, after all, and how much time was there? Ava already had a pacemaker and an artificial heart valve. Anna, thank God, had only the usual: arthritis, glaucoma, osteoporosis, high blood pressure, nothing serious.

Irving said, "If you don't laugh, you'll cry, take your pick."

"Serious things like AIDS you shouldn't joke about," Anna insisted. "Have some respect."

"For what? I should take the world seriously? Why should I? What's the world ever given me that's any good except maybe my children?"

"And then even they don't visit," Anna remarked strictly for his benefit only, since her daughters, when she was home in LA, called her every day.

"Not *my* children. My daughter is married to a millionaire," Irving corrected Anna. "She sends a limousine for me every Sunday, I go to eat Chinese, Italian, whatever I want, cost is no object."

Ava called over from the card table, "Tell the truth, Irving. Tell my sister you eat with the chauffeur, not with your daughter. When does *she* come? The last time was when you fell out of the elevator and broke your elbow."

"Never mind. The chauffeur is like a son to me," Irving called back. "Better than a son. Don't lose your concentration, Ava—those cardsharps over there will cheat you blind if they get one chance."

"I'm ahead four dollars, already, Irving," Ava informed him, ". . . and the night is young." Each time, she pronounced his name "Oiving," and Anna winced. The Bronx still lived in full color in Ava—nothing could winnow it out. The Bronx sat on Ava's tongue like a wart. Anna herself was certain she had no trace of any crude accent. She tried to speak like an American descended from someone who came over on the Mayflower.

"Listen to this one," Irving said. "Two old men are playing golf, but their eyes are so bad they can't see where the ball lands. A third *alta cocka* comes by and says he has perfect eyesight, he'll help them out. He'll watch the ball for them. So one of them hits the ball and then asks, 'So did you see where it landed?' The *alta cocka* says, 'Of course I saw, I got perfect eyesight.' 'So where is it?' the golfer says. 'I forgot,' says the old man."

"An Alzheimer joke! For shame!" Sadie said. "With Ida sitting right here and poor Herman upstairs, putting on his socks backwards this minute."

Irving's attention was drawn away as a fire truck and an ambulance raced by, their sirens screaming. "What's your hurry?" Irving asked, waving his hand at them in dismissal.

Anna's eyes had adjusted to the darkness, and she watched Irving's bald head wobbling on his turkey neck. His ears were huge; they hung on his skull like some strange invention. Certain animals, when she saw them on nature programs, made her feel this way. They adapted to their environment without regard for polite shapes. She didn't want to have to look at their hanging pouches or spiky chins or poison sacs. Old people, too, grew strange parts, took on camouflaging skin pigments, adopted peculiar postures and gaits. Anna hated belonging to an indelicate species.

"Another cowboy bites the dust," Irving said as the taillights of the ambulance disappeared. "Who knows who'll be next?"

"Comes an earthquake we'll all be gone," Anna pronounced.

"Here we have hurricanes," Irving told her. "At least get your catastrophes straight."

"A flush!" Ava said with a cry of glee, laying down her cards. She swept the pile of coins in the kitty toward her.

"Believe me, you can't take it with you," Irving predicted. "Slow down, Ava, enjoy the sights."

"I'm done, anyway . . . it's time for us to go up," Ava said. "*Wheel of Fortune* is on in five minutes." The four ladies pushed back their chairs and stood up. Ava tapped the cards into a neat little square and set the deck down on the table. She gathered up her big pile of quarters and dropped them in the jacket of her flowered pantsuit. She adjusted her mink.

"You ladies live by the game shows," Irving said. "But look, right here, isn't life the biggest game show of all?"

"You're giving away trips to Hawaii?" Sadie asked him. "If you're giving away free cruises, we'll stay and watch you."

"I told you before, Sadie—you want a cruise, I'll take you on a cruise."

"When I'm that desperate, I'll let you know."

"I'm going upstairs now, Anna," Ava said. "Come with me.

"Maybe I'll stay here a while. I could do without the *Wheel of Fortune*," Anna said.

Ava shot her a look, the same kind of look she'd sent her when Anna had been flower girl at Ava's wedding in 1914 and stepped on her train, causing Ava to stumble. "Come up," Ava demanded. "Irving sits here all night. Irving is always here. You'll see him when we come down again from nine to ten to watch the sideshow going by," Ava assured her.

"Your sister thinks this is the army, she lives by a schedule," Irving mumbled into the dark. Anna had noticed this was true: Ava woke at eight, ate toast dipped in coffee poured into her saucer, watched the *$25,000 Pyramid*, watched *Cardsharks*, watched the daytime *Wheel of Fortune*, came down for poker till Meals on Wheels arrived, ate lunch from Styrofoam boxes with the other ladies on the porch (a drumstick, yellow wax beans, a slice of white bread, a cup of bouillon soup and some Jell-O). After lunch, a nap, then an *I Love Lucy* rerun, then down to the porch for card playing till dinnertime, then up for dinner, then down again for cards, then up again for TV, then down again for one last blast of bus fumes on the porch. On certain days there were doctor appointments, and once a week the trip in Hyman Cohen's hotel station wagon to the Food Circus.

As Anna walked by Irving's big feet to follow Ava into the lobby, he reached out for her hand. He had the nerve to grab it and squeeze it for a couple of seconds before he let it go. She looked down into his blue eyes and saw him smiling up at her. "Laugh a little, sweetheart," he said. "There's no good jokes six feet under."

A strange sensation woke Anna; the room glowed blue with particles of light reflected from the shimmering signs of the Crown and the Cadillac. No air came in the lowered windows. Ava never ran the air conditioner: she said it was too noisy, but Anna knew it was the expense. Ava had always been a miser. When they had talked long distance, arranging the visit, Ava had promised Anna a room of her own "right across the hall from mine, one with its own TV," but when Anna had arrived at the Colby Plaza, the first thing Ava said was, "I got a cot in my room for you so you wouldn't have to be all alone. It worried me, you should be all alone in a strange place."

The cot is cheaper, Anna thought, but then was sorry to think badly of her sister who was soon, no doubt, to depart this vale of tears. Ava lay only a foot away breathing noisily through her open mouth. The segments of her false teeth shone like some plastic toy. The room made Anna feel claustrophobic: two beds, a stove, a sink, a refrigerator, a dining table, a dresser, a TV, a recliner chair. All Ava's worldly goods were here; from her huge, human life—a husband, children, big decisions to make—to this: *Wheel of Fortune*, Meals on Wheels, poker, little tiny portions of milk frozen in margarine containers to last the week. (Anna already lived this way in LA; it wasn't news to her but to see that her powerful sister had come to this was a shock.)

She tried to go back to sleep. She kept remembering how Irving had grabbed her hand. An old turkey. A no one. Still, his fingers had felt alive. There was heat and strength in them. She had felt something, a feeling. This was astonishing, to feel something and to think about it. To bother to think about something and to feel pleasure from it.

Anna tiptoed out of bed, put on her clothes, and went down in the old elevator to the lobby. The light of dawn was just arriving through the windows; the desk clerk, a Cuban named Jesús who always wore a dirty black suit, was sleeping on one of the old couches. Anna didn't know what to do with herself. The cards from last night, she saw, were still on the table outside. She could play solitaire. She could actually walk to the ocean and watch the sunrise.

Would it be dangerous? To go alone to the beach? Did they have muggers in Miami Beach? Never mind muggers, she would go anyway. At her age forget everything. Doom was just as likely hiding in her arteries as on the sand.

Irving was still outside on the front porch, sleeping in his chair, his head back against the stucco wall. Had he really been there all night? Anna stared. She thought she could see dew condensed on his bald head. His white shoes glowed in the dimness. Maybe he was dead. She went over to him and tapped on his skull. He jerked upright.

"Dummy," she said with relief. "You don't have a bed?"

"I wasn't sleeping," he said, straightening his eye glasses. "Just taking the air."

"Who cares?" Anna said. "I'm going beachcombing."

"I'll come with you."

"I'm going alone," Anna said. "I need an adventure. When did I ever see the sunrise? In California, you only get sunsets. And at the end of the day, who's going to run to the beach?"

"Here no one runs, we all walk," Irving explained, as he creaked himself out of the chair. He offered Anna his arm. "But allow me to come along and be your bodyguard."

They saw it happen, a fuzz of pink over the blue horizon, a blur of white cloud, and then the emerging burning ball, coming up on a fountain of flame.

"That alone," Irving said, standing against the rail of the narrow boardwalk while seagulls screeched and wheeled overhead, ". . . and you could believe in God."

"You believe?" Anna asked.

"What am I, some kind of sucker?"

"Smart people, really smart people—some of them are believers."

"I'll take my medicine straight," Irving said. "I'll face the firing squad without a blindfold."

"It would be nice to believe something," Anna said. "Then you could have reasons, you could have meaning, you could have a social center, you could have someone to say a prayer when you're dead. This way, like for my husband Abram, I had to hire a stranger, a baby calling himself a rabbi, he reads from a printed sheet 'This was a good man, a good husband, a good father.' A know-nothing."

"If I were going to believe, I'd choose Jesus," Irving said. "He's the best deal around. But no one in Miami Beach, Florida, in the Jew-nited States of America, thinks he's worth two cents."

"They prefer Moses?"

"He can't hold a candle. All he did was talk to God in the burning bush. The trouble is, when you're this old, you should have something to hang on to."

"How old?"

"Ninety-two," Irving said. "Come June."

"My husband died at fifty-five," Anna said. "You had a whole lifetime extra over him."

"It's never enough," Irving said. "It doesn't feel like I even started yet."

They began to walk along the wooden boardwalk. Two seagulls lit on the railing and walked right up to them. They stared boldly, craning their beaks forward.

"They want something," Anna said.

"So who doesn't?" Irving answered. The sun was well out of the ocean now, getting redder.

"Look," Anna said. "Is that beautiful or is that beautiful?"

"You're what's beautiful," Irving said.

"Don't get carried away, Irving," Anna said. "My week is up. I'm going home tomorrow, and anyway I'm not available."

"My mistake. The first day I saw you on the porch we should have got acquainted. I should have talked to you sooner. You got a boyfriend?"

"My heart belongs to Arthur Rubinstein," Anna said.

"He's younger than me? Richer?"

"Never mind," Anna said. "It's not going anywhere with Arthur and me."

"Even at our age we have a right to pleasure," Irving said.

"Don't lump yourself together with me," Anna said. "You're old enough to be my father. Look how you can hardly walk and I'm limber on my toes like a ballet dancer."

"It's these rubber soles," he explained. "New shoes. They glue me down. It's like wearing suction cups."

"You want to go on the sand?" Anna asked. "You want to stick your toes in the water?"

"In my heart, I'm running down to the waves already," Irving said, stopping to lean on the rail, breathing hard. "I'm splashing you with water. I'm ducking you under."

"And I'm jumping over waves," Anna said, looking out at the blue wide ocean.

"I'm tickling you," Irving said.

"I'm laughing," Anna said. She turned her head away from him.

"So how come you're crying?" Irving asked after a minute.

"Because it's a pity," Anna said, wiping her eyes with a tissue. "What we used to have, and what we can't have anymore."

"At least let's take what we can get," Irving said. He held out his hand. Anna studied it. Then she crooked her fingers in his. He brought their hands up to his mouth and kissed Anna's fingers. "I'm doing more than this with you," he said. "Much more. You understand what I mean?"

"Don't have a dirty mind," Anna said.

"I'm doing everything," Irving said. "Every sweet thing. We're in heaven."

Anna was silent.

"I'm going too far?" Irving asked.

"No," Anna said. "I appreciate it."

The next afternoon, the last of her visit, when the Red Top Cab had been called and was to pick her up in one hour for the trip to the airport, Anna put on her new silky flowered dress and got everything else into her suitcase. Ava was already down on the front porch playing cards. Anna realized that if she stayed here for a year, the sister business wouldn't improve. Ava wasn't going to get sentimental. A big bossy sister stays a big bossy sister. To cheer herself up, she sprayed herself five times with Ava's expensive perfume, and by the time she rode down in the elevator with her suitcase she smelled like a lilac tree. She would be lucky if in two minutes there weren't bees landing all over her head.

Irving was spiffy in a plaid jacket and a red bow tie.

He saluted her from his chair. "Forgive me if even on this farewell occasion I don't stand up," he said. "One knee isn't so good today."

"Stand up anyway, Irving," Ava called over to him. "Use it or you'll lose it."

"He lost it already," Sadie said, with a hoarse laugh. "Otherwise I'd go with him on a cruise."

"I didn't lose it, sweetheart," he said, getting red in the face. "I just don't give it away to big-mouth yentas." He turned to Anna. "You're lucky you're getting out of here. If I could go with you, I'd run in a minute."

"So where am I going that's so special?" Anna said, suddenly seeing a picture in her mind of her tiny dark apartment, of her pianos, two of them, with the lids down over the keys, of the milk going sour in the refrigerator.

"Maybe you could get a room here," Irving suggested. "You know," he called over to the ladies at the card table, "I don't think Hyman rented the room yet from after when Sam Kriskin died."

"No thank you," Anna said. "I'm not interested in living in a dead man's room."

"He didn't die in the room," Irving assured her. "Only on the way in the ambulance. Not a single bad thing happened in the room. Kriskin was an immaculate person. That man was as clean as holy water."

"What's the rent?" Anna said. It was a question she didn't expect to ask. It was meaningless, it was to make talk. It was stupid to have brought it up, what did she care? In LA she had a very good rent-controlled apartment, and, besides, she would never leave her daughters, what for? To come here and sit with some old man?

But Irving's blue eyes shone like electrified marbles, and he was already getting up slowly from the red metal chair. "We'll go in the lobby, Anna," he said. "We'll find out the rent, maybe you'll stay, then what a time we'll have, you and I—we'll go across to the Crown every night and watch the floor show, we'll go out to dinner on Sundays with my daughter's chauffeur, we'll buy a VCR and rent a movie . . ."

Irving started to walk without his feet. Anna saw his upper body move toward her, but his shoes, his white shoes with the red rubber soles, stayed glued to the cement and she saw him go down like a boulder.

When she opened her eyes the next instant, he was face down on the cement porch and no one even noticed it. Ava was dealing a new hand of cards.

Irving, rolling on his round belly, was silent. He turned his head slightly to the side, and Anna saw his cracked eye glasses and blood on his forehead.

"Oh God," she cried out. "Look over here!"

Irving whimpered a little and stayed on his face.

"Oh—help me pick him up, *please!*" Anna cried. She could not bend down alone because of her osteoporosis and her arthritis and her collapsed vertebrae.

"We don't pick anyone up here," Sadie said from the table. "We each got our own problems. In no time flat we could all land in the hospital."

"They fall here every day," Ida added.

"How many times has Irving fallen anyway?" Mickey asked, and all the women looked skyward, as if they were figuring.

Anna couldn't bear it, to see him gasping and jerking like a beached fish down there, his forehead on cement. She rushed into the lobby and grabbed a cushion from one of the sagging couches. She carried it outside and slid it under Irving's forehead.

"Don't move him," Ava said. "Something could be broken."

"The last time nothing was broken," Ida said.

"But the time before, remember, it was his elbow."

"This was a softer fall than that one. That time, he stepped out the elevator before it was level. Everyone heard him go down."

Anna ran inside again and yelled to the Cuban clerk. "Jesús! Call the doctor, dummy!" He seemed to be counting out colored postcards of the Colby Plaza. He was counting in Spanish.

Outside again, Anna knelt over Irving. "Irving, can you hear me?" He rocked on his round stomach to answer her. "Are you okay, Irving?" she asked him. "Are you comfortable?"

"I make a nice living," he said.

Anna looked at him, then stood up, shocked.

"A joke," he said. Then he spit out a little blood.

"Jesús!" she yelled into the lobby "Did you call?" The man looked up from the desk, puzzled. It occurred to Anna that he was drunk.

"Hey," he said suddenly. "That old guy can't be on that pillow." He ran out to the porch and grabbed the cushion from under Irving's forehead. "If he bleeds on this, Hyman Cohen will blow a fit! These are his new pillows!"

"Ten years new," Ava called over to them.

"Jesús! Come here!" She called him like a dog, slapping her leg. "Help me pick him up this minute!"

"There's no hurry," the Cuban said. "They'll pick him up when they come."

"Who?"

"The paramedics."

"Did you call them?"

"They have a standing appointment here," Sadie said from the card table as she lit another cigarette.

"Go," Anna said, shoving the Cuban. "Call them!" She watched him till he went in and picked up the phone.

While they waited, Anna sat down on the steps of the Colby Plaza and maneuvered Irving's face, still pointing down, into her lap. She stroked the few hairs on the back of his bald head.

"Don't worry, Irving darling," she whispered. "You'll be fine, this is just a little nothing. We all have days like this. I myself fell in a hole in a parking lot a year ago. I still have a bone spur on my foot from it."

Irving was crying.

"It hurts you somewhere? It hurts a lot?"

He nodded his head. His weight in her lap felt like the weight of one of her babies. She thought the feeling of taking care had disappeared forever, and now here it was again.

"Here they come," Ava announced.

A shuddering vibration shook the street, and a fire truck pulled up at the curb. Four firemen jumped off; they were wearing black rubber trousers with yellow suspenders.

"Aah, it's you again, isn't it?" one of them said to Irving. Irving was sobbing without restraint now. She could feel his hot tears seep through her dress. She found his hand and squeezed it. He held on very tight.

"Don't worry, Irving dear," she whispered into his ear. "It's only this life-and-death business we're having here. Don't take it seriously."

The firemen were turning him over, opening a big black box, taking out rubber tubes, gauze, fancy machines. If the firemen were being the doctors, then were the doctors running up and down ladders putting out fires?

The paramedics clumped around in their huge rubber boots. "Anything hurt?" they kept asking Irving. "Where does it hurt?"

"He's fine," Ava called from the card table. "The man is made of steel. I warned him, never wear shoes with rubber soles. And I told him, always get up slow, get your balance first. But no, a big shot, he was in a hurry to impress my sister."

Anna shot her a look, like the look Ava had shot Anna in 1914.

"Here comes the ambulance," one of the firemen said. "Are you going to the hospital with him?" He was addressing Anna.

"Yes," Anna said, and at the same instant Ava called out, "No, of course she isn't going. Let his daughter go."

"My daughter never comes," Irving cried, crushing Anna's hand now that he was sitting up, propped by the firemen.

"I'll come with you," Anna said. "Don't worry,"

"Don't be a fool," Ava said. She was finally talking directly to Anna, paying her the attention that she hadn't given in the whole visit, pulling her up by the arm. "You'll have to wait there seven hours. That's how long they make you wait in Emergency. It's stacked to the ceiling with old people who fell down."

"I have time," Anna said.

"No you don't," Ava said. "The cab is here,"

Anna had forgotten entirely. The Red Top. The airport. The plane. LA. Her pianos with the shrouded keys.

"Take her suitcase," Ava instructed the driver who had come up onto the porch and was staring, open-mouthed, at Irving. Ava pushed Anna toward the steps. Her mink's head, slithering on her shoulder, showed its tiny razor-sharp teeth.

"Take her to the airport," Ava instructed the cab driver. "And you . . ." she said to the ambulance driver, "you get going and take *him* to the hospital."

Irving reached out to Anna, and Anna reached for Irving. But the forces were too strong, the time was too late. They were too powerless. Two minutes later they were rushing in opposite directions—she could feel the wind tearing them apart, the seagulls were going every which way over the ocean—and Anna couldn't tell if the sirens she heard were approaching or receding.

Starry Night

LOOKING OUT THE WINDOW of the bus, Anna could see a pandemonium of gold and glitter—the whole world rushing around crazily, buying presents. On Wilshire Boulevard, people were stabbing each other with the sharp edges of their packages. Christmas season was a mean season—fat Santa Clauses ringing their bells in everyone's faces, carols blasting out of loudspeakers, "Let-Us-Adore-Him" and "Christ-the-Lord" in every song. Christmas was a terrible imposition on the Jews. Anna, who had no use for rituals, had made it a special point all her life to ignore Christmas. She left the radio off, didn't venture out, read only the newspaper's front page, which had no ads. Long ago she had told her children, "No presents for me. All I want from you is that you should be happy." Her youngest daughter was a suicide's widow and had health problems; her oldest girl had money troubles. The truth was she should have allowed them to give her store-bought presents. With her fancy rules, they could give her nothing.

Now, two days away from Christmas, she was on her way to the doctor's. All the old people on the bus seemed lame or asthmatic; they were probably all going to the doctor's, and, like her, they were going alone. What could she expect from a world in which a woman of seventy-eight had to take three buses by herself to visit a doctor? At least, in the old days, doctors had made house calls.

An old man was making his way up the aisle, stopping beside each seat. He swayed beside Anna as if he might land in her lap. He was unshaven and wearing a tattered coat. Thrusting his fist under Anna's nose, he offered her a choice of red-striped candy canes. She turned her head sharply, dismissing him. He had probably put cyanide in them. He bent closer, shaking the cellophane bouquet beside her ear until she locked eyes with him and willed him away.

Well, soon she would be done with Christmases and all the rest of it. How long? She couldn't guess. The years no longer had any definition—one year was like the snap of a finger, no time at all, a mere one seventy-eighth of her life, almost too small a space to count. When she had first learned to play the piano, at seven, a year had been one seventh of her life. To get from her dull Hanon exercises to her first Chopin nocturne had been an eternity of scales, chords, harmony exercises; endless afternoons of winding her metronome and letting its upright brass ticker measure out the practice hours, the beats, the notes that carried her like tiny black birds, away from the raucous life on the lower east side of New York, and later from the wastes of Brooklyn.

Now Anna had trouble with her eyes: the birds waiting on the staff, as if poised on telephone wires, were bunched erratically, blurred together, bumping one another as they waited for her signal. She had trouble with her fingers, too: when the birds began to fly they became lost in black, dense clouds, their delicate shapes concealed, their formations blotted. Her trills, once absolute bells of clarity, sounded now like the rumble of the "el" thundering by when she was a little girl.

A tremendous blast caused Anna to jump halfway out of her seat. A black boy carrying a radio as big as a house had just turned up the volume, and "Silent Night" was coming at her like the open palm of her father's hand. Automatically she pressed her lips together and held her breath. Her father was dead sixty years and he could still do this to her! Though he had been out of Poland eight years when she entered the public schools of New York, he had stubbornly forbidden her to sing Christmas carols with the other children. She was allowed only to move her lips during the school's Christmas performances on such phrases as "round yon virgin" and "holy infant." He had instructed her, fiercely, with his hand held up and ready to smack, to weld her lips shut, to be certain that not a flicker of her breath passed through her vocal cords when the forbidden phrase "Christ the Lord" came up. He had been like a madman on the subject, though in most other ways he was a kind and reasonable man.

Anna noticed suddenly that all the old people on the bus were now sucking on red candy canes. They looked like a gathering of lunatics. All of them on their way to their doctors, or to nowhere. Being alive was such a commotion and took so much effort. Why shouldn't they suck on something sweet? What better was there to do?

"So I have a joke for you, Mrs. Goldman," said Dr. Rifkin, her eye doctor, as soon as he walked into the examining room. Silver tinsel hung from the rubber plant against the wall, and the doctor had a little red-and-green Christmas wreath pinned to his white coat. "Four *Yiddishe* mamas get together to play cards." He motioned Anna into the chair where he would tell her how fast she was going blind. He was tall, homely, and overweight. If her daughters had married doctors, they wouldn't be having health problems and money problems.

"The first lady says, '*Oy.*' The second one says, '*Oy vey.*' The third one says, '*Oy vey is mir.*' The fourth one says, "*Ladies, ladies! We promised we wouldn't talk about our children!*' "

Dr. Rifkin laughed loudly at his joke and motioned for Anna to put her chin in the cup. Anna flinched at his deep laughter. She wasn't in that class of women, she resented being thought of as a *Yiddishe* mama and she never played cards.

"So how is life treating you, Mrs. Goldman?" the doctor asked, turning wheels on his machine.

"I don't see well and my fingers don't move where I want them to when I play my Mozart sonatas," she said pointedly.

"Then you're extra lucky to be Jewish. You know why?" he asked, holding the eye dropper right over her head. "You can always play on the keys with your nose!"

Anna frowned, letting the numbing drops freeze the surface of her eyes. He darkened the room, and a burning blue light materialized in front of Anna's face. She stared into the heart of it, feeling it burn into her mind. The doctor's head loomed an inch away. Not since Abram's death, except for these visits to Dr. Rifkin, had she felt a man's breath or heard his heavy breathing. When the measurements were taken and the lights turned on—with the doctor again a safe distance away—she steadied herself. It was her opportunity to introduce a new subject.

"Doctor—how often do you think my daughters should have their eyes examined now that I have this condition?" Anna could never ask doctors enough questions, and they never gave her satisfactory answers.

"Oh—once every year or so."

"Not more often?"

"If they want to go more often—sure."

"Shouldn't they go every six months, so if this same problem turns up due to bad heredity, they won't go blind?"

"Mrs. Goldman," said Dr. Rifkin, "what's the difference between a Jewish mother and a vulture?"

"I have no idea," Anna said coldly.

"A vulture only eats hearts after they're dead. A Jewish mother eats her heart out all her life."

The Christmas tree in the waiting room was broken out in an epidemic of angels; around its fake moss base, empty gift-wrapped boxes were piled. A curly-haired little boy of about four shook each box and then sadly set it down. Anna sat across the room from his parents with her heart pounding. She was to have laser surgery in half an hour. "Your intraocular pressure is way up," Dr. Rifkin had told her. "Not much point in depending on the drops any longer. I'd usually schedule you for another day, but I'm going away for a couple of weeks and we should nip this in the bud. If you can wait till I'm done with my next patient, I'll tell Sally to get things ready, and we'll get this over with. It doesn't hurt, it doesn't take long, you shouldn't have much pain afterward, just a little irritation."

"How do you do it?" Anna had asked. "I've heard it's done without knives, without anesthesia."

"You want me to tell you everything I learned in medical school in two minutes?"

"I just want to know something about what to expect."

"It's magic," said Dr. Rifkin, patting her rudely on the arm. "Don't worry about it. Don't you think I know my stuff?"

The receptionist had asked Anna to sign a release, so if she died it was no one's fault. The procedure was going to cost a thousand dollars. No wonder the doctor could tell jokes all day. She hoped Medicare would pay some of it. In a few minutes she would be taking part in a magic trick. A vulture would be pulled from her heart, pluck out her eyes, and replace in their sockets two cold blue marbles. A man in a black cape would saw her body in half.

"Do you have a candy cane for me?" the little boy said, coming to Anna and putting his hand on her knee.

"Donny, come back here and don't bother the lady. Not everyone gives out candy canes."

"It's okay," Anna said, regretting her suspicions on the bus. "I have grandchildren. I wish I had a candy cane to give him. He's a sweet boy." Anna wondered what was wrong with him; glued in the middle of his forehead, like a great eye, was a silver snap. The boy touched it.

"Don't wrinkle the lady's skirt. Behave yourself," the boy's mother said. His father added, "Don't touch your electrode." The parents were young, and looked terrified. She knew they weren't from Beverly Hills. Anna didn't dare ask them what she wanted to know. *Is your boy going blind? Does he have a brain tumor? Something worse?* The boy had climbed on the couch beside Anna and wiggled his bottom against the backrest. His hand on her thigh was warm through her skirt. The boy's mother, sitting across the room with the father, said apologetically, "He probably thinks you're going to read to him. His grandmother always reads to him. You look a little like her . . . my mother."

Anna felt the boy's warmth all down her side. His head brushed against her arm. She could smell his talcum powder, which reminded her of her own sweet babies, of that vanished other life. "I have nothing to read to him, but I can draw him a picture."

"Oh, he'd love that. Donny, come here and give the nice lady your colored pencils. She'll draw a picture for you."

The boy scrambled off the couch and ran across the room for the little flat box of pencils and a pad of paper. "I always come prepared," the mother explained. "We have to wait for hours sometimes."

"Where are you from?" Anna asked.

"Nevada."

"That's a long way," Anna acknowledged.

"We don't mind coming far," the father said. "We would go farther. We would go anywhere."

"Wherever the experts are," the mother explained.

"Well, Donny—I only know how to draw one picture." Anna said. "I'm a one-picture artist. I used to draw a picture for my little girls. Shall I draw it for you?"

The child nodded his head energetically. The electrode mirrored the artificial candles flashing on the tree and sent bursts of red light into Anna's sensitive eyes. She took the boy's warm little hand and held onto it for a minute.

"Well, now, here we go."

On the tablet she drew in pink the heart-shaped face of a girl. "Let's call her Wendy," Anna said. With the yellow pencil, she gave Wendy tight corkscrew curls and wavy bangs. Her eyelashes, done in black feathery strokes, were long and demure. Her mouth was a little strawberry rosebud.

"What is Wendy doing?" the child asked, looking up at Anna as she drew little red *x*'s to the edge of the paper.

"She's giving you a hundred kisses," Anna said. "Like this." She lowered her head and kissed the boy on his forehead, next to the silver circle. "She wants to be your sweetheart."

"Thank you," the boy's mother said. "Thank you very much."

From down the hall, someone called Donny's name.

"Here we go, Donny boy," his father said. Both parents stood. The father hoisted the boy to his hip.

"Good luck," Anna said. "I wish you all the luck in the world."

Anna still had the pad and pencils in her lap. She began to draw a house. It was a child's version of a house, one-dimensional, with a door and two windows, and a chimney on the roof which had a spiral of smoke spilling from it into the sky. Inside was a happy family. She drew the sun and birds flying. She made the birds into little black notes and drew telephone wires for them to perch on.

Then, as if by magic, Anna saw the pastel chalk drawing of a cottage in the country materialize before her eyes. At the edge of the cottage a stream flowed by under a weathered wooden bridge. The season was fall, and the leaves lay in brilliant shifting hills along the road. Dr. Pincus from Brooklyn was drawing the picture, sitting on the edge of the bed of Anna's oldest girl, Janet. He had just told them Janet had pneumonia again. The snowflakes which had fallen from his coat were melting on the rug at his feet. Janet had already had her painful injection and lay limp, tears on her cheeks; every December since she had started school she had been too sick to attend or take part in the Christmas play. On this day she seemed to take little comfort from the doctor's reassuring voice telling her that her fever would fall, her chest would stop hurting, her cough would subside. Dr. Pincus had looked around the room and asked Anna if she wouldn't mind bringing to the bedside Janet's blackboard, mounted on a rickety easel. The doctor had stayed there with Janet for a long time, sitting on the edge of her bed, drawing the landscape very carefully in pastel chalks: a woodfire sending smoke from the chimney, a chipmunk on a fencepost, a high and distant formation of geese honking across the sky. When last of all he had drawn a graceful young girl with swinging braids—unmistakably Janet—skipping rope on the wooden bridge, Janet had laughed weakly, and Dr. Pincus had said, "That's my girl. That's what I've been waiting to hear."

Janet, that winter, had again missed being in the Christmas play at school, but she had healed. She had lived to grow up and have money troubles. It was Dr. Pincus who had urged Anna and Abram to move with their children out of the bitter winters of New York. Twenty years ago Abram had died in California of leukemia. Doctor Pincus was surely dead by now. Doctors had stopped making house calls, and Anna was about to have her eyes pierced by laser beams.

"Here's a joke for you," Dr. Rifkin said in the operating room. "A middle-aged woman comes home from the doctor and says to her husband, 'The doctor tells me I have breasts like a twenty-five-year-old.' The husband answers, 'And what did he say about your fifty-year-old ass?' 'Oh,' says the wife, 'he didn't mention you at all!' "

Dr. Rifkin guffawed. Anna sat like a block of ice while the nurse strapped her head into a contraption.

"Hold your head very still now," the doctor said. "Here we go."

Meteors flew into Anna's old eyes, deep into her brain, where she felt her precious memories hiding their faces. Again and again the doctor fired flaming star showers at her, in the shapes of her husband and children holding out their arms to her, and in the forms of quarter notes, eighth notes, sixteenth notes. She waited for a whole note to come flying to her.

"That's it, Mrs. Goldman," the doctor said. "Go home and no jumping rope this afternoon. Come back in one week. No—make it two, I'll be in Hawaii. Happy holidays, and don't worry. Worry never did anyone any good and never changed the outcome of anything."

"You don't have to tell *me*," Anna said.

When Anna got home, she fell back on her bed in gratitude and relief that she was alive and still had her vision. She turned on the television on her nighttable and saw a great throng of people looking heavenward, their mouths wide open, like baby birds about to receive nourishment. The conductor was on a high podium; the young and the old in the great auditorium had open songbooks in their hands. Their faces were aglow as they sang:

For unto us a Child is born,
Unto us a Son is given . . ..

The words flashed across the screen as they sang; the eyes of the singers sparkled with light while the camera moved slowly from face to face. Anna was about to switch channels—what did she need this Christmas junk for?—when the camera stopped and held fast upon the face of a very old woman. She was older than Anna, her features no longer unique, but sunken into a mask of great age. Yet her mouth quivered with passionate energy, and her eyes reflected light as bright as laser beams. Anna sank back on her pillows and attended with half her mind until she heard the soprano sing some words about "the Saviour, which is Christ the Lord."

She stiffened—the same old thing. Anna could feel her father's angry gaze upon her: *Turn that off! Hold your breath. Move only your lips. Don't sing! Clasp your mouth shut! Never say those words!* With an exasperated flap of her hand, Anna held her father off. She felt a flare of fury blaze up in her. She was only interested in the music, didn't he know that? He had bought her her first piano. He had taken her to hear Caruso sing at the Metropolitan Opera house. He, of all people, should know that music was music and nothing was going to change her at this point in her life.

What fascinated Anna was the evidence of pure happiness which shone on the faces of the singers. There wasn't a mean streak showing anywhere. The camera presented her with an intimate, almost embarrassing, close-up view. She could see pock marks on some faces, little beauty marks and dimples on others. She was much closer than she ever could have been in person—only an inch away from a fat woman; squeezed in with a crowd of young people wearing sweatshirts adorned with the words "Sing Along Messiah"; almost touching a handsome bearded man who looked like Christ Himself. She was right there beside a pregnant woman, brushing arms with a father bending over to point out to his son the correct place in the score—she was with husbands and wives and children, and they were all as happy as Anna had ever seen anyone in her life. The conductor waving his wand was happy. The violinists in the orchestra were smiling as they played, the trumpets shot rainbows of light into the air, the harpsichord strings vibrated and caused a shimmering high above in the great vaulted ceiling of the hall. The soprano sang:

> *Rejoice greatly, O daughter of Zion . . .*

Anna, a Jew, was definitely a daughter of Zion. If *she* wasn't, who was? It was too late to discuss this with her father. Anna had lived a long time, and all her life, without question, she had turned her eyes away from the steeples of churches, away from paintings of Jesus in museums, away from gold crosses on the necks of men and women in the street. Anna's eyes burned as she studied the rapt singers. She listened, unthreatened, with the ears of her natural skepticism:

> *Then shall the eyes of the blind be opened, and the ears of the deaf unstopped, then shall the lame man leap as an hart, and the tongue of the dumb shall sing.*

Suddenly slapping her bed with the palm of her hand, Anna addressed her father: *Papa, listen to the music!* Something was causing happiness to shine on those faces. Something made that old man on the bus give out his candy canes, made Dr. Rifkin, for all his joking, sit there behind his magic machine-gun to do what he could do to keep Anna seeing the world. Someone had invented that one-eyed silver electrode to shine in the middle of Donny's forehead.

Anna felt, without doubt, that every one of the singers was beautiful. It was not like her, it was not her way. Normally she would have made private notations to herself about this one's fake blonde hair with dark roots showing, or that one's bad skin, or the morals of the careless young that the world turned out these days—those braless sloppy girls and the boys with green hair and gold studs in their ears. Old women with scarves around their turkey-skin necks could never fool her. She always had ready, in neat bars of music, a song of many ungenerous verses waiting to be sung. But the music in her head had modulated. She wondered if the surgery had changed her vision in some profound way. She felt like putting her arms around each person in the singing throng—the scarred, the fat, the heavily made-up, the too pretty to be true. When the chorus sang:

Surely he hath borne our griefs . . .

Anna thought she would buy her daughters presents. Maybe she would ask them to buy her a present. What did she want? A record of Handel's *Messiah*? Her father had his hand up, ready to hit. *Leave me alone!* she told him. *So what if I don't hold my breath when those words come around! You've made a big mistake. You worry too much.*

She felt funny, a little like laughing. A little like singing. She wasn't much of a laugher or a singer. She hadn't sung in perhaps seventy years. But she lived alone in a little apartment—who was going to judge her? Sitting up straight in her bed, she smoothed back her hair as if she were about to take her place in the crowd and be shown on television, her eyes twinkling with light. Nervously, she began to sing along as the words appeared on the screen. It took a while for her to get used to the sound of her own thin, wavering voice rising in her darkened bedroom, but soon she gained volume and strength, and finally, with confidence, she brought herself in tune with the others.

Hear No Entreaties, Speak No Consolations

Anna was diminished. If she thought she'd been compromised when she lived in the retirement home, she now realized that the other had been fireworks, a festival, a parade, a county fair, the "Star-Spangled Banner." This. This was . . . she didn't have the words for it. This was a hovel in a graveyard, this was the . . . paws of an animal on her back as some two-hundred-pound dumb cluck turned her from side to side every two hours. This was the supreme insane asylum as moaners and screamers sang a chorus every night of "Call the Police, Oh Momma, Momma, come and get me, I've missed the train, untie me, when are they serving me my sand?" You could hear anything here, and you did. You could scream anything and no one cared. You could be slumped over in your wheelchair in the hall and beg a passer-by to call the police and get you out of here—and no one would help. You could tell them you were being held here against your will, that you had plenty of money to pay a lawyer, that you wanted to go home, that you could afford to hire round-the-clock private nurses, and they'd pass you by, nice-looking, decent people, here to visit their screaming mamas and papas, but as soon as they entered this charnel house, they were in a special hell whose sign above the entrance specified: *Hear No Entreaties, See No Atrocities, Speak No Consolations.*

Anna had seen her own daughters do it (to her satisfaction): pass right by some babbling crone who was slipping down out of her restraints (whose chin was snagged on the straps of her wheelchair), pass right by without so much as a glance as she begged and pleaded. Why should they help anyone here, anyway? If her daughters were coming to see *her*, they shouldn't waste one second on some crazy old coot whose mind was in Minnesota and who had one foot in the grave.

Anna was shackled: straps and ropes and chains and tubes entrapped and surrounded her; Houdini couldn't have got out of this place. Two cords (which since her stroke she couldn't pull) were for the light switch and the call-buzzer. There was a silver chain that attached and locked her five-inch TV to the bed table (otherwise it would be stolen in five minutes). On her wrists were plastic bracelets, in various neon colors, identifying her, her medications, her doctor, her room number, and one bright red bracelet blazing out "Do Not Resuscitate!" There was no chance she'd have the good luck to have her heart stop; the bracelet might as well have read "Miss America 1993" or "Lottery Winner, Five Million Dollar Jackpot." In fact, Anna could see no way that she could possibly die. She couldn't fall (her hand was paralyzed and had no strength, her hip was broken and she couldn't walk), she couldn't starve or even choke to death since she no longer ate anything by mouth, but was on a feeding tube that pumped "Gevity" (a milkshake-thick potion of enzymes and vitamins designed to threaten her with eternal longevity) into a hole in her belly, she couldn't take poison (nothing was in reach of her two working fingers but the On/Off button of the TV next to her bed), she couldn't depart this world via pneumonia, the supposed friend of the aged (since the minute she coughed they'd start pumping antibiotics into her feeding tube—and besides, she'd had the pneumonia vaccine injected into her), she had no history in her family of cancer or cirrhosis of the liver, and she never had smoked or taken a drink. Clearly this was going to be one deadly long last chapter.

"So what do you do all day, Ma?" her daughter Janet asked during one of her many obligatory visits in the second year of Anna's incarceration, "Do you just sit there with your mind blank?"

"I'm never blank!" Anna snapped. "Never."

"What do you think about?"

Anna stared at her daughter; how do you tell a child who is still running to Las Vegas for vacations, still redecorating her home, still looking forward to her daughters' weddings, still dyeing her hair, that there were things to think about that no one could dream could *ever* be thought about? How much truth was a mother allowed to reveal to a child, even if the child were fifty-five and the mother eighty-five? How much protecting was there left to be done?

"I think about Daddy," Anna said. That was neutral; it could be taken as a sentimental, reverential reflection. She saw her daughter breathe with relief. The fact was Anna hardly remembered him.

"I think about him, too," Janet said. (She had her purse in her lap, clutched in her fingers, as if she wanted to leave as soon as possible.) "He was a wonderful father," she added, smiling at Anna to reassure her that no mistake had been made in Anna's choice of a husband. "He was always so full of life, he enjoyed things so much, he had such an appetite for living!"

Anna screwed her lips shut. This wasn't the track she was on, she wasn't going to accommodate to this. Her mouth was dry as old corn flakes. (She was entitled to a spearmint-flavored swab if she wanted it; the nurse would jiggle it around on Anna's tongue if she complained loudly enough, but she didn't want even that, hadn't swallowed anything, food, water, even sucked on a Lifesaver, for more than a year now.)

"Oh, he was such a good father," Janet went on. "He would have done anything for the family, for his children . . . He often said how much he loved us . . ."

Impatiently, Anna cut her off. "I just want to be in the grave next to him!" There, it had burst forth despite her pledge to herself that she would tone it down for this visit. Her daughters often left her bedside in tears, and Anna occasionally felt the slightest pang of guilt about how far she pushed them. But these outbursts were her pleasure, and she couldn't deny herself, even in the interest of sparing her children. "*That's* what I think of in my blank mind, since you want to know! I think of that space next to him, that blank space in the Jewish cemetery, right next to where he's laid out. I want my coffin, I want my peace, I want to be in it. NOW!"

Janet got a scared look on her face—her daughter was not young any more, she was getting heavy around the hips, she had already given up her womb and her gall bladder to the surgeon's knife. *My God,* Anna thought, *one day my darling baby is going to be tied up in one of these torture chambers, too.*

On TV, she had seen a computer-artist change a woman's face from age eighteen to age eighty-eight in a series of quick overlays. She stared at her daughter's face and repeated the process privately, lengthening her daughter's nose and chin and bringing them toward each other, creating wrinkles, bags under her eyes, dewlaps, jowls, turkey neck, long hanging earlobes, liver spots; finally she removed her daughter's teeth and let the mouth that had nursed from Anna's breast undulate and pulse like an octopus. She was transfixed by her own projection, but her daughter was chattering on, unaware of what lay ahead for her.

The curtain, which had been drawn shut between Anna's bed and The Crab's bed, billowed slightly with movement on the other side. Anna knew exactly what the old witch was up to, clacking the beads of her rosary, rolling around the room in her wheelchair to look at one sickly picture of Jesus after another that decorated the walls on her side of the room. Her daughter would be in here any minute, Christmas trees hanging from her ears. The woman must think she was an interior decorator, bringing in paper turkeys to glue on the wall for her mother in November, elaborate crèches in December, red Valentine hearts in February, green shamrocks and leprechauns in March, yellow Easter baskets in April. The rest of the time, when she visited, she leaned head-to-head with The Crab as they listened to soap operas and reruns of westerns turned to top volume. Deaf as Anna's roommate professed to be, she could hear like a lioness the instant Anna hummed her private aria, her prayer, her wish, her command, her passionate entreaty: "I wish I were dead."

"You spoil my digestion when you say that," The Crab complained to her the minute a nurse pulled the curtain back. "It's bad for my appetite and makes me feel as if I'm in a mental institution."

An appetite? Anyone who had an appetite here *belonged* in a mental institution. Before Anna had had her stroke, she was forced to partake of the food they served on this toothless wing: green slime for salad, brown mush for steak, red and yellow ribbons of Jell-O, pink liquefied syrup they called cake.

"To think," Anna said to her daughter now, "that people want to live to a great old age. They should have their heads examined."

"Would you rather have died young like Daddy?" her daughter challenged her. "Dead from leukemia at fifty-five? Never to live to enjoy his grandchildren? Or see the world change the way you have?"

"So he didn't get to see a microwave," Anna said. "But think how lucky he was that he never got old. Am *I* lucky—to see every power taken away, piece by piece, till nothing is left? Look at me. I used to play the piano, I used to walk, I used to eat, I used to smile. Now I'm a piece of meat, they turn me over like a roast, they poke things into me, I'm an open village, anyone can come into my private roads." She saw her daughter throw a look of exasperation at the ceiling. Anna looked, too. What were those reddish spots up there—blood? Had someone's high blood pressure, once-upon-a-time, burst through the top of her head and shot a geyser up to the ceiling? Was that someone's lucky stroke out of here?

"If only you had a better attitude, Mom," her daughter began. "Other people in here, after a few months, accept their situation, they don't carry on like you do, they recognize that when a person lives this long, this is the price you pay; when you get to be very old, your body finally wears out. At least be grateful your mind hasn't worn out; you know everything that goes on, you're as sharp as ever."

"That's my problem. I'd be better off a vegetable. I could babble all night and think I was a flying cow."

"But Ma—after two years here, can't you at least try to accept . . . ?"

Accept? Accept? What was she talking about? Anna didn't want a sermon. She already got sermons from the nurses, who told her she made too much fuss about every little thing, sermons from The Crab, who didn't approve of her death wish and told her she had to wait until The Good Lord called, sermons from the aides who soaked her gown every time they injected medicine into her feeding tube and then blamed her for letting the tube clog up.

The Orthodox Jew who owned the place marched into her room (and the rooms of the two or three other Jewish residents) on High Holy Days, holding up a ragged piece of matzo or a couple of Chanukah candles and giving sermons about "Our Heritage," and "Our Magnificent History." He was maybe twenty-five, with a beard like an octogenarian, and hard little black eyes. What did he know of heritage and history? Anna could see he hadn't lived life at all; he was a small-minded, tough, mean businessman, making babies with his orthodox wife who wore a babushka like from the old country. Anna knew he sat in his office all day peering at charts on his computer and schemed ways to have the nursing home make more money. He watered down the prune juice, he served horsemeat, he refused Anna her disposable diapers.

Even her daughters didn't know about the diapers—what the nursing home did to Anna after she came back from her second surgery. (The first—she reminded herself—was to get the circulation going in her leg so they wouldn't have to cut off her rotting toe; the second was after her stroke, when she tried to get out of bed in the hospital and broke her hip. Why they'd bothered to replace her hip she didn't know. She hadn't walked a step since.)

It was then, upon her return to the nursing home, that the aides starting using diapers. They claimed it was easier than having to run when she called for a bedpan every ten seconds, easier than hearing her complain of pain when they hoisted her on it, then complain again when they left her on it too long before they came back to take it away. So Anna got diapers. What did she care? She knew the seven ages of man. Why should she be different? Like Methuselah, like anyone who lived past eighty, she was becoming an infant without teeth, a baby who peed in bed, who couldn't walk, who couldn't turn over herself, a baby who was going backward into the sea of time till soon she'd sink under, her head disappearing, and be gone. (But not soon enough!)

When Medicare stopped paying for the diapers after a hundred days, the Orthodox Jew and his henchman came in and told Anna they'd have to call her daughters and report that her time on Medicare was up. If her family wanted diapers for her, they'd have to pay fifty dollars a box for them.

"Not on your life," Anna had told the men (who looked to her like Tweedle Dee and Tweedle Dum with beards). "I won't have my children wasting a penny on me. If your aides weren't so lazy, if they were willing to bring me a bed pan, if they treated me like a human being, I wouldn't be in diapers to begin with. So now you figure it out. It doesn't matter to me if I don't have diapers. I'll just wet the bed."

The men stepped into the hall to hold a feverish consultation. They argued in great agitation as if over a point of law in the Torah—this pettiness was in their genes. Also, they had seen Anna carry on and knew she wasn't bluffing.

The solution they reached was a device now in place between her legs—some kind of thick rag (supplied by the nursing home) which, at intervals, was pulled out by an aide and replaced with a new one.

No, there were tortures in this existence her daughters had not yet begun to imagine: the bowel impactions, for example, which had happened to Anna several times due to her inactivity and her lack of solid food. When this occurred, when the aides noted that a week had passed without results, they set upon her some young Mexican aide (sometimes a young fellow just over the border and working cheap) who was given license by the nurses (who hated to do it themselves) to thrust his gloved fingers into Anna's private recesses to unstick the stalled products of digested "Gevity." She had to submit. She had no choice. She sometimes screamed in pain during the procedure. And in recent weeks she imagined the worst, that maybe one certain aide enjoyed doing it to her, came in during the dark hours after midnight and turned her on her side, did things to her behind her back, said it was orders on her chart from the doctor. He took a long time doing it, with her turned on her side, away from him. She couldn't see his face or tell exactly what he was doing (and maybe not doing things only to her). She didn't know his name. She didn't even know if he worked here. Who would believe her if she told anyone her fears? And if she reported him and he was fired, who knew what he would do, come back with a gun and kill her? Kill her children! Never mind. What did it matter? She wasn't a woman. She was no longer human, no longer a sexual being.

When her turn came to be showered here, by male aides or female aides, it was all the same, they sat her naked on a chair with a hole in it, wheeled her under the cascading blasts of water—first too cold, then too hot. They used a washcloth first on her body, her private parts, and then, last of all . . . on her face. She was outraged; she sat there, freezing, burning, singing her tune, "I wish I were dead," saying it out loud and to herself, shouting it, like a Hallelujah chorus, filling her mouth with water and spitting out the words.

So how did her daughter have the nerve to tell her she should have a better attitude?

Her attitude had worsened after she had learned the cost of her hospital bill from her hip surgery. She still couldn't believe it. *Eighty-seven thousand dollars!* For consultations and tests and machines and technicians and therapists and surgeons and heart specialists and lung specialists and blood specialists and brain specialists and stomach specialists and several psychiatrists to find out why she wanted to die. (Their brilliant diagnosis was: "Depression possibly related to recent health setbacks.") All this knowledge for Anna's benefit, all these geniuses gathered around her singing gibberish:

There was an old lady who fell out of bed,
We can't make her well,
We can't make her dead.

No wonder Medicare had no money left for her diapers. But what bothered her was the stupidity of it. Eighty-seven thousand dollars? Anna had never seen that much money in her life, not at one time, not in one place. But to think what money like that would have bought her at another time of her life, another place. An education! Music lessons with a master teacher. A house for herself and her husband and children. Freedom, space, the ocean, the mountains, rivers, eagles flying overhead. Maybe even vacations (which she and Abram could never afford to take), a night in a hotel, good meals in restaurants, a car that wasn't fifteen years old. She couldn't bear to think about this; the tube in her stomach, the machine pumping in the "Gevity"—this alone cost eight hundred dollars a month, more than Anna had ever paid for rent, ever, anywhere, in all the places she had lived in her life. For the conveniences she had now, a narrow bed, a five-inch TV, and all the complimentary tortures of this existence, someone was writing a check for thousands of dollars every month to the Orthodox Jew with his beard and his matzo crumbs.

"How can I get in touch with Dr. Death?" Anna asked her daughter. "This Kevorkian doctor. I want to speak to him."

"He would never consider you, Ma," her daughter said. "You're not terminally ill. You're not even dying." "What would you call this?" Anna asked.

"That's not the point. You don't have a fatal condition."

"I have the human condition."

"Yes, but you're not *dying. Not right now.*"

"Excuse me," Anna said. "Are you suggesting I'm dancing the night away?"

"You make it hard for me, Ma. I don't know what to say. If I could fix you, I would. I'd do anything if I could. But I'm only human, too." Her daughter looked over toward The Crab's side of the room; Anna knew what she was thinking. When The Crab's daughter visited, the two of them chatted briefly, played three hands of gin rummy, prayed to Jesus, watched TV, and then said a brisk goodbye. No operatic crescendos, no Sarah Bernhardt pronouncements, no farewell deathbed scenes. But The Crab didn't have Anna's grasp of the nature of existence. She didn't see the long view and therefore couldn't make judgments. She didn't excoriate the universe; she simply didn't have the brains for it.

"Janet, have a little human sympathy for me." (She knew she should leave it alone, but she couldn't.) "I have nothing to do here all day but think of how I'm in pain, how I'm suffering. How they turn me over every two hours. How I have a bed sore at the base of my spine. How my right arm is swollen and paralyzed. How my heels hurt. How I have a pain in my chest all the time."

"Ma, maybe if you thought of something else besides yourself. I always offer to bring you books on tape and a cassette player. You could listen to all the great books you never read. You could finally get your education!"

"I'm not interested. What do I need an education for now? To help me in my future career?"

"To enlarge your horizons. You could listen to tapes of all the music you love. For pleasure. Beethoven, Chopin, Mozart. "

"Just thinking of a piano makes my heart break. Hearing one would kill me."

"So it would kill you. I thought that's what you want, anyway," Janet said. "Look, I'm sorry, Ma. I didn't mean that. But what is, is. This is where you are. This is your fate now. You have to make the best of it."

"Give me liberty or give me death," Anna said.

"If I actually handed you a poison pill, would you take it right now?" her daughter demanded. For an instant, Anna thought her daughter was going to produce one from her pocket.

"You know I can't swallow anything by mouth," Anna said in self-defense. "I'm on a feeding tube."

Anna checked the large-print schedule taped to the wall and saw that there was an "activity" taking place in Unit Nine. She was getting bored by her own histrionics.

"You'll wheel me over, I'll enlarge my horizons," she told her daughter. "They drag in all these unconscious souls who sleep and drool the whole time, while some poor girl from Mexico, who can hardly speak English, asks us if anyone knows how much two-plus-two is, and then she reads us recipes from the paper for chili beans. Tell me, Janet, are any of us going to be cooking chili beans in the near future?" Anna motioned with her movable fingers to her daughter. "Go get the nurse now and tell her to unhook me from the feeding tube. It's pumping me so full that I'm gaining five pounds a week. I never weighed more than 105 in my life and now I'm 133 pounds. Tell the nurse I want to be put into the wheelchair."

Anna braced herself for the ordeal. Two male aides came in and, chattering to each other in Spanish as if Anna were not there at all, they rolled and jerked her around on her bed. First they needed to put on Anna's cotton robe. They needed to change the wet diaper-rag. They needed to undo the feeding tube from its socket and insert the sealer plug. Anna's daughter waited discreetly in the hall while they got her dressed and lifted her into the padded wheelchair. Anna screamed repeatedly as they pinched her skin, hoisted her roughly, dropped her down too hard, nearly broke her ribs as they let go of her. When her daughter finally wheeled her down the corridor past the reflecting window of the beauty parlor, Anna turned away her head. "I haven't looked at myself in a mirror since I've been here. Why would I want to look at a corpse?"

"Jesus loves me, this I know, for the Bible tells me so."

The song coming from the activity room hit Anna like a hot wind. "I forgot. Bible Study is on Thursday," she told Janet. "Turn me around." They were in the breezeway between units; the goldfish fountain gurgled and sloshed gum wrappers among the mottled, bloated-looking fish. White-coated aides, the beautiful dark-haired young men and women on their breaks, sat on the hard metal chairs and flirted, teased, laughed, as if this place they worked in were a carnival, a celebration on the outskirts of town where the freaks were incidental, where the true purpose of their work was pleasure, laughter, and seduction. They had shining skin, ebony hair, brilliant smiles; they were aching to start making their thousands of babies together, Anna could feel the urgency in their voices.

Janet had stalled the wheelchair; Anna didn't really want to go back to her room and stare at The Crab, not after all her arduous preparations, repositionings, and mechanical adjustments, nor did she especially want to hear that Jesus loved her. Clapping could be heard from the activity room; a man's deep voice exhorted everyone to join in.

"Oh, wheel me in, anyway," Anna conceded. "What can we lose?" Janet turned her in a circle and pushed on. Inside it looked like a train station full of the lame and the halt waiting for passage to Lourdes. Anna wondered how it would be now if she'd been raised a believer. Jesus up on a cloud, arms extended, to welcome her into heavenly bliss, Jesus to forgive her meanness and sarcasm, Jesus happy to bathe her brow in the waters of peace. Jesus her handsome lover there to soothe her pains, console her for her losses, cherish her tenderly for eternity.

Instead, what legacy did she have from her own pale religious beginnings? Nothing but the memory of a father who forbade her to sing the name of Jesus in Christmas carols at the public school. And now what did she have? An Orthodox Jew-businessman with a long beard waving matzos at her.

Janet bumped her over the threshold and found a place for Anna under a vent that already was blowing cold air on her neck and would probably give her pneumonia that wouldn't kill her. Janet herself took a seat on a torn plastic couch beside a Down's Syndrome woman (she could have been fifteen years old or thirty) wearing a pink apron with bunnies on it.

Anna scrutinized the crowd; she didn't recognize a single person. These inmates were *young*—they had to be from some other circle of hell, not the toothless wing or the Alzheimer's wing. The young man conducting Bible Study, the one with the deep voice, was very tall, very handsome. He wore tight blue jeans with a silver belt buckle, and a plaid shirt open at the neck with a bolo tie hanging loose on his hairy chest. He was talking now in deep, low tones that resonated right up through the wheels of Anna's chair and shivered into her lacelike, filigreed bones.

"Are you impatient?" he asked. "Are you tired of waiting for the miracle? Do you think it will never come?" Anna looked her daughter's way and rolled her eyes. Janet seemed to be listening attentively, without hostility. "Do you wake up every day and think, 'Today I'll be saved? Today I'll be released and go home to my Heavenly Father?' "

There was a murmur of agreement in the room. Anna glanced around again, looking to see if any of the usual senile vegetables, the living dead, the comatose catatonics, had been wheeled in. But around her were only the hollow-eyed young, the MS victims, the severely retarded, the quadriplegics, the Lou Gehrigs, the anorexics past the point of no return. Her heart skipped a beat then landed in her gut like an anchor thrown from a ship. (Was this going to be her fatal heart attack? Here, now, with Jesus flapping his wings overhead?)

"My wife left me years ago," the handsome man said, "and every year, on our anniversary, I ask myself, 'Is this the year she'll return to me?' I always set out some flowers on the hall table, and I look out the window for her, hoping to see her, with her beautiful gold hair, coming up the walk. Like all of you, I'm tired of waiting. I'm full of despair. But then one day it occurred to me: the longer I've waited, the closer I am to the day it will happen! So you see? *We're all closer! Every one of us. We're almost there!* Don't you just feel it? If the miracle wasn't yesterday, isn't today it may be . . . tomorrow! Even tonight! Because it's coming, we all know that, don't we?"

A shimmer of assent, like the whirr of hummingbirds' wings, fluttered across the room. Anna felt the breeze of it lift the hair on her neck (unless what she felt was the air vent). Just in front of her was a tiny girl-like woman on a downy fluff of deep padding, in a wheelchair designed like a reclining couch. The girl was emaciated, weighed less than a bird, couldn't have been more than twenty. Her short fine hair was cut like a boy's. She was watching the handsome man with her huge, dark eyes, beautiful eyes, she was following his every movement, taking in his power, his sweetness. Anna had an impulse to call out to him, "Never mind about your wife, come and take care of this girl, she's lonely, she needs you. Put your arms around her. Kiss her with your lips. Give her a taste of love before it's all over."

Now Anna noticed a young man strapped upright into a wheelchair, his face newly shaven (she saw a spot of blood on his cheek, the aide must have nicked him), but he had red lips, blue eyes, he was beautiful. He, too, was listening to the handsome man who promised the coming miracle. Next to him was a wasted young man, displaying the angles of his skeleton. He looked like the AIDS victims Anna had seen on television. Perhaps he had tasted too much love and was dying of it. She saw spastics and cripples and mutes—with their faces radiant and lit from above.

"So let's sing a song of praise now," the handsome man said. "We have much to be thankful for since every one of us will very soon know ultimate love in Our Father's embrace. Just hang on, brothers and sisters. These troubled days are just a lightning flash on the vast skies of eternity."

He pushed a button and a scratchy recording came blasting out of his tape player on a card table: "Jesus loves me, this I know . . ."

Those who could sing, joined in. Those who were unable watched the sunbeams dance in front of their eyes and imagined their deliverance. Anna saw her horizons widen. She saw her mother and father waiting for her on a cloud in heaven, their arms outstretched. The gentle face of her husband was smiling out of the blue skies at her. He waved, with the hand wearing his horseshoe ring; his eyes were sparkling with anticipation. She could feel herself in his strong arms, feel the power of the hug he was waiting to give her.

Anna reached over toward her daughter with her two good fingers. Janet grasped her hand tightly, bending her head and kissing her mother's fingers, one by one, over and over.

"Everyone here is young," Anna whispered to her, "but I'm very old. I've lived my whole life."

"Yes, you're very old, Ma."

"I've had the whole thing," Anna said, amazed. She actually felt peace descending on her, heavily, without grace, like a pelican coming to land on a rock. "There's nothing more for me to do. I just realized, darling—I'm at the very end. I don't have to worry anymore. That's all there is to it."

Anna in Chains

Anna had sung her song, her mantra, her aria for the last five years to anyone who would listen, to a world audience, bigger—she estimated—than the Pope himself commanded.

"Shoot me, get me a gun, bring me a poison pill! I want to be dead! I want to be in my grave! I want to die."

When the aides didn't answer her call bell, she loudly intoned the stanzas of her libretto; when her daughters visited (then went out in the hall to get something for her from the nurse), she whispered it. In the dark of night, when the other crazies up and down the hall were singing their own songs, she chimed in with her lyric: "*Dead oh dead oh give me—dead.*"

"You don't mean it," her roommate, The Crab, told her. "Don't be like the boy who cried wolf."

Anna knew all about the boy who cried wolf. Like her, he had been rehearsing for the real thing, for the moment of greatest need—but no one seemed to understand that a person had to practice, had to find the right tone, the perfect modulation, the impeccable rhythm, as in any piece of music. Anna knew all about music—she was nothing if not a musician.

Besides, the reactions engendered by her litany entertained her during the endless hours of her incarceration. Just as when she used to play the old upright piano—briefly—in the chapel of the nursing home (she had only a few weeks of being ambulatory before her stroke, before her broken hip), and people used to wag their heads in awe at her rendition of the "Moonlight Sonata," she now—when she sang her tune ("*Bring me cyanide, bring me arsenic!*")—took satisfaction in watching all those about her rushing away in alarm.

Each tender new young Mexican aide scurried to the nurse with the desperate news: "The lady in room 615 says she wants to die." Anna cocked her ear for the reply: "Oh—that one. She says that all the time. Pay no attention."

"It's a sin," one young black-haired beauty reprimanded her as she changed the wet sheets on Anna's bed. The child, angelic of face, with dazzling black eyes, was only eighteen and already had three babies that her mother cared for while she worked. "You mustn't say that anymore. You have to be patient and wait till Jesus calls you."

"I don't know from Jesus," Anna said. "And I don't want to."

News of her daring got around. All the aides at the nursing home were recent arrivals from Mexico and staunch Catholics; all the nurses were Protestants; the owner was an Orthodox Jew. Those who attended Anna feared she was daring God—tempting destruction to rain down upon all of them. An earthquake might strike, a fire might rage through the nursing home. What did Anna care? She'd take death any way it came, the sooner the better. Besides, she didn't believe anyone was up there listening to her dares. She had once seen her suicidal son-in-law fling a can of beer up into the branches of a tree, screaming, "Fuck you, God!"—and *that* she had to admit was going a little too far. But the poor demented man was dead now, and God had had nothing to do with it. Her daughter's husband had done himself in with means Anna could never find the strength or technical ability to execute.

She reflected on the suicides that had passed through her history. In 1933, a first cousin of hers named Bertha had secretly married an Italian bartender. For the first year, too ashamed to tell her family she'd done the forbidden thing and married a non-Jew, she lived at home with her parents and only met him once a week, in the back room of the bar where he worked, to have sex with him in the storeroom among the liquor bottles. When one day Bertha's mother discovered a wedding band hidden in her daughter's box of sanitary napkins, she locked Bertha out of the house. After the young bride had moved in with her Italian husband, it turned out he found Bertha too dull and demure for his loud family gatherings. One Sunday morning—as the story went—he told her he didn't want her coming to his brother's wedding, he would have more fun without her. As soon as he left the house, she stuffed towels in the cracks under all the doorways, put the cat out, and turned on the gas.

Gert, Anna's younger sister, told the story repeatedly as a cautionary tale, as a warning against intermarriage, and as purely ghoulish gossip. In fact, Gert had always had a fascination with suicide. She often recounted the story of her best friend, Tessie, who was in love with a dentist. The dentist had given Tessie an engagement ring and convinced her "to go all the way" before their marriage. But he broke the engagement when he fell in love with one of his patients. (Gert relished adding: "And this 'patient' had a bust bigger than Jane Russell's. Men are animals, they can't control themselves.") Tessie, as Gert told the story, climbed up onto his fire escape one night, knocked on his window, and slit her wrists. The dentist wasn't even home—all Tessie's efforts were for naught. The dentist, putting out some buttermilk to cool on the fire escape the next morning, found her there, dead, with her blouse open and a suicide note in her brassiere.

Gert had always kept a little Swee-Touch-Nee tin tea box in her handkerchief drawer filled with yellowed newspaper clippings about suicides. Anna thought about her sister, now rich as a queen, having buried two husbands, the last one of whom had squirreled away half a million dollars. He'd bought Lane Bryant stock in its early days, correctly predicting that women would keep getting bigger and fatter and would keep buying Lane Bryant clothes. Gert lived now in a fancy Beverly Hills retirement home, from which she never stirred to come and visit Anna. Anna's daughters pled excuses for Gert: the hour's ride was too much for her, she suffered from arthritis, she soon needed cataract surgery, she had to stay near her bathroom because her bladder was so weak.

Anna was not impressed. Her sister, always busy doing good work for Jewish causes (for which she always got medals and plaques at donor dinners to hang on the walls all over her apartment), didn't have the kindness of heart to come and visit her helpless, paralyzed, invalid sister. To do a "mitzvah" for her own flesh-and-blood was beyond her goodness of heart.

The truth had been evident from their childhood on—Gert had always been jealous of Anna. She had always wanted everything Anna ever had—including Anna's husband and Anna's daughters. Luckily for Anna, there wasn't a single thing about Gert that Anna had ever envied.

One rainy afternoon, after the nurse had pumped the afternoon medications into Anna's feeding tube (she could feel the pulverized pills, diluted by water, rise up cold and sour into her throat as the nurse shot them into the tube with a fat syringe), a tall, unshaven, toothless old man, wearing a bathrobe and blue nursing-home slippers, padded into Anna's room. He was carrying a Bible. His skinny wrist was decorated with colorful plastic bracelets including a red one (like one Anna wore) indicating "Do Not Resuscitate!"

"I understand there's a woman in here who keeps saying she wants to die," he announced. "Is that you?" he demanded, sticking his grizzly face a foot away from Anna's.

"What's it to you?" she said.

"I came to save you," he said, brandishing the Bible. "You won't want to die if you accept the Lord."

"*Beethoven* is my lord," Anna said. She gestured toward the plastic bust of Beethoven she kept on her side table, the only decoration she permitted, whereas her roommate had junk everywhere—fake flowers, stuffed bunnies, crucifixes, leprechauns.

"Him! That deaf German? He can't give you everlasting life, Lady. Do you know Satan hears your wishes? He's going to *have* you if you're not careful."

"So let him have me," Anna said. "I'm no bargain."

"Do you ever think about the devil?" the old man demanded.

"No," Anna said. "Never."

"Well, *he thinks about you*."

"Oh, go away. I ought to know what I want to think about," Anna said fiercely. "I'm eighty-eight years old, as old as there are keys on a piano."

"You could be saved! You should find the Lord!" the man said, wild-eyed, beginning to back out of the room.

"Is he so stupid that he's *lost*?" Anna yelled after him. "Just stay out of here, you lunatic. You . . . nothing. You . . . no one!"

"Are you my children?" Anna said to her daughters when they next visited her.

Anna's daughters exchanged a glance. "Yes, we're your children, Ma," they both said at the same moment. They pulled the two pink plastic chairs allotted to visitors closer to her bed.

"My memory is losing me," Anna said. "What did my husband die of? What did he look like?" She really couldn't remember. "Do you girls have any children?"

Her daughters began their patient, extended explanations. One had three daughters, one had two sons, one of the sons had two babies, a boy and a girl—the names swirled around Anna's head. These descendants of hers meant nothing to her—did they ever come and visit? She let her daughters talk and took none of it in; while they set the record straight she would have a little time to rest and think about what pleased her.

On the other side of the curtain, Anna's roommate, The Crab, mumbled, "blah blah blah." She hated when Anna's daughters visited, because apparently they all talked too much for her taste. So what? The Crab always had a rosary in her hands—let her commune with the Lord if she felt neglected.

After a while Anna said, "That's enough about family trees. What else can you tell me?"

Her daughters exchanged another glance. This time an alarm went off in Anna's head. She caught something in their look—they were keeping something from her.

"What is it?" she demanded. "What happened? Are one of you sick?" Her girls were no spring chickens. If one of them had cancer, Anna would kill herself! Under no circumstances did she intend to outlive her children.

"It's about Aunt Gert," her older daughter said finally.

"What about her?"

"She's been very depressed lately," her younger daughter said.

"What could she have to be depressed about!" Anna demanded. "She lives in some fancy Beverly Hills place where they take them on tours to see movie stars' houses and the shark from *Jaws*."

"She's old, Ma. She lonely, she's widowed, like you. She's sick, her back hurts, she's going deaf, her eyes are failing."

"So? I can't walk! I can't eat! I'm paralyzed. I'll never play the piano again. Do you see me being depressed?"

"Never mind. Maybe we shouldn't talk about this."

"Let's talk about it. So what else about Gert?" Anna felt a sense of alarm that Gert was about to gain some critical advantage over her.

"Well, the truth is, we think she tried to kill herself."

"How, by eating pork?" Anna asked.

Her daughters were silent.

Anna had to think about this. Finally she said, "Is she dead?"

"No. It seems she took too many sleeping pills. When she didn't come down for breakfast, they sent someone up to her room, and found her there."

"So what happens now? She's not going to *live* with one of you girls, is she?"

"No, but the fact is we'll have to visit her more often, keep a close eye on her."

"I wouldn't bother if I were you," Anna said. "All she wants is attention."

Anna's daughters exchanged the "Let's get going look." She saw them both stand up at once.

"Okay, Ma. We'll be back to see you soon."

"Gert should have had children of her own if she was going to need so much attention. I hope she knows she isn't going to get it from *my* children."

"Don't worry. We know we belong to you. You never let us forget it."

All night Anna was distraught. She hadn't felt this worried in a long time. Gert, even without an Italian husband, without a dentist or a fire escape, had almost accomplished what Anna most longed for—oblivion. Now Gert would probably have a fancy psychiatrist (a luxury Anna had never had in her entire life), and the next time she took too many pills they'd take her to that hospital in Beverly Hills where all the movie stars went—George Burns, Elizabeth Taylor. This was not acceptable.

Anna considered her options. Even if she had pills, she couldn't take them by mouth. She would need a mortar and pestle to grind them up and then would have to bribe someone to shoot the mixture into her feeding tube. If she had a gun, even if she knew how to use one, she was righthanded and her right hand was paralyzed. What were the words of that Dorothy Parker poem? Anna had memorized it in her youth—about how razors pain you, rivers are damp, acids stain you, drugs cause cramp—and the rest of it, gas smells bad, nooses give, guns aren't lawful, you might as well live. Dorothy Parker was only playing with words—she'd had something to live for, all that fame and money, till she drank herself to death. If Anna had some Manischewitz wine here, she would gulp the whole bottle down at once. (She could still *use* her mouth, she could still swallow. She simply chose not to, she let the feeding tube do all the work.)

The tube, then, was the only way she could kill herself. The "Gevity" that slithered day and night into her guts had to be cut off, stopped. If her sister Gert had the guts to take sleeping pills, Anna could at least starve herself. There were two ways to do it—stop the machine from pumping, or pull out the tube itself. Could she do either one?

For days and nights, Anna pondered this subject. She organized her thoughts; she hadn't been a legal secretary for nothing. She knew how to reason, she was simply waiting for the moment to act. On shower days, which were Tuesday and Saturday, the aide always turned off the feeding tube pump and unplugged the feeding tube from the segment implanted in Anna's belly in order to wheel Anna into the shower room. Once or twice, after she returned Anna to her bed, she forgot—in her hurry to get to the lunch room and have her enchiladas—to restart the pump. But eventually the nurse or the aide discovered the error and corrected it. Besides, Anna had heard that starving to death could take a month or more. That did not actually appeal to her very much. She had always been an impatient person, and she liked immediate results. However, if that was her only option, she could deal with it. She was sure the appropriate opportunity would present itself—she simply had to be alert enough to seize the moment when it arrived the way the wolf, in the ancient story, finally seized the boy.

On a Monday when Anna had already been disconnected from her feeding tube and hoisted into her wheelchair, waiting to be taken to the scale to be weighed—which was the monthly ritual here—the old guy in the blue slippers came back, peered into her room, and guffawed. "Hah, Lady—I see you're still alive, whether you want to be or not."

Anna knew the moment was upon her.

"Oh hello again," she said. "How nice to see you.

What's your name, by the way?" she asked sweetly.

"Ludwig," he said.

"So you remember our talk?"

"What talk?"

"I wonder if you would wheel me down to the chapel."

"You want to pray?"

"I've had a lot of time to think. I've come around to a whole new way of seeing things."

"I think you should wait till Sunday when they have a priest here to say Mass. He does the whole business."

"No, I want to go now. I have no time to lose."

"I have more time than money, myself." The old man shuffled into the room, unlocked the brake of Anna's wheelchair, and began pushing her down the hall. She didn't like the way he was driving—maybe he was drunk, he reminded her of a drunk, with the stubble on his face, without all his teeth—but his driving record wasn't foremost in her mind. He was pushing her so fast she felt the wind on her face. Wildly they sped past the nursing station, past the shower rooms, past the activity room—she hadn't been on a trip like this since the roller-coaster in Coney Island.

He pushed open the door of the chapel. Two skinny stained-glass windows threw green light into the room on either side of a wooden cross. In the corner, just as she remembered it, was the upright piano.

"Could you leave me right there?" Anna asked. "In front of the piano?"

"I'll wait while you pray," he said. "Otherwise, you could be left here till Sunday."

"Don't worry," Anna said. "You go on ahead. I'll be fine. Just push me in a little bit closer to the keys, maybe I can play a hymn."

It was that easy. He probably didn't want to sit around while she played hymns. He just left her there—he didn't even preach to her. He had probably already forgotten why he'd come, one of the benefits of senile dementia.

In the muffled silence of the chapel, Anna bowed her head over the keys. The greenish light descending in long rays upon the keyboard was full of sun-lit dust motes. With enormous effort Anna lifted her left hand from her lap and laid it on the keys. She remembered a song from her childhood songbook, and began to hum it:

Seated one day at the organ,
I was weary and ill at ease . . .
And my fingers wandered idly
Over the noisy keys . . .

Anna tried to play a chord but her shaky fingers had no strength in them and collapsed on the discolored ivories without calling forth even one clear note.

"It doesn't matter," she said aloud. "I didn't come here to play at Carnegie Hall." Using all her strength, she wrenched her buttocks from the seat of the wheelchair and tumbled to the floor. She began to roll. She had had much practice in rolling, the aides rolled her from side to side every two hours, day and night, in her bed to keep her from getting bedsores.

Anna rolled herself around to the far side of the piano—it took her an hour or two to cover the distance—and succeeded in wedging herself in the space between the back of the piano and the wall. That was all. Now she would die here, unobserved, slowly departing life in the shadow of the great instrument that she loved, the piano that was the passion of her life. She would die heroically, suffering as Beethoven suffered, and thus doing she would accomplish all her goals, mainly beating her sister Gert to suicide, and finally dying and getting out of this place.

Anna woke in chains. She was bound, hand and foot, to the rails of her bed. She seemed also to be in some kind of a straitjacket—she couldn't tell exactly. The feeding tube was humming away beside her, she was clearly alive and in business again.

"Get me a doctor!" she screamed, and was surprised at the fierceness in her voice. She had never called for a doctor in the past, she had only called for death. Perhaps she had suffered brain damage, being stuck behind the piano for so long. "A doctor! A doctor! Get me a doctor!"

At some point in the day, a handsome bearded fellow materialized beside her bed. He looked like Abram, her dead husband, when he was young. His eyes were greenish-blue and had a Jewish sweetness in their gaze. The boy—he couldn't be more than thirty—pulled up a chair and took Anna's paralyzed hand tenderly in his own.

"Hello, Anna. I'm Dr. Arthur Kramer. I'm a psychiatrist and I've been called in to help you. My plan—with your permission—is to visit you often from now on with the goal of getting you back to a place where you can enjoy life again."

"Would you really call this 'life'?" Anna demanded. "Tell me the truth, Doctor. I know you're a smart boy, a dummy doesn't go so many years to medical school. Is this condition I have what you'd call 'life'?"

Anna indicated her shackles. She rattled the bed rails with what little strength she had in her good hand. Something about the vulnerability in the boy's face suggested she could take liberties with him. He looked a little frightened, in fact. She might even be his first geriatric patient.

"It *is* your life, whatever you call it, Anna. It's what you've got."

"So who needs it? Would *you* want it?"

"I don't think we should talk about me, Anna. We're here to talk about you. We're going to do a lot of talking, and I'm going to start you on some medicine that may help you adjust."

"Adjust to what?"

"The many losses you have suffered, the losses we *all* suffer as we age. My job is to teach you how to grieve your losses."

"Maybe you should find another job then," Anna said. "I don't need a teacher for suffering. I'm already an expert in the field."

"Maybe you'll see it differently after a while. Perhaps in time you will, with the wisdom your years have given you, be willing to take on the new challenges of great old age and try to conquer them."

"Do you always talk this way?" Anna said, "because though you're a very nice boy, I don't have much patience."

The doctor was looking down; Anna had a sense that he might have choked up, even have tears in his eyes. She wanted to take him in her arms and assure him that her torment wasn't really as bad as it looked to him, that she liked to exaggerate for effect. On a good day she could even consider this life of hers an adventure.

"What's the matter, Arthur? You have a grandma about my age?"

He raised his head. "Will you work with me, Anna? I'll try to be brief when I explain things to you."

"Tell me something. You're married? You have children?" Anna asked.

"I have a wife, yes, and a son, a little boy," the doctor said.

"I understand. You have to earn a living," Anna agreed. "Look, so I'll cooperate, Medicare will pay you. I'll let you come and keep me company and talk till your half-hour or whatever is up. But you should know I don't really believe in this psychology baloney. You talk but I don't have to listen. I'll ignore you, which is exactly what I do when my daughters come to see me. But I want you to understand, Arthur-the-psychiatrist: there's nothing you can teach me about life. I've lived three times as long as you have. So if I'm not paying attention, you'll be kind enough not to force yourself on me. Maybe I'll be thinking about how I danced with Abram at my wedding, how the gardenias he gave me smelled like the entire Brooklyn Botanical Gardens in springtime, how the edges of the corsage were already turning brown when we got to Atlantic City for our honeymoon. You can rest assured—I have enough to think about till the end of time."

Anna Passes On

Once her dying got underway, Anna could not really complain about the way the process moved along. She had waited seven years for this moment to arrive, sobbing, begging, and beseeching anyone who passed by her room in the nursing home—anyone who wasn't a wheelchair prisoner or a babbling vegetable—to help her get out of this mess. Neither threats nor the ultimate pleading of her desperate soul had had any effect on those who held the power. *They* felt well. They were alive and walking around the world and were simply convinced it was the best way to be: *here*.

Anna knew better, her two daughters knew better. Year after year (seven years! Twenty-five hundred days!) they came like the good girls they were to visit her, chained as she was to her bed, one arm paralyzed, her legs useless, her stomach fed by a plastic tube, but they had no solution. For all those mornings and afternoons Janet and Carol had sat at her bedside, hopelessly, earnestly, attending to her, bored to be there and scared to see where they were ultimately headed; they agreed with Anna that not being anywhere would be a blissful improvement for their mother over her present existence.

Anna warned them constantly: they mustn't do anything illegal and end up in jail. Neither one was familiar with firearms, neither one had access to heavy barbiturates and no one could figure out how to get her to a bridge railing. Ropes, razors, and drinking drain cleaner did not appeal to Anna nor did a plastic bag over her head. Even so, Anna held a continuing, daily conversation with them. With the privacy curtain pulled around the bed, she whispered, "I want to die, children," and they answered, as in a catechism, "You will, Ma, you will. We just don't know when."

Her roommate, The Crab #25 (they were all the same), on the other side of the curtain, would yell to them, "Jesus knows when. He'll call you when he's good and ready."

"Oh drop dead," Anna would reply.

Sometimes, for her own entertainment, she'd perform a little operatic scene, singing out her long catalog of miseries, pains, losses, deprivations, and torments . . . or she'd invoke her need to be "quiet in the grave next to Daddy." Sometimes she'd just stare, catatonic, at the ceiling, until her daughters thought she'd actually had the final, fatal stroke. But no, surprise, she was always there, back in business, infinitely present, never dead, never stupid, and never done with it all.

One month after Anna turned ninety, after she'd passed the threshold beyond which no one could logically say she had a future to live for, the substitute nurse, changing the bedclothes, coughed her Christmas bronchitis into Anna's face, thereby transferring to Anna the precious, deeply desired germ. Anna's lungs embraced the bug like an egg engulfing a random sperm, nourished it into a colony, then filled slowly with poisonous fluid. Her end—at last—burgeoned in her chest like a growing fetus.

When Anna's fever rose to 104 degrees and her pulse became erratic, it finally dawned on her daughters that an opportunity was upon them. Janet leaned close to Anna's ear: "Ma, you're really very sick this time. If you want us to, we'll try to get you out of this."

"Do it," Anna gasped in a brief, painful exhalation. Her voice gurgled upward through fathoms of seaweed as if she were talking underwater.

"Do you mean it? Are you absolutely sure?"

She wanted to interrogate her daughters further. How would they get her out of this? By what method? *When*? She knew how important the right questions were—she had been a secretary for two New York state senators from the time she was eighteen, just after her father died and she had to go to work to support her mother and sister Gert. The senators found her so clever that they urged her to go to night school and become a lawyer. However, they wanted her to continue to work for them by day, which plan would have left her no time for studying, eating, or sleeping.

Now, everything she'd never done in her life flashed before her eyes. She could have been someone great and important. She could have been a famous pianist. On her bedside table, lined up to break her heart now that she could not play a note, were the busts of Mozart, Beethoven, Tchaikovsky, Schubert, and her beloved Chopin. No more music in her paralyzed fingers. And now even her extraordinary gift of speech was done for.

Her daughters held a brief conference, their heads turned away from her. "Ma—" Janet said, "the truth is you probably don't have more than six months to live. If the doctor verifies that, it means we can legally request hospice care. A special nurse would be sent here to take care of you. She'd give you morphine, and then you'd just go to sleep. The main thing is that you wouldn't suffer anymore."

Not suffer? What would be left if she didn't have suffering? But her eyes were wide open; she hoped they twinkled. She blinked agreement—*Yes, yes, yes!*—with all her might.

When the girls went to call the doctor, she contemplated the clock on the wall. *Get me out of this*, she begged the endless round of time. Could she really hope for a change? She'd go anywhere to reach the end of this existence, even to a hole in the ground. She'd ride in a hearse! Have a new view! Life was always life—this trip to death was just more of it.

When her children were little, Anna used to reassure them: "Darlings, you will never be dead so don't ever be afraid. Till the very end of your life you will be alive. You will live till the very last minute, and after that you won't be there to care." What she had told her precious babies was truer than even she had imagined. Alive was always alive, even when dead was better.

When her girls came back from the nurses' station they were smiling as if they'd hit a jackpot: "Your doctor agreed, Ma! He'll order the hospice nurse to come tomorrow. He never thought you would last this long. He really thinks you're a wonder."

Anna took considerable satisfaction in this—though of course it was not news to her that she was a superior person.

"You'll just float away on the morphine, Ma, you'll feel nothing at all—and that will be it," Carol said.

Already Anna could feel relief: like the Red Sea, the ocean of pain was parting in her body. She managed one last wheezing command through the bubbles of phlegm flooding her chest: "Today!"

Not that it was so simple. Her daughters, bless them, were like boxers in the ring, fending off the regular nurses who still insisted upon pressing antibiotics into Anna's feeding tube or forcing inhalators down her throat.

"No more!" her defenders said. "She's had enough. Stop!" They fought the nursing home administrator, a man with a long black beard who came in to argue life at any cost. Her daughters stood firm: "No hospital! No respirator! Don't even think of it!" He was an orthodox Jew who didn't want an empty bed in the nursing home. He laid out God's law. Jews did not take death into their own hands. Anna's girls argued human mercy. He looked at Anna with disdain, with loathing, and left the room. So much for Jewish compassion. The Crab on the other side of the curtain kept muttering, "Only Jesus knows the time. You will go to hell for this."

Her daughters had to—bodily—pull a pulmonary therapist from Anna's bedside and throw her out along with her suction machine. "We're done with all that, don't you understand?" Janet cried. "We have the okay! My mother is *leaving here!*"

This last stop, where she and everyone else on earth was headed, was what her poor Polish mother had feared every time Anna caught a cold, every time she left the house to take the trolley to school. The same terror sent her thin and nervous father to shul to pray that death would not befall his children. Worry and prayer both came to nothing as it did in all cases. Here Anna was: the great and famous moment was nearly upon her. She was about to lose the spark every tiny ant and worm wants to keep hold of, the force that makes flies evade the swatter and convulses fish off their baited hooks. It seemed a trifle now, life, all those swarming needs, disappointments, broken promises, dashed hopes—even the glorious days (if she ever had any, but she must have, mustn't she?)—all of it was just so much exhausting ado about nothing.

Her girls were not so far from the end of the road themselves. If Anna was ninety, they must almost be old women. Her babies were moving along the treadmill not so far behind her.

Thank God, Anna murmured, *Thank You for not letting either of them die before me*. Surely it was a blessing that they would outlive her. (Unless a massive earthquake struck in the next few hours, they would.) It was meant to be that children should outlive their parents.

But what was happening to her? She never allowed herself to think in terms of "blessings," and "meant to be's". . . Not for a minute had she believed Someone was Up There blessing them, that a Grand Plan existed for which mortals cannot know the reasons. Had she actually allowed "Thank God" to pass through her brain cells? Who had slipped this phrase into Anna's mind? The reason was a lack of oxygen, of this she was certain.

That night, the hospice nurse, a young Chinese girl, materialized in Anna's room like a slender angel. "You'll have no pain anymore," she said to Anna. "This will ease your breathing. Just relax now." She slid a needle deftly into the vein of Anna's left wrist and strapped it there with tape. She upturned a small glass bottle, filled a syringe with its contents, and very slowly injected the fluid into Anna's vein.

"That's all there is to it," the sweet girl said. "You'll feel much better very soon."

Instantly, Anna felt a wave of warmth and peace spread through her. She closed her eyes and that was that. Dead . . . or as good as. No more thinking, no more suffering. No more food. No more air. No more Santa Clauses giving out perfume to the old crones. The nurse gently removed the oxygen cannula from Anna's nose, turned off the feeding tube pump, disconnected the tube that fed Anna's belly. They were closing up shop. Anna was done, excused, pardoned, dismissed.

She heard the clink of glass hitting tin as the nurse disposed of the morphine container in the waste basket. She took Anna's pulse, she brushed the hair off Anna's forehead, she turned off the light above Anna's head and left the room.

In the morning, though Anna was, for all practical purposes, dead, a death watch ensued. She was glad to see the nurses move The Crab to another room, for the sake of delicacy. Janet, her husband, and their eldest daughter, Bonnie, arrived (her granddaughter definitely had too much gray hair for a woman so young). Carol came in with her son, a gorgeous young man six and a half feet tall. He had in his eyes the beautiful wild look of his crazy dead father, but he was totally sane, a miracle. Next, Anna's sister Gert arrived, leaning on her cane, earrings dangling from her ears, necklaces from her neck, at eighty-eight still the little cockroach sister, the galling brat, and now she walked in with the cocky air of being the winner. (For this alone Anna might consider staying alive, just not to lose the game.)

"Open your eyes, Anna," Gert said. "Say good-bye."

Anna was already congealed as cold lead; what did her sister expect, miracles? Gert turned away, grumbling. "A negative person," she said to Anna's girls. "Your mother was always so negative. Your father would have been happier with me."

But even triumphing over Gert could not tempt Anna back. She was already high above them, swinging on her heavenly swing, her two pianos perched on a cloud, her music ranged around her in a semicircle like a rainbow in the sunlit heavens. Light as a bird, Anna had flown up to heaven, and all it had taken was an ounce of clear fluid. If word got out, the whole world would be doing it, all the old Chinese in their gray pajamas and black cotton shoes, all the old Jews in their skullcaps and prayer shawls, all the old Indians in their turbans and saris—there would be a run on needles and little glass bottles; someone smart could make a fortune.

Her family hung over her bed not knowing what to do or where to stand or what to say. Anna would have liked to smile sweetly and grace them with forgiveness, but Jews never had much interest in sin and redemption. Once a year they fasted, ostensibly to cleanse their sins and start the year anew, but Anna had never known a Jew who thought he had committed a sin.

Deathbed scenes were historically quite moving; Melanie's death in *Gone With the Wind*, for instance, was heart wrenching. But then Melanie had been young and beautiful, tragically deceived and deeply forgiving, all of which Anna was not. Nor had Anna a besotted but gorgeously handsome Clark Gable crying in the hallway. Anna's husband Abram, whose face she could no longer recall, had been dead for thirty-two years and was barely a wisp floating at the back of her mind.

Aside from calling out for Jesus, Anna's many and various roommates who had died had, in their death throes, called upon their mothers: *Mama, Mama, I'm afraid! Mama, hold my hand.*

Fear had never been Anna's concern; her main emotion throughout life was indignation. Even now she was thinking whoever had designed this living business should have seen to it that the end was not so messy and miserable. Why wasn't there a cutoff date, maybe at age eighty, at which time the subscription ended, and everyone knew it and was ready for it? A simple pill or a shock administered to the breathing center of the brain and that would be that. This arrangement was too hit-and-miss. Some were lucky and died in their sleep (no one she ever knew). A few others had a five-second massive coronary and it was over. But look at her, seven years chained to this bed. What kind of joke was that? What kind of a joker had cooked up this arrangement? A lunatic, an imbecile.

So who could she call on for help in her last moments? Certainly not the lunatic. As for her mother, her mother had never held her hand or reassured her about anything. She tried to conjure up her mother's face but got an image only of a white head of hair and a voice admonishing her to wash the floor. *Wash the floor, Anna!* Her mother: Sophie, a Polish-Jewish washerwoman, a cook and a chicken plucker from Kutno, a peeler of potatoes in a shtetl somewhere in the wilds of eastern Europe. What would she know about comforting a child? What did she ever know? *Eat! Sleep! Wash the floor!* Sophie had been a great buxom beauty whose first husband had run off with a young girl, forcing her to send the children from that marriage—Sam and Ava, Anna's half brother and half sister—to an orphanage. While they lived there, Sophie had become a midwife to earn her living and pay for the Jewish divorce, "the get." What did she get afterward: she got Moishe the tailor, the man with constipation, who fathered Anna and Gert. Anna tried to recall what she knew about her father. Almost nothing, that he worked over a sewing machine ten hours a day, that he made her take castor oil every night, that he inquired daily about the movement of her bowels.

Gert had a gold mine of stories about their father. She always took Anna by surprise in that sly way she had, when she came up behind her and said, "Do you remember the time?" Anna never remembered Gert's memories; she was sure her sister made them up. This one was a dirty story. Their father, with all his straining and trying to move his bowels, had terrible hemorrhoids. One night the doctor sent Anna's mother to the drugstore with a little slip of paper. "My husband is so sick," she told the druggist. "He can't stand the pain. The doctor said I have to get this . . ." and she handed him the scrap of paper.

"Oh, you can't want that!" the druggist said. "You must be mistaken."

"Yes, we have to have it, the doctor said we have to use it tonight!"

If you use it tonight, you could end up killing him," the druggist said. The instructions given Anna's mother by the doctor were to bring home what the druggist gave her, fill it with ice and apply it to her husband's private parts.

"You know what it was?" Gert challenged Anna. "It was a condom, Anna! Isn't that a laugh? She was supposed to put ice in the condom! But the druggist thought it was for . . . you know what!"

Very funny, Anna thought now, Gert with her condoms. Anna hadn't even known the name for those things till a few years ago, from the talk shows talking about condoms all the time and should they be passed out to little children in schools. Even Abram, in all his years of being married to Anna, kept a box of them hidden under his socks and didn't once say the word to her face.

Now Gert was stroking the cheek of Anna's handsome grandson, saying "Smooth, like a baby's tushy." Gert with her dirty mind—even at the side of a deathbed.

Anna's granddaughter, Bonnie, was holding Anna's hand and singing to her, a beautiful song about white sands and gray sands. Danny, Janet's husband, was standing over by the wall, reading the letter pasted up there from the mayor, congratulating Anna on reaching her ninetieth birthday. She noticed no one in the room was actually crying. Her family had no idea how long this death would take—it could test a person's patience. Anna could see that her breath was coming in short, shallow gasps, with long intervals between. Her chest heaved, and then rested for many seconds. When the hospice nurse came in to check, she whispered to Anna's family, "She's having agonal breathing now."

Agonal, Anna thought. *The last agony*.

But suddenly, Anna had a shock! The stage hands were wheeling in the tunnel, the famous tunnel she'd heard about on Oprah, the tunnel filled with all the people from the past who would be there to guide Anna into the next world. It looked a little like the Holland Tunnel, a long arc of white tiles (quite a few missing), and filled with stinking car exhaust. But it also had a McDonald's in it, and a replica of P.S. 9, Anna's elementary school, as well as the Ferris wheel from Coney Island. This was a major production. Anna was surprised anyone would go to so much trouble for her. She saw her first grade teacher wearing a big white feather in her hat (now maybe Anna could make up for an unforgivable grammatical error she had once made when meeting her teacher on the street), and there was her sister Ava carrying an Ebinger's cake (to make up for all the unkindnesses she'd done Anna).

That light at the end of the tunnel was too bright—and also in her eyes. But who was that tall figure with the unruly head of hair ambling toward her; who was that sweet-faced man, smiling that loving smile, holding out his hand to Anna? Her husband's face materialized after all these lost years, his wonderful brow, his blue-green eyes, the smile that took her in and wrapped itself around her. She could feel her heart stopping at the sight of him.

At her bedside, the nurse was urging her family to say goodbye and leave. A good idea—Anna had so many last-minute things to think about now.

The nurse counseled them: "You know, the dying find it hard to die while the family is here. She feels your energy and that's what's holding her back. But hearing is the last sense to go—so you could all say a few words of farewell to her."

"Happy New Year, Mom-Mom," her granddaughter whispered in her ear, shocking Anna with the news. New Year's Eve! What a convenient night upon which to die! How fitting. How economical! She wouldn't have to pay even for one minute of the new year, not one minute of the new month, in this hellhole. If she could exit before midnight, even her tax liability would end here.

There was a flurry of all the heads of her beloved people bending over her bed, some tentatively stroking her good hand, her forehead. It was an ordeal for them, she understood this. She was wasted, emaciated, hollow, a bag of bones. Her eyes had rolled up into her head, her mouth hung open, her bony chest heaved with irregular gasps.

Don't worry, she wanted to say. *I'm up here already, I have my beautiful auburn hair falling full down my back, all my fingers are ready for Mozart, my heart is open to Chopin. My beloved Abram is going to kiss me at the stroke of midnight. Go home, children. This is nothing at all, this getting of wings. Go home and live a while longer. Welcome the New Year. No one ever dies; it's just a fairy tale.*

Anna's Archive

In the driveway of Carol's house, conveniently situated catty-corner from Janet's, Anna watched her daughters disposing ruthlessly of her precious papers. Sitting in plastic garden chairs, they examined then flung these scraps of paper and notebooks and folders and flyers, her carefully collected medical bills, her filled calendars, lists of all the drugs she had ever taken, notes from all her classes, records of every phone call to people who had cheated her, a card file of all her customers from the antique store, her jury duty summonses, these and other precious notations they dumped—without ceremony—into a huge green plastic garbage can.

She felt it was premature for them to be doing this when their mother was not yet even warm in her grave. (Warmer, at least, than her remains were now in the mortuary refrigerator.) Not that Anna expected her children to lug her material leavings with them for the rest of their lives, but this seemed a precipitous rush to get rid of her, bag and baggage. Yet she understood her delayed burial presented many difficult hours for them to get through and this activity might be—in their view—an appropriate act of remembrance and devotion.

"Hold on a minute, my God, what *is* this?" Carol exclaimed, pulling out of a carton the moldy remains of Anna's brown corduroy jacket. Black pellets fell from it onto the cement of the driveway. "Rat droppings! Yuck!" Carol jumped up and flung the jacket away from her. "Now we'll probably catch the hanta virus. It lives forever in rat droppings—then the droppings dry into a powder, and you breathe it in and you die."

"So I guess then we won't be separated from Mom too long," Janet said. "We can just follow her lead and join her in the afterlife."

"I'm not in such a hurry," Carol said. "Are you? Wait here a minute and don't touch anything. I'll be right back." She went into the garage. Anna noticed a breeze blowing, warm for January. In fact, it was like a picnic out in the driveway—tree branches sighing, birds chirping, the sky bright and blue overhead.

Nature was not actually so bad. Anna couldn't understand why she had shunned it all her ninety years—never bothered to admire a sunrise, a lowering sky, the buds of spring, the chirp of baby birds. Probably because such matters were mindless. Anna had no patience for lack of thought, for slowness (what was slower than the growing of a tree from some kind of nut?), for repetition without purpose. Whereas in Chopin, in Mozart, if a theme were repeated and moved steadily through a sonata in varying patterns, it was there to bring the listener's heart to life, to bring someone musical (like herself) to her knees with its beauty and design.

Now Carol came back looking like an alien from outer space. She had a painter's mask over her mouth and nose and huge yellow rubber gloves on her hands. She handed a duplicate set to Janet. "Put these on. We're not breathing in hanta virus if we can help it. If I died and my sons inherited this house, they'd sell it and blow it all in two months."

So Anna's daughters went back to work shuffling through the minuscule record of their mother's life: her written remains, mere scraps of paper, lined notebook pages with meaningless lists, business cards of others, IRS tax returns, canceled checks. Where were her great creative works? Her opus? Her poetry, her musical compositions, her art? What petty remains were left of her were going into a cracked garbage can—and those sending them there were the only substantial creations of her life: her children.

Not enough, not enough, Anna concluded. Thirty or forty years hence her girls would be in the grave as well, and where would Anna be found? In the shape of the thumb of one of her grandchildren? In their inherited bunions? Even her renditions of "White Christmas" on the piano, performances that Abram recorded on plastic records back in Brooklyn in the '40s, were long crumbled and devoured by time. Maybe a few of her pieces were on those cassette tapes that Janet's husband, Danny, liked to make at family events. But it was little enough to show for a lifetime. Anna recalled how, as a little girl, she used to play make-believe piano on the edge of the wooden kitchen table in her parents' apartment in the lower east side of New York till one day her father gave in and bought her an old upright piano. Where did her longing come from? Her father's love of Caruso? Some distant rabbinical scribe, some cantor in the old country? She had never wasted time on these sorts of questions and wasn't going to now. Music was Anna's passion, and she knew she'd had it in her to be a great musician.

"Remember how Mom used to carry her music to the eye doctor's office? The way she would say, 'My glaucoma is so bad! I can't read my Mozart! I can't read my Chopin!' "Carol was looking with disgust at the pile of Anna's music notebooks in her lap.

"Of course I remember," Janet said.

"Weren't you embarrassed to death, the way she made such a fuss? As if, since she played music, she was more entitled not to go blind than the other old ladies who only watched soap operas?"

"She always needed to prove she was special," Janet said.

"Because she *wasn't* special," Carol said. "Look at this!"

She was holding, Anna could see, the bulletin from the Hollywood Senior Multipurpose Center.

"Volunteer of the Month: Anna Goldman," Carol read aloud. "Listen to this information she gave them: 'Anna Goldman was born in New York and lived there until her family moved to Florida and later to California. She has two daughters of whom she is justly proud. The elder daughter is a writer and teacher of international fame, and the younger is talented and celebrated in art and sculpture. Both are married and have families."

"Notice she doesn't say that one of her daughter's husbands was a wife batterer, and killed himself. Notice how she inflates your 'international fame' and my 'art genius.' She always used to say, when the three of us were together: 'Here we are, the musician, the writer, and the artist.' We were three invisible nobodies, Janet, that's what we were."

"If it made her feel worthwhile to brag about us, why should you have minded so much? We didn't turn out so bad."

"Well, if you think you're that special, you have the same problem Mom had. She had to be in the limelight. She had to puff us up because we were really never good enough for her. I always minded! I was always so ashamed of her."

Anna felt a pang in whatever portion of her being was still extant. She had always believed her children thought as much of her as she did of herself. Maybe more, since she had the added power of being their mother.

"Throw it all out," Carol continued. "Don't even read that stuff in her folders or her notebooks. Our mother was a hollow lady, Janet. I don't even know if she loved us. Maybe she only loved herself."

A hollow lady! Sharper than a serpent's tooth! But could it be true she loved no one but herself? Maybe not even herself?

There, in the balmy air of the driveway, Carol and Janet were having a tug-of-war. Carol was trying to pull a bunch of notebooks out of Janet's lap and toss them in the trash. "One second, don't do that!" Janet was pleading. "These are Mom's notes from her music class. I just want to look at them."

"Don't waste your time. Mom was just a parrot. Listen to this . . ." she said, leaning over Janet's shoulder and reading: "*'Baroque Period, 1600-1750, Bach died in 1750 and Handel stopped writing in 1750—hit by blindness. Handel lived in England. Bach lived in Germany.*' Her notes are totally mechanical. She never had an original thought."

"Where is all this anger coming from so suddenly?" Janet asked her sister. "I think you're just tired and stressed out. We've been stretched pretty thin these last few days. Maybe we need to take a break. Have a cup of tea. I just can't imagine what Mom did to you to make you this angry."

"It's what she didn't do! She never knew what I needed! I wanted nice clothes, and she bought me junk on sale that I looked awful in. I wanted to wear my hair long, and she made me cut it short with little bangs. She never knew who I was! She never thought of me as a person with needs. She wasn't sensitive to anything I needed."

"And would you say we did better with our children?" Janet asked. "Were we so sensitive?"

"We did better than Mom did. At least I tried to hear what my kids were saying. Mom didn't listen to anyone. I don't even know if she had any sense of the kind of man Daddy was. I don't even know if she loved him."

Anna felt unduly stirred by these accusations, unfairly attacked since she no longer could defend herself. Her girls glared at one another. She knew, from her own troubles with high blood pressure, that their systolic readings had to be up in the danger range. She hoped one of them wouldn't have a stroke and then they'd have to cancel Anna's funeral.

Janet had wrested one of the notebooks from Carol and was reading something in it, a big blue faded loose-leaf. Carol turned away and continued dumping papers into the garbage can, mumbling under her breath. "Why did she save all this junk? All her complaint letters, this one to Campbell's soup: 'There aren't enough noodles in your chicken noodle soup!' To Van De Kamp's bakery: 'I found a bran muffin in your box of chocolate cupcakes.' To the police department: 'I had gone out to do my civic duty and vote, and what did I get but a parking ticket!' All that energy wasted. All that misplaced indignation. And these nonsense jingles she wrote to every stranger she met, to kiss up and curry favor. Listen to this one:

To Evelyn and Joe, (whoever on earth they were . . .):
Here's a heartfelt double tribute
That I'd fondly like to state
One-half goes to Evelyn
The other to Joe, her mate.
They're a very special couple
Who aim to please us all
They sing, they dance, they have a talent
It's almost ten feet tall . . .
When the news is grim and papers shout
Of recession, uneasy peace, and fright
These two just turn the tide and say
'Everything's all right . . .'
And since this is their birthday month
Evelyn's the twelfth and Joe September three
We wish them forever good health and cheer
From you and you and ME!"

Carol put her finger down her throat. "Shall I throw up here or in the bushes?"

"Have a heart. She just did it for fun. It was almost a reflex of hers, to put everything into rhyme. But here's something different," Janet said, in a different tone of voice, looking down at a sheet in her lap. "Come here and look, Carol. Here's something that isn't a complaint letter or a nonsense jingle."

Carol came and leaned over Janet's back to see what it was. She squinted in the sun, shading her eyes.

"Read it to me, I can't focus out here . . .it's too bright."

"She wrote this among her notes from the music class at UCLA. It's dated November 1, 1967. That was Daddy's birthday, two years after he died. This page has notations from a lecture on Debussy and Chopin. But listen to what Mom wrote on the edge of the page:

The cool damp earth the cake,
Each candle a star

Peaceful birthday my darling
Wherever you are."

Carol and Janet looked at one another.

"Mom wrote a real poem," Janet said. "She wrote Daddy a love poem."

"So you believe she really loved Daddy after all?"

"I think it *proves* we're children of a love match," Janet smiled. "You and I, we're love children."

"Alright, so we'll keep this one piece of paper, even the whole notebook," Carol conceded. "Maybe we could even make copies of this poem for our children."

"If you don't mind, I'd like to put the original in a frame and hang it on the wall."

"Good, you keep it. And I'll come every day to your house to visit it," Carol said.

Late that night, Janet came outside to her front yard to call her cat. It seemed to Anna that a moonbeam was illuminating the row of trash cans at the curb near Carol's house. The cracked green garbage can, the can without a cover, was filled to overflowing with Anna's papers, the edges of envelopes and the tips of folders like so many glistening points of a crown glowing in the strange, hushed light of the moon. Anna watched her daughter pause and stare at the can, take a few steps toward her own front door and turn and look again. Anna could see what her daughter saw, how the moon was a spotlight on her earthly remnants, the darkness like a stage from which actors were calling out all her written words.

Janet went quickly back into her house and came out immediately holding a large yellow plastic bag. She rushed across the street to where Anna's trash heap shone in the moonlight. Working fast, she grabbed handfuls of her mother's papers and transferred them to the bag, stuffing them down till they were compressed, then adding others. She was bent halfway into the garbage can when a police car cruised by and slowed to a stop. Janet straightened up and waved at the officers: they waved back, no questions asked. Anna—because she had helped her daughters with the down payments on their homes—was glad to be responsible for the fact that they lived in one of the safest towns in America.

An owl hooted and the chilling cry of a coyote spun upward from the distant hills while Anna's daughter, intent on her mission, went on rescuing from the garbage the treasures of Anna's archive.

Anna felt revived by the night wind. She could still know relief and its attendant pleasures. Now all her words would be preserved, and a good thing it was—for her descendants, her heirs, and for the nourishment of posterity.

The Desert of the Mysteries

The main problem with marriage, Anna thought, was that it put an end to looking further. When Abram took her to see the musical *The Desert Song*, she listened to the tenor's honeyed voice croon, *"The desert is waiting, come dear with me, I'm longing to teach you love's sweet mysteries . . ."* and decided then and there she might as well let Abram be the one to show them to her. Something notable had to have inspired all those movies and the love poems Gert was always clipping from the newspapers. The tragic arias of every opera depended on love's mysteries, and Chopin's heart had to have been in this desert when he wrote his nocturnes. Though Anna had no patience for sentimental nonsense and scorned Gert's habit of pressing flowers in her "Thought for the Day Album," she knew at one time or another she'd have to choose some man and go with him to those vaunted places.

The lawyers in the offices where she worked were always after her—they smelled of starched shirts and the ink that oozed from their signatures onto their desk blotters. She imagined that life with a lawyer would be one long contract with many stipulations. She didn't want to marry anyone smarter than she (or who thought he was) or with more education. The man she finally chose—when he turned up on the front porch of the Brooklyn house, brought along as Gert's blind date for the party she and her friends were giving—seemed shy, pliable, agreeable, unthreatening, and had a sweet, winsome smile. He looked, in fact, a little like Clark Gable.

When, on the night of Gert's party, Anna came home from dinner with yet another dull lawyer, she discovered Abram rocking rhythmically on the porch glider, smoking a pipe that smelled of butterscotch tobacco, and keeping himself hidden from the noise and chatter inside the house.

She gave him the barest nod and went upstairs to change her clothes—or so she had always thought. This meeting with Abram was the part of the story she and Gert always fought over: Gert swore Anna went upstairs after her date and then came down in her *negligee*, with her hair loosed from their pins and flowing down her back. As Anna remembered it, she had changed into a blouse and tailored slacks and had left her hair in a bun. But—whatever the case—she surely had every right that night to step outside on her own front porch to take the night air. Gert argued for the rest of her life that Anna had ruined her chances, that Abram would have married her if not for Anna's turning up at that moment and showing herself off in a sheer nightgown.

To clear things up for herself, Anna—with the special privileges of the unburied dead—now had a chance to revisit the scene and see the truth for herself. She came back on this particular spring evening. The house was bright with noise and the voices of strangers; Anna saw, for one thing, that the lilac tree was in full bloom and heavy with clusters of fragrant blossoms. Anna had never paid attention to nature. A tree was a tree and a bird a bird; if the tree didn't fall on her and the bird didn't deposit its droppings on her head, she had nothing against them. Flowers in general always seemed a waste to her: on the bush they withered and died (especially gardenias, which had no useful life span at all), whereas cut and given as a gift, flowers were also useless. You had to put them in a vase and a few days later you had green slimy water to dispose of as well as the flowers themselves.

Yet, this night, as she came up the walk with David Bloomenstein, an attorney at her firm, a man with acne and a left thumbnail black with fungus, she was overpowered by the sweetness of the lilac blooms. She staggered a little at the onslaught, as if a drug had been given her.

A short time before, at dinner with David Bloomenstein, he had proposed marriage and had the nerve to try to force a diamond ring upon her. He guaranteed the ring had no time limit on it: she could take forever to decide when (or if) they would marry. He said he was sure she would learn to love him. Anna had adamantly refused the ring. He refused to take it back. She insisted that he must or she would leave it on the table at the Chinese restaurant among the shards of their fortune cookies. He said he didn't want it if she wouldn't accept it—it was meant only for her. She dropped it on the white tablecloth: "Then let the Chinks have it!"

She thought "Chinks" was a word anyone would use, indicating both the restaurant and the Chinese who ran it, but from the look of dismay on David Bloomenstein's face, she knew she had said something ugly. If she wanted to think of the owners as "Chinks," it was her business. She didn't care for such fussy sensibilities in a man, and she refused to be disapproved of.

Still, she could tell there'd been a fatal error, not that she cared. The lawyer took her home, anyway, coldly but politely escorting her to her front door. When he dropped her arm and bid her good-bye, she stood on the porch till he drove away. She had to compose her face for going into the house where a foolish party was in full swing. She could hear charades being played inside, and dance music was on the Victrola. At that moment she saw the ruby glow of a match held over the bowl of a pipe and heard the strong inhalation of a man's breath as he lit his tobacco.

Anna, with not a romantic cell in her body, felt her bones turn gelatinous. What he said to her, what she said to him, she could not remember (and could not make out even now, in her visitation): but she remembered the deepness of his voice, the way it vibrated through the floorboards of the porch and into the core of her being.

Her high heels were pinching her toes; she told him (she didn't yet know his name) she would come out again as soon as she changed her clothes. Inside the house the party was raucous, a circus of jokers and teasers, a bunch of young men from the neighborhood, fellows without a brain in their heads trying to impress Gert and her girlfriends who were in a club they called "The Sorority."

Anna went upstairs. She passed Mama's room where Mama sat on the side of her bed, soaking her feet in a pan of hot water. She went into the room she shared with Gert (the big front room was rented out to Mr. Vicci, the boarder, who paid $2 rent each month), and she took off her heels, her stockings, her suit jacket (still pinned to it was the orchid corsage David Bloomenstein had given her). Her skirt, her slip, her underwear, they all came off—she felt she could breathe once the elastic stopped pinching her. Then she put on . . . (here Anna looked closely, to find out the truth of the matter once and for all) . . . her peignoir set! So Gert was right! The historical truth was that she had gone back downstairs in her sheer nightgown. But of course with a matching robe over it. There was nothing untoward to be seen, just a shimmer of mauve chiffon robe over a lighter lavender chiffon gown. (Who had given her this honeymoon set, and when? She could not recall.) And—this was also true: she let down her hair. Well, why wouldn't she, with the pins sticking in her scalp, and the hair pulled taut around her forehead? She could feel the relief even now, as she shook it loose and it tumbled over her shoulders.

She passed through the crowd of party-makers without a glance toward them (if Gert saw her, it couldn't be helped, could it?) and went out to the front porch.

Abram's long legs made the porch seem small—she had to step over them to take a seat on the wicker chair. They talked a little: nice night, nice party. They exchanged names. After a while Abram said, "I don't really know your sister, you know, so I wonder if you think it would be alright for me to ask you something. Someone gave me a pair of tickets to the ice rink on Ocean Parkway." He fished around in his jacket pocket and held them up for her to see. "Are you game to go ice skating with me?"

"I don't skate," she said.

"Me neither," he said, and laughed. She realized this was a man she could manage. She knew the tickets had been brought along for Gert. He had moved fast, even though he talked in a slow Jimmy

Stewart drawl. She was still arranging her frothy nightgown around her legs and already they had a date. So there it was. The famous thing that happened to other people had happened to Anna: love at first sight.

Gert liked to say after the wedding that Anna never wanted to be married. Otherwise, why had she burst into tears after the ceremony in the living room and run upstairs, her lace handkerchief to her mouth? Why did she go to pieces while all the guests were still there? (Years later, Gert told Anna's daughters she thought she knew why. She told them their mother was afraid of what Abram would say when he discovered she wasn't a virgin!) Gert and her salacious mind! Prurient Gert! Anna could never get over the vulgarity of her sister. To whom could she possibly have "given" her virginity? And why would she have? Sex was the furthest thing from her mind, then, now, and all the years in between. She was crying on her wedding night, all right, but crying for a different reason entirely. In "The Desert Song" the lovers flee into the night on their camel; they don't have to live crowded into the same house with the bride's old mother and her old maid sister. That's why she was crying! Heartsick in the realization that she wasn't going into the desert of the mysteries with her handsome lover, but back into the bedroom next to her mother's now that Mr. Vicci, the boarder, had been evicted.

Anna and Abram were forced to run away to Cleveland to get some privacy. Where was Cleveland? Anna, who disdained geography, had no idea, except that it was far away from Gert and Mama in Brooklyn. Abram's job, selling pajamas in the men's department of Abraham and Straus, did not hold much promise for the future. She had resisted Abram's proposition that they go and find their fortunes further west until the morning Mama opened their bedroom door ("Don't pay attention to me, I'm just here to get your laundry") just as Abram was lifting Anna to get her poised on top of him because he told her she'd have more feeling that way.

Her anger, not her shame, was the thing that convinced her she wanted to leave—anger at her mother and Gert for having to live with them, anger at her father for dying young, anger at Abram for not being satisfied to do it in the dark, in the night, under the blanket, the usual way, and anger at herself for letting him get her into such a compromising position in a room that had no lock on the door.

Together they looked at road maps to Cleveland where Abram had heard from his brother Sol there were certain opportunities having to do with gambling machines. Sol was already out there doing business. He was sure Abram and he could make some money together. Abram, who was looking for his life's work, thought this might be it.

"Don't worry about Mama and Gert," he assured Anna. "We'll send them money for rent and food the whole time we're away, and if—after I learn the ropes—the business works out there, I'll set up the same business back here in Brooklyn."

This Abram of hers hadn't just married her. He had married the lot of them: Gert and Mama, too. He'd taken on their full support. Was he made out of pure gold, her husband? My God, how Anna resented his goodness. She wanted her own life even if it meant leaving her mother and sister to fend for themselves. But Abram wouldn't think of it. He was a better man than she. He was too good to be true. Even if he had enjoyed a few burlesque shows in his day, even if she knew he had a pack of playing cards of naked women in his handkerchief drawer, even if he thought Anna should have more feeling in bed, how could she hold it against him?

For her, indignation was a natural reaction. She found it a relief to hold everything against everyone—it was almost her religion. For reasons she did not question, her life energy had been powered by fury. She was actually surprised (now that she was dead) that it hadn't kept her living forever. She crackled like a burning bush, throwing flames at the world for not letting her get educated, for not giving her the best piano teacher, for not introducing her to a rich and important husband, for making her take care of these two helpless women. If she'd married a rich lawyer she'd have a house with a decorator by now. She was angry at herself that no lawyer had ever appealed to her as much as Abram. She was seduced and attracted by his gentleness and kindness and therefore angry at him the rest of her life for having so much of those qualities that he never got ahead in the world.

Abram's younger brother, Sol, was a Valentino look-alike, always in black shoes polished to a shine, a rakish thin mustache on his face, a wink in his eye. Women loved him, women—unlike Anna—who couldn't see through to his slyness, his crooked nature. He was dumb and shrewd at the same time, a combination Anna had no use for, a man without a vocabulary, a man who said things like "She don't want to see me," and never knew the difference. His stupidity gave him courage, he took chances, he got mixed up with every lowlife around and thought anyone in a striped suit was a powerful kingpin.

Sol's business in Cleveland involved installing claw machines in bars, diners, cafés, and dance halls. The machines required customers to put money into a slot, then aim the claw down into a pile of tantalizing gifts: leather wallets, wristwatches, china dolls, pearl earrings, rings, and necklaces. The goal was to capture a prize. When Sol brought a machine to their apartment to demonstrate it to them, Anna tried it and found that the prize fell from the claw's grip every time.

"It's robbery," she told Sol.

He laughed.

She tried again: the claw hand was imprecise, it was impossible to get it positioned. If she did grasp a prize, the claw went limp, its springs collapsing and allowing the object to drop back into the pile.

"Try it this way," Sol instructed her, and showed her how to position the claw behind the object so that—as it dropped down—

it also moved forward and landed on the prize. "It's not easy but it's possible."

After he left that night (to go out with one of his bleached-blonde floozies), Anna confronted Abram. "I don't like you mixed up in this business. It's gambling."

"What's so bad about that? Isn't all of life a gamble?"

Abram, the philosopher, comforted himself every day, convinced that if he wasn't rich, it didn't matter because "the best things in life are free." If he didn't own a yacht, he could still rent a rowboat in Prospect Park and go fishing. If he didn't own an oceanfront house, he could still go out to Coney Island and sit on a bench on the boardwalk and contemplate the mystery of the sea. The ocean was his, the seagulls were his, the big tankers out on the horizon were his. The pelicans diving for fish were his.

But they weren't Anna's, and she had no interest whatsoever in pelicans.

At least they had privacy in Cleveland. Mama and Gert were not underfoot. Anna could make meals for Abram without garlic and onions, which Mama always used and which Anna hated. She wanted to prove to her husband, who had a streak of impossible Jewish piety, that if she served butter in his mashed potatoes alongside a steak, God would not strike him dead for the sin of putting meat and milk together. How could Abram, or anyone, believe those Old World tales in which God was always about to strike someone dead for some foolish act like eating bacon? What God? Where was God? Had he turned up to save her brother from drowning or her father from dying young of a sore throat? Had he stopped Anna's mother from marrying, for her first husband, a bigamist? Why should Anna worry about what God wanted the Jews to eat?

Sol lived in a room in a hotel in downtown Cleveland; he spent time there only when some lady friend did not have him stay over at her place or when Abram happened to forget to invite him over for dinner. Sol filled up Anna's apartment with cigarette smoke and the scent of his shoe polish. He didn't seem to sense her obvious distaste at everything about him; in fact, he seemed to think she was grateful for his offering Abram this chance to get rich. He'd tilt back in one of the kitchen chairs with the air of entitlement that the rich carry with them—he'd drop his cigarette ash into the dessert dish that had been filled previously with applesauce or canned peaches. He was always plotting: to buy more machines, different machines, to fill them with cheaper items, to invent new kinds of machines. He thought they could sell other things, like dirty postcards, from vending machines. He had a collection of these that he brought over one night, laying them out on the kitchen table in a fan, like a winning poker hand. While he and Abram talked business, Anna, pretending not to look, peered over their shoulders as she cleaned up the dishes. Her eyes were riveted on these women: young women, with delicate faces and tendrils of curly dark hair framing their graceful features—but naked! Posed with a single rose in her hand, or her toe held forward, about to step into a marble tub, or with a feathery shawl resting on her shoulder, each woman looked as if she belonged in a poem or a Shakespeare play, each having a radiance and sweetness about her form.

Anna could not understand how they would pose for a camera this way, to know that their private parts would be slavered over by men like Sol, to know their images would be sold and bartered from pocket to pocket. Why was she here serving lamb chops and string beans and applesauce to a man who was trying to convince her husband to sell pictures of naked women in coin machines? What did Sol think when he looked at Anna in her linen skirt and wool sweater? What did Abram think when he studied these women? Did he wish his wife were one of them?

She knew Abram wanted her to have more feeling, but Anna was convinced she had been born with something missing: she had no animal instincts. She didn't sweat. She didn't like food (meat with its gristle, eggs with their slime, milk that turned sour in the bottle). And she didn't like the mess and grunting of sex, the untidiness of it, the invasiveness of it. She knew she had to put up with it, she knew it came with the wedding ring, but could other women really enjoy it?

Gert, ever the thorn in her side, actually said to Anna's daughters one day, in her old age, "Your mother thinks her shit doesn't stink." Anna was shocked by this, truly disgusted, horrified, to see so frankly revealed the pit of slime in which her sister's mind swam. The irony was, in fact, that Anna's bowels—all her life—were literally knotted in slime, an "irritable bowel," the doctors told her (they always asked her if she was especially worried or tense about anything!). What she never told them was that her father had been fanatic about bowels all his life. He asked Anna and Gert daily if they'd had their bowel movements. Anna refused to discuss this with him. Therefore, because she wouldn't answer him, he forced cod liver oil into her mouth—a disgusting, fishy, spoonful of poison! My God, Anna thought, now that life was all over for her, if only she had been able to live it like an angel: unsweaty, unfed, unboweled, unsexed.

Soon after they got back to Brooklyn, soon after Abram installed dozens of claw machines in bars and dance halls and cigar stores in Brooklyn, Governor Dewey declared gambling machines illegal and ordered that they all be thrown in the East River.

Abram's scheme to get rich and buy Anna the privacy she craved never came to pass. At least he did this one thing: when they moved back into the bedroom next to Mama's in the house in Brooklyn, Abram screwed a lock and bolt on their bedroom door. Time and time again he tried to lead her into the desert of the mysteries. He whispered imaginary tales to her, he told her to pretend she was someone else, a fan dancer, a veiled beauty in a harem, he urged her to forget herself. He would be a sultan, she a belly dancer in his harem. He would be King Herod and she would be Salome. She would do the dance of the seven veils to delight him. But the bolt on the door never stopped Mama from knocking and asking for laundry, and though once or twice Anna tried to imagine herself Salome, and once or twice the mistress of Chopin, she never achieved the key to the secrets found in the desert of the mysteries.

ANNA GETS WINGS

TODAY ANNA was to disappear permanently from the face of the earth. "The sun shall not smite me by day nor the moon by night," she reminded herself. "Six feet under." "I'm goin' where the sun don't shine." "Kicking the bucket." "Dead and buried." "Cold as a corpse." "Dead as a doornail." "Cashed in my chips." "Bought the farm." "Gave up the ghost."

Heir now to these literary gems, Anna was impressed. Dying brought a person into the realm of poetry and eternity, of eulogy and flattery. The bad news, however, was that she'd be silenced for good, her lips buttoned for time immemorial, till death she did part, which was, after all these years of living and fearing and fighting, today.

No more limericks, jingles, complaint letters, no etudes, gigues or nocturnes, no chocolate cakes on her birthday, no flashing of her pretty legs, no pencil and pad at her fingertips, the end of all further opportunities to have her say! What if she turned out to be awake in her grave for the rest of eternity? Stuck there without even a crossword puzzle! She hoped her daughters had ordered a bell installed in her coffin, one with a wire going up to the outside should Anna, by some chance, come back to life.

She had long ago dreamed that her husband Abram had been cured of his leukemia by embalming fluid, but since they had cut out his heart for the autopsy, he was prevented from rising up from his casket. Luckily, no doctors had asked her children if they could cut Anna into pieces. She was probably too poor an example of anything anatomical, too dried up, empty, her bones a latticework of splinters, to be of use to medical research. She hadn't wanted her organs reused either, though do-gooders were always urging people to give their eyes, their kidneys, their gall bladders, to others. Did she want some stranger peeing out of her kidneys, seeing out of her eyeballs? She didn't think so. Besides, her organs were at death's door, like the rest of her, and of no use to anyone.

Out in the living world, all her kin were busy. Janet was answering phone calls from dozens of people (most of them interested in financial gain now that they'd seen the two printed lines in the obituary column—Anna's name, her date of death, and "Proprietor, Goldman's Antiques"). The vultures—some of them dealers Anna used to do business with when she had the store—were calling to ask Janet, with voices full of insincere piety: "Did it take your mother long to die, did she suffer, was she in pain, poor thing, and what happened to the antiques left over from the store, do you want to sell them?"

Sitting at her kitchen table, Carol was on the line with FedCo, asking the price of cold-cut platters. (She could have called Canter's—the only decent Jewish deli in Los Angeles—but it was too expensive.) "Nothing but the best" was not a phrase Anna had taught her children to live by. Now she was feeling the consequences of her philosophy—she'd have third rate corned beef at her funeral reception, seedless Christian rye bread and prune Danish made with lard, with not a single salty black olive or a plate of pickled herring in sour cream on the table.

She'd warned her girls numerous times that she didn't want any transients at her funeral, no flowery baloney in the newspaper ("adored wife, beloved mother, devoted daughter, cherished sister . . ."), wanted no strangers who would cry crocodile tears and stuff themselves with food pretending they were brokenhearted Anna was dead. Most of all she didn't want a rabbi who had never laid eyes on her announcing in stentorian tones how good she had been in her life and how generous to everyone in need, that she was famous for her mitzvahs—visiting the sick, honoring her parents, donating to charity, and doing a good deed a day.

What if there *were* someone at the gates of heaven (*what if there were a heaven!*) asking Anna how many times she had succored the sick? She had been sicker for longer than anyone she'd ever heard of and had she been succored? Why did people even pretend it was in human nature to help others? Religion just tried to scare you into it. Anna had never been one to respond to threats. If anything, they made her more stubborn and ill-tempered. But now that she was up at the wire, crossing it, in fact, she wondered: should she have been kinder? And to whom?

If there were no atheists in foxholes, were there atheists in morgues? Anna knew that once underground her pretty legs would be consumed. *"The worms crawl in, the worms crawl out, they crawl in your stomach and out of your mouth."* She'd sung the song in the childhood alleys of the East Side of New York. "So give me God," she challenged the universe. "Give me heaven. Give me an afterlife where I get to dance with Abram till dawn, and after that I'll cook him sunny-side-up eggs, bubbling in the pan and sparkling with crystals of kosher salt." At least Jews cooked with salt that tasted like salt. Jews had taste, and Anna, a Jew in spite of it all, had excellent taste; she always knew which side was up. But now she was going down, six feet under. She felt—beneath her indignation, her outrage, her certainty—a chilling shudder of fear.

The morgue—refrigerator and dressing room combined—was not as lugubrious a place as she had imagined. Two Russian immigrant women were doing the dressing of the dead, babbling to one another in their shrill tongue, and slitting everyone's clothing down the back. They used a giant tailor's shears, like the one Anna's father had owned. The dead weren't cooperative, their elbows did not bend, so the women dressed them as if they were wooden dolls without joints.

Anna winced when they slashed her quilted red bathrobe down the middle of the back—a waste of a perfectly good piece of cloth. They chattered over her face, packing cotton behind her lips and stitching them closed in an extremely unnatural position. Though she no longer felt any of her body parts, she was offended to have her lips redesigned as if she were whistling, which she had never done in her life, believing that a whistle was a crude way to render music of any kind. Now she was especially glad she had demanded a closed casket, unlike her sister Gert, who had so much vanity she wanted to be on display in her evening gown. (Though this would not happen for some time, apparently, which fact annoyed Anna.)

Though Anna had none of the famed powers of ghosts, she would still have done her best to knock the lipstick out of the Russian's hand had the lady dared to try to color Anna's lips. When a person was dead she ought to look like death.

Now between the two of them (were they washerwomen or brain surgeons, you never knew with these Russian women) they maneuvered Anna's remains (she could have been a dead horse for all the respect they paid her) into the cheapest casket offered by the cemetery, a cloth-covered carton, the match to one Abram had been buried in thirty-two years ago. She didn't even want to imagine what was left of him now. She'd seen a movie with Sean Connery who takes a young girl (his mistress as well as his niece) to the Alps ostensibly to climb mountains with her. The villagers discover, on their climb, the body of a young man lost in a climbing accident many years ago and frozen in the ice. When they bring the man back to the village, his fiancée, now a crone as old as Anna, bends over his frost-covered body and sees his beautiful, youthful face gleaming up at her through the ice crystals. That's how Abram lived in Anna's mind, not at the age he died, fifty-six, which was young enough, but long before that, the face with which he courted her, with his wavy hair parted in the middle, and his sweet smile that melted her resistant heart.

A body in a box was what she had come to. She'd seen this before with her father and her mother and her husband, and the end result of a life always violated her trust in any goodness in the world. To think that even babies someday would come to this outrage! No matter what had gone on before, how glorious and successful the life, how much beauty and love and happiness had been the lot of the liver, there was the moment of the box, the closed box sitting on a pedestal, motionless as a mountain. And inside, a human being with the lid down over her face and darkness within. A fancy way to dispose of garbage.

Even though Anna wasn't really in there, it took her breath away to think she might be. Her children didn't know the truth and imagined their mother was in the box. Her granddaughters were clinging to one another in the anteroom of the chapel, refusing to look upon her face in the moment the casket had to be opened for reasons of identification.

"Forgive me but it's required," said the cemetery representative (an old man with a paunch in a dark suit), "—we must ask that the family certify that this is their deceased in the casket."

"Who else would it be?" Janet said. She, with Danny beside her, and Carol holding her hand, approached the box. Her daughters' expressions reminded Anna of when she had taken them—as young children—into the "Hall of Horrors" in the fun house in Coney Island. There they encountered a floor covered with wet spaghetti, spiderwebs brushing their faces, bats swooping down from the eaves, and skeletons popping out of the wall on springs. "It's all make-believe," Anna had explained to them, and she wished she could say it now. *All for effect*, she wanted to assure them. *Nothing's going on here—it all ended back there in the nursing home room when I stopped breathing. That was the happy end. Believe me.*

"Yes, that's our mother," Janet told the man in the dark suit. She reached inside the box and touched Anna's bony fingers resting on the quilted cloth of the red bathrobe. She knew her daughter would wince—this was not a humane entertainment. Anna herself had touched Abram's dead face in the coffin (a face made rosy with suntan colored liquid makeup) and to this day could feel the cold, clay chill on her fingertips.

Janet leaned over and put a book of music in the coffin—Anna's tattered book of Chopin nocturnes—as well as a sheet of paper with directions to Janet's house for the gathering after the funeral. Then she signed the paper the man held forth, after which he decorously replaced the lid over Anna's face putting forever out of sight that sewn-together mouth.

The family was offered the choice of sitting in the veiled area, out of sight of the mourners, or in the front row of the chapel.

"We'll sit with the others," Janet said, "but first I have to do something . . ." She reached into a paper bag and withdrew from it Anna's beloved musicians—the plastic busts of Beethoven, Schubert, Mozart, Chopin (he was in alabaster, from Italy)—and even Bach, though Anna could take him or leave him, and lined them up at intervals on the lid of Anna's coffin.

A stroke of genius, Anna thought. In the hush of these funeral places, usually sopping with flowers and organ chords, this was almost anarchy and smacked of idol worship. Anna felt her heart lift: maybe she would have a funeral befitting her spirit after all.

Who were all these people filing in? Anna was certifiably friendless, and yet she saw shades of the past arriving: Corrine Blume, who had taken music appreciation classes with her at UCLA, Arum Hartunian, the rug dealer who had run a fancy Persian carpet store across the street from Goldman's Antiques, Elsie Herriley who had shared a desk with Anna at the first job she held when she was eighteen. And wasn't that her eighth grade teacher, wearing a red suit and a hat with a tall white feather? The bald man was definitely Irving, the delicatessen owner who had given her free Indian nuts from his store on the lower east side of New York, and coming in now were her two New York state-senator employers, Raybinold and Scribner who had introduced her to the high society of New York life. Tessie Fineburg was wafting in the door—her high school friend who had killed herself on the fire escape of her lover/dentist who had betrayed her, and there—in the very back of the chapel—was a row of Anna's old boyfriends. How young and sweet-faced they looked, before they went to war to fight Hitler, before they had bad marriages, or bad children, or bad heart attacks. If any were alive, they'd be ancient geezers, yet here they were with their faces like young Gods, and bodies to match.

Just then a sparkling light caught her attention, directed it upward, where she saw, high up in the balcony, her beloved Abram, the boyfriend she had married. He sat alone, his face shining down upon her like a golden sun, its rays lighting and heating her soul till she felt atomic, as if she would vaporize into droplets of gold.

What a thrill this was, this Life Reunion, more astounding than her passage through the grungy Holland Tunnel on the day she died.

In the chapel, the mourners spoke in hushed whispers, filling out cards to be turned in to the family to announce who had been there. The ghosts would not leave cards, Anna knew, only her daughters' few friends would do that. Of course, her sister Gert was there in the front row with Janet and Danny, her face set in a sour expression, obviously annoyed that all this fuss was about to take place over Anna—which was clearly a waste since she was already dead and beyond appreciating it. Gert, who had already failed to die once—by her own hand—and left a bloody mess behind for Anna's girls to clean up, had given explicit instructions about her death to Janet and Carol: the next time she died, she wanted to be featured in her green chiffon evening gown, so all who passed her coffin could admire her beauty. In fact, Anna could tell Gert wished it were she, right now, in that box on the stage, so she could get her due admiration without further delay and be there to witness it.

Anna heard sobs and saw that her granddaughters were embracing one another and crying. Already they missed her. Such beautiful grown-up young women who carried Anna's genes for brilliance, for music, for language. Not that this aptitude had gotten them so far in life or got them wonderful jobs. Not that it had helped them find rich and powerful mates—but it had prepared them for what music and language were made to provide: beauty and poetry. This was Anna's legacy to them along with a few pieces of antique jewelry, and she was proud of it. She wanted to reassure them that death was only death, neither more nor less than anything else in their lives, their first merry-go-round rides, their first day of school, their first periods, their first kisses. This was their first death (Anna had been through so many she knew the song and dance by heart) and they were trembling as if it were the end of the world.

The secret was this. There *was* no end of the world. As long as you were in it, you were alive and the world was yours. Once you were buried, as Anna would be today, you weren't there to worry. One should relish, delight in, the thought of "nothing." Eat it like candy. Savor it like hot fudge. Nothing was the absence of *everything*. "Nothing" meant *no more of this mind dancing!*

And now strains of "The Entertainer" were coming down from the speakers on the chapel wall. Not any "Entertainer" but Anna's special rendition, played by her own fingers on her own piano. Heads were turning to discover the source of the music. Her granddaughters had a look of awe upon their faces as they heard Anna's own musical accompaniment to accompany Anna's funeral. How brilliant of her daughters to know that no music would suffice but that from Anna's soul itself. Hearing the music that was embossed in the very fibers of her being, she felt a flood of love overtaking her, a tidal wave, an ocean of joy that had no boundaries, no limits, and no conditions.

If music be the food of love, play on, she reminded herself. For so long Anna had been starved of nourishment, had savored nothing for the seven years she was chained to the feeding tube, and now . . . this veritable feast! Her hunger was enormous, she blew up like a balloon, like the Goodyear blimp; she felt herself expanding to the bursting point, filling with the generosity and good will that she had fended off all her life. In a moment she would explode with this sudden unfamiliar love of all humanity and be scattered in a blaze of falling stars upon the universe below.

Her eldest granddaughter, Bonnie, took the stage carrying her violin. She announced softly that she would play a Celtic folk tune called "I'll Always Remember You." The violin tones spread over the room, settling on their heads like a river of silver tears. Myra, Anna's youngest granddaughter, joined Bonnie in a duet, with Myra singing a Hebrew folk melody and Bonnie accompanying her. The guests of Anna's Life Reunion were wiping their eyes, one after another.

Then Myra stepped to the podium.

"I want to talk about how good Mom-Mom was to her grandchildren. We always called her *Mom-Mom*. When Bonnie was a little baby, she couldn't pronounce 'Grandma'—it came out 'Mom-Mom'—and that's how, halfway through her life, my grandmother got a new name and became Mom-Mom, the person we loved. Mom-Mom was not a soft or sentimental person, but she was very kind to us. Although we could see that she was formidable in her own way, she never intimidated us. When we were little, we visited her in her apartment in Fairfax. Her grand piano with the beautiful green antique lamp on it dominated her tiny apartment. She had a little tiny kitchen; the three of us would go in there and she'd put us up on the counter with our legs dangling. We'd sit there and she'd open the refrigerator and take out the Oreo cookies. She kept everything in the refrigerator, the cookies, the crackers, the cereal. I will never forget the delicious taste of those cold Oreos. I was always happy and excited when we went to visit her. I often wonder about the person she was before she was Mom-Mom, when she was a young woman growing up in New York. I never met that person, but I knew Mom-Mom and I loved her and I miss her very much."

Thank you darling, Anna wanted to say. She wanted to fly to her grandchild (who was trembling as she spoke her words, standing two feet from Anna's remains) and wrap her in the heat of the last movements of her seething molecules—which would shortly be dispersed to the universe.

Bonnie, still holding her violin, stepped up to the podium.

"I brought my wire music stand today, though I have a much fancier one now. Mom-Mom gave me this one for my birthday when I was ten years old. I've had it ever since. I'd like to share one or two small memories with you. One of the best things about her was being able to see her in her antique shop. When I was in college and had my own car, I used to go there and visit her. She would play the piano and I would play along the top line of the music . . . and she ignored her customers! When she bought her last car and was trying to remember a way to remember her new license plate, which was '600 TCI,' she said, 'The 600 part—that's easy. The TCI, well, Tough Cookie I.' It worked!"

Anna had forgotten all about that. Wasn't it strange how others carried in their memories facts about your life that you, for the life of you, couldn't have recalled?

Now Jill, her middle grandchild, stepped up to speak. Though no one knew it yet but Anna, she was two months pregnant with Anna's great-grandson. Jill glowed with her secret—she was grieved less than the others because she knew that Anna's replacement was on the way, a new vessel of life, replete with the family talents, to have his day in the world.

"I especially remember and admire Mom-Mom's independence. In the years when we knew her as children, she ran the antique store alone, went out 'on calls' every weekend, carried furniture onto the sidewalk in the morning and back into the store at night. She was always well-dressed, chipper, energetic. She braved the LA freeways to visit us. She sometimes dropped in on a surprise visit, arriving at the back door bringing a bag of food and treats, delighting us. She was glamorous: she wore skirts and elegant shoes and a pin on her collar. She was modern and decisive: she liked her hair white and short. She didn't like to cook and ate her meals out. She loved her grandchildren and let us know it. And we loved her.

"It was very hard to see her lose that independence. My mother and aunt worked very hard—to their limits—at the impossible task of trying to make her last years easier.

"My grandmother as I knew her was courageous, independent, and beautiful. Her talent with words and music gave pleasure to us all, whether in a Chopin nocturne, her virtuosic Scrabble playing, or in a sharp and witty retort. We will miss her. But she is part of us all."

Anna had tears in her eyes, herself, she who never had patience with sentimental ceremonies. But the woman her granddaughters were painting seemed far more generous and loving than she knew herself to be. Could it be she had been wrong about herself? That she was really as wonderful as they said?

Now her youngest daughter was beginning to speak—her baby girl who had had such grief in her life.

"I wish this gathering today could be for one of Mom's recitals. In a way, it will be. We'll hear her playing more of her own music shortly; I think she'd love to go out in a blaze of Chopin. Mom was a brave trouper. For seven years she was held behind enemy lines in the nursing home, a prisoner of her body. But between the shrieks of 'I want to die!' was the motherly advice: 'Sweetheart, did you have lunch? Sweetheart, I wish you could meet some nice man. Sweetheart, you're so pretty.' She, till almost the very end, had the ability to laugh at jokes I would tell her, sometimes at her expense. Once she asked me, 'How come my mother doesn't visit me?' 'Well, Mom' I told her, 'Let's see, Grandma would be about 125 years old now. It might be hard for her to catch the bus.' She would laugh and I loved the playfulness we shared. Beside her wonderful ability to play the piano was her way with words. She loved Scrabble; seven-letter words were a piece of cake for her.

"At the end of our visit, we would say our good-byes. She would always say, 'Thank you for coming,' and I would reply, 'You're my mom, you don't have to thank me.' I would open the outside door to the parking lot, turn, and wave, and she waved back, often with tears in her eyes. But this last time, New Year's Eve, with Mom deep in a morphine coma, close to death, I turned and waved just in case. I love you, Mom. The biggest gift my mom gave me was that I am lovable and I didn't have to do anything or be anything but myself.

"Looking through my mom's papers, I came across a note my dad had written her many years ago. 'Dear Anna, after twenty-five years I still think I picked the right one.' Well, that was written thirty-eight years ago and finally the two of you will be joined again today. I love you both."

When Carol stepped down from the podium, Anna had serious second thoughts about dying. If she was really that beloved by her grandchildren and her children, maybe she should stick it out a while longer!

Janet took her turn to say her piece, recounting how an old man in the nursing home had said to Anna, "You won't want to die if you find the Lord," and Anna answering, "Is he so stupid that he's *lost*?" There was a rumble of laughter from the audience, and Anna had to smile herself, remembering the old geezer's reaction. Janet then said, "My mother told us she wanted to be buried with Chopin's music, and indeed, today she will be. In a very important way, my mother has been my muse and my inspiration. She was a force, a mystery, a support, a wonder. I don't know what it's going to be like in a world where I can no longer say 'I'm going to see my mother.' "As Janet stepped down from the podium, wiping her eyes on a handkerchief, once again Anna's rendition of "The Entertainer" burst forth from the chapel speakers. The guests began to smile and tap their feet. She was impressed all over again with her skill on the ivories. How glad she was that her children had forced her to play for their tape recorders on various occasions; otherwise her music would have vanished forever. Following the ragtime piece was Chopin's Nocturne in C Minor (not her best rendition, Anna thought, but pretty substantial) followed by "Sunrise, Sunset," that heart-twister of a song that made you face how old you had grown and how the young were there to replace you. None so old as Anna, however, who was glad to say she had taken on the title of nonagenarian before bowing out.

"Ladies and gentlemen," the funeral director said, "do not stop to greet the bereaved till after the interment at graveside. Please stand, one row at a time, and file past the deceased to pay your respects."

Anna watched as her family, as well as the shades and ghosts of her past, walked down the aisle and up a few steps to the stage where the coffin was displayed. They made a circle around her final remains. A few patted the cardboard of the casket. Her sister bent down to kiss the lid (the hypocrite!). Her granddaughters were sobbing and clutching one another's hands.

Anna remembered what one of her aunts had written in her eighth-grade autograph book. "May your life be like a snowflake, that leaves a mark but not a stain." She saw today that she had actually made a sizable splash. With everyone missing her and crying, she felt almost sentimental herself.

There was no mistaking the significance of the pyramid of dirt that stood beside Anna's grave: *Dust thou art and to dust thou will returneth.* That mountain of dirt, gouged up from the belly of the earth, would shortly be pressed down over her remains. Anna tried to imagine how, exactly, her disintegration would come to pass and how long it would take before she was mere fodder for worms. Not that it bothered her—it was appropriate that her body, broken beyond repair, would finally be consigned to oblivion. Nothing as ugly as she'd become should furthermore be seen in the light of day. She was pleased to know that her vanity was intact and had lasted well beyond her last breath.

But all this rigmarole about death, all this pomp and circumstance! Anna wondered where it had originated, the solemn digging and burying and dirging, all the hushed verbiage about grieving and closure and "life must go on." What an elaborate pretense that the dead body was sacred (burned or buried, it was nothing more than refuse) and that it must be marked by burnished bronze or marble or carved angels and visited over the years with flowers and tears and wails.

What pained her was to see her three beautiful granddaughters standing at the rear door of the funeral coach as her coffin was pulled out and each of them was assigned a handle. Then the pallbearers—the girls, Anna's youngest grandson, one of her sons-in-law and a hired hand from the cemetery—made their way down the hill. She could see the anguish on her granddaughters' faces as they realized whatever was in there bumping and sliding about in the box was their former grandmother. It was brutal, really, this ceremonial torture. Better to have it end with no witnesses and no speeches.

Her casket was laid on metal pipes that were connected to pulleys. Though Janet and Carol had respected her wishes for no rabbi, Anna could see that some signal was lacking for continuation of the ritual. The Mexican workers at the pulley controls were waiting for the sign. The guests were looking around for the next segment to begin—and there was only silence.

Anna understood that a rabbi would have served to produce this transition, yet she still believed she was right in not wasting $300 on some meaningless gibberish a rabbi would babble.

A man wearing an embroidered yarmulke on his head stepped forward to the graveside—the husband of Janet's childhood Brooklyn friend. It was convenient for Anna that his parents had given him a good Hebrew education, for he quickly dispatched the whole business by saying the Mourner's Kaddish very quickly—satisfying the Mexicans and the guests and maybe God and even Anna (who at least, since it was free, didn't turn it down because who knew whether or not it might open some doors for her in the afterlife.)

The Mexicans turned the pulley wheels, the ropes hummed, Anna's body was lowered slowly into the deep rectangular hole, and the sun came out on the hills beyond the freeway.

The cemetery representative made a little speech about "Now you are invited to step forward to these shovels and make your last gift of kindness to your loved one. Tradition tells us this is the ultimate act of charity you are able to offer to the deceased, since it is one she can never pay back to you."

"Charity," Anna heard her sister Gert mumble. "When did my sister ever do an act of charity in her life?" In any case, Gert came forward first, Anna's little sister, now an old woman of eighty-eight, fat in the belly, wobbly on her legs, thick in the chin, sour in the face. With almost a look of vengeance on her face, she grabbed one of the shovels in the dirt and flung her clod of dirt over Anna's coffin. Two more dull explosions of dirt hit the casket and she stepped back, satisfied. This burying of Anna meant that Gert now had moved up to the top of the line, the place she had always been jealous of Anna for occupying. What a hopeless privilege, Anna thought. All it meant was that you were the next to die.

When the last car had driven the guests away, back to Janet's house for cold cuts and hard-boiled eggs, when the grave diggers had putted away in their little tractor to dig the next grave, when Anna was finally tucked in for eternity next to Abram, when the afternoon passed to evening and the sun gave way to moon (neither of which would smite Anna again), Anna accepted her fate. She had been here on earth and now she was gone. The opera had reached its climactic conclusion, the curtain had come down, the characters of Anna's drama had bowed and moved offstage. The house lights were black.

Anna was ended.

Thanks to Jacob Smullyan for bringing this book into the light, and to Jeffrey Moskowitz for helping me through a difficult year.

Merrill Joan Gerber has written thirty books, including *Revelation at the Food Bank* (Sagging Meniscus, 2024), *The Kingdom of Brooklyn*, winner of the Ribalow Award from *Hadassah Magazine*, and *King of the World*, winner of the Pushcart Editors' Book Award. Her fiction has been published in the *New Yorker*, the *Sewanee Review*, the *Atlantic*, *Mademoiselle*, and *Redbook*, and her essays in the *American Scholar*, *Salmagundi*, and *Commentary*. She has won an O. Henry Award, a Best American Essays award, and a Wallace Stegner fiction fellowship to Stanford University. She retired in 2020 after teaching writing at the California Institute of Technology for thirty-two years. Her literary archive is now at the Yale Beinecke Rare Book Library.

www.ingramcontent.com/pod-product-compliance
Lightning Source LLC
La Vergne TN
LVHW041109080826
845145LV00007B/1741